THE CHARM BUYERS

THE CHARM BUYERS

Lillian Howan

[signature] 10/14/17

A Latitude 20 Book

University of Hawai'i Press
Honolulu

22 21 20 19 18 17   6 5 4 3 2 1

Library of Congress Cataloging-in-Publication Data

Names: Howan, Lillian, author.
Title: The charm buyers / Lillian Howan.
Description: Honolulu : University of Hawai'i Press, [2016] | "A latitude 20
   book."
Identifiers: LCCN 2016034518 | ISBN 9780824858520 (pbk. ; alk. paper)
Subjects: LCSH: Tahiti (French Polynesia : Island)—History—20th
   Century—Fiction. | Hakka (Chinese people)—French Polynesia—Tahiti
   (Island)—Fiction. | LCGFT: Novels.
Classification: LCC PS3608.O8966 C47 2017 | DDC 813/.6—dc23 LC record available
   at https://lccn.loc.gov/2016034518

University of Hawai'i Press books are printed on acid-free
paper and meet the guidelines for permanence and
durability of the Council on Library Resources.

Designed by Milenda Nan Ok Lee

For my mother, Thérèse Sou Kin Moux Howan,
and my father, Yin Chong Roger Howan,
and for Bruno Leou-on

Contents

Contents

PART THREE *The Charm*

PART FOUR *Chessboard*

PART FIVE *Huahine*

Major Characters

Marc Antoine Chen: the narrator. Born in 1970.

Tamerlan Chen: father of Marc. Brief marriage to Sylvia Tan (Marc's mother). Black pearl cultivator. Married to Cecile Li.

Sylvia Tan: mother of Marc. Brief marriage to Tamerlan Chen (Marc's father). Black pearl cultivator. Married to Tiurai Tunui.

Odile Tunui: Marc's half sister. Daughter of Sylvia Tan.

A-tai: Marc's great-grandmother. Grandmother of Tamerlan Chen.

Marie-Laure Li: cousin of Marc Chen. Half sister of Cecile Li, the current wife of Tamerlan Chen. Mother: Georgine Li, née Tan, younger sister of Sylvia Tan. Father: Ten-kwok Li.

Charlemagne "Radish" Li: cousin of Marie-Laure Li. Close friend and business partner of Marc Chen.

Cecile Li: expert comptable, graduate of Hautes Études Commerciales. Current wife of Tamerlan Chen. Half sister of Marie-Laure Li.

Jonathan Li: usually referred to as "Monsieur Li." Eldest cousin of Marie-Laure Li, Radish Li, and Cecile Li. Close friend of Tamerlan Chen. Believed to have obscure magical powers.

Marise De Koning: usually called "De Koning." American-born apprentice of Monsieur Li. The De Koning family is multiracial: Tahitian, French, Chinese, Dutch, Greek, and Irish.

Madame MuSan: restaurant owner. Aunt of Philippe MuSan.

Philippe MuSan: politician. Friend and former lover of Aurore du Chatelet. Nephew of Madame MuSan.

Major Characters

AURORE DU CHATELET: The Marquise du Chatelet. Painter. Educated as a *notaire* (lawyer specializing in contracts and documents).

VETEA TCHONG: the subject of one of Aurore's paintings. Farmer. Worked at the atoll of Mururoa, a nuclear testing site.

HINERAVA POROI: a child who befriends Marc, the narrator.

THE CHARM BUYERS

PART ONE

ISLANDS

Chapter 1

The things you've heard about me—they're true, especially the lies. Some say they love me, some say they hate me, but all will tell you it's true, every word they say. And what if their words paint different pictures, so different they couldn't all be true? They'll say, of course, that it only shows how deceptive I am, how you can never trust me.

Other people give you your face. So the saying goes, but A-tai, my great-grandmother, always said that this was the type of nonsense that only fools believed. Your face was your face and no one gave it to you or took it away.

As for what you see—maybe I'm remembering something that never existed: the good son, my mother smiling at me and her family saying what a handsome little boy, just like my mother who, even now, is famous for her great beauty. Sylvia Tan, they say—and then in the next breath, people will say how beautiful she is. My father, Tamerlan Chen, fell in love with her when she was seventeen. She was riding her horse at the Hippodrome track where the road to the cemetery begins, the road of shadows and bright flowers dying in the careless sun. My father was eighteen. My grandfather had died the year before and every day my father went to the Chinese cemetery, the *Chemin du Repos Éternel* in Arue, to bring new flowers to my grandfather's grave. It was when my father drove down the dirt road from the cemetery that he saw my mother riding her horse, a white horse brought from the Marquesas Islands.

They married before the end of the year. I was born the following year, in 1970, and by then the marriage was self-destructing, breaking into thousands of fierce pieces, falling apart for good when I was three, and that was when I went to live with A-tai.

At first, my great-grandmother's place seemed strange, because for her, it was all the same, the world outside the walls of her house and the world inside. Outside she raised fish, black tilapia, in a cement basin, and inside she grew turtles that swam in basins rimmed with green algae. All around the walls were jars and bottles with seeds and leaves steeping in dark, bubbled liquid. At night, I slept on a cot among the small mountains of debris that filled her rooms. A-tai hung a curtain of mosquito netting over the cot and the lizards climbed, racing around the filmy white netting.

When I fell sick, A-tai brewed a medicine, something with an onion root and leaves and the crumbled bits of the horrible things that would make you well. The taste was bitter and when I drank, nothing happened at first, except that I'd feel even worse from the taste.

At night, as we ate dinner, A-tai told the stories she learned in the village in China, a village with a name that meant something like "a corner of sand." We ate bitter melon or *ature* fish or chicken cooked in rice wine from a brown glass bottle. A-tai said that I ate as much as her entire village. She said that they always made a little plate of pickled tofu or pickled salted greens and then the trick was to keep their eyes on the plate of pickles as they ate their rice. Just looking at the pickles made your mouth water, A-tai said, and you could imagine you were eating all types of delicacies, when in fact every mouthful was the same—rice, rice, and rice, and you were grateful even for that. When they ran out of rice, they gathered seaweed to eat, and at the end of the war, they were eating nothing but seaweed. The stories of the war were grim and hard and I always wished that the stories would end—but there were the nights when A-tai talked instead about better times when her great-uncles were thieves and robbers. She laughed and shook her head, talking about their adventures. Her eyes grew large, as if she were a child once more. Their loot! Such treasures! Jade and gold and pearls. They were wild, her great-uncles. They were horsemen and they wore their hair long. At night, I dreamed of A-tai's brigand great-uncles, riding with their stolen treasures, riding on their horses—and as I slept, the sound of the lizards chasing each other over the mosquito netting turned into the deeper sound of horses racing and racing away into the night.

4

One day when I was ten, I returned home from school and I thought it was a day like any other. A day slipping away, a day like a hat folded out of yesterday's paper. The words that A-tai didn't know popped into my head, *rouge, blanc, Napoleon, un, deux, potiron* . . . and I talked about *la forêt lointaine,* the faraway forest, the blue forest, the whatever I said didn't matter forest.

A pile of fruit, mangoes and bananas, most of them black from the heat, sat on the kitchen table with a swarm of flies. Footsteps approached and, as I looked up, my father walked into the room.

He seemed from another world—at the time, I could not say why, only that his clothes smelled of laundry soap and the burning heat of an iron. Standing next to my father, A-tai was bent and shriveled. I was already a few centimeters taller and she said that I was growing fast, but when my father came to visit, I knew that I would never be tall. In my father's presence, A-tai and I were like the creatures in the fairy tales I read at school—crooked, misshapen creatures hidden with the junk along the walls, the sour-smelling jars, and the darkness of the rooms. I was living in a cave.

"Marc Antoine," said my father. He spoke to me in French. "You're coming to live with me."

I glanced at A-tai. She nodded at me, as if something good were happening. She walked to a corner of the room and picked up a wicker basket filled with my clothes, already washed and folded inside.

My father grimaced, as if a bad smell arose from my clothes. "Leave those."

A-tai stood, holding the basket as my father walked to the door. "I'll buy him others," he said.

I stood up and took the basket of my clothes from A-tai, kissing her on her cheeks. Her skin felt soft and I began to cry.

My father called me from the yard, from the piles of rubble, the leaves smoldering from the small fire A-tai burned to keep away the mosquitoes. In the car, I held the basket of my old clothes, never letting go.

My father took me to the barber. I sat in the plastic chair and the seat seemed to sweat beneath me. I watched my hair falling on the floor. One of the barber clients, a distant cousin of my father's named Feng, said, "Your son, he's so shy."

"His great-grandmother raised him," my father replied.

"Does she still tell those stories?" Feng asked.

"What stories?"

Feng continued, laughing and oblivious. "Those crazy stories."

"I've never heard any crazy stories," my father replied.

"If you don't know, then you don't know," Feng said, waving one of his hands in the air.

The barber had finished and a girl began sweeping the fallen hair. She was around my age, a skinny girl wearing a faded blue dress. The girl swept the pile of hair into a dustpan and glanced at me. My father and the barber had walked to the cash register. The girl picked up the dustpan in one hand and then she smiled at me, a sly sort of smile. I looked back at her and she was still smiling.

"If you don't know, then you don't know," Feng said again, only he was speaking to himself, sitting on one of the barber chairs and waiting his turn.

You don't know—for some Hakkas this was a continuous chant, repeated several times a day. Ask them a question and their response was the same: *you don't know?* If you didn't know, you didn't know, and no one was going to explain it to you. Another way of looking at it was that if you didn't know, it meant that you didn't belong to that inner circle of those who already knew. You were on the outside and you could stay there forever, always trying to look in and seeing nothing. Whatever the reason might be, there would never be an explanation. You either knew or you didn't.

It wasn't as if there were a large number of Hakka, the first group brought to Tahiti a hundred years ago by boat from southern China. My father—making sure that I always calculated percentages and interest in my head—said that in the town of Papeete, if you started counting a hundred people, maybe five or six would be Hakka, and in the outer districts the number would be even fewer, clustered around a Hakka grocery store you passed on the side of the road. In the remote islands outside of Tahiti, there were always two or three of these stores and there were boats and ferries run by the Hakka, carrying passengers and vanilla beans, chickens and bananas. If you asked how the business was going, the response was usually the same: *slow*. Business was slow, even if the store was crowded with customers, especially on Sunday mornings, so the answer really didn't say anything.

I always felt that I was fumbling, trying to put together the pieces of the slippery jigsaw puzzle of how things worked—and I was never certain if I was fitting the pieces correctly or if the scattered pieces in my mind even came from the same puzzle.

My father left on occasion, for weeks at a time, and I stayed with his younger brothers, but never again with A-tai, my great-grandmother. I was never told the reason—whether there had been a disagreement between my father and A-tai or whether I was considered too old to live with her. I knew only that, until my father returned, I remained in the large and chaotic households of my father's brothers, my uncles who felt benevolently indifferent toward me.

My mother had remarried. She had a daughter named Odile and people said that my mother was very rich, married to a Tahitian black pearl producer. She sent for me on occasion and I would arrive wearing a freshly ironed white shirt and dark shorts, my father leaving me at the green iron gate by the street. The gate opened between the trimmed hedges of pink hibiscus, into the interior garden. A dog would be barking and snarling at me from the end of his long chain, a maniacally fierce dog, lunging at me, his neck held back by the chain. Red-veined crotons and *tiare* gardenias bordered the lawn and a tree of Chinese green grapefruit grew in a far corner over the pond of golden koi.

The barking of the dog would bring out my mother, appearing between the double French doors. She would run out to me. She was tall like my father and smelled wonderful, an expensive sort of smell. Always, for a moment, I would think that I never seemed to grow and then my mother would sweep me into her arms, gushing over how handsome I had become while the dog barked with unceasing fury.

Wrapped in my mother's arms, I felt that I would remain there always, enclosed in her fragrance with the sweetness of her hair against my cheek. She would release me slowly—reluctantly, I always thought—and I would follow her inside the parlor with its polished wood chairs and pillows of traditional *tifaifai,* quilted in flowers and leaves. My mother would ask how I was doing, nodding her head and listening, but after a short while, she would turn her head to the door, as if she had heard a sound I couldn't hear. She would stand up from her chair and, kissing me on the cheeks, would disappear into the interior rooms, leaving me on my own. I was free to enter into the house or remain in the parlor, but her time with me had ended.

I would wander with a sour feeling of disappointment through the house, occasionally hearing my mother talking with one of the maids in another room. It was always the same: my mother running out to greet me, her embrace, our brief parlor visit, and her departure. I did fair in school and then I did poorly; the teachers agreed that my French was dismal and I repeated a grade; my father had a new girlfriend, replaced by yet another new girlfriend—but year after year, my visits to my mother remained the same.

Once when I was sixteen, I followed my mother into the parlor to find my cousin Marie-Laure sitting in one of the chairs.

"Your Aunt Georgine is in New Zealand, so Marie-Laure is staying with me," said my mother.

Marie-Laure smiled at my mother and, for a moment, I felt my mother's indulgent affection for her, the daughter of Aunt Georgine, who, at nineteen, had married Ten-kwok Li, becoming his third wife. Ten-kwok's eldest son from his first wife was the age of my father, but Ten-kwok had taken an obsessive fancy to Aunt Georgine, who everyone agreed was as lovely as a doll.

I often saw Marie-Laure—she was two years younger than me—and I always wondered if it was difficult for Marie-Laure to grow up in a family of such beautiful women when she herself was so plain. Her nose was squat and her mouth was too large, like a doughy gash across the bottom of her face. She usually had a sprinkle of pimples over her forehead and her hair was thin and tangled easily, bunching around the back of her neck.

My mother once told me that Aunt Georgine had given birth to Marie-Laure after two days and nights of excruciating pain—everyone thought that Aunt Georgine would die, but then Marie-Laure was born, a tiny shriveled baby. "She was ugly," my mother said, her voice soft and warm with affection. My mother loved Marie-Laure, the child of her beloved youngest sister. And Aunt Georgine adored Marie-Laure, her only child, it turned out, for something had happened during the process of Marie-Laure's being born and Aunt Georgine could never have another child.

Marie-Laure sat serenely in her chair. I thought to myself that if I had been raised with so much indulgent attention, I would have that same air that Marie-Laure radiated, a calm, ugly girl of fourteen.

"We're leaving for the market," my mother said, kissing me on the cheeks and walking out the door with Marie-Laure.

My father expanded his business, starting another black pearl farm in the Tuamotus that year, and I spent my summer on the atoll, a solitary ring of sand twenty kilometers long, surrounded by the endless ocean. I did odd jobs, helping my father with his paperwork, working for several hours each day in his tin-roofed office.

"Why can't you work like this in school?" my father asked.

I said nothing—the answer was obvious. I hated school but I loved the atoll, the clear blue sky, the clear blue sea, the solitude. I could think in the silence.

A year passed before I visited my mother again. She had a new dog, an elegant Doberman Pinscher who barked at me from the second-floor balcony of her house. I followed my mother into the parlor to find Marie-Laure sitting at one of the antique Chinese tables carved of elm wood. She was fifteen and as plain as ever.

"Marc," she said, rising from her chair, and I kissed her cheeks.

My mother inquired politely after my school, and I watched Marie-Laure gazing back at me with her liquid dark eyes as I explained that I was failing and that my father was threatening to send me to France for my military duty as soon as I turned eighteen.

"He won't do that," my mother cried. "I'll talk to Tiurai for you." She left the room, as if to call my stepfather, but I knew that she wasn't coming back.

"Would you like something to drink?" Marie-Laure asked.

"I'll be leaving soon," I replied.

"But you just arrived," said Marie-Laure. "I was going to get something from the kitchen." She wore a sacklike dress of green gingham, her body thin and shapeless. She noticed me looking at her dress and smiled. "I just finished sewing this," she said. "I know—I'm not much of a seamstress."

"You don't have to wear it," I said.

"From the look on your face, it must really look bad." She smiled again and walked out the door.

I sat in the empty parlor among the *tifaifai* pillows. I had borrowed my cousin Harris's motorcycle and I was thinking of going to the *roulottes* by the waterfront that evening to get something to eat.

Marie-Laure reappeared at the door. "Are you coming?" she asked.

I found myself following her down the long shadowy hallway to the side entrance of the house. Orchids grew in blue and white porcelain pots by the door leading outside to the kitchen, a separate building fringed by a row of chicken cages. A large white refrigerator loomed inside by the kitchen entrance and Marie-Laure opened its door, taking out two bottles of orange soda. I sat down at the kitchen table, a long rectangle of *tou* wood. Marie-Laure placed one of the bottles before me and sat down across the table.

"You want something to eat?" she asked. It was the usual Hakka politeness—always asking if a guest was hungry.

"You want to get me something?" I asked.

She drank from her bottle of soda, her eyes watching me.

I leaned across the table. "A gun," I said—and why was I saying this, but did I care? "Get me a gun."

Marie-Laure took another sip of soda and placed the bottle on the table. "I was thinking of doing a *tour de l'île* tomorrow," she said, meaning a drive around the island.

"With my mother?"

She shook her head. "Your mother is going to Bora Bora tomorrow with your sister Odile. They're visiting Aunt Genevieve."

Aunt Genevieve—of course. Another favorite sister of my mother.

"Is that your cousin Harris's new motorcycle?" Marie-Laure pointed her hand out the door, towards the street.

"You know all the gossip," I replied.

"I don't gossip." She stood up and opened the refrigerator door again, taking out a bowl of red grapes. I watched as she washed the grapes, flipping back her ratty hair and then bending over the sink. I heard that Marie-Laure was preparing to take the baccalaureate the next year, having skipped a grade ahead.

"You have time to go around the island?" I asked.

Marie-Laure placed the bowl of grapes between us.

"Don't you have to study?" I asked.

She popped a grape into her mouth. "Sure. But the drive won't take long," she said. "You're driving fast."

Chapter 2

You could drive around the island of Tahiti in two hours, in a day, in two days. You could pass the slower cars, the pickup trucks with their loads of mothers and kids in ragged T-shirts, the bicycles turning in lazy circles by the side of the road, the bony yellow dogs trying to cross—if you never stopped, the drive could take less than two hours, provided that you weren't entering or leaving Papeete during the morning or late afternoon traffic jams. At the other extreme, you could visit every relative living around the island—your aunt who ran the general store in Papeari, your uncle who worked at the gas station in Mahina, your countless cousins who were expecting babies or who had just given birth, your grandmother who lived with your aunt who lived with your great-aunt . . . this type of *tour de l'île* could take an entire day or two or three days.

"You're out of your fucking mind," said my cousin Harris. "You aren't old enough to drive—there's no way you're taking Marie-Laure around the island." We were eating steaks and fries at a *roulotte,* a van with a grill and a row of cheap plastic chairs parked by the waterfront. "Why did I lend you the motorcycle?"

"So lend me your car," I said. Harris drove an American sedan, dark blue and peppered with rust spots.

"What the hell's wrong with you?" Harris pulled out a pack of cigarettes from his shirt pocket. "Didn't you hear what I said? No *tour de l'île.* You're seventeen. Look—anything bad happens to Marie-Laure and your mother's entire family is going to kill us."

"She asked me," I said.

"Well, being around you was a bad influence." Harris lit his cigarette, tilting back his head and exhaling a thin stream of smoke. "It was her idea, wasn't it? The little buddha herself. And look at you, her devotee."

"Shut up."

"Don't get me wrong—I have nothing against her. Your mother's family loves her."

I picked up my empty soda bottle.

"You want to know why?" Harris asked. "It isn't because of her looks. She's an ugly kid—everyone knows that. The island's full of beautiful women and she isn't one of them."

The only reason Harris had a better reputation than I did was that Harris had that clean-cut, good Chinese boy look. He had the earnest smile, complete with a dimple on his right cheek. His face was broad and his expression seemed so guileless, his eyes almost sparkled.

"They all say that you look like your mother." Like I wanted to hear this. "She's a great beauty—everyone knows that," said Harris, picking through the fries. "Beauty is everything. The reputation of the whole fucking island was built on beauty. The sacred illusion. That's why a family of beautiful women loves Marie-Laure. She isn't about illusion and illusion is hard work in the end. Or maybe that's just how Marie-Laure seems— after all, she has you sweating, because you promised to drive her around. Even if you don't have your license and it's illegal. Or maybe that just proves the point—she knows you can drive. It doesn't matter what the rules seem to be. All that matters is how things really are. The ugly truth, calm and pure." Harris waved the pack of cigarettes in front of me. "What—you're not smoking? What do I know? I'm probably all wrong about Marie-Laure."

I arrived at my mother's house around six in the morning. I opened the gate but there was no sign of the dog, and, for the first time, I entered the garden unaccompanied by the sound of barking and snarling. Marie-Laure was seated, reading a book in the parlor.

"Your mother and Odile left early, an hour ago," she said. "I'm sorry—I should have told you." Her hair was plaited in a braid down her back.

"I'm sorry," I said. "I can't take you around the island I don't have a driver's license I'm not old enough." I spoke in one long, painful breath.

Marie-Laure stared at me and I felt the earth tensing beneath my feet, preparing to swallow me whole.

"So when will you be old enough?" she asked.

"Soon. After Christmas."

"End of December?"

"Near the beginning of the year." I tried to look bored, like I couldn't care less, my thoughts foundering as I drowned.

Marie-Laure studied the cover of her book, as if she were pondering something written there. With her hair pulled back, her forehead looked wide and square like a lump. She was wearing a dress—a dismal dull green—and sandals that showed the stubs of her toes. "Well," she said in a quiet voice, "I'll wait until then." She smiled at me, casually dismissing the issue. "Have you had breakfast yet?"

"Yes—not really."

"You have—you haven't?" She left through the door into the garden and I followed her along a path through rows of white ginger. She paused, opening a tall metal gate. My mother's Doberman rested in the interior yard beyond, by a bowl of water in the shade of a long, wide awning. The dog walked towards Marie-Laure as we entered and crossed the yard.

I seldom saw this part of the household, set further from the street than the main house and the kitchen. When I was a child, I was vaguely aware that the household was several different buildings, some of them connected, extending towards the sea. Different relatives lived in the buildings—two of my mother's unmarried sisters, a bachelor great-uncle, and a widowed sister of my stepfather who lived with her youngest son. A continuous flow of relatives stayed for differing lengths of time: my stepfather's cousins from the Tuamotus and various older children of my mother's siblings. They took up residence in the innumerable rooms, throughout the household.

I followed Marie-Laure up a flight of wooden stairs until we arrived at a terrace, partly shaded by an old mango tree. An enclosed room was built on one side of the terrace, beneath the branches of the tree. The roof extended beyond the room, so that there was a shaded area beneath the tree and the roof, still cool in the early morning hours. A glass-topped table and three plastic chairs stood in the shade. The Doberman walked beneath the table and plopped down with a heavy grunt, but Marie-Laure shooed her away, to the shade under the tree.

"I brought some tea from the main kitchen," said Marie-Laure, disappearing through the door of the room. She reappeared with a tray holding a metal thermos, two cups, a baguette, and a sticky jar of jam, and set the tray down at the table. I sat down beside her, the leaves of the mango tree a canopy of green overhead.

A low rumbling began, barely perceptible at first. Marie-Laure poured the tea into my cup, but the rumbling increased, coming from somewhere above. Marie-Laure stopped and set the thermos down, my cup only half filled. The Doberman lifted her head. I looked at Marie-Laure who looked back at me. She reached for my cup, holding it down with her hand, and then I understood—an airplane was approaching. My mother's house was in the flight pattern, as airplanes came in to land at the airport across the water in Faaa. The landings were scheduled early in the morning or at night, so I'd never heard an airplane approaching before, although my mother always complained about the noise.

The rumbling grew louder, increasing to a roar, accompanied by a loud whining—the sound of engines. The table and the chairs began to tremble and then the cups, the thermos, everything was shaking. There was the scream of the engines, a strangely thrilling sound. Marie-Laure and I looked up to see it: immense and close beyond belief, shining metal passing swiftly, directly above.

Even after the airplane had passed and the rumbling disappeared in the distance, we sat frozen and silent as if our voices had been drained by its roar.

Marie-Laure picked up the thermos and poured tea into my cup. "I forgot to ask—do you want coffee?" she said.

"Tea is fine."

She placed the thermos down and stood up from the table.

"Where are you going?" I asked.

"I won't be long—I'm getting coffee from the main kitchen."

"But I always drink tea," I replied, lying because I always drank coffee. I picked up the thermos and poured tea into Marie-Laure's cup. "Sit down—your tea will get cold."

Marie-Laure cut the baguette with a knife. A flock of *vini vini* birds flew past, into the branches of the mango tree, and in a neighboring house, a television droned in a masculine voice, a newscaster reporting the early morning news.

Harris called the following week, talking about a party, a big party thrown by one of Marie-Laure's cousins on her father's side. "But you can get in," said Harris. "Go ask Marie-Laure."

I knew the talk about this party was overblown—it was an island, after all, where everyone kept running into the same people all the time. You could talk about something as much as you wanted, but it was always the same thing in the end.

"I'm going with Jocelyn," said Harris. He was obsessed with Jocelyn Loong, or, more accurately, he was obsessed with her insanely wicked body. "You can come with us but you'll have to find your way back—why don't you get a ride with Marie-Laure?"

"What makes you think she'll be there?"

"Oh, I talked with the ugly buddha—they're really close on that side of her family. She'll be there. Better yet, why don't you go with her?"

"You're lending me your car?"

Harris's laugh was about as genuine as the alligator-looking bag that Aunt Georgine once brought back from Hong Kong. "Why don't you go ask Marie-Laure? She'll get you a car. She just has to wave one of her froggy little hands around."

Marie-Laure was playing chess with her cousin Radish when I arrived at my mother's house. They played using a timer and they played swiftly with silent concentration, their hands darting around the chessboard. Radish was my age and had passed the baccalaureate the year before, at the age of sixteen. He was tall and mild, the sort who sidestepped arguments. The family referred to him as "an odd child." Marie-Laure adored him.

Marie-Laure looked up from the chessboard and Radish extended his hand. "Good game."

"You took almost all my pieces."

16

"You won," Radish said.

Marie-Laure noticed me for the first time, standing outside the parlor by the garden door.

"Does she always win?" I asked.

"You should have said something," said Marie-Laure. "How long have you been standing there? Harris said that you'd be here, that you needed a car."

So much for social subtlety on Harris's part, I thought.

"He said that you wanted to go to Irina's party."

"Harris is going to Irina's party," I replied.

"Yes—with the lovely Jocelyn Loong." Marie-Laure began placing the chess pieces back on the board.

"I'll be in the kitchen," said Radish, rising to leave the room.

I waited until he left and then I asked, "Would you like to go to the party?"

Marie-Laure kept her eyes on the chessboard. "Are you going?"

I felt something strange and unexpected, stirring somewhere between my throat and my heart. A silence fell over us. "It's tomorrow night," I said finally.

"If you're going, I have something for you."

I followed her out the door, but she turned to me in the hallway. The shadows seemed to smooth her features, her eyes deep and black. "Wait here for me," she said.

Someone was chopping in the kitchen, the rapid-fire sound of the cleaver on the cutting board echoing in the hallway. A lizard slept on the ceiling. After several minutes, I heard footsteps approaching and Marie-Laure appeared, holding something wrapped in a plastic bag.

"This is for you." She placed it in my hands.

"What is it?"

"I asked one of my friends—she went to Paris over the Toussaint holiday."

I unwrapped the bag. There was a shirt and pants folded inside. The fabric felt expensive, like nothing I had ever worn before.

"Promise me you'll wear them tomorrow," said Marie-Laure.

"I'll pick you up here at seven," I said. "I'll be here with Harris." Marie-Laure kissed me, quickly, close to the side of my mouth, and left.

No one was in the parlor when I arrived the next evening. I heard the Doberman barking unseen from the interior yard. Someone had left the television on, the announcer of a French game show talking to the empty chairs. I crossed the parlor, and went down the hallway to the outside kitchen.

Marie-Laure was serving dinner to two small girls seated at the kitchen table. The girls were around six and seven and they looked up as I walked in.

"Wow," said the older girl.

"Be careful," Marie-Laure said to them. "The soup is still hot."

"You look like those French people on TV," the older girl said to me.

"Rosine—what did I say?" Marie-Laure asked. "You'll burn yourself." She stirred their bowls with a Chinese soup spoon. "Wait, wait. Moeana, don't touch—I just told you." Marie-Laure wore a pale blue dress and her long hair, usually ratty and tangled, was combed, falling smoothly down her back. She placed the soup spoon down and turned to see me, lifting her eyes for a moment and then glancing away.

The girls blew over the surfaces of their bowls.

"Would you like some soup?" Marie-Laure opened the lid of the soup kettle, her back turned to me as she spoke.

"No—I'll wait while you eat."

We were all taught to be patient, how to wait and wait, ever since we were children. I had seen grown men sitting silently, waiting in pickup trucks, waiting in front of stores. It seemed the mark of adulthood, the ability to wait—an ability that little children lacked, always fidgety and restless. When you fished in the early hours before the sun rose, you waited, like the sky and the land, like time itself.

"I'm not going," said Marie-Laure.

I sat down at the table. The little girls began drinking their soup, the older girl, Rosine, smiling over her bowl at me.

"You're pretty cute," I told her, and she giggled.

"What about me?" Moeana demanded.

"You're very pretty too," I said, and they giggled together.

18

"You should leave or you'll be late for the party," said Marie-Laure.

"I don't have to go—there's nothing special about this party," I replied. "It's a party like all the parties—everyone's drinking Laurent Perrier, and if it's a Chinese party, they have those longans or litchis drowning in champagne."

"Then you're ridiculously overdressed for sitting in the kitchen," said Marie-Laure.

I looked down, examining my shirt. "Someone made me promise to wear these clothes—and like the well-trained Hakka male I am, I've been taught to obey her every word."

"What a bunch of crap," said Marie-Laure. "Every Hakka male I know is thick-skulled and stupid and never listens, no matter what you say. No wonder we spent a thousand years wandering around China. Nomadic by stupidity."

Rosine laughed and then turned to Marie-Laure. "Go to the party with him."

"Get out," Marie-Laure said to me, her voice rising. "Before I throw you out."

"Go ahead. Try." I didn't know what else to say—I didn't know why she was so upset.

Marie-Laure stood in a rush and ran out the kitchen door.

"Hey—there you are." It was Harris, walking into the kitchen from the garden. I had forgotten about him, waiting in the car. "Where's Marie-Laure?"

"She's not going," said Rosine. "She's in her room."

"Well then, let's go." Harris clapped his hands together, as if I were a trained dog.

"No—I'm going to talk to her," I said.

Harris grabbed my arm. "I've got to meet someone. I need you to go with me."

"You mean Jocelyn? I don't think you need me around."

"No—someone else. Business." Harris motioned to me without smiling. "We really have to go."

The little girls stared solemnly from across the table.

"She's not going with you to the party," said Rosine.

"Why—what happened?" I asked.

"You don't know?" Moeana replied. They fiddled with their soup spoons but no longer ate.

I slapped the table with my hand. "What happened?"

"Nothing happened." Rosine looked at me as if the answer was obvious to everyone else.

"We're leaving." Harris took me by the arm and walked us out the door.

Harris drove through the narrow side streets surrounding my mother's house. In the middle of the street, dogs lay in clumps, rising and moving away as we approached, their eyes glowing in the headlights. Thick-skulled and stupid—is that what Marie-Laure had called me?

The evening before, as she had placed the clothes in my hand, there had been something luminous about her, something you could almost see in the shadows of the hallway, as if her calm radiated from something visible only in the night, in the darkness.

I stared out at the trees by the road—bananas, mangoes, breadfruit, their outlines tangled in the shadows. "Edouard's at Fare Ute," said Harris.

"It's your business," I said.

"You want a cut—is that what you want?" Harris was asking. "It's the best, brought in from Raiatea or Tahaa, someplace there, very high quality."

"Look—I really don't care."

"Your loss. I'm telling you," said Harris and then he continued, babbling on.

I knew Marie-Laure—she would wait until I left before returning to the kitchen for the girls. They would be sitting now in her room built under the old mango tree, the little girls curled beside Marie-Laure beneath the web of mosquito netting. Would they be asleep? They would be restless, perhaps, so that Marie-Laure would tell them a story. I had heard my share when I lived with A-tai—stories I rarely thought about anymore. Stories about war, about her great-uncles, stories about magic. Stories told at night, in the dark. During the day, there was work, things to buy and sell, accounts to be settled, but at night came the stories of the past, things forgotten and now remembered, tales of wanderings and horses and terrible sacrifice. "We come from the North," A-tai said, but it was so long ago. No one talked about why we, the Hakka, had left this North or where it was located: in China? Further north? It was vague like everything else, real only in the voice of the storyteller.

Why had Marie-Laure changed her mind about going to the party? Her dress, her long, smooth hair—didn't she want to go? It was like everything else I knew—the things that no one said out loud, so that the more questions I asked, the more hidden the answers remained.

A-tai sometimes talked about charms and magical talismans. She talked about how you had to keep a charm hidden so that its power could protect you. It was the only way the charm worked: as long as it was kept secret, something known only to you and no one else. These were the stories that I knew, tales of magic. The charm was always kept hidden where it remained—true, powerful, and magical. It had its own will, its secretive desire, at least according to the story, something half-remembered.

Chapter 3

Harris pulled over to the side of a road in Fare Ute, north of Papeete, and parked behind a dark Peugeot. The Peugeot doors opened and two men stepped out.

"The tall one's Edouard," Harris said.

He wasn't from Tahiti. I knew because I had never seen him before.

"He's from Raiatea—they're both from Uturoa," said Harris. "I don't remember the other guy's name—everyone just calls him Ha Gow."

They were nineteen, twenty years old, a few years older than us. Edouard stood by the window on the driver's side, and, even in the shadows, I could see the veins bulging from his arm muscles. "Who's the other *mec?*" he asked.

"My cousin," said Harris.

The street was deserted. We were parked by the chain-link fence of a construction yard, closed for the night, a heavy chain wrapped around the gate. Edouard cleared his throat and spat on the ground. He walked back to his car.

Harris opened his door. The air outside smelled of diesel fuel and the sea, the heavy smell of salt and chemicals.

We walked to the Peugeot, and Edouard settled himself in the driver's seat. Harris reached into his pocket, but I put my hand on his arm. "Let's see it first," I said.

Edouard looked at me for a long moment and produced a plastic bag with about a half kilo of *pakalolo* inside.

"Give us a sample," I said.

"Fuck you," said Edouard.

"If it's good, we'll do business with you again."

"Who the hell are you?" Edouard spoke quietly, as if this was the way he always spoke.

"He's Tamerlan Chen's son," said Ha Gow.

Edouard looked unimpressed.

"Black pearls," Ha Gow added.

Edouard glanced ahead at the road, still empty of cars. No one passed through that area of the industrial zone at night. Edouard took out a cigarette paper, opened the plastic bag, and rolled a joint. I passed it to Harris—I didn't know the first thing about *paka*. On the black pearl atolls, most producers—Robert Wan, my father—had a zero tolerance policy, enforced by regular inspections of everyone's living quarters. No one was going to get drunk or stoned on such a small stretch of sand surrounded by hundreds of miles of ocean. My father said, "I don't want to deal with drunks or potheads in the middle of nowhere." Living with my father was the same as living on the atoll—any hint of *paka,* and he would never let me anywhere near his pearl oysters.

"You don't know shit," Edouard said to me.

"What—about cheap operations like yours? I wouldn't waste my time." It was true—I didn't know shit.

"Rich pretty boy," said Edouard.

"If you dealt with rich guys, you wouldn't be in the sorry fucked-up shape you're in," I said. "You'd be looking at a million francs instead of a hundred here, a hundred there."

Harris kept his hands in his pockets and then, after a moment, began fumbling with a pack of cigarettes.

"You think you know it all," said Edouard. "You think we don't know anything, coming from the *van-tui*."

The *van-tui,* the backcountry, had a romantic tone when A-tai spoke of it. The remote places, the remote islands, distant, untouched, but when Harris and I talked about the *van-tui,* it meant a boring place, stupid and backward.

"You're right," I said. "I do know it all. I know that if you wanted to hide a million francs, you'd grow it in the *van-tui*."

Edouard leaned out the window and looked past me. We all knew what tough and bad looked like—we saw it in the movies and on TV. But

Edouard had something else—he knew how to wait, how to measure out time.

"Business, business," said Ha Gow from the passenger seat.

"You bring it in, we'll distribute it," I said.

"You're a rich piece of shit," said Edouard. He offered his hand. "Edouard Ma."

"Marc Chen," I said without shaking his hand.

Edouard extended his hand again. "Monsieur Marc Chen. But I might as well tell you, we don't have a million francs of *paka*."

"We'll talk later," I said.

"I'm going to France. Military duty. But I tell you—if I promise you a million francs, I'll give you a million francs," he said.

"Is this *la jet-set?*" Ha Gow asked.

"You're looking at it," said Harris.

Chapter 4

Five minutes after I arrived at the party, I knew that I could do without *la jet-set*. The atmosphere was suffocating and it wasn't due to the heat. Harris disappeared with the paka and the luscious Jocelyn, leaving me to stand about in various darkened rooms. The women were exquisitely beautiful, but I was related to almost all of them, and they certainly weren't interested in talking to me when there was much bigger game to hunt.

"Marc—you know I saw your father the other day." It was Philippe MuSan, a glass of champagne in his hand. "Let's get you something to drink." MuSan was in his fifties, his grey hair curly and casually rumpled, and he wore the indoor-lighting pallor of the politicians at La Présidence, the Presidential Palace. I followed him past a fountain—a statue of a small boy pissing into a koi pond—and up the stairs. "Did you just arrive?"

"Yes. It feels like eternity," I said, then realized that I was speaking to myself; MuSan had disappeared into the party.

"Eternity. As in condemned to hell?" MuSan reappeared holding a second glass of champagne. "You know, your father said something about your military duty."

"He intends to have me sent to France."

"France isn't as bad as you think." MuSan put the champagne into my hand.

A woman appeared at his arm. She was partly sheathed in a very tight black dress, her hair a pale ripple over her shoulder. "Aren't you getting me a glass?"

MuSan smiled elegantly at her. "Later—when you're old enough."

There was a motion to the side: Harris waving, trying to get my attention from the balcony.

"Do you know where I'll be sent?" I asked.

"You have any particular preference?"

Somewhere not too cold, I thought. "Where it doesn't snow."

MuSan motioned towards the balcony. "Your cousin Harris—he's been waiting to talk to you."

"He'll live. He has a very beautiful girlfriend. She's somewhere here."

"Mademoiselle Loong. Your father mentioned her. She's the niece of my first wife," MuSan added by way of explanation. He sipped his champagne and I wondered why the subject of Jocelyn Loong had surfaced in a conversation between my father and MuSan. "You'd better go check on your cousin before he falls off the balcony."

The house stood on a stretch of black sand that curved out to sea, ending at the tip of Point Venus. The view was spectacular during the day, but from the balcony at night there was only the blackness of the sea and the sky. "So what took you so long?" asked Harris.

"So why did you want to see me?"

"Jocelyn was going to pick up some friends. I thought you could go with them—you looked so bored. But they left already."

A breeze floated over the balcony from the sea. I had a headache. It was December and hot, the middle of summer.

"Hey—Harris. You've been hiding from us." Two women glided up on either side of Harris, two French women. My mother once decided to send me to riding lessons at the stables near the Hippodrome track—my father said that this was such a crazy idea, but every week A-tai made me get into the pickup truck driven by her friend, the dumpling vending woman, who would drive me across town. The French girls stared at me and they whispered into each other's ears. I hated every single lesson. A-tai said that the French stared at my mother because they couldn't believe she could be so beautiful, and I looked just like my mother. No, I said—those girls stare because they're mean. But A-tai said that my mother had spent a lot of money on these lessons and I must not waste her money.

I walked down the stairs to the glass doors opening to the garden. The blonde in the black dress glanced at me. She was standing by the stairs. It didn't look as if Philippe MuSan had changed his mind about getting her a glass of champagne—her hands were empty, but she was smiling, an intimate, contented smile. I knew that her mother was a *demi* like Mu-San, part Chinese, part French, but I couldn't remember her name. She continued looking in my direction, as if she were going to walk towards me, but then she walked back through the party, disappearing beneath a string of lanterns.

"You won't believe what she did," another woman was saying.

"He was really stupid," someone replied.

The sounds of the party drifted over the beach—the music, someone laughing, the murmuring of voices. I stepped outside the house and the garden. I walked out, further and further along the sea. The moon was swollen and almost full, and the waves rolled low and steady. Silence fell over my thoughts, the voices disappearing in the distance.

Someone was burning leaves and the smoke hung in the air. A light flickered in the ocean, the lantern of a boat fishing in the night. A crab raced along the beach, disappearing sideways into its hole. Long waves rose and rippled far along the shore.

There was a motion in the darkness: a woman walking by the sea. Her dress shimmered as if it were spun of moonlight, a tiny sliver of a dress. I could tell, even in the shadows, that she was no longer young, but she was beautiful, the edge of the water curling around her. "You're Marc," she said.

She approached, her hair cut short in dark waves.

"How do you know my name?" I asked.

She was holding one sandal in her hand, jeweled with an impossibly long heel.

In the distance swept the beam of the lighthouse at Point Venus. She walked closer and I could see her light-colored eyes and something else: sadness, a hopefulness when she smiled.

"I'm Aurore," she said.

We walked back to the house and I followed Aurore through the garden, along the lawn where she picked up a garden hose lying by a row of ginger. She turned on the water and began rinsing the black sand from her feet.

It was her house, I realized—one of her houses—and she had lent it for the night, for the party. I had heard of Aurore du Chatelet, that she was a lawyer—a *notaire*—and a painter, that she was related in a complicated way to the Comte de Paris and that her husband was living in France, in Rambouillet. She was part of the general gossip of the island, the *radio cocotier,* and yet even gossip kept a certain awed distance from her.

She threaded her way past the clusters of guests, the tinkling of glasses. She paused to nod when someone called her name across the room, and then we were walking past a hedge of torch ginger, towards a small house, a *fare* set in a corner of the garden. She opened the door. A fragrance of nocturnal flowers, the Queen of the Night, rose in the air with the flutter of wings, a moth rising from the vines that grew by the *fare.*

She turned on the light, an ordinary motion—like picking up the garden hose—but I was watching a secret. She was extraordinary, I knew, and for whatever unknown reason, I had been selected to watch her act as if she were mortal, like watching a celestial presence in disguise.

Books lined the walls of the *fare* in glass-covered shelves, a protection against the appetites of termites. I glanced over her books, pausing at the one that Marie-Laure had been reading. "*The Dream of the Red Chamber,*" said Aurore. "It's an English translation in five volumes—this is the second. It's one of the better translations." Aurore slid the glass open, taking the book from the shelf. "The first volume has been sitting for weeks on my nightstand." She passed the book to me. "You can borrow this if you like."

"You should keep it," I said.

Aurore was quiet—too gracious, I knew, to ask the obvious question: if I had already read this book.

"I'm not much of a reader," I said. "I only know about *The Dream of the Red Chamber* from what my great-grandmother told me."

Aurore smiled, making no movement to take the book back.

"Maybe I would know about it from you," I said.

"You're shy," said Aurore. "Or maybe it's the way you appear. It's very charming."

"I'm only telling the truth about what I don't know."

"What did your great-grandmother tell you?"

I picked up the book, placing it on the desk. "It's like *The Three King-doms,* but different—*The Three Kingdoms* was written about war." How dumb I sounded: it was like this but it wasn't like this, it was different.

"*The Dream of the Red Chamber,*" said Aurore. "You might say it's about illusion. On another level, it's about love—love between cousins."

"It was written a long time ago," I said. *We don't do that anymore,* I almost wanted to add, wondering if Aurore thought of such things between cousins as strange, the practices of an alien world. "Would you like something to drink?"

She laughed, silvery and bright. "Are you going to bring me something to drink?"

"Champagne? What would you like?"

"Ah—what would I like." She was standing across the room by the books. She spoke as if it were not a question.

I held two glasses in my hand, weaving through the crowd of guests, which was growing thicker as the night grew late, and all I could think of was Aurore. You decide, she had said.

"Marc." Someone grabbed my shoulder.

I almost spilled the champagne and I turned angrily, trying to slip free.

It was my father, his hand still on my shoulder. "I've been looking for you," he said.

No one ever said that I looked like my father. He had a broad forehead and long, piercing eyes, and he wasn't handsome, but he looked important, as if he had already arrived at the places that everyone else was only dreaming about. "Harris said you needed a ride."

"I'm staying," I said.

"How are you getting home?"

"With Harris."

"He's left already."

I knew how I appeared to my father—his dropout son rushing through the party with two glasses of champagne.

"We're leaving," said my father.

I stepped away. I walked outside past the torch ginger. The door of the *fare* was ajar and I slipped inside. The fragrance of the Queen of the Night drifted through the air, the ghost-pale flowers blooming outside the door. The room was empty.

The book rested on the table. I placed the glasses down and a clock ticked on the desk. "Aurore," I called.

The door opened and my father entered the room. "The Marquise du Chatelet is not here," he said.

"I'll wait," I replied.

My father left the room, leaving me alone. I sat down at the desk. I knew how to wait. I had practiced for a long time.

Chapter 5

We heard about it the day after. The *radio cocotier,* the coconut radio, the island gossip made up in speed what it lacked in accuracy.

"Haven't you heard?" Harris asked, his call waking me.

From the yard outside rose the crowing of roosters.

"You're awake, aren't you?" Harris said. "You've got my car."

I was lying on a mattress next to some lumber piled on the floor. I had left the party too late to drive to my father's house in the mountains over Papeete.

"Elodie De Koning," said Harris. "You saw her, right? She was standing next to you at the party. Black dress, really tight. Huge *ti-tis.* You heard how she left the party? With a friend of Philippe MuSan. Old enough to be her father—no, her grandfather."

A rooster crowed outside. I had fallen asleep on the upstairs floor of my Uncle Alexandre's house. An extension cord lay thrown next to the pile of lumber with boxes of tiles stacked along the walls—the upper floor had been under construction for as long as I could remember. Wires stuck out from the walls and there was the smell of cement and concrete, things left unfinished.

From the window, I looked over the eastern mountains, the pure color of the sky in the morning light. People talked about how beautiful it was, the sea and the sky and the flowers, but there was always that underlying feeling that Tahiti was an island and you always ended up driving the same road around it. Not much new, not much to think about. So beautiful, they said, and then they left.

I drove away in Harris's car before Harris could arrive later in the morning to collect it. A maid was sweeping the stairs as I pulled up to Aurore's house. Orchids flowered along the staircase and a red frangipani bloomed by the entrance. The maid wore her hair in a dark braid.

"I'm here to see the Marquise," I said.

The maid nodded and disappeared into the house, leaving me to wait at the bottom of the stairs. It was quiet, with only the sound of the sea, a sound like faraway thunder, the waves falling on the beach behind the house. A white seabird glided through the sky. The calm and cloudless sky—unlike my thoughts running around and around in angry circles. What was I doing here? As if I never learned. Aurore had appeared just as I was leaving the night before, her hand resting on my arm. I'm sorry, she said. Come here tomorrow. Her eyes glittered as if she were crying. Were those really tears? Promise me, she said.

The maid reappeared at the doorway. "Come back later," she said and continued brooming.

I drove the car in reverse down the narrow access road from the house. I was driving too fast, the car hitting a dip in the road with a jolt, but I drove faster and the car continued backwards. The dogs started barking from behind the gates of the neighboring houses. I saw the main road in the distance, the road back to town. Aurore appeared, walking around the corner from the main road, a baguette tucked against her arm. It was the middle of the morning, later than the normal time for picking up bread. She waved and smiled.

I slowed the car to a stop. She was wearing sunglasses, a red blouse, and white shorts; her legs were long and tanned.

"You're here," Aurore said.

She seemed so happy to see me, so guileless, that I found myself leaning over and opening the door.

"I'm sorry—you were waiting," she said.

I felt so nervous, I didn't trust myself to say anything. In the morning light, I realized that Aurore was around the age of my father.

"I was worried I wouldn't see you." She slid into the passenger seat.

The maid had disappeared from the staircase as I drove up to the house. Aurore opened the door, stepping lightly outside. I heard the sound of sweeping, the maid brooming somewhere inside. The orchids, the flowering plants crowded, luxurious and dark, around the staircase.

Aurore turned, waiting for me before the stairs.

I should leave, I knew—mumble an excuse and drive away. What did I know? Marie-Laure once said that I spoke Hakka "like those old Chinese poems"—her exact words, not that I had ever heard any of these poems.

"My grandmother says we're butchering the language and only Marc Antoine speaks the way it should be spoken," said Marie-Laure. "She says that it's because of your A-tai that you speak so beautifully." My A-tai, who was over eighty and a lot of good that did me, carrying around useless knowledge from a century earlier, but of course I clung to Marie-Laure's compliment, replaying it a hundred times in my mind—how she said that I spoke Hakka beautifully, how I spoke beautifully—until her calling me thick-skulled and stupid erased anything she'd said before.

I opened the car door and walked to where Aurore was standing. A chicken scratched at the ground by the stairs, the dust scattering over where the maid had swept the tiles clean. I moved to shoo the chicken away with my foot, but she turned a black bead eye towards me and continued her scratching.

"Just leave her," said Aurore.

I bent down, picking up the hen and turning her backwards so that she couldn't peck at me. I carried her to the edge of the garden, releasing her by a bush of *tiare*. She rushed away from me into the neighboring garden. Aurore was still waiting for me and I walked with her up the stairs into the house.

I washed my hands in the kitchen sink. Glasses dried in rows on the counter.

"How did you get that?" Aurore pointed to a white scar on my hand, running over the knuckles of my fingers.

"I cut myself on some coral."

"A venomous coral, with that kind of scar," she said. "Something to drink?"

"What are you drinking?"

"Mineral water for now."

She poured out two glasses.

33

"*Santé*," I said. She tapped her glass against mine. I kept my hand around the glass, not moving. I couldn't stop being nervous. "You're a *notaire*." I was beginning to say things just for the sake of saying something.

"I haven't worked as a *notaire* since I left France," she replied. "If you stop painting for too long, it's difficult to start again."

"I'm in the process of buying a boat. If you like, I'll take you wherever you like and you can paint." Why was I saying this? It was like the night before with Edouard at Fare Ute, only there no one had known any better than I had.

"What makes you think I want to paint the ocean?" Aurore asked.

I tried to stop. "I wouldn't know."

She smiled as if I were making sense, as if she actually wanted to talk with me.

"I'm just assuming that you'd want to paint somewhere outside of town," I said. "It's not particularly pretty in town."

"You don't think I'm going to do a series of ugly paintings? 'Ugly Tahiti,' I'll call it. It'll be a sensation. 'Sensationally Ugly Tahiti.'" She laughed, as if I were part of a secret that amused her.

I found myself looking at the walls, at the ferns and the white moth orchids growing from the volcanic stone wall that rose by the stairs leading to the upper floor. The water of the fountain tinkled, falling from the statue at the foot of the stairs.

"I don't keep my paintings here," said Aurore. "They're at the house at Mataiea."

I looked down at my glass, the fine lines of bubbles rising in the mineral water. When I glanced up, Aurore was watching me, her eyes jewel green beneath the dark wave of her hair.

"Are you working at the Perles du Paradis by the waterfront?" she asked, meaning my father's store in Papeete—he had a smaller store at Le Paradis, the hotel on the road leading to Faaa.

"No," I said. "I'm actually going into business for myself." Business, business. I knew that this was how the Hakka Chinese appeared: all about business, the one-room stores, the *libre service* markets, the bread trucks, the dressmaking stores, the car showrooms, the giant tankers of oil that docked at Fare Ute.

"Business—in Papeete?"

A dove cooed from somewhere in the trees of the garden. It would be easy to stay, to remain for hours.

"I should be going," I said. I knew: it was inescapable and by sunset I would be back, driving a car I had wrangled from my father's house above Pic Rouge, something that I hoped looked decently sleek so that I could drive Aurore from her house in Mahina to her house in Mataiea, where I would try not to talk too much, try not to blabber about things I knew nothing about, and finally lapse into desperate silence as we sat on the veranda of her house.

I was completely ignorant about art, but I sensed something unusual and passionate about her paintings that hung on the walls at Mataiea. The paintings were landscapes and still lifes—tamarind pods around a *moripata,* an old-style flashlight; a bowl of custard apples; a series of paintings of *fe'i* bananas. The dark colors, the deep curves of fruit, luxuriant and overripe. She would tire of me and my silences—I said this to myself over and over, because I didn't know what else to think—but Aurore watched the darkness settle over the coconut palms and the expanse of her garden down to the sand by the sea, not black like the fine volcanic sand near Point Venus, but white, a grainy ivory sand. From time to time, I glanced at her. I couldn't stop looking at her, the curve of her, eyes and mouth, and always, she turned to look back at me, saying nothing and yet improbably serene, as if she were happy and as if it were enough.

Chapter 6

Even in the beginning when there was nothing but promise and anticipation, I knew I could never speak about Aurore. It had to be as if I had never seen her, that I never thought about her all the time, that I was spending my days borrowing money from Harris and various relatives, bickering over the interest I owed them. I barked and argued, I pleaded. I had watched my father negotiate and I tried to do the same.

My father was capable of great charm, irresistible because it was real. You were important, you were the most important person in Tahiti, in all of French Polynesia, and, for that matter, in France and China as well—my father truly believed this when he negotiated with you. He considered your best interests, he wanted the best possible result for you—and for himself, but it would all be arranged so that you and he, everyone, would benefit—and how could you resist his detailed proposals, already anticipating your slightest objections?

"You're not your father," said my uncle Florian, the uncle of Marie-Laure, the younger brother of Ten-kwok. "I need more details. I can't invest in something I know nothing about." His eldest son, Radish, sat at the table with him. He stood as Uncle Florian stood and held out his hand to me. "I'd like to help. Come back when you know what you're doing."

Radish opened the door as I rose to leave. "I'll walk you outside," he said, following me down the steep wooden staircase leading from his father's office at the back of their house in the Patutoa district on the outskirts of Papeete.

We didn't speak until we reached the open drainage ditch where mosquito fish darted along the side of the street.

"This is about *paka* isn't it?" said Radish. He rested the side of his neck against his long fingers.

"Are you interested in what I have to say?" Uncle Florian was right—I wasn't my father, charming and subtle.

"There's talk." Radish shrugged. "I'd rather hear it from you."

"Aren't you going to France for your studies?"

"I'd rather stay in the islands."

"And not go to France?"

"It sounds good only because everyone tells us it's good. You haven't answered my question," said Radish. According to Marie-Laure, Radish had chosen his name when he was seven, announcing that he was old enough to do so. The older Hakkas had chosen their names when they were no longer boys. They liked lucky names, French names, or military names: Napoleon Liu, or Cesar Chang. There was even an Attila Tan, living on a remote atoll in the Tuamotus. This had all changed, and boys now had names right from the start, but Radish hated the name on his birth certificate, Charlemagne Li, and decided to rename himself *Lo-pet,* a word that meant a type of radish.

"You'll need a bookkeeper," he said.

"I don't have any money. Why do I need a bookkeeper?" I replied.

Radish swatted at the mosquitoes on his arm. I started walking down the road—Harris had reclaimed his car, and my father's fleet of cars was parked at his house above Pic Rouge. Radish ambled next to me. "You should go into transportation," he said. "You're buying a boat, aren't you? You can ferry passengers. You should start between Uturoa and Tahaa. It's a short distance; you don't have to go outside the lagoon."

The sun was hot. Even the street dogs had disappeared, running to the shade of the trees.

"But you won't go into transportation," said Radish.

"You were just telling me this was a good idea."

"We'll need a car," said Radish. "You don't have enough money to buy a boat, but I know where we can get a car."

"*I* don't have enough money, but *we* need a car?"

"Half and half. We'll split it. The money and the car."

I was already lost, thinking about Aurore—how I had seen her once, riding in the back of a car, although I could have seen her several times

without being aware of it, her image blurring into the general category of
the French, a small scattered number compared to the much larger Tahitian population—even the Hakka Chinese seemed more numerous. I was
walking in the *centre-ville,* crossing the street where the flamboyant trees
grew, their parasol branches shading the street near the administrative offices of the Haut Commissaire. A whistle blew and a gendarme appeared
so that I halted in the middle of the street. The gendarme held out the
flat of his hand against where I stood. With his free hand, he motioned
to two cars, letting them pass, one after the other gliding swiftly around
the corner. The windows of the first car were rolled tightly shut, but the
back window of the car that followed was rolled down and I saw Aurore
seated inside. At the time, I did not know who she was. I saw only the
sunlight falling on her as she passed so that I was still looking down the
street after the cars had vanished.

"He's the son of Pico Pearls," Radish was saying.

"All right."

"Are you listening?"

"I have other things to do," I said because I had no idea what he was
talking about.

Radish studied my face and shook his head. "You didn't hear what I
was saying—and I was saying, we should go and see him."

"Pico?"

"His son. He runs the store in Moorea."

"Well then, call him," I said. "I'll see him tomorrow night."

"How about right now?"

"What's the hurry?"

"You should see him tonight," said Radish. "He'll lend us the money."

"Not tonight."

"Do you have a good reason?"

I didn't reply, acting like I didn't hear.

"All right," he said. "But you'd better have a good reason or else you're
a fool."

"If I'm a fool then you can leave."

We walked beneath the sun, a lone pickup truck passing us on the road.
The color of the sky faded in the heat, the blue disappearing into the glare
of light.

Azure, cerulean, *bleu d'outre mer*, the tubes of oil paints nestled side by side inside their wooden box. Aurore closed the lid delicately shut as if the paints were sleeping lightly. Her lips brushed against my ear. We sat on the veranda at Mataiea, the breeze from the sea rustling the gift-wrapping paper. Aurore looked over the lagoon, the mirror of the sunset, orange and darkening purple. "You always hear that it's beautiful here and it's true, but it's not only that," she said. "It's finding such gentleness." She said this in the way that you talked about pain.

Her arms were folded, the lines on her forehead furrowed deep. The waves lapped quietly on the sand. "It's dark, isn't it?" She let me sit so close, I could almost touch her. It would be easy. Crazy and easy and it would never happen. "The sweetness," she said. "It's all so dark. Kind and horribly dark."

The gift-wrap had fallen to the floor, a corner caught between the slats of wood. Aurore bent down to pick up the paper, shiny and printed with a pattern of flowers. She tugged at the paper and as it came loose, she held it between her fingers, fluttering in the wind coming in from the sea.

Someone was playing a guitar, the music floating from a distance. I couldn't tell if it was only the guitar or if someone was singing—the music was too far away.

"I should bring you another gift," I said. "You must have all the paints you need."

"No, to the contrary. Oils—they're expensive and I'm imprudent."

Living in too grand a style, Uncle Florian would say. He belonged to the old Hakka: living in dilapidated wooden houses, wearing the same faded clothes and looking like fishermen, shuffling in their plastic sandals no matter how much money they had. They're *gnat-shee,* Radish said—they bit their shit, they were so frugal.

Imprudence felt luscious by contrast. I sat alone on the veranda, alone with Aurore. When she had brushed her lips against my ear, I thought I would lose my mind.

"It's been a long day for you," I said. "I should be going."

"You're very charming."

"You told me this at the party."
"I haven't lied to you—it's true."

I drove too fast, back to Papeete. The road was dark. Only the occasional store or gas station was illuminated, their doors closed for the night.

I was crazy, I told myself. Why did I do these things—like leaving the way I did, turning and walking away? I was crazy, so crazy about Aurore that I couldn't even admit to myself that I was hopelessly infatuated with her, that I wanted her, but there was something else, at the corner of my mind, flickering like a night moth flying away in the darkness only to reappear again, caught in the light.

I was crazy and a fool, but I was still thinking. Why was Aurore talking to me? I wasn't so stupid that I couldn't figure it out—what was it that Edouard had said—a rich pretty boy, someone who caught her fancy for the moment, it seemed.

The last thing I wanted was to be someone's pretty boy. It was there at the party, the unseen network, the social niceties to which I was oblivious, but I knew enough. I knew they existed: the rules you could break, the rules you couldn't break. It was a sophisticated game, and I wasn't going to start playing when I could never learn the rules.

The questions started from the beginning: why did Aurore disappear at the party? Why did she ask me to return? All I knew was the maddening way she kept me so close. This wasn't the answer, just the reason I ignored the questions.

The road curved through a forest of *mape* trees. The trees were tall, the branches woven thick, the shadows beneath the trees like an endless cave. The forest was haunted, according to the stories. You could smell the perfume at night, the perfume of beautiful women long dead.

Chapter 7

I tried to forget Aurore. I went about my usual business, which was to waste another day trying to borrow money. Who was rich, who was wealthy? You couldn't tell from appearance alone. The old Hakkas dressed and lived the same, wearing rundown clothes and living in rundown houses, some of them little more than plywood and corrugated tin sheet shelters.

My father and his friends were younger, occasionally indulging in signs of wealth: the cars they drove, a bottle of finely aged cognac—but even then, this was combined with more humble possessions so that they lived with a mixture of expensive and cheap.

Uncle Florian said that it was only among the French that you found people who could waste money all the time, buying impractical houses filled with overly exquisite furniture and difficult lovers. The French were temperamental. Who knew what they really wanted?

I visited Uncle Florian again in his office. I listened and nodded my head. "Why aren't you working for your father?" asked Uncle Florian. "Smart man, your father."

My father the smart man was in the Tuamotus. I had told my father that I should move to the Tuamotus and work in the pearls where there was always too much work, grafting, harvesting, extracting, my father fretting and checking the water flowing through the atoll. The smallest increase in temperature and the *Pinctada margaritifera* oysters grew slower and slower. His answer was the same: I was staying in school. I wasn't going to school—I didn't go to class for weeks—but when I said this, my father raged at me, saying that he didn't want to hear anything about this.

Islands

The week after he left, I dreamed I was on the atoll. The sunlit clouds drifted in the sky, the reflections drifted in the water. The rippling clear lagoon, the floating clouds, the silence. It was beautiful and then I awoke.

A picture of Elodie De Koning smiled from the front page of *La Depêche,* next to a picture of a record-breaking large tuna caught in the Tuamotus. In the picture, Elodie appeared fourteen or fifteen, looking even younger than I had seen her at the party, and she was lounging in a tiny orange bikini on the deck of a yacht with one of my father's friends, a black pearl producer who, according to the newspaper article, had just proclaimed himself "The Emperor of Pearls." I returned to the upper floor of my uncle's house and opened the newspaper, reading as I sat on the mattress and drank my coffee. The windows and doorways were unfinished and empty. My father said that Alexandre, his younger brother, could never finish anything he started—look at the upper floor of his house. Uncle Alexandre had given me the key to the grandiose front door, imported from Hungary. He placed me in charge of the bill of lading for the door, sending me to the dock when the ship container arrived. The key had a carved handle, elaborate as the key of a fairy-tale door—and completely ornamental, since the windows of the upper floor had no glass and any-one could climb inside.

It was hot as the end of the year approached, and I started sleeping on the upper floor where the unfinished, open windows made the nights bear-able. The roosters crowed through the night and there was the mournful sound from the ship horns in the evening and early in the morning, the ships departing from the harbor of Papeete as the day ended and just as it began.

I flipped inside the newspaper, following the article.

"The story of the day," said Radish as he walked through the doorway.

"The garbage of the day."

Radish sat down on the mattress, stretched his long legs before him, and watched me reading the paper.

"I saw Elodie at the party," I said.

"I know—you were supposed to go with Marie-Laure."

"Supposed to—she didn't want to go."

"You should know," said Radish. "She'd never go to that party. She's too smart."

Too smart to go to the party with me?

Radish looked up at the blank wall. "Are you listening to what I'm saying?"

"I waited for her and she just left," I said.

"So tell me—what was the point of her going there with you? You'd just meet someone else, and she knew it. I mean, look at that photo of Elodie with her *ti-tis*. Elodie was there at the party, right?"

From the open windows came the voice of a woman talking in a neighboring yard. She was talking on the phone or to herself—the sound of her voice both clear and yet so garbled, I didn't know what she was saying.

"You don't have to lie," said Radish. "You can be sleeping with the Queen of France. I don't want to know. I'm just telling you why Marie-Laure didn't go to the party with you."

I felt a strange stirring, somewhere inside, like the night when Marie-Laure first talked to me about the party. It was the reason I decided to go—for her, for the way she stood in the shadows of the hallway. "Is she still at my mother's house?" I asked.

"She's back at her parents' house. Her mother came back from Austria, or some Baltic cruise—I don't know, I don't clutter my mind with these things." Radish waved his hand like he was swatting at small bugs.

"What did Marie-Laure say?"

"That she didn't go to the party with you. She's been upset about it all week."

"What?"

"All right," said Radish. "How about I agreed to come here because I hoped she'd stop crying over you all the time?"

I looked down at the newspaper. I felt my heart beating like it would fly away, turning wild, something unpredictable that you could never catch.

Radish had a motor scooter and we rode to the Fautaua River where Marie-Laure's father, Ten-kwok, had built a house. When we arrived, five of Radish and Marie-Laure's cousins—they were from that side of the family rather than from the side I was related to—were walking to the river, looking like a line of ducks heading to the water. They stopped when they saw Radish. The older two were boys around thirteen years old, dressed in wrinkled black swimming trunks. The younger ones were seven or eight, the two girls in faded underpants and the boy completely naked.

"Are you swimming with us?" the older boy asked.

"Is Marie-Laure at the house?" Radish asked.

The older boy shook his head while the younger cousins stared at us, one of the girls swishing a stick through the air.

"Do you know when she'll be back?"

"She hasn't been here all day," said the boy. They stood for a moment looking down at their feet and the dirt. The younger girls started down the road again and then they were all shuffling to the river. They broke into a run, screaming and shouting, scrambling over the boulders at the river's edge before splashing into the water.

Money—now that was easy to understand: you had it or you didn't have it. Pay me back, twenty percent.

"I told you Stellio would lend us the money," said Radish as we left Pico Pearls.

"We still have to pay him back," I replied. "In six fucking months with fucking interest."

I felt sick, wondering how I was going to pay it all back. Radish bought a stack of notebooks from the Prince Hinoi bookstore and entered the numbers. We brought a table up the stairwell to the upper floor where he sat by the window with a view of the eastern mountains and the peaks of Le Diadème. By the afternoon, the clouds had moved over the mountains, throwing the slopes into shadows.

Someone knocked at the door. I looked at Radish—no one ever knocked at the door—and then I walked to the empty windows and leaned my head outside. It was Marie-Laure wearing a green and white dress, her long hair tied with a ribbon. She held a package in a white plastic bag.

I opened the door and she kissed me with a formal air on the cheeks. "Hey," said Radish, smiling, and she threw her arms around him.

"How's the studying?" I asked.

"Fine." Marie-Laure walked across the floor to the windows facing towards town, the harbor hidden in the distance.

"You can study here," said Radish.

Marie-Laure turned, her back against the window. "At least there's a breeze here. It's horrible in the house—you can't breathe, it's so hot."

"We'll share the table." Radish stood and reached for the pack of anti-mosquito coils kept in an empty wall niche. "Have a seat." He propped a broken piece of mosquito coil on its aluminum holder.

I searched around my pockets, producing a booklet of matches. Radish placed the mosquito coil under the table. I followed, kneeling down and striking a match to light the coil. I looked over at Marie-Laure—she was untying the plastic knot around the package. Her dress was plain but there was something different about her, a reserve, almost elegant. She plucked at the knot with her fingernails. The knot unraveled and she smoothed the plastic away from a round tin standing inside. From a side pocket of her dress, she produced a rusty vegetable peeler with a broken plastic handle. She pried the lid of the tin with a flick of the end of the vegetable peeler, turning the tin with one hand and repeatedly prying the lid until it opened.

Radish looked inside. "Puffed rice!" he said, sounding like a child. We both peered into the tin where rectangles of puffed rice cookies, dotted with tiny squares of ginger, lay stacked in spirals.

"My great-aunt made these this morning," said Marie-Laure. She tilted the can towards Radish, who selected a rectangle, removing it carefully from the tightly wedged spiral of cookies. Marie-Laure removed the next rectangle, holding it between her fingers and turning to me.

I reached out to take the puffed rice from her, but she shook her head. "Your hands," she said.

I glanced down to find my hands smudged and dark. I couldn't remember how they had become that way. When I looked back at Marie-Laure, she lifted the cookie, motioned towards me impatiently and slid it inside my mouth.

Marie-Laure and I stood by the window, looking in the direction of the sea. We could see only trees, tall breadfruit and mangoes, and the neighboring yards with their lines of laundry, but there was the breeze, coming from the sea. It was evening, the sky a purplish blue and the underside of the clouds orange as flames. At first we were mostly silent and then we were talking, about nothing really, talking just to talk, our elbows resting side by side. Radish left, saying he would return, but I knew from the hurried way he left that he was gone for the day.

"He's in love," said Marie-Laure.

"With whom?"

"Ah—that's a secret. I can't tell. Then it won't be a secret." In the evening light, her hair appeared reddish, glowing in the sunset. The birds in the trees chattered wildly, the last burst before their nocturnal silence.

"Do you tell him everything?"

"Yes." She lowered her voice. "Are you jealous?"

Of course I was jealous. "No, of course not."

She smiled at me—she knew I was lying.

"I have to go to this *cocktail* with Uncle Alexandre next Saturday night," I said. "Why don't you come with me?"

"No—I have to study."

"You're not studying now."

"Well, I will be. Soon."

"The *cocktail* will be tedious. Boring. I won't have anyone to talk to if you're not there."

"You can talk to me all the time, if you want. You can talk to me when you return from your boring *cocktail*."

"Why won't you go?" I said, suddenly serious.

She shrugged, chewing for a moment on her lower lip. "I heard you were looking for me."

"I've been looking for you all week. I went with Radish to your parents' house in Fautaua."

"This isn't like ancient times," said Marie-Laure. She started talking in French.

"What are you talking about?"

"You know what I'm talking about." She kept her voice quiet, almost a whisper. "It's why I'm here. I heard you were looking for me and I knew I had to talk to you. I'm going to pass the *bac* and I'm going to France." If anyone else had said the same words, it would have sounded presumptuous, but when Marie-Laure spoke, her words sounded modest, saying the simple truth.

"I don't see why you didn't go to Irina's party with me and I don't see why you can't go to the *cocktail*—it's next week; you can study until then."

"It's not that I can't go," she said. "I can't go with you."

"Why not?" I asked.

"You know as well as I do." Her words were calm, sharp as a razor.

I wanted to say, *Radish said that you were upset. That you were crying.*

"That's it, then," I said.

She stepped away from the window and walked inside. In a moment, I would hear her footsteps going down the stairs. I walked across the floor and caught her by the arm. There was no lighting and the floor was dark. If she had moved away, I would have let her go, but she made no motion. I ran my fingers along her hair, smooth and slippery soft. She reached up and kissed me on the mouth and I kissed her back. It was so easy. I held her and kissed her and I could not let go.

Chapter 8

No one did this anymore—it was like those ancient tales when men wore long hair in a topknot and women had elaborate combs stuck in elaborate hairstyles. Once it had been common, but now it was unthinkable. In the world of *The Dream of the Red Chamber,* it seemed that the only people you ever slept with were your cousins, but now, three hundred years later, it seemed as likely as wearing long silk robes in the street—no one did that anymore.

In the late afternoon, Marie-Laure brought her books to the upper floor and studied at the table with Radish. They seemed closer than ever, bound by their private secrets. I drove her back to her house near the Fautaua River before the night grew too late and Aunt Georgine would begin to worry about the whereabouts of Marie-Laure.

I bought Marie-Laure a woven hat decorated with ivory-white *mautini* flowers. I hammered a nail into the wall and she kept the hat over the bed. I slept with her every evening—I could not have enough of her—and always we were silent and there was a strange ease between us. I had slept occasionally with other girls—passing flirtations, sudden passions that vanished quickly. There was always a certain awkwardness, moments of fumbling. But Marie-Laure would lie nestled in my arms, as if she had always fit there, her hair against my skin, and when we moved it was without friction, sliding together as if we had been made as a whole in secret.

Marie-Laure had a friend, an Australian whose yacht was docked in the harbor of Papeete. I never saw this man, but she talked about him all the time. He was much older, in his mid-fifties, and he was in films, a producer. He had traveled the world. They had met at a dinner at Aunt Genevieve's. I knew that in his circles, it wasn't looks that counted because such a man could have a dozen beautiful women and he was already tired of beauty. From what I could see on television and in the glossy magazines that my aunts read, these kinds of people were always tired and they knew about all the variations of fatigue. He told Marie-Laure that she could call him Martin and she was invited to his yacht on a regular basis, although her mother made sure that she was accompanied by one of her male cousins, usually Radish.

"Why didn't you ask me?" I said.

"Oh, like I'm stupid," Marie-Laure laughed.

"I'm male and I'm your cousin."

"You'd be so jealous—you would spoil it all, sitting there with your dark look."

I began buttoning my shirt, but Marie-Laure slid her hands beneath, kissing me.

A few days later, Marie-Laure brought me a box, placing it in my hands. It felt heavy for its size. "Where did you get this?" I asked.

"Martin. He would have given it to me, but I told him I was giving it as a present and I had to buy it from him."

I unwrapped the paper to find a polished wooden box inside. I opened the lid.

When I didn't move, Marie-Laure looked inside, as if she were checking to see if we were looking at the same thing. "You asked me—remember?" said Marie-Laure. "The day we talked about the *tour de l'île*."

She didn't have to say anything. I knew what it was—I had seen enough movies: a Smith & Wesson Model 29 .44 Magnum.

The revolver gleamed darkly, and I placed the lid back on the box and set it on the table. "You should return it," I said. Firearms were illegal—you couldn't buy or sell arms, and approval for a permit was unlikely, granted only for special purposes, usually for members of private hunting clubs. It was impossible for anyone to get me a gun, and I had known this when I asked Marie-Laure.

"Too late," she replied. "Martin left already—he sailed yesterday morning. I'm sorry you don't want to keep it."

She seemed so sad that I tried to kiss her. "You want me to return it," she said.

"No—I'm keeping it."

"You're only saying that," she replied, unconvinced.

"You see this in the movies." Harris held the Magnum in his hands. He heard that I was living on the unfinished third floor of my uncle's house and he decided to visit. "Where did Marie-Laure get this?"

"An Australian film producer," I said. "He was passing through Papeete."

"You think this is the original—the one they used in the movie?"

"Are you stupid?" Of course not—but now that Harris had mentioned it, I wasn't actually sure for a moment.

"I've heard about him. He produced those action movies, the crazy ones. They say that Marie-Laure caught his fancy. Maybe the novelty appealed to him, an ugly girl for a change."

"I would watch my language," I said in a voice so quiet and angry that Harris looked at me strangely.

He opened his mouth as if he were about to say something.

"Who knows," I said. "Maybe it's the one in the movie."

"Did he give it to Marie-Laure as a present?"

"No, she bought it from him."

"He made her pay for it?" Harris seemed offended.

"She insisted. She said it was going to be a present."

"For you?" Harris turned the Magnum around in his hands. I knew he wanted to fire it.

"Don't even think about it," I said.

"Why do you think he'd let Marie-Laure have this?" Harris asked. "I know—she bought it from him, but he doesn't need the money. From what you tell me, he was just humoring her. He didn't want to hurt her pride. I think it's true—what they say, that he really fancies Marie-Laure. And why shouldn't he?" I felt Harris watching me and I kept my gaze on the revolver.

It began raining late in the afternoon, the landscape strangely illuminated in sunlight against the dark thunderclouds. The colors seemed overly bright, green trees and yellow light. The clouds gathered thickly in the sky but the sun beat fiercely through the opening in the cloud layer. The rain started in heavy drops, one by one, until it poured in sheets.

Rainstorms carried their sudden dangers. The rain pounded and poured over windshields so that it was impossible to see. Rivers rose and swirled, spilling over boulders. The newspaper reported the inevitable casualties: car pileups and boys seen for a moment, playing at the water's edge, taunting one another and sliding down the rocks. The water was unpredictable and unforgiving, the bodies disappearing, washed out to sea.

Chapter 9

My father arrived unexpectedly the next afternoon. It rained in a steady downpour. Marie-Laure was studying while Radish read *Strategic Chess Openings,* moving the pieces on a chessboard as he followed the diagrams. I was on the phone talking to Edouard. "I'll call you back," I said when I saw my father walking through the door.

"When's the baccalaureate?" he asked Marie-Laure. He seemed to stand higher than the door and his voice echoed through the floor.

"Too soon," she replied.

He turned his glance to me and the smile vanished from his face. "Did you ask your uncle if you could stay here?"

"I took care of the door," I replied, pointing at the carved oak entrance.

"That was months ago," said my father. "I came back from the Tuamotus last night. Torea told me you haven't been home for weeks." My father had a housekeeper and a gardener; it wasn't like his house was being neglected. I looked around the floor—my clothes were piled in a jumble. Papers and empty bottles lay scattered over the bed.

Radish and Marie-Laure sat gloomily, but they weren't in the line of fire. "What have you been doing the past two weeks?" my father asked me. "Nothing, by the looks of it."

I retreated into silence.

My father stood over me. "We're leaving—but first you're going to clean up your mess. I'll be downstairs talking to your uncle."

He left and Marie-Laure began gathering her books from the table. "What are you doing?" I asked.

"I'm cleaning up."

"Why? I'm the one he's mad at," I said.

Marie-Laure swept her pens into her book bag.

"He won't stay long." I put one hand over her books. "Wait—he'll be leaving for the Tuamotus by the end of the week."

"You should leave with him. It's your business too."

"I won't leave you."

"Don't be ridiculous," said Marie-Laure. "What are you going to do—teach me calculus? I'm fine on my own." Radish rose from the table and left, closing the door quietly behind him.

Marie-Laure walked to the bed and began picking up the empty bottles. I took her hand. She pulled sharply away.

"Someone will see us," she said.

"So let them."

"You're crazy."

"All right," I said. "I am crazy."

She kissed me, softly at first and then passionately. I ran my hand along her back, pulling at the zipper of her dress.

My father lived above Pic Rouge in the mountains over Papeete. When he had begun building his house, the older Hakkas said that no one would live there with him—it was so remote, so far in the mountains that the air sometimes turned cold at night. In the old style, you lived with an assortment of relatives—your parents, your children, unmarried sisters with married sisters, chickens, pigs, cats, and dogs all running around together. A-tai said that in China, many families lived in one building; living space was arranged by kinship so that your closest kin lived in the room next door and your most distant kin were in the room across the courtyard. My father said that thinking about this gave him a headache. He needed to think and he couldn't think when dozens of relatives were crowded all around, telling him what to do.

There wasn't a real road leading to my father's house, just a dirt trail so that most of his cars were breaking down all the time, turning into expensive car sculpture. I learned how to order parts using my father's credit card so that I could drive his cars when he was away in the pearl farms in the Tuamotus.

My father drove me back to his house in a black Italian import, his favorite, the one car that he said was completely off limits to me. I had searched his office meticulously trying to find the car keys so I could drive Aurore in that car, but the keys were hidden so carefully, I had to settle for another import. My father loved this car. I felt his mood softening as he drove into the mountains. I looked out the window at Papeete receding further below, the boats in the harbor looking like toys.

"She's smart," said my father, breaking the silence between us. "Ten-kwok says that Marie-Laure wants to go to the University of Montpellier." The rain had stopped and the air was cooler. "I'm taking you to the Tuamotus," my father said suddenly. "We're leaving on Monday."

"What about school?"

My father laughed out loud. "So now you want to go to school." The paved road ended, turning into a dirt track. My father's mood grew somber. "Ten-kwok talked to me this morning. He said that Marie-Laure was spending too much time with you."

"She studies. It's quiet on the upper floor."

"Do you have any idea what you're doing?" From his calm tone of voice, I knew that he already knew about Marie-Laure and me. Gossip, gossip, people with nothing better to do, making up stories, only this one had hit its mark.

"I'm going to marry Marie-Laure," I said.

"Completely out of the question," my father replied. "You're leaving Monday morning."

"I'm going to marry her."

"You haven't been to school all year," said my father. "You grow up and then you can talk about marriage."

"What about you? You got married at eighteen," I said.

"What about it? The biggest mistake of my life. It was clear to everyone else—but I was eighteen and didn't have any sense."

"You just said it yourself: Marie-Laure is smart."

My father kept his eyes on the road. "Yes, she is."

"So there's no problem."

"The problem is you. I went to Pico Pearls and paid off your debt to Stellio. What the hell were you thinking? He had the nerve to argue with me about the interest. I came back from the Tuamotus because everyone was calling me, complaining about you. You've shown nothing but poor judgment. All I hear about is the trouble you're getting into. Ten-kwok said that he didn't want you dragging his daughter into your mess, and I agreed with him. You couldn't have picked a worse time."

The road curved through guava and brush to a pair of iron gates. Beyond the gates rose a grove of bamboo surrounding the road. I got out of the car to open the gates; they creaked on their hinges as they swung back so that my father could drive the car past. The road continued into the forest of bamboo, over a bridge passing above a stream. On the far side of the stream stood a tall *bai yu lan* tree, the slender petals of its white flowers lying fallen on the road.

My father's house stood beyond a circular driveway, surrounded by a garden, an abundance of the rare and the ordinary: ginger, hibiscus, orchids, vines of barbadine and passion fruits, trees of ylang ylang, cherimoyas, rambutans, mangoes, and litchis, and trees whose names I didn't know. The silence was broken by a pair of black birds flying with a loud flapping of wings from a tamarind tree. Clouds passed overhead, cumulus clouds heavy with moisture, darkening the sky.

Years later, someone would show me a map of the area around Papeete and I would study it, trying to find the location of my father's house. I would find Pic Rouge and Pic Vert, but there was something different about the mountains and valleys—nothing corresponded to the twists of the road or the way the peaks of the mountains looked when I had stood at my father's house. The old generation was suspicious of abstract representations of how things were—books and maps were fine if you didn't know what had happened or what was there, but they believed that if you knew, you didn't need words or lines to show you what was real. I was from another generation, though, a generation that trusted maps. I turned the map in different directions and, in my mind, I tried to align what was written there with what I had seen, searching for the place where my father had built his house. From the grand front room of his house, a glass wall overlooked a valley, isolated and verdant, the mist curling in waves against the mountains of the interior. The clouds that enclosed the far valleys, the solitude—there was a moodiness I felt when I sat in this room. My father had chosen the place for its spaciousness, the mountain air, but I felt the brooding emptiness, oppressive and indifferent.

My father sat in one of the many chairs. He drank his tea from a green porcelain cup while I lit a cigarette—I had found a half pack left behind by one of his girlfriends. "You know, I went to see Ten-kwok on business," said my father.

I exhaled, staring at the black calligraphy paintings on the wall.

"I've hired Cecile. She's an *expert comptable* and a graduate from Hautes Études Commerciales."

Cecile Li, Marie-Laure's half-sister, the daughter of Ten-kwok's first wife. "She's in Paris," I said.

"She's here." My father stood up, walking to the glass wall and looking over the valley disappearing into the evening shadows. "She's coming with us to the Tuamotus."

"Why?"

"Because she's our new manager. I've hired her to reduce our losses—we're hemorrhaging money," said my father. "I was talking to Ten-kwok about a loan. He said he'd waive the interest, since we're family."

"Ten-kwok's giving you an interest-free loan. Is this why I can't marry Marie-Laure?" I asked.

"Her father complained, saying that Marie-Laure seemed infatuated with you. He joked about it, saying that perhaps we should marry our children together like they did in ancient times, *Dream of the Red Chamber,* that sort of thing—but he said I'd have to show him another son, not someone spoiled and *maozhung* like you." *Maozhung*—useless, worthless, a defective product. My father continued, describing the details of how worthless I was: failing my classes, never going to classes, dealing in drugs—*I'm not dealing in drugs,* I argued—flirting "outrageously, tastelessly, and publicly" with the Marquise du Chatelet, who was forty-one years old and married. My father paced along the glass, angrily turning and retracing his steps. "Ten-kwok told me that he didn't want to see you around his daughter. He said that you weren't going to ruin her life and that she was going to France. He told me that I didn't know—obviously, because I didn't have a son who could pass the baccalaureate—but he saw how Cecile had to study. Marie-Laure was going to do the same and she wasn't going to get distracted by you. I had to listen to him talking about how smart his daughters were."

I heard my voice, attempting to explain: it wasn't the truth about me. "It's not true," I said. It was exaggerated, it was twisted around . . . All right, some of it was true, but not in the way my father thought.

"You were at the party," said my father. "You were waiting for the Marquise. I saw you myself. Didn't I tell you it was time to leave?" My father had stopped pacing. He was looking out the window, his back turned to me. The view outside had turned dark, the valley swallowed by the night.

I went to the upper floor when I returned from the Tuamotus three months later. I was leaving the next day for France, for the army. My hair was shaved and I had the required inoculations, three on one arm, three on the other. It was arranged so that I would spend as little time as possible in Papeete—arriving one day and leaving the next. My father had made good on his promise to Ten-kwok Li.

Everything on the upper floor was the same as when I left. The chessboard that Radish used was still on the table, the chess pieces awaiting their next move. No one had returned.

Marie-Laure's white hat hung on the wall. I lifted it from the nail. A brown spider was hidden inside—and something else, a pouch with a long string. I opened the pouch to find a piece of stone, greyish white with green veins, a jade piece. It was carved in the shape of a fruit with curled leaves, a magical fruit, something imaginary. A-tai had spoken of magical charms, things you kept hidden, things you never spoke about. It had passed quickly—ten days, two weeks—the days with Marie-Laure. She had slipped the charm inside the hat—to protect us, to grant us luck, good fortune, a long life together, all the reasons why people keep charms.

If something is precious, keep it well hidden. If you love someone, never speak of them. I couldn't remember who had said this, A-tai or one of my aunts, but it was true. There was what you showed, how things appeared, and there was the way it really was. I could go to the most remote island of the Tuamotus, I could go to France, but the truth would still remain, hidden, secret, forgotten, always waiting, forever and ever passing like a day.

PART TWO

GHOSTS

Chapter 10

I returned to Tahiti too late for the Feast of All Saints. The flowers on the graves had wilted by the time I arrived in November and the roses on my grandfather's tomb in the Chinese cemetery had crumpled. I took the *tiare lei* that my sister Odile threw around my neck at the airport and laid it on the slab of grey marble. Every tomb had its roof, sheltering the dead from the sun and the rain. We walked away in the narrow space between the rows, overgrown with grass.

Two years had passed since I left Tahiti. Odile was thirteen and tall. I was twenty.

"Was it bad?" asked Odile.

"The army? They offered Edouard a promotion to *tireur d'élite.*"

"Why didn't he take it?"

"How should I know?" He didn't want to stay in France and he was tired of the army. He dreamed of going home.

Mango trees grew at the edge of the cemetery. At the crest, at the top of the long slope of graves, lay a family plot of the Tahitian royal family. An ancient *tiare* bloomed from one of the graves. I looked up at the black seabirds turning in the sky. Odile's face was blank, her eyes measuring me. "People talk."

"Well, you don't seem like the gossiping type."

Odile walked down a gravel path to where the car was parked. I remained standing for a moment by a row of tiny graves, the tombs of infants, next to a grave of one of the MuSans, someone who had hanged herself at nineteen.

Odile ran the air conditioner inside the car. I opened the door and sat in the driver's seat. The interior smelled fake—fake air, a false lack of heat.

I drove the car past the tombs, their white paint glowing pink in the evening light. "You've forgotten," said Odile. "No one comes here in the evening." No one visited the cemetery after five, for fear of the *tupapa'u,* the spirits of the dead.

"I haven't forgotten." I didn't want to see anyone.

My father announced his engagement, his wedding set for May. He was hosting two engagement parties, a private dinner for the family and then an elaborate party with an endless guest list. I was expected to stand next to my father greeting guests, shaking hands, listening to the talk about the uncertainties of the black pearl market and my father's reassurances—sound planning, financial organization, exciting new design—although he obsessed about the same worries in private.

Odile kept a jar of black pearls the size of marbles: silver, peacock blue, iridescent green, and purple, each pearl with a blister, a pucker, a defect that made every pearl in the jar worthless. I turned the jar in the light. We were at my father's house, where Odile was staying in one of the guest rooms. My father was always fond of Odile, his paternal affection giving rise to rumor. There was Odile's stick-straight hair and narrow eyes— the *radio cocotier* agreed that she was proof that my mother had continued sleeping with my father long after their acrimonious divorce.

"Ask for a jar of real pearls," I said.

"These are real pearls," she replied.

"Defective pearls."

"You're full of shit," Odile said, taking back the jar.

I sat beside her on the *tifaifai* bedspread, green and white. With my fingers, I traced the pattern of leaves and the curving lines of breadfruit. Odile's room was at the end of a hallway. A window opened onto a balcony overlooking papaya trees and coral-flowered balsam. White clouds floated through the sky, clouds of light.

"You know, Cecile wants me to a wear a dress to the party," said Odile.

"So wear a dress," I replied.

"Don't make me throw up. They might as well skip the engagement and just get married."

"It's a show. It's publicity."

"Yeah—she'll get to hear all over again about how she saved the Perles du Paradis. You were in the army—you didn't have to hear about this all the time."

I heard about it, even in the army: the story about Cecile Li, *expert comptable,* resurrecting the floundering business of Tamerlan Chen. There were other stories, darker ones—about how she was marrying out of love but my father was marrying out of gratitude, that he already had a mistress, beautiful and much younger, that he always had girlfriends and could never settle with one. According to these stories, you wondered how my father had the time to do anything at all.

At the airport the night before, my father had looked tired and worried, embracing me when I arrived. He asked what I wanted to eat. "Steak and fries," I replied.

My father fried the steaks as I sat in the kitchen. With the presence of Cecile, I expected newer appliances, an upgrade in furniture, but the house seemed unchanged—the kitchen still had its propane-gas stove and the same blackened pans. My father cut a thick slice of butter, melting it on my steak. "Cecile says it's bad for the heart."

"She's right," I said.

"I heard Edouard considered reenlisting. They said you could be sent to Chad."

"It's rumors. There's no truth to it."

"How do you like your steak?"

"Slathered in fat."

"You know Edouard's eldest sister married one of my cousins," said my father. "They had a store in Tahaa before they moved back to Raiatea."

My father seemed drained, as if something weighed on him. He continued speaking, optimistically outlining the plans to expand the Perles du Paradis, but there was an underlying weariness I had never seen before. He watched me eating my steak.

"Aren't you going to eat?" I asked, my mouth full of fries.

He glanced at the steak on the plate before him. "I'll have it later."

Odile placed the jar of pearls on the nightstand by her bed. "Put it in a better place," I said.

"Someone told me these were worthless," she replied.

"You'll tip it in your sleep—the glass will break."

"You haven't heard, have you?"

I picked up the jar and walked across the room, placing it on a shelf next to a bottle of glue.

"Cecile will get half the business," said Odile. She watched me, her lips pressed into a narrow line. "Cecile made your father sign an agreement. It limits your share. Cecile said she wasn't going to work just so that he could give it all to his son."

The sunlight fell in a long slant from the window to the floor, the dust floating, suspended in the light. I passed my hand into the light, watching the dust swirl.

"Your father said it wasn't legal—he was arguing about it downstairs with Cecile. She had her *notaire* draft the papers. Your father finally signed the agreement last week."

"Why are you telling me this?"

"Because you didn't know." Odile crossed her legs, sitting at the edge of her bed. The birds sang outside, *vini* birds swooping past the balcony.

Chapter 11

When I first returned, I spent my nights trying to sleep. The roosters crowed at all hours and strange calls echoed in the valley—nocturnal birds and sounds that came from the wind, the trees, the night itself shifting within the earth. I had been dimly aware of these sounds before I left, but I had always slept in one stretch, awaking heavy and forgetful.

I wondered now how I could have slept through the weird creaking, the whistles and animal calls from the night forest. Each night, now, I would wander downstairs to the main room, usually falling asleep towards dawn.

The garden was as beautiful as I remembered, but it was overgrown, the vines of barbadine running unpruned and wild. At first, the entrance gates had creaked as I opened them. I had oiled the hinges, and wondered why my father had never installed automatic gates. Soon I realized that my father was no longer interested in the house.

Except for the first night when I arrived, my father did not stay above Pic Rouge. He was building a new house by the sea at Taravao near the *presqu'île;* the construction was almost completed, and when I returned, he had already moved to Taravao with Cecile. It was his present to her, a dramatic house with wings like a bird overlooking the water.

Nothing was said—I was never told that I could not live at Taravao. My father drove me there and showed me the sweeping double staircase and the lotus pond, the leaves the size of umbrellas and the flowers perfect and lush, rising above the water. Cecile greeted me at the door and gave me a tour of the rooms. I was welcome, she said. I could stay as long as I wanted.

Three weeks after I returned, my father and Cecile celebrated their engagement at a dinner party. They were all there—aunts, uncles, and cousins, distant family related by name or families related by allegiances so old the reasons were explained by a dozen versions that no one I knew cared to listen to anymore. My father appeared relaxed and jovial, dressed in a floral shirt and dark pants. Cecile wore a long rose-pink dress and a strand of silver-blue pearls. Her father Ten-kwok arrived accompanied by Aunt Georgine.

Ten-kwok shook my hand and grinned, grabbing the back of my head. "You're back!" he said. He had a tendency to shout, even if you were standing right in front of him.

Aunt Georgine smelled of expensive floral perfume, lavishly applied, as she kissed my cheeks. Cecile's mother Mei wore a gold and orange sleeveless dress, her arms heavy and white and her eyebrows etched in black. She sat next to Cecile and my father and my grandmother Madame Chen. "A silly woman," A-tai said whenever she spoke of my grandmother. A-tai always considered her the young and frivolous bride of her son—it didn't matter that Madame Chen was past sixty and that for over twenty years she had been my grandfather's somberly dressed widow, offering platters of oranges and pomelos before his picture, displayed like an altar in her front room.

Odile and I were seated at the table next to Madame Chen. Odile had agreed to wear a dress—not a frilly dress, she emphasized. "I hate this dress," she told me when we sat down at the table.

The restaurant was air conditioned, but with the large crowd of guests the air seemed to grow warmer. I stood and shook hands, kissing cheeks and nodding my head. Yes, I was happy to be back. Yes, my hair was growing. Yes, the winters in France had been cold, much colder than I had ever imagined.

"Where's A-tai?" I asked.

"Someone went to pick her up," Odile replied.

The food began to arrive, plates of piglet in coconut milk, tamarind duck, gingered fish—a lavish nine courses. My father had reserved a chair for A-tai at the table. The chair was still empty.

"Do you want a soda?" I asked Odile.

"So," said Odile, ignoring my question, "did you see Marie-Laure in France?"

"She's still in Montpellier," I said.

"I heard she has a boyfriend."

"You heard correctly," I replied, motioning to the waiter.

"A whiskey sour," said Odile.

"She'll have a soda," I said to the waiter.

Odile shook her head and the waiter walked away before I could order for myself. Across the table, Cecile was talking to her eldest cousin, who lived in Huahine. He admired her necklace. He said something that made her laugh.

"Marc," said my father. Cecile's cousin turned to me. He was around forty. I had seen him on occasion in Papeete, and Marie-Laure said that he sometimes sent her books.

"Monsieur Li," I said.

He shook my hand and I saw, for a moment, a dark stone set on a gold ring. Monsieur Li had sloping shoulders and long arms and long, slender fingers—there was something about him that, even though he was as tall as my father, made him seem less intimidating. Marie-Laure said that he had once won a prize for translation, an obscure Chinese text from the Warring States period. He spoke to me in impeccable Hakka, speaking with precise words in the formal nuances of the language instead of lumping everything into vague, general words the way we always did. He asked about my return from France, and I found myself telling him that I was having trouble sleeping. Monsieur Li listened sympathetically and suddenly I knew why I was talking to him at length—he shared the same calm demeanor as Marie-Laure. For a moment, I felt the room dip.

"I'm fine," I said, shaking my head.

My grandmother Madame Chen took Monsieur Li's arm. "Why don't you sit with us?" she asked.

"I have to keep Ten-kwok out of trouble," he replied. Monsieur Li was brilliant, said Marie-Laure—but other people said he did crazy things, like keeping a photo of Pouvana'a a Oopa. He put oranges from Taravao and flowers before this photo, like you would before a photo of your father if he were dead. My father told me that Pouvana'a was thrown in prison in France for all those years on nothing but lies. The real reason was so that Pouvanaʻa would be far away before the airport was built and the army began arriving and the CEP, the *Centre d'Expérimentation du Pacifique*, began in the Tuamotus. Pouvanaʻa demanded independence from France. And did my father keep a photo of Pouvanaʻa for everyone to see? No— otherwise people would start thinking he was crazy like his friend Monsieur Li.

The room swam again. I continued standing and there was a rushing, like a wind through my head. I walked away. I tried to breathe. I felt my heart pounding. I walked to the restaurant bar, the faces swimming before me. Someone tapped my arm, but I continued walking.

There would be a toast, everyone's glasses filled with champagne. I was expected to say a few words, congratulating my father and Cecile, his fiancée. I tried to picture how I would stand, my hand raised, holding the slender glass, everyone crying *Manuia, santé.*

"Let's go, here," said Radish, his hand on my arm. We stood by the entrance door to the restaurant. I broke into a sweat. "You look green."

"You look like a sixteen-year-old trying to grow a mustache," I said.

"Fuck you too," Radish replied.

I'm throwing up, I thought.

"It's better in here," said Radish, but I opened the door into the breathless heat. The car was parked beneath an acacia tree, the fallen twisted seeds littering the windshield. It was stifling hot inside and I turned on the air conditioning, rotating the dial as high as it would go.

"I'll get some brown sugar and water," said Radish.

"I'm all right."

"You look the color of puke."

"Does it really work?" I tried to talk, my head spinning.

"What?"

"You know—sugar and water."

"How am I supposed to know? It's what my grandmother always gave us," Radish replied. "She used to tie a string around our finger when our nose wouldn't stop bleeding. You have to do it on the right finger—I can't remember which one."

My forehead felt damp and cold and I closed my eyes.

"Here—I'll drive," said Radish.

I had to go back. I had to give the toast. There were the guests, my father. I felt sick. The more I thought about all those people and how I was going to speak, the sicker I felt. If I kept my eyes closed, if I thought of nothing at all, my head slowed its spinning and rushing, hurling like it would explode into pieces.

Radish drove to the sea. He parked and we leaned against the car, looking out at the waves, the thin line of foam visible in the darkness. He didn't talk. I kept my mind on taking one breath, then another and another again.

Chapter 12

Most of the guests had left by the time Radish and I returned. The gravel lot in front of the restaurant was almost empty. Inside the restaurant, the waiters carried away platters of duck bones and fish bones. A girl who looked around fifteen picked up the empty champagne glasses and put them on a tray.

"Why weren't you here?" Cecile asked, and I shrugged.

"Where's my father?"

"He drove your grandmother home. Since you weren't here."

Uncle Florian accompanied one of the great-aunts to the door. "Make yourself useful—go get the car," he said to Radish. The great-aunt sat down heavily on one of the plastic chairs by the door. Radish turned to me, raising his hand before walking outside.

"Was A-tai here?" I asked Cecile.

"Since you're asking, why don't you bring her the food?" Cecile walked to one of the tables, lifting up a bag the size of a small suitcase. Cecile was so angry, I had nothing to lose.

"How was the toast?"

"There was no toast," said Cecile. "Your father insisted on waiting for you. He told me that you would show up. He waited and waited."

A-tai rested on her bed, the room shadowy, lit by a solitary night-light plugged into an electric socket. Smoke rose in a thin line from the mosquito coil burning in a corner of the room. A sewing machine sat on a table by the bed, heaps of fabric lying in piles around the table. A picture of Jesus Christ was taped to one corner of a mirror, the tape cracked and yellow.

"Who's there?" my great-grandmother asked.

I lifted a stack of fabric from the table to a chair and placed the bag of food down.

"Ah—it's you." A-tai raised her hand from her side.

The bitter smell of herbal ointment hung in the air as I approached the bed. "Didn't anyone come to drive you to the party?"

A-tai made an impatient sound. "Yes, and I told them to go away. Wasting my time. What am I going to do at that party?"

"Everyone was asking for you."

"Go get a chair. Get that one by the table. You should sit down properly—what's the use of being so handsome when you're going to ruin your back bending like that?"

I placed the chair by her bed.

"Let me look at you," she said, peering up at my face. I bent closer and she burst into a sudden laugh. "Your father's a fool. He should have married you off to Ten-kwok Li's daughter. She's not stupid—I bet she chased you around." A-tai laughed again.

"Marie-Laure's intelligent. *Fwei-lin,*" I said. An intellectual, a scholar.

"And an intellectual doesn't deserve a good-looking husband?" asked A-tai. "I don't understand how your father thinks."

"She's in France," I said.

"Yes—with a Russian man. Your father's so stupid."

"His parents are from Poland. I've met him. He's getting his doctorate in chemistry."

A-tai snorted. "Where's your balls? You should go get her."

"My father said they're giving you a new medicine."

"Poison—useless poison," said A-tai. "I was dizzy this morning, but now I'm better. What did you bring me?"

"The food from the party."

"Well, bring it here," she said impatiently. "Let's take a look."

I peeled the aluminum foil from the plates and brought them over to the bed: squab with fried salt, crystallized prawns, white-baked chicken, the piglet in coconut milk. "I'll have some of the fish with rice," said A-tai.

She chewed the pieces of fish slowly. I poured her a glass of tea from the heavy blue and white teapot by the sewing machine. A-tai wanted to know how everyone looked—my father, Cecile Li ("She's really pale," I said and A-tai agreed, adding that Cecile always looked like she was having trouble digesting her food), my grandmother Madame Chen, and Cecile's mother, Mei.

"Was there enough food?"

"There were plates and plates of leftover food," I told her, but A-tai looked worried. She asked what food had been served, making me repeat the list three times.

"I hope your father remembered to order enough food," she said finally. She grew suddenly tired; the color drained from her face and she closed her eyes. "Leave me alone. I'm going to say my prayers."

I wrapped the plates back up in their foil, and placed the dishes in A-tai's refrigerator. There were a few bottles of pickled turnips and greens in it; otherwise it was empty.

The kitchen was smaller than I remembered, and someone had cleared away the pickling jars that once lined the walls. A Chinese calendar hung on the wall by the refrigerator, the days of the month printed in red characters. When I returned to A-tai's room, she had fallen asleep, the spit foaming on the corners of her mouth. I picked up the empty bag from the chair and walked to the door.

"Marc," she said, without opening her eyes.

I walked back to the bed. Her hand felt light, like a small bird inside my hand.

"Open the drawer. The bottom one, next to the door."

I slid the drawer open. A quilt was folded inside, sewn from small triangles, each triangle the size of a plum.

"Bring it here," said A-tai. "Let me see."

I unfolded the quilt—it was too large to hold between my arms and I laid it over three chairs. The triangles had been cut from scraps in every color, in several different patterns, all carefully matched, an arrangement of hundreds and hundreds of triangles.

"I meant to give it to you on your wedding," said A-tai.

Who knew when that would be, I thought.

"Take it with you now." Her face had turned grey and she spoke in a whisper. "There's nothing wrong, saying good-bye. Moving from place to place. We're leaving—going from here to there. Always leaving, always saying good-bye."

No—no more goodbyes, I wanted to say.

"Now let me see you again," she said and her eyes flickered open for a moment.

At night the sky seemed alive with stars, a glittering blanket. It was beautiful and cold, the stars appearing so close, but in reality they were untouchable and more distant than I could ever comprehend. I watched the stars from the steps of the house at Pic Rouge. The solitude was crushing.

My head felt cool, like it had been washed in some sort of liquid. I wondered what had happened to me at my father's engagement dinner. They were angry now, I knew—Cecile and my father. I should have tried to explain it to them, but I was never good at talking when it counted the most. And what could I have said? That the room started spinning around, that I felt sick for no good reason at all? The more I thought about speaking, giving the toast for my father, the sicker I got—was I going to say this? That would have sounded worse than no explanation—it would have sounded like I was going crazy.

All the time that I was in France, I had wanted to go home. It was grey and cold and even when it had seemed beautiful, it still felt grey and cold inside. I had counted the days until I could return. It was different for Marie-Laure—I knew from her voice over the phone. She was excited when she arrived at Montpellier. Everything was so new and she was homesick, but she had been happy in an unexpected way. It was all so different, she said, and she felt like a different person. From the way she said it, I knew that this difference was a type of happiness for her. I also knew what she didn't say and perhaps didn't know then—that it would be different when she saw me and that this type of difference was a sadness that cut you deep and hard. She would rush to see me at first and then it turned awkward. The ease we once shared together had disappeared.

At the train station as I waited for the train back to Niort, to the army base, Marie-Laure had clung to me and I had pushed her gently away, kissing her sad brow.

"I'll write to you," she said.

I nodded and then I shook my head. I spoke the truth. "It's different."

"When will I see you again?" she asked, but I knew that there was no returning.

"You know," I said. "We'll always be cousins."

"Nothing will change that," she replied. Her voice was so serious, I couldn't tell if she was happy or sad—but perhaps it was like that fact: it was something that didn't depend on how we felt. It was just the way it was.

But when I sat on the stairs of my father's house and thought about how Marie-Laure had reached up to kiss me, the last kiss, I felt a terrible sorrow. I had returned. I was back under the dazzling stars of the tropical sky, but the stars were not alive. They were far away and, although they seemed romantic from a distance, in reality they were chemicals and gases that burned with unimaginable ferocity. I had come back to the place I had longed for to find it empty and different in a way that I couldn't explain and that I couldn't escape. I had returned and had nowhere else to go.

Chapter 13

My father came to the house above Pic Rouge two nights later. He said that Cecile had complained about my behavior at the engagement dinner. "I don't want trouble between you and Cecile."

"There's no trouble," I replied without enthusiasm.

"You can stay at this house and you can stay with us in Taravao. But you have to start working."

"Tell me when," I said.

"Listen to you. It's your attitude. It's disrespectful." My father stood at his usual place in front of the glass wall overlooking the valley. "Cecile says that she's tired of you acting as if we owe you something."

I was tired of my father being disappointed, tired of his being angry.

"I signed a partnership agreement," my father said. "It just needs your signature. You have a share and Cecile has a share. But I'll be frank with you—Cecile says that the partnership is a mistake. She says that you've never worked for the Perles du Paradis."

Never worked—that was a lie. "What about all the work I did in the Tuamotus?" The summers I spent there, the months before I was sent to the army. Didn't I want to work?

"She's talking about the business now. It's different. It's been re-organized."

"Well, I'm sorry if I wasn't here—I was in the army, remember?"

My father sat down on the divan and shook his head. "I thought you'd grow up. You were heading for nothing but trouble. Why do you think I sent you to France? And now I'm offering you a part in the business and instead of being grateful and working, you just sit around. I don't know." He stood up as if something had bitten him.

I looked down at the ground. I looked up at the calligraphy on the wall, swirls and lines that meant nothing.

"What about the partnership? Most people would jump at the opportunity."

"It's not going to work," I said. It was one thing to work with my father, another to work with Cecile. She didn't like me and I knew it.

"And what makes you so sure?"

"Cecile doesn't want to work with me."

"Don't talk like that. How do you know? You haven't worked with her."

"I don't have to."

"What kind of attitude is that?"

I kept my head down.

"Cecile deserves more. Someone who's respectful for a change."

Something started throbbing inside my head. "What the hell does that mean?" The sound of my voice was strange and cold.

"You don't get it, do you? You think that everything is going to fall into your lap. You think that money grows on trees. You have no idea what it takes. No idea at all."

"Forget about the partnership. Give me a third and you can give the rest to Cecile," I said.

"Give you money? Give you more money? That's all I've been doing. How about paying back money? Are you capable of that?"

"A loan, then."

"All right," my father said unexpectedly.

I swallowed. I was trying to breathe. "I'll pay you back."

My father named a figure. "Let's start with that. I'll give you a year to pay me back."

He was angry, but all the same, he was offering a generous amount. I stood up. I thought of walking out of the room, away from the throbbing in my head.

"It's fair." I forced myself to shake his hand and to look into his face. What I saw was terrible—my father's shame and fear. I had already failed.

I knew then that I wasn't going to think about what I was doing or why I was doing it. I wasn't going to fucking care. It started then. *Don't ask questions. Don't fuck up. Don't disappoint me.* I made sure the deliveries were made, that the *paka* was distributed, that it was profitable.

I paid the money back in less than a year. At first I screamed and shouted. There were debts, and deliveries that didn't arrive as planned, everything going wrong at once, and then the money started coming in. By the time of my father's second engagement party, Edouard suggested expanding distribution to the Tuamotus. I paid the money back to my father in five months, in April. It was the way it worked; it was just a matter of doing it.

In the end, I found there was not that much difference between dealing in pearls and dealing in *paka*. Once I had worked in pearls. Now I worked in *paka*. You bargained hard, you selected only those you trusted. You worked all the time.

Chapter 14

In early May, my father and Cecile married in a civil ceremony at the city hall of Papeete. Cecile's cousin Monsieur Li and I were the witnesses, signing at the bottom of the marriage certificate.

The wedding reception was celebrated at a beachfront hotel, the guests flowing out from the restaurant onto the plush lawn beneath the coconut palms. I appointed Harris, the son of my father's sister, to give the official toast—he was the right combination of style and wit—so that I could sit unconcerned at a separate table with Radish and Edouard.

Cecile seemed genuinely happy. She was in love with my father, they said. He had his reputation, the rumors inflating the number of his indiscretions. Who could take it seriously? But they did and whatever gossip there was never spoke about how it weighed on my father. He did everything to make Cecile happy. He could have all the girlfriends the rumors claimed and he would still be obsessed with Cecile's happiness.

My father and Cecile posed for endless photographs. Cecile wore earrings of diamonds and blue pearls, the deep steel blue of the sea at sunset. Happiness made her beautiful for a day.

Cecile wrote an official guest list but my father kept inviting more and more guests. People who worked for him, important clients, minor clients, his classmates from elementary school, his classmates from the Catholic *lycée,* the brothers and priests who taught at the *lycée,* anyone who was even remotely related to the Chen family and the Li family, the entire older generation of the Hakka community, the fishermen who regularly sold him tuna, anti-independence politicians, pro-independence politicians—they were all his guests, sipping *prestige cuvée* champagne.

"Excuse me, excuse me."

I knew enough not to look in the direction of unfamiliar voices. I hated the unexpected camera flash and, for the most part, I succeeded in remaining unphotographed, unnamed, and uninteresting as far as the local press was concerned.

"Excuse me—aren't you Tamerlan's son?"

"No, he's left already."

"But Monsieur Li pointed you out to me."

I turned to reply, the usual noncommittal comment to deflect attention, but I stopped before the words began.

A woman smiled and extended her hand. "I'm Monsieur Li's apprentice." She looked vaguely familiar, but I couldn't place her. She was around eighteen, with baby-fine dark blonde hair. "Marise De Koning."

"You're a De Koning."

"There's a lot of us. We're a big family—you probably know my cousins. I've only just moved here." The De Konings, the family of Elodie De Koning—the blonde at the party so long ago, it seemed, the party at the house of the Marquise du Chatelet. The De Konings were Tahitian, French, some Chinese, and a variety of everything else thrown in.

"So why are you looking for me?" I asked.

"I didn't have anyone to talk to, really. Monsieur Li said that I should go talk to you."

"You're very direct."

"It's an American thing—so I've been told. My mother was born in Raiatea, but she lives in Oregon."

"I've been told that I'm not very good at talking." I glanced around the lawn: Edouard was chatting with a contact from the Tuamotus and Radish was sipping cocktails with one of Cecile's friends. He turned in my direction for a moment and I motioned to him to come over.

"Where I grew up, there weren't too many De Konings and that's what everyone called me: De Koning."

"Shall I call you De Koning, then?"

"That's what Monsieur Li calls me," she said. I wondered what she was studying—obscure Warring States texts?

"You called?" Radish asked.

"This is Marise De Koning," I said. "She's the apprentice of Monsieur Li."

"An apprentice," said Radish. "What are you studying—magic?"

"You might say that," she replied.

"You should teach him, then." Radish waved his cocktail glass in my direction.

"Abracadabra," I said.

"I've heard that you speak Hakka very well. Monsieur Li's cousin told me I should talk to you." De Koning was gushing. I wondered if this level of enthusiasm was also an American thing.

"Marie-Laure?" I asked casually.

"She calls Monsieur Li every week. She's going to Spain for the summer—her boyfriend's family has an apartment in San Sebastian."

"San Sebastian." When I was in France, I had seen a postcard of San Sebastian, the resort hotels curved around its blue glistening bay.

"Any time you need a reference on Hakka terminology, feel free to call Marc," said Radish. "He's amazingly knowledgeable."

"He's babbling, talking nonsense." I placed my hand on Radish's forehead, like he was running a fever.

"He'll bring you the answers," said Radish.

"In Huahine?" asked De Koning.

"He's out that way a lot."

"What do you do?"

"A bit of everything," I replied.

The wedding cake was a five-layered *Gâteau des îles* decorated with white *vanda* orchids and white frosting. Odile complained to me that it looked like plastic, like something you would never eat. She wore her hair slicked back. In heels, she stood taller than me. "They still say you're prettier," she said.

And shorter, I thought. From what I heard, gossip about me had grown stale: I was a disappointment, one of the failed sons of the *nouveau riche*.

I bought a secondhand twelve-meter yacht from a Singapore businessman vacationing in Bora. In the weeks before my father's wedding, I moved out of the house above Pic Rouge and stayed on the boat docked at the harbor.

"A friend of mine is thinking of selling her yacht," said Philippe Mu-San. The reception had meandered into the late hours. "It's beautiful—twenty-five meters. You'll be able to take a bath."

"I'm bathing," I said.

"What—with a tea kettle? You need this yacht. It's docked at Marina Taina—come by Saturday morning."

Business was good, but I couldn't afford a twenty-five-meter yacht.

"You're thinking you can't afford this?" asked MuSan.

"I'm looking for a *notaire*," I replied as if that explained my disinterest.

"Now that's the sign of adulthood—you need your own lawyer. Any particular specifications?"

"Someone discreet." Someone I could afford.

"I'll mention it to my colleagues," said MuSan.

My father was smoking cigars with Monsieur Li, Robert Wan, Uncle Alexandre, and Uncle Tito, my father's two younger brothers, and his *notaire,* Maître Lesage. He waved his hand towards himself, gesturing that he wanted to speak to me. I walked towards his table and my father stood, placing his hand on my shoulder. "Marc," he said, "I haven't talked to you all evening."

He left the table, pausing to shake hands with Monsieur Li and Robert Wan. "Until your next wedding," Wan said, laughing.

I walked with my father through the reception, pockets of guests gathered at the tables. The dance floor was empty except for Harris's two younger sisters slow-dancing with their boyfriends. Half the guests had left, leaving behind crumpled napkins, smudged glasses, plates of shells and bones.

"Take a slice of wedding cake to A-tai," said my father. He raised his hand and a waiter appeared, asking what he wished. "Three slices of cake. In a box." He turned to me. "You had enough to eat?"

He looked as if he were about to tell me something. Cecile was no longer among the guests, although Ten-kwok was laughing with his friends, standing by the entrance in a haze of cigarette smoke. We stood some distance from the tables, looking like we were talking casually. "I have some idea what you're doing," my father said. "Some sort of *pakalolo* distribution."

I opened my mouth to speak, but my father held up his hand.

"Let me finish. This isn't a lecture. You're old enough to make your own mistakes. I'm just giving you some advice: put your money in something legitimate. Better yet—you've made your point, you've repaid me, you have your own business: it's time to get out and go into something else. You think we weren't all bandits and robbers at one point? A-tai told you enough stories—but that was different. They didn't have a choice then."

"I'm looking at a *terrain* in Huahine," I said.

"Land is good, although you'll have to get yourself a good *notaire*. I'm telling you, titles are always a mess. Always. You buy from a family and some nephew will come in, or some uncle, or family from Rangiroa, and they'll all be saying the same thing: they never agreed to the sale. Get yourself a good *notaire*. Talk to Maître Lesage or why not Maître Leclerc? But be careful." He leaned closer, speaking in my ear. "You buy it now and they'll know how you got that money. The way people talk—they'll never say that you're clean." The waiter approached carrying the cake in a paper bag decorated with a bow. "Go take the cake to A-tai," my father said. "Before it gets too late and she falls asleep."

A-tai had fallen asleep when I arrived. Aunt Suzette, one of my father's sisters, was washing dishes in the kitchen. "I already brought her dinner," she said. She wore her good clothes, a turquoise-colored dress with a white lace collar and blue high heels. "Wasn't your father's wedding lovely?"

I opened the refrigerator to put the paper bag with the wedding cake inside, but Aunt Suzette snatched it away. "She can't eat that. All that sugar."

"Well, you should tell her that my father sent it to her," I said.

"Then she'll want to eat it." Aunt Suzette held the bag firmly in her hand and I knew it was lost forever.

I walked into the room where A-tai was sleeping. She looked smaller asleep, as if she had drawn herself inwards, gathering in her breath and her skin. The room was dim, lit by the single night-light, but I knew that even in the sunlight, the room would look dingy, every single thing cheap and worn.

MuSan was right—I bathed on the boat using a tea kettle, an old black kettle I had found under the sink at the house at Pic Rouge. I boiled the water in the kettle and then mixed it with a bucket of cold water. It was the way I had always washed myself at A-tai's house, soaping myself with a square of oily yellow soap and pouring the bucket of water over me.

"Is that you?" A-tai spoke, opening her eyes.

"It's Marc."

"Little stupid," she said. "I know who you are—you don't have to tell me."

"I've come from the wedding."

A-tai's eyes clouded for a moment, trying to remember. "Your wedding?"

"My father's wedding."

"I'm thirsty," she said.

I stood up to bring her a glass of tea.

"No tea," she said.

"*Lang pui shui?*" Cold boiled water?

"The bottle in the refrigerator is empty. Go fill it. Bring me water from the spring."

"Now? It's the middle of the night," I said. When I was a child, A-tai always sent me to fill the bottle with spring water, sending me to one of my uncles' houses to ask for a ride to the spring that ran by the side of the road in Faaa. Sometimes I had to wait all day until someone would take me in their pickup truck to fill the bottle for A-tai.

My father had lent me his favorite car, the black Italian import, in a burst of generosity. I was leaving the reception when he called me back, tossing the keys so suddenly that I almost dropped them.

"Is this mine?" I had asked him.

"For a few days, until I return."

It was late at night, but a pickup truck was parked by the spring at the side of the road. Two women sat in the back. They whistled through their teeth and laughed as I got out of the car.

"Good evening, ladies," I said.

"You thirsty?" asked one, a white *tiare* in her hair.

"My great-grandmother is."

They burst into laughter and jumped out of the truck. They wore T-shirts and shorts and their feet were bare.

"After you," I said.

"But we have many bottles and you have only one," said the woman with the *tiare*.

"You were here first."

"We were here, long before you. But we can wait," said her companion, speaking with a strangely deep voice, her face hidden by her long hair.

The water flowed out of a pipe, splashing as it hit the ground and spilling into a metal grating. I let the water fill the bottle, overflowing as it reached the top, and then I bent down and drank. The women hooted and laughed until I turned around.

There was no sign of them. Through the darkness came the solitary sound of water running from the spring. The pickup truck had vanished as well. I walked out to the main road but it was empty with only a dog wandering across.

Chapter 15

People saw ghosts all the time. Crossing the road at night, sitting in rocking chairs, riding motorcycles in the cemetery. The island was crowded with ghosts but I told myself that there was another explanation, that the women I saw at the spring didn't just vanish into the air. They had left in the pickup truck without my noticing—I told myself this was true and the only explanation. They were not *tupapa'u*, not ghosts.

"You all right?" Radish asked. We were sitting on the deck of the boat the following morning and Radish was talking about investments in land, going through a list of possibilities: a lot in Huahine Iti, various parcels in Teahupoo, a *motu* in Raiatea.

"Fine."

"You didn't get enough sleep?"

"Is something wrong here?" I asked.

"I don't know—you look weird."

"We're wasting time. Why don't we go see the land in Teahupoo?" I felt odd, out of sorts, and it was only once we were out of Papeete, driving in my father's car to the other side of the island, that my thoughts began to clear.

"My friend's got a speedboat," said Radish. "He says he'll lend it to us. We can take it to Te Pari."

"I thought we were going to Teahupoo," I said.

"Te Pari."

"Why? We're not going to buy anything in Pari. There's no road out there."

"We'll take the boat. Besides, it's Sunday. We won't find anyone to show us the land in Teahupoo." Radish appeared mild, but after working with him I saw beneath the surface, that he liked getting his way—he was just more patient and clever about it.

"Why didn't we take my boat, then? Now this is going to take all day."

"We'll be back in Papeete by mid-afternoon," said Radish. "We'll be back by two."

By two, we were still waiting around for Leo, Radish's friend in Tautira, having been assured by Leo's younger brother, his girlfriend, and various neighbors that Leo had gone to Pueu for some fishing gear and would certainly return at any moment.

"He went down to the store there," Leo's brother said as we waited in the driveway. "You can't miss it. It's just down the road. Not far at all." A number of piglets were running around the dirt driveway. "You want to buy one?" he asked. "I'll give you a good price."

The price of the piglets remained about the same for the first hour, but by the end of the second hour of waiting, Radish managed to bargain the price down. "We'll take the black and pink one," said Radish. He was putting the piglet, wiggling and squealing, into a rice sack when Leo pulled into the driveway.

I glanced at my watch—I didn't care that it was considered rude to look at the time. It was ten minutes past three. "Let's get going," I said.

"Let's have some beer." Leo opened the trunk of his car. He was short, thick-necked, and muscular, his skin a deep reddish-brown. "They didn't have any in Pueu, so I drove out to Papeari."

It would take another hour—drinking beer and then Leo looking around for the keys, driving out to the boat, checking to see if there was enough gas and finding that the tank was nearly empty, mixing the gas with motor oil and filling the tank. Long after I turned surly, Radish remained good-natured, shaking hands with Leo and promising to return the boat before dark.

"No hurry," said Leo. "You can camp out there. Why not? Under *la belle étoile.*"

There were no roads entering Te Pari, the southeast edge of the island. The coast was wild. Radish said that he knew of a place upstream from the coast. An older cousin sometimes took him there on weekends. He drove the speedboat over the open water. "It's just up there." He pointed to coconut trees at the water's edge and the cliffs in the distance. We grew silent, the movement of the boat following the waves up and down, our thoughts quiet in the deep blue of the sea. It was the same when I had followed my father to the Tuamotus—there was something about the immensity of the ocean and the sky that made the usual circle of thoughts fall still.

Radish slowed the motor and turned the boat towards the land, and I saw the mouth of a river appearing between the trees. Except for the seabirds drifting through the air, we were alone. Radish guided the boat upstream, the river-shore thick with raisins-of-the-sea and *purau* trees. "We used to come here every weekend," said Radish. "I haven't been back for months. I came here after my military service. If you could call it military service—it was just pushing paper around."

Radish drove through the shallows and cut the motor. I jumped into the water and Radish threw me the rope. The water was cool—cold river water flowing down from the mountains mixed with the warm shallow water of the ocean.

"We'll go through there." Radish pointed to a grove of *mape* trees.

The sunlight filtered down through their branches and leaves, making flickers of light in the dark shade of the trees. We walked over the sandy earth, stepping over the roots running along the ground. The air felt dense, muffled and hushed. You could try to talk, but it was like swimming against the waves of the deep ocean. It was easier to fall into silence.

Water collected beneath the trees, resting in the shallow curves of the roots, gathering into a liquid ripple and then a stream. We turned through a line of trees and stopped. A pool stretched before us. The sun glittered on the surface of the water, the light falling from a break in the trees. Radish stepped out onto a finger of sand. I bent down and scooped up the water, soft to the touch, like satin. Radish peeled off his clothes, wading into the water and diving in.

I walked out along a tree branch bent over the water, so clear that I could see the stones resting on the bottom. Radish emerged, tossing the wet hair back from his face. "How is it?" I said and he grinned. I took off my clothes and jumped in.

The water felt smooth, parting as I glided through. I swam to the far side and turned on to my back, looking up at the pattern of leaves. I felt transparent like the water, like the air and the sky above. Radish sat on a rock by the side of the pool, the sun on his skin.

When Radish talked about military service, he had a choice: paperwork in an administrative office or the barracks in France. He could decide where to go, but for my bad school record, there was no such choice—as if I would ever choose to be sent to France, to a place that cold. I had never been cold before in my life. I had no idea what it was, that it was something that scraped at your bones, eating you from the inside so that you couldn't escape. There was the monotony of endless hours of guard duty, the monotony of drills and inspection and cleaning everything over and over. Never had I ever seen anything that was stripped completely free of dust—there was dust and dirt everywhere in Tahiti—but now I was in the polished grip of immaculate cleanliness. A cold, cold hell, and the only consolation I felt was at target practice, gripped by a furious focus that made it almost bearable.

Marie-Laure kept a notebook by her bed, a notebook bound by a spiral of metal where she wrote down her dreams, pages of her beautifully swirled writing. What I could remember of my dreams would barely fill half a page, a few lines.

"Why do you want to remember this stuff?" I asked, but the moment I spoke, I knew it was the wrong thing to say. I had done nothing but say the wrong things during my stay with Marie-Laure in France. I couldn't remember the words, only the feeling afterwards that I wanted to swallow those words or to spit them out so that they would never exist—like all the memories I wanted to forget, the things I wished I had never done, the stupid feeling that made me want to peel every layer of skin away and become completely invisible and forgotten, so that I didn't have to remember.

I took in my breath and sank beneath the surface of the water. I saw the leaves floating on the top and nothing else—nothing. It was transparent like the feeling in my arms and legs, the stillness of breath locked inside me. If only I could hold my breath forever and remain beneath the water.

But already I felt the growing tightness inside my throat, in my head and my chest, and I was swimming to the surface, breaking into the air and gasping, breathing without even thinking. There was the sunlight and the canopy of trees and the blue open sky and the stillness. There were no words, nothing that I had to swallow or spit out or hide. It was silent, like forgetting, like never having to remember at all.

We sat on a rock beneath the sun. The air had turned dark and golden with the end of the day and the birds were loud in the trees.

"We should get out," Radish said.

"Didn't Leo say we could stay here and return the boat tomorrow?"

"I'm talking about business."

I stared out over the water. "We're making money."

Radish shook his head, crossing his arms over his legs. "It's changing. Already they're talking crystal meth. Things will get ugly."

"We'll arm ourselves," I said.

"You don't know what you're talking about."

"There's a yacht at Marina Taina. Twenty-five meters. A real yacht—not a rinky-dink boat like I have now. I'm going to look at it tomorrow."

"Well, you can go without me."

I nudged Radish on the shoulder. "Don't worry so much."

"I'm telling you: we should get out."

"We'll get out. So stop worrying." I stood up on the rock overlooking the pool, the fading light on the water.

The sun had set by the time we returned the boat. Radish drove to Pueu, to the Chinese store where he had left the piglet in the rice sack. The owner's daughter had let the piglet out—she complained that we were gone so long. Radish and I ran around the store trying to corner it, before the store owner grabbed the piglet and put it, squealing, back into the sack.

"You guys are *maozhung*," he said. "Completely worthless."

The car was parked on the gravel in front of the store. I opened the trunk. "Are you out of your mind?" asked Radish. "The piglet will suffocate in there."

I opened the car door. "Put it in the back, then."

"No—it's riding with me," said Radish sitting in the passenger seat. His hands were covered in mud and there was another splash of mud on his neck.

"You smell really bad," I said.

"Better than you," Radish replied. A car pulled into the gravel lot. The door opened and a red-haired man got out, nodding his head at us. Radish stopped and watched him enter the store.

"You know him?" I asked.

"He was on TV—an Australian guy. Some antinuclear activist. He was talking on the news."

"You should put the piglet in the back," I said. "It smells."

"No way."

"You're such a piece of shit."

"Fuck you," said Radish, laughing.

The passenger door of the Australian's car opened and I turned my head. It was Aurore. She wore a black swimming top and a dark blue skirt. She glanced at me before walking into the store.

Now I searched through everything I could remember about the Australian. He was tall—would Aurore think him handsome?—and this is what gnawed at me, although I'd never admit it: did they look like lovers? After all, they hadn't entered the store together, but maybe that was a sign too.

I hadn't seen Aurore for over three years, but the way my thoughts were spinning, it was like yesterday. I turned the car from the gravel and drove onto the road. Radish held the rice sack with the piglet inside.

"Are you going to your parents'?" I asked.

"Are you looking at this yacht tomorrow?"

"Tomorrow morning."

"It's too much money," said Radish. "It'll put you in so much debt."

"We'll expand."

"We're getting the hell out," he replied. "Can you keep the piglet?"

"On the boat? Are you crazy? Why don't you take it to your parents? They can cook it in coconut milk."

"No—I'm keeping it."

"Well, okay. Fatten it. But not on my boat."

"If I take it home, someone will slaughter it when I'm not there."

"Then you'll eat it." What the hell was the problem, I thought. Radish could make such a big deal out of nothing.

The piglet was out of her sack when I awoke the next morning. She ran around the deck while I watched the morning news, a grainy image on a portable TV with bad reception. It was the usual: Gaston Flosse had been reelected President in April and already there were accusations of misused public funds. I threw the piglet half a baguette. There was something eerie about piglets and their ability to escape. You put them in boxes, in sacks, and sooner or later, the boxes and sacks would be empty—I never knew if piglets gnawed or wiggled their way out.

The phone rang.

I watched it ringing. I hoped it was Aurore; I couldn't wait to pick it up. I knew I should let it stop.

I said something polite. *Bonjour.* How are you?

"Philippe gave me your number," Aurore said. "He said you were looking for a *notaire*."

"I talked to him at my father's wedding."

"I'm sorry I missed the wedding," said Aurore. "I just missed it. We arrived yesterday—we were visiting *les îles.* I asked about you. I thought I'd seen you."

I wondered what the real story was, why she hadn't said hello to me the day before at the store. *We were visiting les îles*—who did she mean: the Australian and her?

"They rented the house in Mahina so I'm staying at Mataiea. Why don't you come by tonight, for aperitif?"

I watched the piglet sniffing around the edge of the deck until she discovered something in a corner. She rooted it out with her nose, squealing before disappearing into the cabin.

"I have to be somewhere tonight," I said.

"Tomorrow night, then."

Tomorrow I was supposed to be in *les îles,* on business with Edouard. I was too busy. And what did I know about Aurore and her true reasons for seeing me? I wasn't seventeen anymore. I could think for myself.

"Tomorrow around five?" She spoke with the same directness, a seeming lack of pretension. "It could be later if you like."

I watched a frigate flying motionless in the sky, holding still, buoyed by a current of air. I was lulled by the rocking of the boat, the sea deceptively gentle within the harbor, which was ugly and industrial with ships of smoke grey, rusting containers, and the sorts of crews that routinely threw garbage overboard.

"I saw you yesterday. We could have spoken then," I said.

"I couldn't believe it," she said. "We just docked at the Baie de Phaeton and Al was getting cigarettes. I guess I couldn't speak—I couldn't believe it was really you—and when I came back out, you were gone, you had left already. I'm sorry—you must think I was rude."

Yes, she was rude, but now there was something in her voice, something I could taste, something I wanted. "No," I said.

"I told Al all about you—he's my colleague. They're planning to shoot a documentary on the CEP. His wife won an award in Sydney last year. She's a wonderful film editor. Why don't you come by tomorrow?"

The phone rang all morning. There was Madame Evelyn Wu, the owner of the yacht at Marina Taina. She was leaving in the morning, it turned out. She was visiting her sister in Tahaa and she couldn't show me the yacht until later in the week. A mechanic called about a motor part for one of the boats in the Tuamotus, and then Edouard called and asked when I was arriving.

"I'll be there on Wednesday," I said.

"Wednesday—why?"

"Look, it's just a day later."

"You can't wait a day later. I thought you said you'd be here tomorrow."

"I'm telling you now. I'll be there Wednesday morning. I'll leave on the five o'clock flight."

The silence bristled.

"I'll stay there a week," I said.

"You say that because you're not here. You don't have any idea what's going on."

"Isn't that why you're there? To make sure things get done?"

In the army, Edouard's accuracy for shooting targets was consistent, predictable, terrifying. He hit the target standing still, he hit it moving, dead-on, right through the center, black silhouettes pierced through the heart. He knew I was changing the arrival date for reasons that had nothing to do with the best commercial interest of anyone.

"You were supposed to be here tomorrow," he said.

"I'll be there Wednesday morning with the money. You need someone to babysit you until then?"

"If I tell them to wait a day, they'll want more. Bad for business."

"Tell them they're lucky we're paying them so much," I replied.

Business was business, no matter what. It was always the same: if you needed something delivered, you always had to wait for them. If you were paying someone, they never wanted to wait for you. It was human nature, a constant headache, a pain in the ass—making sure things weren't delayed, making sure costs were down, making sure you bribed the right people.

"What the fuck is wrong with you? You have to be here tomorrow."

"Do I have to hold your hand or something? I arrive the next morning and they get paid."

"They'll say they'll come to Papeete."

"They come here," I said, "and I'll never deal with them again. The way you're talking—this is the last time we're doing things this way. This was fine when we didn't know what the fuck we were doing. It's too risky. The money's wired into their accounts from now on. Nothing direct from us."

"You're talking like the *popa'a*. They talk like that. Wire money into some account. They never want to get their hands dirty. They never want to show their faces."

"We show our faces too much," I said. "We'll end up in prison."

"It's your money too," Edouard replied, but he didn't say what he knew, that I was always obsessed with everything arriving and leaving on time and that the only reason I was delaying now was because my obsession had changed. And if I wasn't obsessed with business as usual, that could mean only a woman, another type of madness.

✺

My father flew in from Huahine that evening. He was staying in Tahiti the following day, checking on business before flying out on his honeymoon. I met him at the airport.

"How was the flight?" I asked.

"Smooth. Short." My father was alone. Cecile was still in Huahine. She planned to meet him at the airport the next evening, before their flight to Santiago. "You've kept my car in one piece?"

I handed him the keys but he smiled and shook his head. "You drive."

"You're in a good mood," I said.

"I saw Jonathan in Huahine," said my father. Cecile's cousin Monsieur Jonathan Li was about the same age as my father.

"I met his student at the reception."

"Apprentice," said my father as I opened the car door.

"Okay: apprentice—she called herself that."

I drove the car out of the airport parking lot, past the flower and shell *lei* vendors. "Are you going to Pic Rouge?"

"Taravao. Cecile wants me to pick up some things at the house." My father seemed relaxed. He usually spent his time with Monsieur Li talking and drinking coffee at a roadside stand in Huahine, an isolated place in the middle of nowhere. They spent hours talking.

I turned the car south on the main road, towards Taravao and the *presqu'île.*

"You've got problems at work?" asked my father.

"The usual."

"People want more money, deliveries are delayed, things aren't selling as fast as they should be."

"That sums it up," I replied and my father laughed. "What did you and Monsieur Li talk about?"

"He went to China. He said I should go with him next time."

"Why did he go to China?" I wasn't sure what Monsieur Li did for a living. I knew only that the older generation was superstitious, warily consulting those with arcane, semi-medicinal knowledge about herbs, horoscopes, the right time to do this and that.

"So you noticed his apprentice," said my father.

"Marise De Koning?"

"She's pretty."

"Maybe she's interested in you."

"I'm too old," my father said, laughing again. "Besides, I'm married."

"You should get married more often. It puts you in such a good mood." I couldn't remember teasing my father so often or my father laughing in response.

"It's the honeymoon stage."

I wondered if my father's good friend Monsieur Li had given him something for the honeymoon stage—roots, strange powders and elixirs.

"Jonathan showed me something." My father spoke as if he were reading my thoughts. "He found it in China."

I was driving behind a Deux Chevaux going too slow, the road winding so I couldn't pass.

"He said he met the nephew of his teacher. They went to a village in the delta outside Shanghai."

"Looking for something magic?"

I was joking, but my father was serious. He pulled something out of his shirt pocket. I glanced at him. He held an envelope in his hand. "It's a kind of charm—it works as an antidote. Jonathan knew about it from a friend, a lawyer. He says the Americans are starting to invest in China. It's risky. This lawyer went to Shanghai because an amusement park venture went bankrupt."

"Monsieur Li met him in China?"

"He knew Mr. Pelevin from before."

I heard the rustling of paper and something clinking like coins. I looked over at my father—he was putting the envelope back inside his pocket. The road straightened and I accelerated, passing the Deux Chevaux. "Do you need the car?"

"While I'm in Santiago? Are you asking if you can borrow it?"

"For a few days longer. I'll return it to Pic Rouge. Or Taravao."

"Keep it until I return," said my father and the road stretched ahead, dark and straight.

I awoke in the night, everything silent inside the cabin of the boat. Some-one laughed in the distance, leaving one of the clubs along the water-front. A noise had startled me from sleep: footsteps, someone walking above on the deck. The darkness pressed against me. I felt among the pa-pers on the shelf near the bed.

It was Radish. He popped his head into the cabin.

"What the fuck?"

"I came to get the pig," he said.

"You and your stupid pig. Do you know what time it is?"

"It's not good for her, being on a boat."

"She's a pain in the ass. I threw water on her all afternoon."

"I found a place for her."

"I could have shot you. I didn't know it was you. I could have shot you, all for your worthless pig."

Radish walked into the cabin. I waved my hand over the pile of papers by my bed. He sat down on the edge of my bunk and picked up the revolver.

"Marie-Laure gave this to you, didn't she?"

"You didn't think about waiting until morning and getting your pig then?" I rubbed the side of my head. "What time is it anyways?"

"One in the morning—something like that."

"You're out of your mind," I said.

I lay on the bunk after Radish left, cradling the piglet in the rice sack. The pieces of the day played in my mind, my thoughts turning round like a dog chasing its tail. Edouard, Radish, the pig, the yacht, the heat and darkness around me, my father looking at the envelope in his hand: a charm, an antidote—against what? I had forgotten to ask.

Come over at five, Aurore had said. *You can come later, you can come at seven at night.*

I was awake. The words and my thoughts and the sound of Aurore's voice—it was all waiting, it didn't matter how late. It was waiting, some-thing shimmering, and I almost knew what it was—yes, I almost knew, falling blind into sleep like a stone.

PART THREE

The Charm

Chapter 16

"They're only rumors," said Marise De Koning. It was three in the afternoon and, except for a man eating by the window, we were the only customers in the restaurant. A calendar advertising Chinese beer hung over the cash register. De Koning was finishing a plate of *ma'a tinito*. "I don't believe you're some sort of scum." She twirled the noodles around her fork and paused, the fork in mid-air. "I wasn't supposed to say this, was I?"

I began to laugh.

"I don't believe any of it."

"Don't lie," I said. "It'll spoil your looks." I hadn't seen De Koning in over four years, since my father's wedding, and she had gained weight, turning voluptuous—she had her own rumors.

The waitress appeared with a glass bowl of litchis. De Koning looked over the fruit, selecting one and breaking the skin, the flesh beneath glistening white. "You're so serious," she said. "Do you ever relax?"

"You've been to a Chinese store."

"My grandfather's Chinese," she said, peeling another litchi. "He had a store in Raiatea, in Avera."

"All right, so he had *bon-bon chinois*."

"*Bon-bon chinois*—I love *bon-bon citron*."

"Well, you didn't see your grandfather sitting in his store, relaxing and eating *bon-bon citron*, did you? Even though he sold it all the time." His supply of *bon-bon chinois*—Chinese candy, sweet pickled lemons. No store owner sat around eating the candy. "It's bad business."

The waitress picked up the bowl of discarded litchi peels and seeds and handed me the check.

"They'll do *ma'a Tahiti* tomorrow," I said.

"*Poulet fafa?*"

"Why don't you meet me here? Say around two."

"Why do you eat so late?"

"Work." The usual—too much work. "When are you going back to Huahine?"

"In a few days." De Koning stopped as if there was something more on her mind. She kept a careful silence—why, I didn't know.

De Koning talked about rumors and, for whatever reason, there were still the rumors about smuggling when, really, *paka* had turned too risky. Unbelievably lucrative, but Radish kept nagging at me like an old woman, saying over and over that all that money wasn't going to do me any good if I was sitting in Nuutania Prison. When I left, Ha Gow and most of the crew had stayed and worked with other *paka* growers. "They don't know when to quit," Edouard said. We took the money we made and we put it into land. I hired a *notaire*, Maître Leclerc, and he drafted the papers. We bought land and houses and *fares* and rented them out. Edouard and I spent our time fixing broken screens, replacing light bulbs, and caulking showers and tubs. Boring and completely legal. The rumors said what they wanted—that I was clean only on the surface—but there was little truth to what they said, so little. The rest were lies.

A deep gold illuminated the windows of Aurore's house at Mataiea. Coconut palms stood over the sweep of the lawn. I drove along the curve of the driveway, parking in front of the stairs leading to the veranda and the entrance door. The sky was vast with stars.

The front room was empty and I entered the dining room, the table covered with papers. I swept them to the side, placing the bowls and plates of takeout on the corner. One of Aurore's paintings stared from the wall, a portrait of a roadside vendor gazing over a table of limes and mangoes. Aurore was working on another portrait, drawing the preliminary sketches. Someone had commissioned the painting and Aurore rarely accepted commissions.

She sat on the back veranda built over the garden. She let me kiss her and then turned away absently.

100

"Do you want to eat here or inside?"

"Here's fine," she said.

I brought the bowls and plates to the veranda, setting them on the table.

"How was lunch with Marise De Koning?"

"Late. The flight from Huahine was delayed."

"She's gained so much weight. Although she's still very lovely. No wonder Monsieur Li keeps her as his apprentice."

I uncovered the nearest bowl of takeout. "Shrimp and green beans." I knew where the conversation was going—a dead end, avoidable only with early intervention.

"She has enormous breasts."

"Pass me your plate," I said grimly.

Aurore rose from the table, leaving the veranda and entering the house.

Monsieur Li had called from Huahine, asking if I could pick up De Koning from the airport. Obligation. Not that I complained—De Koning was easy to look at—but it was obligation. I couldn't say, "I can't do this because I'm with the Marquise du Chatelet." Secrets were impossible on an island, and, for the past four years, Aurore and I had done the impossible. We were secret.

The food remained untouched on the table. One of Aurore's cats, a dark grey one, slept on a wicker chair, and the dog slept at the top of the stairs. There wasn't much to keep secret anymore—we were acting like an old couple and not in a contented, comforting way.

My cell phone rang. "You have a moment?" asked Radish.

I wondered what was wrong this time. "Half a moment."

"It's the shipment—we should talk in person. I think you should see this."

Beyond the garden, the waves fell on the sand, a low rumbling as they receded only to rush to the shore again and fall. I had promised never to leave, I had promised Aurore over and over, fevered and desperate, but now there was endless time for thoughts to roll out and still I couldn't leave.

I ate alone. I thought of bringing the food to Radish, living at the house with his parents, two brothers and two sisters, his wife on another island, on Raiatea. It worked better that way, Radish said, unenthusiastic about

101

marriage right from the start so everyone knew they would stay married. They had nothing to gain and nothing to lose.

I put the food in the refrigerator. I turned on the TV and watched the news. When I awoke, the TV was still on, playing an American movie. I went out to the veranda. The night was old.

The glass door slid open and Aurore walked outside. Her hair was pulled back, tied carelessly so that a strand of hair curled around her neck. She walked without speaking to where I stood. She reached out and I smelled the turpentine on her hands. With a finger she etched a line over my brow, pausing and then tracing my mouth. She moved closer, her finger stroking my skin, as if she were drawing me.

There were ancient Chinese painters who painted with their fingers, Aurore once said. They painted with their hands, their palms, the fingernails.

They were drunk, I said.

They were, she replied. It was a requirement, drinking a lot of rice wine.

She was going to do the opposite, she said. She would get intoxicated by painting me.

"This isn't going to happen," I told her. I didn't want to be drawn, sketched, painted. I didn't want to hang on display on a wall of her house. As it was, I became invisible.

Chapter 17

Radish stored the merchandise in a room behind his parents' house in Patutoa. Audio equipment, crates and boxes sitting on pallets—Radish knew the location of everything.

"You told Stellio his speakers arrived?" I asked.

Radish shrugged, his arm resting on a crate. "I called him. He paid—it's his problem," he said, leaving the room and walking into the garden. He stopped at a shed under a breadfruit tree and pulled a set of keys from his back pocket, looking for the right one and opening the padlock. The door swung open.

A fan turned inside, ventilating the interior. I looked for a light switch along the wall. Radish picked up a flashlight from a chair and swept the light over the concrete floor, the beam illuminating a dozen aquariums. The aquariums seemed empty at first, without water, filled only with branches scraped clean of leaves. I walked to one, looking through the glass.

"They're quiet."

Radish crouched down. "Look—this guy's awake." A black and red snake rested against the glass.

Except for the breathing holes, Radish kept the aquariums tightly sealed and allowed only his younger brother Arthur into the shed to feed the snakes their diet of mice. Radish was meticulous and kept everything clean. He even washed his pig regularly, and watered her with a garden hose as she slept beneath the trees in the garden.

Radish stood and walked to one corner. "This is the biggest container I have, but it's still not big enough. I keep telling them it's a mistake."

The python's head was sleek and black, resting on its coils. "You know how much we can sell this for?" I said.

Radish walked away, shaking his head. "Sell this? What the fuck." He turned and walked back to where I stood. He started shouting. "So he was right—you ordered this. You're fucking crazy, crazier than I thought. I told him no way, already we're breaking a hundred laws by selling the corn snakes. But a python. I told him: take it back. He said you ordered it and—what do I know—it turns out he was fucking goddamned right."

"I have a buyer," I said.

"I don't care."

"Three thousand cash. Paid in US dollars."

"You think I'm as crazy as you."

"We'll split it. Fifty-fifty."

Radish looked at the floor, looked away. "If you weren't so crazy, I'd make you promise this was a one-shot deal. One time only."

"Do you know what this is? A Black-Headed Python."

"You have any idea what happens if he escapes? You have any fucking idea?"

"She—it's a female."

Radish walked to the door and stood in the doorway. "I don't want to hear this," he said.

De Koning ate the *poulet fafa,* the breadfruit, the yellow and purple yams, finishing the food on her plate.

"A beer? Another orange soda?" I asked.

"Are you having another? No, don't tell me—you're leaving for work."

"You want dessert? They have ice cream."

"You should visit us in Huahine," said De Koning. She wore an electric pink dress and gold bangles—I couldn't tell if these were real or cheap. "I'm going back after tomorrow."

"I'll be in Uturoa next month."

"Then come visit us. You can stay with Monsieur Li. He always talks about you." De Koning crossed her arms, resting them on the table. "I'll pass on the ice cream."

"You sure?"

"What flavors do they have?"

"Chocolate. Vanilla. There's this flavor called Hokey-Pokey."

"Maybe next time. Thanks anyway."

"Anytime," I said, finishing the bottle of beer.

"She's not really pretty," I said to Aurore that evening. Aurore was recovering from a headache, lying on the sofa against the green and yellow cushions.

"So you took a good look at her." Aurore kept her eyes closed.

"Not really. Why should I?"

"I was thinking of going to Hitiaa. Tomorrow or maybe the next day. There's an old church there. I remember the light coming in through the windows." She rested her hand against the side of her head, as if she were keeping something from spilling out. "If I don't get another headache, I was thinking of going late, around sunset."

I didn't know anything about painting, only that it seemed to be about light. "Are you going to paint there?"

"No—I'm not sure. I just wanted to look around. It's all ruins, abandoned." She opened her eyes to look at me. Her eyes were a crazy shade of green, deep and dazzling.

"I'll come by in the afternoon. I'll drive you there."

She turned towards me, moving slowly, keeping her head on the cushions. "In the mid-afternoon. So we don't get caught in traffic," she said, shutting her eyes again.

Everything was for sale; it was only a question of how much. My father said this. Some things appeared without price, but it wasn't because they couldn't be bought—it was just that the price was too high. "You don't believe me?" he asked.

I was very young, ten years old. I had just started living with my father and I couldn't tell if he was saying the truth.

My father raised his voice. "You believe me?"

I learned a basic rule when I lived with A-tai, my great-grandmother: when in doubt, keep silent. This rule worked with A-tai, but it didn't work with my father, especially when he fell into one of his moods.

He hit the table, and the bowls and plates jumped.

"Yes," I said.

"You think I'm lying?"

"No," I said.

"Why are you closing your eyes?"

Maybe I was sleeping I thought, my eyes still closed. It was a dream and everything would go away. A dream, a dream, I said to myself.

My father set up a chessboard and he let me think for as long as I liked before each move. There was no timer, no sense of hurry. He said that his father had taught him the different types of chess and now he was teaching me. He taught me Chinese chess and Tahitian chess—the one played by the Fautaua River—and the chess that the French called *jeu d'échecs*. I learned this last and maybe this was the reason that I could never completely master it, so my father insisted that I play this version of chess with him. I always thought, at the beginning of each game of *jeu d'échecs*, that I would win, and the games grew longer as I learned to outmaneuver, to surprise, to play with fewer and fewer pieces. When I first started to play, I grew frustrated because I always lost, but gradually the feeling went away and I just played.

One night when I was thirteen, I won. It was late at night and my father extended his hand, the way he always did, at the end of the game. We shook hands. As it turned out, it was the only game I won. My father won the next few games and then he left for the pearl farms in the Tuamotus where he stayed for weeks. It was much later that I realized that my father had insisted on playing this because he foresaw—even though he continued playing Chinese chess privately with Monsieur Li—that *jeu d'échecs* would become the only version the Chinese played in public. It was the chess that my cousins played, and there was a silk painting in Ten-kwok's house of two Chinese scholars playing *jeu d'échecs* in a pavilion, although Radish pointed out that this was the giveaway that the painting was a recent creation, springing from the imagination of a Beaux Arts graduate living in Punaauia.

"I'm not selling this painting," Aurore always said. Over the years, I heard her say this about almost all the paintings at Mataiea. The ones of the *fe'i*

bananas, the one of the custard apples. The various portraits. She sold two portraits, one of a woman selling baskets from the Australes. Aurore told me the price, an unbelievable amount.

"You want something to drink?" I asked.

"I thought you left." Aurore covered her eyes with her hands.

"You want the migraine pills?"

"This isn't a migraine—it's something else. I wouldn't be talking if it was a migraine."

I stood by the sofa for a moment and then I walked into the kitchen where Aurore's dog sat waiting by the screen door. She was a medium-sized black-and-tan mutt that Aurore insisted on calling Georges. I pointed out the obvious, that she was a girl, but this made no difference to Aurore. I opened the door and Georges bounded outside into the garden.

"I'm sorry," Aurore spoke from the front room. "About the way things are, about things not going anywhere."

"Do you want to go to Hitiaa? To look at the light?"

She laughed, a short laugh—I wasn't sure if it was bitter or happy. "You want to go now?" She sat up uncertainly, as if she were drunk. "It's almost night."

I waited by the kitchen door.

"You had lunch with Marise De Koning?"

"She's going back, to Huahine."

"No—she's not leaving yet. She's only pretending, so you'll think that she'll leave. She wants something. There's something else going on. She's waiting for the right time to ask you." Aurore's voice was slow and even. "Where did you eat?"

"At a Chinese restaurant—the one across from the Bank of Tahiti." I kept my voice casual, like I was already bored with De Koning.

"Madame MuSan's restaurant," said Aurore. "I went there once with Philippe. A long time ago. Madame MuSan was very kind, very polite."

I had heard the stories, about how Philippe MuSan had fallen in love with Aurore several years ago, when she had first arrived in the islands. The stories differed about what had gone wrong—whether she was too fickle or he was too ambitious or whether they were too similar.

"Did you have the *ma'a tinito?*" Aurore asked.

"No—they had *ma'a Tahiti*."

"You should order the *ma'a tinito*."

"We can go there tomorrow if you like." I was talking like a fool and I knew it—I would never have lunch with Aurore in Papeete, in public. The silly quarrels, the public spats in the waterfront cafes; they would never happen. I was sealed in a private world as far as Aurore was concerned, confined to her bed, and this made me insane.

"Madame MuSan—she must be over eighty," said Aurore. She lay back on the sofa, her eyes resting on me. It was a game we played, saying that we were going to drive to Hitiaa, saying that we would eat at this restaurant. Of course, I could say that she was an old friend of my father's, that it was a business lunch, strictly professional, but I knew that, even now, I only had to look at Aurore and everyone would know how I wanted her.

I arrived at Aurore's house the next afternoon and found the dining table, ordinarily piled with papers, almost clean and empty. The papers had been swept to the floor where they lay in disordered heaps. A few sheets remained on the table. I looked through them—they were new sketches, charcoal studies.

There was a platter of *ma'a tinito,* beans and clear noodles and chunks of pork in sauce. Drawn in shades of grey and black, the beans were smoothly curved, the noodles swirled, a translucent tangle, the dark sauce mixed with slashes of meat.

There was a table, a motorcycle helmet resting on a corner, a customer waiting for his takeout, sitting on a chair, his feet in flip-flops. He was dozing, his arms folded across his chest.

There was A-min, Madame MuSan's cook, stirring a black wok, long flames of fire licking the sides of the pan. It was the secret, the intense heat, the fire. The flames leaped in tongues, but A-min swirled the pan so rapidly, his hands remained unscathed. Sweat ran down the side of his face, his forehead wrinkled in straight, deep lines.

I glanced up to find Aurore standing by the table. "When did you draw these?" I asked.

"Today. I started this morning."

I looked down at the sketches—they were real, more than real. They were magic, as if I could step through the paper and enter the restaurant.

"They're for you," said Aurore.

I picked up the sketch of the beans and noodles, sliding my hands under the thick paper like I was holding the platter and would eat what was painted there.

Chapter 18

Aurore kept a thousand books in her bedroom, behind glass along the shelves that covered the walls. The books stood in classroom precision on some of the shelves; on others they lay in jumbles that seemed, if not for the glass, ready to tip onto the floor. She kept books on Tahiti near her bed, books on old Papeete, books of nautical maps. Alone in her room, I sometimes found myself watching her books—not touching or reading them. Watching, as if they would move, shifting their weight, a small movement, something you could hardly see. Of course I knew this was stupid—books didn't move—and I never told Aurore about it. But I watched and I learned the position of groups of books: thick black books near the floor, glossy books of the oceans on the middle shelves. At the end of the top shelf were two books by Henri Hiro—Aurore said she had met him once in Raiatea. I had never read any of his poems. I saw only his televised interview, broadcast as a memorial the week of his death.

"You're not a visual learner," said Aurore.

"I don't read," I said. There was no use making the truth look pretty.

"But you read the paper. And you're intelligent—the way you talk. It's so formal and correct."

The way I spoke—it was A-tai who had taught me to be formal with strangers, especially the French. I was smart, but I was realistic. I knew that if you added the days I had actually spent in school, the cumulative years would take up the fingers of one hand.

Aurore relentlessly analyzed how I thought and why I thought that way. She talked about colonialism. She talked about postcolonialism. She talked about *residue of orality* and how I came from an oral culture, and she used

110

phrases like *the hegemony of the written word*. I resented feeling like a specimen under examination, even if my examiner was tantalizingly beautiful and the examinations led to her bed, at least in the early years of our affair. And it was an affair, hidden and clandestine, and I learned that time in an affair exists in its own space, an enclosed bubble suspended in its prolonged moment.

Aurore's bed was extravagant. I had slept on cots and bare mattresses and on the bunks of my boats. A-tai had slept on a narrow bed covered with a quilt sewn of jewel-sized scraps of fabric. My grandmother Madame Chen still slept in the bed she had shared with my grandfather—an iron bed painted an unexpectedly sentimental shade of sky blue. Aurore's bed was larger than A-tai's and Madame Chen's beds combined, and she covered it with a Tahitian *tifaifai* quilt of brown and dark yellow. Her pillows were embroidered with metallic thread, so that her bed was covered with fabric the color of the earth shot through with gold and silver. A tree of purple flowers grew outside her window. Early in the morning, doves rested among the branches. In other households, it was the time to rise and feed the chickens, the time to walk to the store to buy bread. On the boats when I traveled in the islands, the *Îles-Sous-le-Vent,* it was the time to sail across the clear surface of the ocean, navigating through the passes in the fields of underwater coral. But in Aurore's bed, I spent the early morning hours lost in love, lost in the secret jagged games that she knew.

In the hallway outside the bedroom was a painting of a man named Vetea Tchong. Aurore had painted him with a background of the mountains that rose over the valley of Papara. It was one of the only times I had accompanied Aurore, to the land in Papara where Vetea and his family grew taro and melons and raised a small herd of cows. Vetea's mother was Tahitian and his father was Hakka. Aurore thought that if I conversed with him, he would relax from the solemn pose he always assumed when he sat for his portrait. He was a serious man with silver-grey hair and deep-set eyes and thick fingers with dark wrinkles puddling at the joints. When I first visited him with Aurore, he told me that he was sixty-two and that he was born in Tahaa. His father's parents ran a general store in Potoru near the bay of Hurepiti, and he remembered waking in the middle of the night when he was a boy to find his grandfather baking bread by the light of a lantern, the same lantern they took to fish at night. The bread dough lay in deep bowls, covered with cloth, where the dough was left to rise. We sat on overturned crates in the shade of his garage while Aurore set up her easel to paint, and when Vetea laughed, the gold teeth of his back molars flashed, but at other times, he settled into a stillness as we sat among the farm tools and the empty petrol containers by the wall.

"They sent for a medium when my grandfather died," he said. "They brought the medium, a Hakka man, one of the older Mu uncles, by pirogue from Raiatea. He was living in Opoa. I wanted to stay, but my parents sent me to my aunt's. They said it wasn't good for children to be there when the dead were called."

As I drove back from Papara, Aurore said, "So what did you think about what Vetea said?"

"What Vetea said?"

"About his grandfather, about the medium."

"It was interesting." I glanced over at Aurore to find that she was looking at me, watching closely like I had a strange bug crawling on my face.

"I'm glad it was Vetea who talked about this," she said.

"Why?"

"Because you always get so annoyed when I ask you these questions—about mediums and spirits."

"That was a long time ago. We don't use mediums anymore. My father has a friend living in Huahine—he knows more about this than I do. Monsieur Jonathan Li. You should talk to him."

"There you go. You're annoyed again."

"No, I'm not."

"Yes, you are. You should see your face." Aurore started imitating me: "'No Aurore—we don't use them anymore. You're a crazy *popa'a* who thinks we're backwards and superstitious.'"

"It's not a subject for conversation." I was as superstitious as anyone; I just didn't want to talk about it.

"Well, you talk about it with Vetea."

"That's different."

"How is it different?"

"He doesn't make such a big deal of it. Look—I don't believe in this sort of thing. Maybe old people still do, but no one I know does. There just isn't anything to talk about."

"Then why do you get so angry?"

This irritated me about Aurore—her interest in ghosts and magic and her expectation that I had some sort of exotic knowledge on the subject. "I'm not angry," I said, meaning that I wasn't going to talk any more about this.

Aurore spent several days drawing sketches of the mountains, preparing the background for Vetea's portrait. She sat outside wearing a large-brimmed hat while I followed Vetea as he walked along the farm ditches to check the water flowing from the stream that irrigated his land. Once when we were walking to his field of taro, Vetea told me that he had worked for several years in Mururoa. I knew already—Aurore had told me. I knew this was the reason that Aurore was painting him. She was passionately opposed to the CEP, the *Centre d'Expérimentation du Pacifique,* and the nuclear tests on Mururoa.

"I worked for a long time there," said Vetea. He paused and looked up at a rambutan tree. "You like rambutan? Come back in a month, when the fruit is ripe."

I knew he would say nothing further about Mururoa—about how long he had worked there or what work he had done for the CEP. Everyone had signed papers swearing that they would say nothing.

"My grandfather, he drank a dark tea," Vetea said one day as we walked along a dirt path to the mouth of the valley where the cows grazed during the day. "I've seen Chinese tea, but this was dark. He had a flat cake. Big like this." He held his hands apart as if he were holding a plate.

"The kind of tea you're talking about—it's really old," I said. "They age this tea."

"You know this tea?"

"There's some that's twenty, twenty-five years old." As old as I was.

"That's young tea," said Vetea and he laughed.

The next time Aurore came to paint the mountains, two weeks had passed. Vetea's daughter Maeva had called, canceling Aurore's usual visit, saying her father was ill. Maeva didn't specify what was wrong and when we visited, Vetea looked the same, but he moved more slowly, as if something within him had turned brittle. He sat on an oil drum beneath a mango tree and unwrapped the package I had brought him.

"This is from China?" He removed the parcel from its brown postal wrapping paper. It was a cake of tea, sandwiched between white paper stamped with red and green Chinese characters.

"I got it from a Chinese from Indonesia. He was sailing through Rangiroa." The Chinese had a forty-five-meter yacht and a girlfriend from Vladivostok. He walked with a slight limp and wore an oval jade ring on his middle finger. He told me to call him Pen.

Vetea bent over the tea and sniffed; it had a musky scent of earth and leaves laced with smoke. "It's the same smell. Is it old?"

"Nineteen years old." Like a perfect young mistress, Pen had said.

Vetea turned the cake around between his hands. "Do you know what this says?"

"I don't read Chinese."

"You should learn to read," he said.

As Aurore and I were leaving, Vetea came to the car window. Aurore was saying good-bye to his wife, Emilie. I was waiting in the car, the engine idling, when Vetea took my hand and I felt something dropping into my palm—a Chinese gold chain with a clasp of hammered gold shaped like a W. I reached out to return the chain, but Vetea stepped away and shook his head.

"This is yours."

"I can't take this," I said.

"It belonged to my grandfather."

The car door opened on the passenger side and Aurore sat down carrying a green pomelo. Vetea walked to the door, turning around to wave before entering his house.

Chapter 19

The phone rang as I lay on Aurore's bed. The ringing continued—my cell phone, among the clothes on the floor.

"Is this Marc?" It was late at night and De Koning knew she could still call me.

"Yes." Always so formal and correct, as Aurore said.

"I'm leaving soon."

The day after tomorrow, on the six o'clock morning flight to Huahine. I hadn't forgotten.

"Can I see you?" she asked. "Look, I think we should talk."

"Tomorrow then." From the way I spoke—if Aurore was listening, if she was in the hallway or the next room—I could be speaking to anyone: Radish, Edouard, a client.

A long pause followed—you usually knew these things, if someone was interested in you, and I knew it was something else with De Koning. "Monsieur Li asked me to talk to you."

"About what?" I asked.

"Can we meet for lunch? Early, before noon, at the Chinese restaurant."

"Eleven," I said.

A lizard clicked softly in the dark, from somewhere above on the ceiling. I picked up my phone again and called Radish.

"Do you know what time it is?" he asked, his voice raspy from sleep.

"Someone's interested in the python. We should talk, tomorrow morning."

"You told me you had a buyer."

"They backed out. But it doesn't matter—we'll sell the python before the end of the week."

"Edouard says he's not handling your python."

"Tell him he has to come with us."

"I need someone else."

"How about your brother Arthur? He's good with snakes, isn't he?"

"I don't want him involved. A python—you're crazy. Why do you want to do this?"

Radish always asked: why was I doing this? We made enough money from renting the houses and the *fares*. Why didn't I just stay with land? Legal transactions. Clean and boring, things I could do in my sleep. And that was the reason: all that clean work—I might as well sleep through it all. The snakes were different: they made me think.

"Make up your mind—you want to handle the snake by yourself?" I said. "Or do you want Arthur to help you?"

Aurore entered the room. Her hair was wet, a towel wrapped around her.

"Seven-thirty. We meet at seven-thirty," I said.

Aurore walked to the armoire and opened a drawer, pulling out a *pareu* and then deciding on another before leaving the room. My phone rang again.

"Marc." It was De Koning. "I talked to Monsieur Li. He asks if you could call him. I'd call him right away if I were you."

"In Huahine?"

"You have his number?"

I dialed Monsieur Li's number but the phone rang and rang without answer. I stared at Aurore's books, at the shelves that she never touched and the shelves that she was always reading. Her favorites were the books on divination, bound in grey and dark blue like school books. Twice a year, I followed different members of the family—A-tai, my aunts, and my father—to make offerings and to consult their fortunes. The smoke of hundreds of incense sticks filled the temple. When I was very little, my father would place the incense in my hands and I would follow him from statue to statue, pretending that I was solemn and pious and bowing whenever he bowed. Outside the sun was hot and dazzling, but within the temple, it was gloomy and silent. It was darkly comforting: the smoke, the pyramids of oranges and mandarins arranged as offerings. Someone would always recognize my father or A-tai and there would be plates of red rice cakes, glistening on rounds of leaves, to eat.

Aurore once said that she heard I had problems speaking in front of people, that there had been an incident at my father's wedding. She said this one morning as we ate breakfast.

"Nothing happened at my father's wedding," I had replied. Who was telling her this?

"Then something about the wedding—maybe another party."

I thought of the terrible feeling at my father's engagement party, my running from the restaurant.

"It's a form of anxiety," Aurore said, slicing a red papaya at the table and squeezing a lime over it. "An anxiety disorder. You feel like you can't breathe. It's fairly common."

I poured a thin stream of canned milk into my coffee. "You weren't at my father's wedding."

"You're right. I didn't actually see you."

I drank my coffee and checked my phone for messages.

"I threw up at my mother's wedding," said Aurore. "I was wearing a blue dress. The fabric was very light. Voile, that's what they called it. I was supposed to say something short. Everyone said that I looked lovely in the dress, but I felt so sick. No one would let me leave. They said that I could leave only if I talked. But I couldn't talk and just the thought of it was horrible. I threw up all over the dress. It was ruined and I cried and cried. I wished I was dead. I wished they were all dead."

"They shouldn't force you to talk. Little kids are shy."

"I was twenty-two," said Aurore.

I tried to think of what I should say. Aurore picked out a papaya seed, black and filmy like the eye of a fish.

In the bedroom, Aurore was looking for something, peering among the tiny combs and makeup brushes on her desk. A trickle of water ran from her neck, down her back, disappearing beneath the *pareu* fabric wrapped around her. My phone began ringing.

"Aren't you going to answer?" Aurore asked.

"It's late," I said.

"I thought you were still working."

She had something small, like a wand, in her hand. When I had first started sleeping with Aurore, she told me stories about the forests she knew as a child—the Forest of Rambouillet, the Forest of Paimpont. They were remnants of the old forests that had once covered France, but it was still easy to get lost inside, she said.

I let the phone ring and I took Aurore's hand, still wrapped tightly around the wand. I lifted her hand and saw that she held not a wand but a long, thin paintbrush. She was quiet and preoccupied and I drew her closer, kissing her neck, running my tongue along the curve of her ear.

When Aurore was a child, she lived with her sister and her mother near the edge of a forest. A secret place, the forest. "My mother told me not to go inside," she said. "So of course, I always went there. When I was small, my older sister told me that we were druids, going into the forest to perform magic. We crawled through the underbrush until we reached a clearing where my sister drew circles with a long stick. Magic circles, she said. We stood inside while my sister mumbled strange words. Later I went there alone. I knew paths and passages through the trees, but the forest was always strange. Sometimes I walked for a long time, thinking I was lost."

I wondered if Aurore told all her lovers about the forest. She said she had married when she was nineteen, a marriage that lasted a year, and then she married again in her late twenties. Her husband lived in France and Aurore visited him once or twice a year, traveling to different cities to meet. He was not aristocratic, but his family was very wealthy. Aurore said that her mother never seemed to have enough money—they had lived in a house near the forest on land that belonged to her father's family. A few cousins had money, but most of the family just knew how to spend what they no longer had.

"Did you tell your cousins about the forest?" I asked.

"No—why should I?" She seemed surprised by the idea, and I took it as a sign that perhaps she spoke only to me about the forest. Aurore had a fondness for running her fingers through my hair, and I took to cutting it less and less, to please her. She said she liked the way my hair fell in waves and then curled at the bottom of my neck. Like a girl, she teased me. I replied that my sister Odile always complained that Hakka girls rarely had wavy hair—it was something you saw on boys.

Aurore told me that once, when she was walking alone in the forest, she saw a young girl in the distance. She and her sister sometimes saw people in the forest and there were those who rode horses along the paths, even though it was forbidden to do so—but she had never encountered someone alone. She found herself approaching quietly, walking quickly enough to draw closer but keeping herself hidden. The girl paused from time to time and Aurore stood behind the trees.

"Why did you hide?" I asked.

"I had never seen her before—she didn't come from around where we lived—and yet she was walking like she knew the forest. And she wasn't old, like someone who had once lived nearby and was returning to something familiar. She was around sixteen. I thought she was very pretty. At first I thought she was on her way to meet someone, but then I saw that she was walking deeper into the forest."

Aurore talked about the girl in the forest only when we were alone together late at night. She told me this story many times and sometimes I felt that there was something she was not telling me, something important—but other times, I felt that she had told me everything and that she herself didn't know why she repeated this story to me over and over again. The ending was always the same.

"I followed her," said Aurore. "But she was going deeper inside."

"Why didn't you see where she was going?" I asked. "The forest had to end. You said it yourself: it was a real forest long ago, but only a small part of it was left."

"But I could be lost, following her inside."

"You follow her and the forest ends soon enough," I said.

"And you know so much about forests," Aurore replied.

I awoke before the night ended. Aurore's books and the pillows tossed on one side of the bed—all were different shapes of the same darkness. I slid out of bed and opened the door.

"Where are you going?" Aurore asked, speaking in the dark.

"It's early," I said. "I thought you were sleeping."

The window opened to the back garden. A rooster crowed and then another, anticipating the dawn. "They sound sad," said Aurore. "Bright and mournful. People say that roosters crow to greet the sun—but really, when you listen, it sounds like they crow to mourn the ending of the night."

"I don't think roosters work that way," I said.

"They sound especially sad in the islands."

I wanted to tell Aurore that roosters were roosters and they sounded the same anywhere.

"Where are you going?" she asked.

"I have to be in Papeete at seven-thirty." Unless I left before the traffic began, I'd be stuck all the way from Punaauia, through *la route de colline,* into town.

"Why so early?"

It wasn't that early—most people began work at seven-thirty or eight, before the heat of the day.

It had grown light enough to see Aurore turning towards me on the bed and, even though I knew better, I approached her. "Marc," she said softly, and already I was caught, although I appeared to be standing a certain distance away by the door.

That was how it had begun, years ago, four and a half years, several lifetimes, it seemed. I had gone to visit Aurore, for aperitifs, she said. I had walked up the stairs and entered the parlor to find that I was the only guest. Aurore wore a long dress of some kind of nearly transparent material and she poured me a glass of something. I couldn't remember what it was—a glass of *eau minérale,* wine, champagne. I never even began to drink. She had turned to me, touching me lightly on my hand. It felt unbelievable and exquisitely lush, her fingers on my skin. I was so crazed I couldn't speak, and then I had done the unthinkable. I touched her, on the cheek, on the corner of her mouth, and she closed her eyes and it all became possible.

"I went to Papeete yesterday," said Aurore, and there was something different, a flatness in her voice, as if she were reading to me from a newspaper. "I went to Madame MuSan's restaurant to draw. I ran into Philippe MuSan there; he was having a late lunch."

It was odd, the way she spoke.

"What's this about?" I asked, still standing by the bedroom door.

"He talked to me, about someone in your family, a young woman. Marie-Laure." Aurore sat up on the bed. "Did they tell you? Philippe said that some of your family were coming to Tahiti. He mentioned Monsieur Li, that he was arriving from Huahine to see her."

Monsieur Li asks if you could call him, De Koning said. About business, about some favor he was asking my father—I had assumed this all along.

"Philippe was concerned," said Aurore. "He said that she was so young."

"So young?"

"She's very ill."

I listened to Aurore talking as if in a dream, a bad dream that I'd suddenly entered.

"Philippe talked to me because Al—we worked together on the CEP documentary—wrote this article, something about blood disorders."

"What does Marie-Laure have?" I heard my voice, strangely calm.

"The doctors don't know exactly. They're still running tests."

I replayed the previous day in my mind—Aurore's charcoal sketches, her quiet, her sudden tenderness at night.

"It's so sad," said Aurore.

My phone rang.

"Marc," said Radish, "I have talk to you. You heard, about Marie-Laure? Jonathan just called me. Shit. I can't believe it."

"I have to talk to your cousin. Jonathan, Monsieur Li." I walked across the veranda, the dog following me down the stairs to my car.

"He said he was having trouble reaching you. What do you want to do about the python?"

Forget about it, I wanted to say. "What did Monsieur Li tell you?"

"He wants to see you. It's about Marie-Laure. He's changed his plans—he's here in Tahiti."

"I'm going to Papeete."

"Marie-Laure arrives tomorrow night. I can't believe it. Why Marie-Laure? Where the fuck are you?"

I thought about Marie-Laure during the drive to Papeete. The last time I had seen her was at Radish's wedding, an expensive church wedding with a maid of honor, five bridesmaids, and a flower girl with a basket filled with white and pink roses. Marie-Laure had arrived from Lyon. Her hair was still long, but she looked pale and tired, resting on Radish's arm during the reception. She took my hands and her palms felt so spongy and strange that I wanted to ask what was wrong. She promised to have dinner with me, but when I went to her house that week, Aunt Georgine said Marie-Laure had already returned to France. Radish's wife, Natasha, kept the wedding album, a white book printed with doves, filled with wedding pictures, and Radish bought her a home in Raiatea near her parents, a one-level house by a stream where she kept a basket to catch river shrimp. His wife was very resourceful, Radish said. He visited her once or twice a month.

Chapter 20

It was eleven in the morning, early for lunch customers, when I entered Madame MuSan's restaurant. Madame MuSan sat with another woman at a table in the back. They peeled garlic with their fingers, talking as they worked, a pyramid of garlic in the center of the table, the paper-fine skins scattered over the oilcloth. Madame MuSan stood and wiped her hands on her apron. She was small and bony, her face webbed with wrinkles.

"Let me get you some tea," she said, walking behind the counter and picking up a glass from the stack of clean glasses.

"Your father's new girlfriend, the very young one," said the other woman, a sister-in-law of Madame MuSan named Lita Lee. "She's pretty but they say her *ti-tis* aren't real."

Behind the counter, Madame MuSan pointed to one of the tables. "Why don't you sit there?" she said to me.

"This time Cecile's really angry," Lita said. "She usually just looks the other way."

I sat down at the table and ran my fingers over a crease in the green oilcloth. "My father bought Cecile a *motu*."

"I heard," said Lita. "In Raiatea."

"No, in Bora Bora."

"It's worth a fortune then," said Madame MuSan, pouring tea from a white teapot into my glass and setting the teapot on the table.

"Two fortunes," I said.

"One for each of Jocelyn's *ti-tis*." Lita started laughing.

Madame MuSan waved her hand, like she was shooing a fly. "You're talking nonsense."

"I've heard this rumor," I said. "About Jocelyn Loong."

"It's true then," said Lita.

"I didn't say that. It's a rumor."

"She was your cousin's—what's his name? Melody's son."

"Harris."

"Harris—yes, Harris's girlfriend. They say that your father liked her even then."

"What kind of talk is this?" said Madame MuSan, slapping Lita's arm. "Let him drink his tea."

The door to the restaurant opened and De Koning walked inside.

"Bonjour," she said to Madame MuSan, who went behind the counter to pick up a clean glass for De Koning.

"You heard about your cousin Marie-Laure?" said De Koning, sitting down at my table. "Monsieur Li said that he talked to Radish who said he already talked to you. I guess everyone knows."

"You knew this already?"

"I found out last night, right before I called you." She looked up at Madame MuSan pouring the tea into her glass. "Thank you." She turned back to me. "Did you order yet?"

"No, I was waiting for you." My mind was whirling, thinking about Marie-Laure, and I didn't feel like being polite anymore. "What did you want to talk to me about, before you knew about Marie-Laure? You wanted to see me about something else."

De Koning glanced over at Lita Lee, peeling garlic at the back table, and then she looked back at me. "I came here to see your sister."

"My sister? Odile?" Of course, my sister Odile—I had only one sister.

"That's why I'm here. I met Odile at your father's wedding."

De Koning had met me for the first time at my father's wedding too, but that wasn't what she was talking about. I picked up the menu, a handwritten sheet entombed in heavy plastic.

De Koning leaned forward slightly, her voice quiet. "You're the first person that I've talked to about this."

When I looked up from the menu, De Koning was staring at a point on the table between us. I picked up my glass of tea and drank, then put the glass down, a heavy sound in the empty restaurant. The lunch customers would arrive soon—takeout orders, clients from the bank across the street.

"You met Odile at my father's wedding. Four years ago."

"We met then, but she was with someone else at that time, and then it didn't work between them and we met again. We've been together for a month."

De Koning was American, I thought, talking about these things so directly. I felt my mind spinning, falling off the ground. Marie-Laure was ill, she was coming back to Tahiti, De Koning was with my sister.

"Monsieur Li thinks very highly of you," said De Koning. "He called me last night because he wants to talk with you, about Marie-Laure."

"How ill is she?"

"She has something complicated. Autoimmune. Odile told me that you were very close to Marie-Laure." De Koning shook her head, her caramel-colored hair—she was pretty and I really didn't know what to think. All right, she was attractive and she was with my sister—what was I supposed to think? De Koning wanted me to be the first to know—should I be flattered?

"I'll have a beer," I said to Madame MuSan, who had appeared at our table.

"The tamarind duck," said De Koning.

"What are you eating?" Madame MuSan said, turning to me.

I waved my hand. I couldn't think.

"How about the *steak frites*? Or the fish. There's parrot fish today, steamed with lemon."

"The parrot fish," I said, handing the menu to Madame MuSan.

The lunch customers began arriving. A young Chinese couple sat at the next table, the man wearing a blue shirt and iron-pressed slacks and the woman wearing a lacy dress with pearl buttons along her wrists and neck, the sort of clothes you could wear if you were sitting inside air conditioning all day.

"I'm hoping to learn Hakka," said De Koning. "I was hoping to learn from you."

Why don't you ask Odile to teach you, I thought, but De Koning was smiling, her head bobbing up and down earnestly.

"Are you upset?" De Koning lowered her voice. "I told Odile that we should tell you. I wanted you to be the first to know."

I found that I wasn't so surprised about Odile—maybe it was one of those things that I had known, without ever really thinking about it. I was surprised about De Koning—although perhaps, I had to admit, it was more about my pride. De Koning wasn't interested in me. Not that I was ever interested in her—I was in love with Aurore—but De Koning wasn't even interested in me. I was just the brother of Odile, the older brother, that was all.

"Why does Monsieur Li want to talk to me about Marie-Laure?" I asked.

"Monsieur Li told me that your great-grandmother raised you," said De Koning. "He said that she told you about things. Magic."

"You're the apprentice of Monsieur Li, aren't you? I think you know more about these things than I do."

"My grandfather's Hakka. But I didn't grow up here. And the rest of my family—Tahitian, French, Dutch, some Greek, some Irish. Sometimes I feel like I'll always be on the outside."

"Don't talk like that."

"I wanted to tell you—about Odile. Not just because you're her brother," said De Koning. "I know. I've heard what they say about you. But I don't think you're like that at all. Ever since I met you, at the wedding. You're quite good looking—I guess everyone must tell you that. You must get tired hearing it."

I could hear this again—easily, I thought.

"Monsieur Li pointed you out to me. Go talk to him, Monsieur Li said. And I thought, are you crazy? But you didn't act the way I thought you would. You're shy, I think. And you seemed—I don't know—sort of lost."

"I'm the brother of your girlfriend. It's the only reason you're nice to me."

"I want us to be friends."

"We are friends."

"Don't tease me. I'm serious."

"You were telling me about Monsieur Li," I said. "And Marie-Laure."

"You know Marie-Laure was in love with you. Odile told me this."

"Maybe. If so, it was long ago. A crush."

126

"No, Odile doesn't think that Marie-Laure ever got over you."

"Let me tell you this," I said. "When I was eighteen, or almost eighteen, we were supposed to go to this party together. I went to drive her to the party. I showed up, dressed in these clothes that she asked me to wear. But she didn't go."

De Koning looked at me like she was studying a problem very carefully.

"She wouldn't go," I said.

"How old was she?"

"Sixteen."

De Koning nodded, as if that explained everything. "Monsieur Li wants to talk to you because you're close to Marie-Laure."

"It's only because we're cousins. I think you know that."

"You don't understand about this party, do you? It's obvious."

"Then it's obvious to you but not me."

"I've never actually met Marie-Laure. She calls Monsieur Li a lot—probably because he's her eldest cousin and he knows these ancient texts they're both always reading. The *Li sao,* the Heavenly Questions, stuff like that. Monsieur Li has family pictures, so I've seen what Marie-Laure looks like. I know she's really smart. But she's really plain. And everyone here always talks about how people look. Like 'Marc Chen—he's so cute.' And your mother—she's such a beauty. You go everywhere and there's beautiful women. It's clear what happened. Marie-Laure felt ugly. She didn't want to go to this party with you because she thought that everyone would be talking about how ugly she was compared to you. And you're dressed up in these clothes she got for you, right? So you look great and she feels even uglier by comparison. And then you're cousins. I'm sorry, but that's weird—that's what people would say. That's why she wouldn't be seen at this party with you. And she's sixteen, so whatever people say, it hurts. You can want to die, because of what people say. I should know. And you love that person even more. And it hurts so much, you can't breathe when that person's around you."

Madame MuSan appeared with a plate of the tamarind duck, a wedge of lime between the slices. "I'll bring you more lime," she said, putting the plate on the table.

"This is enough," said De Koning.

I poured tea into our glasses, first De Koning's glass and then mine. "You say that Marie-Laure is ill—what does that mean?"

"She's actually very ill. The doctors don't know how to cure it."

"She should change her doctors."

"Monsieur Li had a teacher," said De Koning. "The teacher's nephew is still alive, living in China, near Shanghai. Monsieur Li sent for him."

"Why?"

"Because the nephew has this medicine, this magic."

Marie-Laure was sick and no one seemed to know how to cure it— and here we were talking about magic.

"What are you telling me?" I said. "Marie-Laure needs something that'll cure her. Not some hocus-pocus."

"The doctors tried. Nothing worked."

"So we're going to rely on this magician. A sorcerer of some sort."

"Monsieur Li said that his teacher was very powerful. That's why he sent for the nephew."

"A quack, for all we know."

"But we don't know. How do you know? You haven't met him."

"I don't want to meet him. There must be a cure for Marie-Laure. We'll take her to Australia or we'll take her to America."

"You don't understand." De Koning sat still, her face very quiet. "We have to try."

"What are you talking about?"

"No, no. We're doing this. Nothing else works. I thought you knew something about this. Monsieur Li said your great-grandmother told you."

"They're stories," I said. "That's all they are." What did she want me say?

"Aren't you going to help?"

"They're not real. They talk about things that don't exist. They're stories told to little kids so they won't cry at night." It was time to grow up. Magical charms and happy endings—just stories.

Chapter 21

I drove past the store displays of toys and *pareu,* the air-conditioned restaurants with their tinted windows and the snack shops with their scattering of flies lying dead on the window sills.

I drove out of Papeete, following the delivery trucks and Vespas along the stretch of highway that had taken forever to build, requiring a fortune, poured into the pockets of those talking smoothly of promises no one could keep.

Marie-Laure was ill. She was arriving tomorrow.

No, I wasn't going to be stupid. I wasn't going to listen to a charlatan from China selling fake charms and useless dust.

A half hour outside of Papeete, I pulled into the parking lot of the Vaima River. A shimmering fever of heat rose from the ground. A Chinese, one of the grandsons of the dumpling vending woman, was selling snacks from a bread truck parked under the trees: gum, chocolate, magic eggs, crumpled bags of Twisties and chips, *bon-bon chinois* stored in barrel-shaped jars.

"How's business?" I asked.

"Slow," he said. I pointed to a display can of soda by the window. He reached behind him, opening an ice chest to take out a can, shaking out the shaved ice from his fingers. I walked to the river to drink. Two women sat smoking cigarettes in the shade of a tree. A group of men were talking, sitting by the river, the water shallow and clear, rippling over the stones on the bottom.

I sat on the concrete slab by the river's edge. A blue eel swam along the far side, among the tree roots. Further upstream, three boys were splashing in the water that bubbled from the deep springs beneath the trees. The water was cold. A girl swam past, gliding underwater, her black hair streaming. She was ten or eleven and plump, wearing bright pink. She rose to take a breath of air and then glided further down the river.

The last time I had gone to the Vaima, I was with Harris and we had tried to catch the grey river fish, swimming so close and lazily it seemed possible to catch them with our hands. Of course we had caught nothing.

The Vaima was the same as I remembered. There were wider and more powerful rivers, the Fautaua, the Papenoo. The smaller Vaima flowed, narrow and clear, fed by pools of spring water. The girl returned, gliding upstream. She remained under for so long, it seemed as if she was breathing in the water. The boys had disappeared and it was suddenly quiet. Even the group of men had wandered elsewhere and there were only the two women smoking their cigarettes.

I stared, thinking of nothing. I gazed at the girl swimming and, suddenly, I felt it rising inside, as if I were going to be violently sick. A choking, uncontrollable sadness. I was crying and it poured out my nose, the way blood gushes out.

Marie-Laure arrived in the night, accompanied by her mother, Aunt Georgine. Ten-kwok went to the airport to pick them up, followed by a crowd of family. Aunt Georgine was wreathed in a hundred leis of frangipani, *tiare*, and orchids, and Ten-kwok held a hundred more leis intended for Marie-Laure, only she was too weak to breathe the heavy fragrance.

Aunt Georgine and my mother decided that Marie-Laure should be taken to my mother's house, that it was closer to the doctors in Papeete than her parents' house by the Fautaua River. Once she arrived at my mother's house, Ten-kwok and Aunt Georgine walked with Marie-Laure up the stairs to the room beneath the shade of the mango tree. I saw only part of her hair, her head resting against Aunt Georgine, and the blue fabric of her blouse from the back.

I stood at the foot of the stairs and watched Marie-Laure disappear. After several minutes, Ten-kwok reappeared at the top of the stairs. My father took him by the shoulders and walked him down the steps,

Ten-kwok like an over-sized puppet. He stared without really seeing anything, back to the walkway from the main house to the kitchen and past the chicken cages to the table inside. My father poured Ten-kwok a cup of tea and then he opened one of the cabinets, taking out a whisky bottle and two glasses and pouring a shot into each glass. Ten-kwok sat with his hands covering his face.

Chapter 22

Aurore waited outside on the veranda. There was the sound of someone playing a *vivo,* a wooden flute, in the distance, a high, thin music somewhere along the beach. Georges lay by Aurore's feet, the dog's head resting by her paws, asleep with the trusting oblivion known only to dogs.

"Did you see Marie-Laure?" Aurore asked. "Did you talk to her?"

"She went to sleep at my mother's house," I said.

Aurore turned in the direction of the music, now fading away as if someone were passing, walking by the ocean. "I fixed some sangria. It's in the refrigerator. Go have some—I already had a glass."

The pitcher sat in the center of Aurore's refrigerator, next to a jar of mustard and some bottles in the back. "Did you eat dinner?" I asked.

"I'm not really hungry," Aurore called out from the veranda.

"My mother's drinking this white fungus soup. She said she's giving me this soup tomorrow. It's good for the skin, something like that." What was the point of my drinking this, I wondered. Marie-Laure was dying in my mother's house and the only thing that my mother talked about was the fungus soup.

"Your mother's so beautiful. She looks like a lady in those Sung Dynasty scrolls."

"You should paint her, then."

"I want to paint you," said Aurore walking into the kitchen.

"A waste of time. Even my mother said that I didn't look so good."

"She's your mother. She just said that so you'll drink the soup."

A pile of envelopes lay on the kitchen counter—Aurore must have gone into town to pick up her mail. I started reading a postcard, turning it over.

"It's an opening, at a gallery," said Aurore.

"Are you going?" The invitation printed on the postcard was for an evening reception.

"I'll probably stop by."

"Why don't we go together?"

"It's not that important. I see her all the time. She's somewhat flamboyant, sometimes too much, like her paintings."

"I'll go with you."

Aurore took the postcard from my hand and returned it to the pile of letters. "How do you like the sangria? It's missing something—or maybe I put in too much lime."

"I don't see why we're not going to this gallery."

"You let me paint you and we'll go to the opening."

"Since when are we bargaining about these things?"

"You know I'm only asking."

"No," I said. "I don't know." Why didn't she just say, Strip off your skin and let me stick you to the wall where everyone can stare at you.

"I'll make a sketch. A line drawing, something simple."

"I'm not a plaything, a sort of toy, something to amuse you."

"What's got into you?" Aurore's voice turned sharp. "You're acting so strange. You're unreasonable, saying these things."

"You're the one being unreasonable. Why can't we go to the goddamn gallery opening?"

"Why do you want to go look at paintings when you can't stand the thought of being painted?"

"That's different."

"Is it? How so?" said Aurore. "You want to go and stand in a room full of paintings—when the whole thing just terrifies you."

"It doesn't terrify me."

"All right, then let me paint you."

It would be easy, taking the glasses of sangria and throwing them across the room.

"What is it? Just tell me," said Aurore. "Why don't you—"

"I don't see the goddamn fucking point." The room began to roar, a soundless whirlwind. It was all I heard, a pounding in my head. I walked outside into the blackness.

A bird made its strange creaking cry from one of the trees. The night air fell heavily, hot and damp.

Sometimes I drove without direction, away from Aurore's house, late in the night. I drove south to Taravao, towards my father's house where I never slept. I heard about his guests, various friends of Cecile's, a couple they met skiing in Chile or one of Cecile's accountant friends visiting from Paris. On other nights, I drove above Pic Rouge. I didn't sleep in the main house, but in a *fare* in the garden near the ossuary my father had built for my grandfather's bones. It was illegal, digging up my grandfather's coffin from where it was buried in the Chinese cemetery, but my father was stubborn. He told me that before, in China, the Hakka removed the bones of the dead after ten years, placed them in urns, some of them housed in elaborate pavilions, others in shelters that were nothing more than a concrete table. No one did this in Tahiti—it was probably against numerous health regulations. French regulations, said my father with an anger that surprised me. I had heard the rumors: that some of the older Tahitian graves were empty, a formality to please the French, and the bodies were buried in secret, in the mountains. My father and Monsieur Li went to the cemetery in the night when I was ten years old and then my father built his house above Pic Rouge and placed the bones in the back garden. A useless idea, my A-tai said—it wasn't like we were in China anymore. She complained, but once the blue-tiled pavilion was completed, she told me that it was really beautiful. It was kept secret. No one talked aloud about its existence, even in the family, and the tombstone at the Chinese cemetery was kept for public displays of offerings: incense, chicken blood, tea, and wine.

When I was a child living with my father, I began sleeping in the *fare*, a one-room bungalow surrounded by the white ginger that grew around the pavilion. The doves cooed in the trees in the morning, in the calm of the garden. Even when my father fell into his rages and moods, there was something untouched that lived there, something unseen in that space where I was alone, where no one stared and laughed or yelled and screamed.

A-tai had passed away the year before and she was buried in the Chinese cemetery in Arue. The view from the cemetery looked over the ocean, to the west. I wasn't sure if that was good or bad, but A-tai said that it looked towards China and that was good enough for her.

"No use digging up my bones," she said. She had decided to stay in the ground.

The door opened and Aurore walked out and stood beside me. I stared out from the front veranda over to where my car was parked.

"Are you leaving?" she asked.

Behind the line of coconut palms and the hedge at the edge of the land, the road was hidden.

"Are you going to Pic Rouge?"

"No," I said, and I heard my voice shouting. I felt Aurore recoil in the darkness.

"I'm sorry about Marie-Laure," said Aurore. "The *métropols* who return to France—even they have mysterious cancers, blood diseases that no one can explain." I had heard Aurore talk about this a hundred times, about the CEP, about the effects of radiation from nuclear testing. "I'm sorry," she said.

Sorry, sorry . . . The night was heavy and black.

My mind felt blank, my thoughts trapped in a hole, someplace out of reach. Yesterday at lunch, I had watched De Koning crying about Marie-Laure. I just sat, unable to do anything, as she cried.

"If it was so safe, they'd do it back in France," said Aurore.

Why Marie-Laure? Sorry, sorry. The words sounded empty and senseless and dead in my thoughts, and I stared out into the night—at things I couldn't see, the invisible forest, the place of long, enchanted sleep.

Chapter 23

I arrived at my mother's house at noon, but I knew from the way the birds sang in the garden close to the kitchen that there wasn't any lunch. The kitchen was empty. No chopping, no cooking, no one slurping soup at the table.

I crossed the walkway to the dining room, the doors open to the garden. Everyone ate at the long table in the center of the kitchen, but when guests, friends of my mother and Tiurai, were visiting, they sat at the round table carved of ironwood in the dining room of the main house.

A woman sat alone at the dining table. Her hair was long and grey and she wore a blue and white cotton dress trimmed with white lace, an old-style gown. She was reading a newspaper. A basket of oranges sat by a pile of papers, green and orange colored fruit, each one smoothly round.

"*Ia orana,*" I said, greeting her.

The woman looked up over her reading glasses. A thin white scar slashed the eyebrow over her left eye.

"You're Sylvia's son," she said.

Before I could answer, she peered at the oranges, reaching into the basket to pick up first one and then another, placing each one aside in turn. She continued looking through the basket until she finally decided on an orange, weighing the fruit in her hand and offering it to me.

"We picked these this morning." She smiled. "You don't remember me. I'm Jonathan's aunt."

"The aunt of Monsieur Li?"

"Yes, but my mother came from the Tuamotus."

"Your father was Monsieur Li's grandfather?" It could take a long time, sorting out how someone was related to you—by blood, by marriage.

"And Cecile, your stepmother," she said. "I'm Vaianu."

"My mother asked me to stop here around lunch. Is she here?"

"*Aita*. The doctors decided to examine Marie-Laure at the hospital and your mother went with her." She sat back in her chair. "You're Marie-Laure's cousin."

In a burst of chatter, a handful of birds flew outside the door. Vaianu sat in the chair and her eyes moved slowly, without hurry, across my face like she was reading me, line by line. I knew the story of how Marie-Laure was born, how Aunt Georgine had almost died and they had sent for Monsieur Li who arrived with Vaianu, his aunt. They knew the old ways—the spiders you gathered in the mountains and where to draw water, the old remedies, people said.

"They'll return this afternoon," said Vaianu, turning to pick up the newspaper. "Come back then."

It was night before I returned to my mother's house. Edouard was retiling the showers of the bungalows, and we went to the *bricolage* store on the Avenue Prince Hinoi to look at tiles. Then a tenant called complaining about the trash left by neighbors throwing a party, and we went to look at the damage. The tenant was renting one of the houses in Paea.

"I'm paying you good money," she said. I had to listen to her complain for half the afternoon before she gave me the rent, all cash, large paper bills in Pacific francs stuffed in an envelope.

Two dogs barked from inside the front gate of my mother's house. Odile ran out into the garden when she heard their barking. She shouted at the dogs until they cowered and slunk away obediently towards the Chinese grapefruit tree in the corner.

"They're new?" I asked.

"A friend brought them from Moorea. I'm keeping them for a day. They think the garden belongs to them." She turned and glared at one of the dogs trying to slip back, close to where we stood, and the dog dashed away. "Did you eat dinner?"

"I ate with Edouard."

"There's some chicken in rice wine soup in the kitchen," said Odile. "And Mom left you the white fungus. It's in a bowl in the refrigerator."

"Good haircut," I said.

"Oh—this." Odile touched the top of her head, as if she had forgotten how her hair looked. "Thanks, I guess." We spent a long moment looking over each other's shoulders. "You're here to see Marie-Laure?"

"Where is she?"

"In her usual room in the back," said Odile. "Near the big mango tree."

I stood on the terrace by the room where Marie-Laure slept. A wind was blowing in the night. The leaves of the mango tree bent and swayed and, far away, something metallic clanged as it rolled down a street.

The windows of Marie-Laure's room were high, long rectangles close to the roof so that no one could look directly inside. A glowing light shone through the glass.

"Is someone there?" Marie-Laure spoke from inside the room. "Who's there?"

I opened the door and Marie-Laure was sitting on a bed beneath a tent of white mosquito netting. On a desk by the wall, a bouquet of roses bloomed, pink, orange, yellow, and red, one of the many-colored rose bouquets sold from buckets at the entrance to the open-air market in town.

"Marc," she said. "It really is you."

Through the veil of mosquito netting, I saw her face, swollen and horribly bloated, her hair tied in a ponytail. I wondered, for a moment, if she truly was Marie-Laure.

"Close the door behind you," she said.

I stepped back outside and reached for the door, to shut it behind me as I left.

"No, no," said Marie-Laure. "Come inside. And then close the door."

I stood for a moment, uncertain, repelled.

"It's not contagious," she said.

"It's not that—it doesn't matter." I stepped inside.

"Come closer. So I can see you. My mother and your mother, they both insist on this mosquito netting. Against the dengue or some other fever." She placed her hand against the fabric so that the netting curved around the shape of her fingers. She sat cross-legged on the bed, a book opened before her. "You can sit down here," she said, patting the mattress near the edge of the mosquito netting.

I remained standing. "I should go. You must rest."

"That's all I do. Rest and rest. It's boring."

"Rest and you'll get better."

"I'm tired of being sick."

I moved the netting carefully to the side and sat on the corner of the bed, outside the netting. Sitting close to her, I saw the grey paleness of her skin.

"Does it hurt?" I asked.

"It hurt at the beginning—the small joints. In my fingers and my hands and in my feet, but they gave me medication. Steroids. It's why my face is swollen like this. I must look terrible." She held her hand out, touching the fine web of fabric. "I can't believe it's really you."

"Why? Do I look so different?"

"No," she said, and then she looked down, at her hands lying on her lap, and we fell quiet.

"I should go," I said.

Marie-Laure looked up. "You're going?"

"I'll return," I said.

"Tomorrow morning?"

Tomorrow morning. "What would you like?"

"Bring me a chessboard."

"What time do you get up?"

"You have to work, don't you?"

"Work—it can wait."

"Where do you live?" Marie-Laure asked. "You know, I asked—but no one seemed to know where you lived. The way they looked at me, it was as if no one had really thought of this before. Odile said that you lived at the house above Pic Rouge, but the way she spoke, I didn't think she was really sure."

With her hand, Marie-Laure parted the white netting. I saw her clearly, her face and her arms. The smell of something unfamiliar and chemical drifted from her. She hesitated and her eyes fell downward. I moved closer and I kissed her on the cheek.

She pressed her cheek for a moment against my face and then she reached up to the border of the netting, letting it fall between us again.

Marie-Laure was seriously ill. I knew this for certain, once I saw her. Her face was unrecognizable, swollen from medication, but more than that, there was a strange and repulsive fragility to her, as if something normal had stopped flowing inside. I didn't need to be told that it was rare—I knew. I'd never seen anything like it before. It wasn't a fever or an infection. It didn't smell like blood and pus and phlegm—all the rotting smells that came with disease. It was something almost alien. Once I saw her, I knew that it was very close. Death—a strange variety, but death all the same. Usually mortality had a familiar mark, and we had seen enough death: the old, babies, people who died of fevers and infection. You smelled the same stench when death came knocking at the door. But Marie-Laure had something different: death in another disguise, changed into another form so that it was difficult to see, to outmaneuver, to outrun and escape.

Chapter 24

Aurore stood before a row of jars filled with earth: the plateau of Taravao, the sand at Point Venus, the river valley of the Papenoo. A few weeks before, she had announced at breakfast that she had a new idea for something she called An Installation and she had gone driving around the island to collect a jar of earth from each of a dozen different places. She kept them on the table of her studio, picking them up to examine the color inside: black river earth, rusty volcanic soil, the leafy mud under a *mape* tree, the sand bordering the house at Mataiea.

"What do you think?" she asked, turning as I entered the studio. The jars stood in a line of different shades and colors of soil. She bent down until she gazed eye-level at the line of earth. Her unfinished painting, the commission she was trying to complete, left her troubled and she was restless, pondering distractions. "Maybe I'll show it to Inez." Aurore's friend Inez was a tall, very thin black-haired woman who walked with a slight stoop, somewhat like a seabird bent over the sand, foraging for bugs. Aurore had never introduced me to Inez, but I saw her sometimes walking in town. When Aurore spoke of Inez, she seemed mysterious, belonging to an unknown world, but whenever I actually saw her, she was just unglamorous and plain and there was nothing alluring in reality.

"Aurore." I was leaving to see Marie-Laure at my mother's house.

Aurore plucked a jar of reddish-brown soil and repositioned it next to one of grey sand. I thought of what I should say: *I'll be back soon, I'm leaving now, I've seen Marie-Laure and now I know, she's sick, very very sick.*

"I'm looking for a finer grain of white." Aurore picked up a jar of white sand.

"Bora Bora sand," I said. The week before Toussaint when the graves were cleaned, white sand was brought from the island of Bora Bora and sold in sacks by the cemetery.

"Will that work? Will you bring me some? Don't bring me too much—just enough for a jar," she said, her kiss grazing my ear.

Marie-Laure stirred, raising her head. "*Allô?* Oh," she spoke from behind the mosquito netting. "Your mother was just here."

I stepped inside and placed the chessboard next to the bouquet of roses fading on her desk.

"I talked to Radish," I said. "He's driving here from the store."

"The one near the waterfront?"

"No, the new one—it's closer to Fare Ute. Not far from here. You want the chessboard on the desk?"

Marie-Laure rose from the bed, her hair rumpled and loose. "I should go wash."

I lifted the netting so that she could stand.

"It's just my head." She stood in place for a long moment. "A headache—that's all." She began walking to the door. I followed her outside to the washroom next to the bedroom door. "You can wait inside, in my room," she said. "You don't have to hover."

I arranged the chess pieces on the board. It was turning hot inside the room, even with the fan by the bed, and I propped open the door with a brick from the terrace.

Marie-Laure walked out of the washroom. Her hair was combed, falling around her shoulders, her face shiny and swollen.

"White or black?" I asked.

"Black," she said. "You can have the first move."

She sat down and the opening moves passed quickly. I paused finally to consider my options, glancing up to see Marie-Laure blinking rapidly.

"What's wrong?" I asked.

She touched the side of her forehead. "It's just hot."

I stopped, watching her.

"Don't think you're getting any sort of advantage," she said.

Someone was walking up the stairs to the terrace, reaching the top, the footsteps approaching the door.

"Radish," said Marie-Laure.

Radish held a bag in his hand. He kissed Marie-Laure's cheeks and took out soda bottles from the bag. "Limonade?"

Marie-Laure picked up a bottle of bright red soda. "I haven't drunk this in years."

"Probably because it's full of dyes they can't sell legally in France," said Radish.

"Here's to being irradiated," I said, opening three bottles. They were cold and I handed one to Marie-Laure.

Radish looked over the chessboard. "Who's white?"

"I am," I said.

"You're in trouble." Radish took a long sip out of the bottle and sat down at the edge of the bed.

"What—checkmate in five moves?" I asked.

"More like four," said Radish.

"Why are you helping him?" Marie-Laure sat down on the chair and waved a hand over the board. "Go," she said to me. "Make your move. Enough delay."

I studied the board, my hand hovering over my queenside bishop before I moved.

"I'm sorry about your A-tai," said Marie-Laure. "You know, someone brought me a pomelo. I'll give it to you for her." She stood up and walked to a corner of her room, lifting up a green *pareu* fabric covering a cardboard box.

"You should eat it," I said.

Marie-Laure picked up a large yellow pomelo from inside the box. "It's beautiful. Here," she said, putting the fruit beside the chessboard. The pomelo was smooth-skinned and glossy, a twig of leaves still attached to the top. "You know, we should go to the cemetery after this. We could take it to her grave."

"You should rest," I said.

"I've been here in this room ever since I arrived. Why don't we go together? The view from the cemetery—it's so beautiful. You can see the ocean."

"Your mother and Aunt Sylvie, they won't like it," Radish replied.

"We won't tell them. We'll go by the back stairs. I'll be back before they know I'm gone." She smiled, her face flushed. "Why don't we go now?"

Radish and I exchanged glances—you didn't have to be a doctor to know that going under the hot sun with Marie-Laure was a bad idea.

"First," I said, "I have to win here."

Marie-Laure sat down. "We'll leave in a minute. After you lose."

"You wish," I replied.

Marie-Laure reached up, as if to remove something from the top of her head. "It really hurts," she cried suddenly. The skin around her eyes began to twitch.

"A headache?" asked Radish.

Marie-Laure opened her mouth to speak, but no words came out. She turned to me, as if she was trying to tell me something, and her eyes rolled back.

Everything seemed to move very quickly and not quickly enough: I stood up, knocking over the chess pieces, and Radish rushed from the bed. Marie-Laure's face continued its strange twitching and her eyes were white like the dead. I picked her up and Radish ran ahead, opening the door. I moved too slowly, carrying Marie-Laure down the stairs and through the garden and out the gate into the car. Radish started the engine and turned, the wheels squealing, onto the road.

Chapter 25

My father stood at the entrance to his house with his dog, a black and brown Rottweiler named Khan.

"Marie-Laure," he said.

"She's at the hospital," I replied.

"Cecile just talked to her mother."

"I can't stay long—I'm going back to the hospital. Is Monsieur Li here?"

"He's in the garden."

The front room, wide and sweeping, looked over the calm waters of the Baie de Phaeton. Past the front room, separated by a wall of glass, was a garden surrounding a lotus pond. Monsieur Li stood by the water, near the deep-colored flowers growing thickly.

"You had a good flight from Huahine?" I asked. These were the polite things you said, greeting someone who had just arrived, asking if the journey was good, asking if it was smooth, and always asking if they wanted something to eat.

"I saw they're rebuilding the airport," said Monsieur Li.

"It's only been two weeks," I replied. The airport at Faaa had burned in September during the riots. My uncles complained that the riots were pointless—you could burn down all of Papeete and it would do nothing. If France wanted to blow up their nuclear bombs in Mururoa, they were going to do it, no matter what anyone thought. "Let's see how long it really takes to rebuild."

"You saw Marie-Laure at the hospital?"

"She's not well."

"Was she awake?"

"No—she's still sleeping. If you can call it sleeping."

"I'll go to the hospital after dinner. You should get something to eat," said Monsieur Li.

I glanced at the pond, the tangle of leaves and flowers blooming over the water.

"Your father, he did the right thing, putting in goldfish instead of koi," Monsieur Li said. The fish swam through the water, flecks of orange and white. It was true: the smaller fish seemed part of the water itself. The koi would have been showy and magnificent, a spectacle to admire—but the goldfish seemed natural, like the water, the stems bending gracefully, the green leaves. It reflected well on my father, his modesty and restraint.

"De Koning told me that you've sent for the nephew of your teacher," I said. "He's arriving from China."

"I did. He should arrive in a day, maybe tomorrow."

"Marie-Laure can't wait that long. You have to do something now."

The door opened and Cecile stepped outside. "Why don't you come in and have dinner?"

"I can't stay," I said.

"Marie-Laure is my sister."

"Yes," I said. Now go away, I thought.

"You aren't the only one who's worried," she said. "This isn't all about you."

"Maybe we can get him a plate of the fish," said Monsieur Li. "He could bring something to Georgine."

"No—he can wait and eat like everyone else. We're all going to the hospital."

"We'll bring the food there," Monsieur Li replied. "Many people will be there—we'll bring them something to eat." He nodded at me and I walked to the door.

"You know, I'm Marie-Laure's sister," said Cecile. "He's her cousin. He can stay here with us and go to the hospital when we leave."

"He's young—he's worried about her," said Monsieur Li.

"And I'm not worried?" asked Cecile. "I'm not going to pack him a plate of food and then pack food all over again to take to Georgine at the hospital. He can wait."

146

The door opened and my father stood at the entrance. "Is something wrong?" he asked.

"I was explaining to Marc," said Cecile. "We're all going to the hospital after dinner. We'll go see Marie-Laure. Why should we pack food for Marc now and then pack food all over again to bring to Georgine and my father and everyone at the hospital?"

"You don't have to give me anything," I said. "I'm leaving now."

"You just arrived," said my father.

"And I'm going back. I left Marie-Laure to come here. I told her I'd return."

"I just talked to Georgine," said Cecile. "Marie-Laure is deeply asleep. The doctors don't expect her to awaken until morning."

"Well," said my father, still standing at the door. "That settles that. We'll eat and then we'll leave for the hospital. We'll bring food for Georgine and Ten-kwok."

"That's what I was saying," Cecile replied.

I thought of Marie-Laure, her fingers in my hand during the ride to the hospital. I kept holding her once we arrived, as they turned her and as she twitched and gasped while they stuck needles into her arms. "No," I said, walking to the door and moving past my father.

"This isn't about you." Cecile raised her voice. "You act as if this is all about what you want. This isn't about you at all. It's about my sister, Marie-Laure. You stand there, giving me orders, when it's my sister who's so ill." Her voice choked and she began to cry.

"Marc," said my father. "Go into the dining room."

The dining table was set for dinner with a white tablecloth, red plates, and a red tureen; not the red of luck or blood, but a flat, stark red. I sat alone at the table. My father walked in with Monsieur Li.

"Marc Antoine," said my father, "you've upset Cecile."

"I'm sorry," I said. What was I expected to say?

"It's a difficult time." My father sat down across from me at the table and Monsieur Li sat down next to him. I felt their gaze pinning me like a bug, a cockroach, a fly. "I know you're worried about Marie-Laure."

I picked up one of the porcelain soup spoons, fingering the handle nervously.

My father lowered his voice. "We all know about you and Marie-Laure. But Cecile is her sister. It's not just about you and what you think is right for Marie-Laure. Now is not the time to start acting like . . ." His voice fell quiet for a moment, as if my past involvement with Marie-Laure were a thread that my father preferred to let drop, falling out of sight. "You are Marie-Laure's cousin," my father said finally. "But Cecile is her eldest sister and Cecile's mother is Ten-kwok's first wife."

"Marie-Laure is very, very ill," I said, standing up from the table. It wasn't the time to discuss the fine points of family hierarchy. "I must go. I promised Marie-Laure that I'd return."

"She's asleep," my father said. "Deeply asleep."

"She had a seizure," I replied. "That's what the doctors say. She's in a strange kind of sleep, a coma. I have to be there; I have to talk to her." I wasn't talking sense, just repeating what someone once told me—I couldn't remember who, maybe it was Radish—that people in comas looked like they were sleeping, but they heard what others said around them.

"It's possible. He could be right." Monsieur Li said to my father.

They looked at each other without speaking, my father with his arms crossed.

"Let him go," said Monsieur Li.

"Go, then," said my father, and I walked to the door and left. I was opening the car door when I saw Monsieur Li coming down the front steps to where I stood.

"You're driving directly to the hospital?" he asked, opening the passenger door and sitting inside.

Marie-Laure slept beneath the fluorescent hospital lights. A nurse was changing a bag of the liquid that flowed into a tube leading into her arm. Aunt Georgine slept in a chair by the bed, but she awoke when Monsieur Li entered.

"She's still the same," said Aunt Georgine.

I sat on a chair by the foot of the bed.

"Go and rest," said Monsieur Li to Aunt Georgine.

"I'm not leaving."

"The doctors say that she'll be up in the morning. You go sleep and you'll be here when she wakes up."

Aunt Georgine kept her eyes on Marie-Laure and then she wavered and glanced at me.

"Marc will call you when Marie-Laure begins to wake up."

"How can I rest?" Aunt Georgine asked, but Monsieur Li led her towards the door. "Wait." Aunt Georgine returned to take Marie-Laure's hand, bending to kiss her daughter's forehead.

I watched Marie-Laure, her eyes closed shut, the black fringe of her eyelashes, a dark blue vein across her eyelid. There was something heavy that weighed on her, something that kept her eyes shut and her mouth silent and still. The convulsive breathing had stopped and now there was only a deep sleep, something that moved in long, smooth curves on the monitor screen near her bed. I took the chair and slid my hands beneath her hands. Her fingers felt cool and heavy, curving to fit inside my fingers.

"Marie-Laure," I said but there was no reply.

My father and Cecile arrived, followed by Ten-kwok and Uncle Florian with a kettle of soup. People entered, standing by Marie-Laure's bed or sitting in the chairs around the room. Their voices fell quiet and some of the women cried. They left, one by one, in pairs and in groups, speaking in sad hushed voices.

When I awoke, the room was dark except for the lights of the monitor. My hands had moved further away from Marie-Laure's hands—or perhaps she had moved. I took her hands again and they felt warm. Her head stirred, turning to the side.

I awoke again and checked the time: a few minutes past four in the morning. There was a rustling—Marie-Laure moving her head again. Another rustle as she moved her arms and her hands and then she opened her eyes.

"Marie-Laure." I bent close to her over the hospital bed.

She parted her lips and spoke, but her voice was so soft, I couldn't hear. I moved closer, placing my ear by her mouth.

"Why are you this close?" she was saying. "Can't you hear me?" Her voice was hoarse and faint.

"I can hear you," I said. "But you're speaking very softly."

"Really?"

I nodded my head.

She closed her eyes for a long moment and then opened them again. Her voice was slightly louder, as if she had been gathering herself for that effort. "Give me a kiss."

I kissed her on the forehead.

"No." She paused for a moment. "A real kiss," she whispered. "Are you holding me?"

"Yes—here," I said, pointing to where I was touching her, on her shoulder, above all the tubes and tape on her arm.

She moved her eyes slightly upwards. "I can't feel you." Her voice sank and then she closed her eyes.

Chapter 26

Three days ago, I thought about a hundred things. The python, the snakes, the bungalows, the *fares* and houses—thoughts that meant nothing now that Marie-Laure slept, sliding into dark places where no one could reach her. All those thoughts I had, about how I was going to talk to Radish or to this *mec* who said he was interested in a beachfront *fare* or how he was paying his rent late this month, just give him one more week—all the things that I thought I was doing right and yes, I had given up *paka* but I kept my profits and put it in land—I was clever, I told myself—all this meant nothing. These thoughts, they were like bugs, scurrying and scattering, and now they were gone.

I opened my eyes and Monsieur Li stood by Marie-Laure's bed. The monitor screen above it glowed in the darkness.

"What time is it?" I asked.

"Five in the morning," Monsieur Li replied.

"Marie-Laure talked a little, but then she fell back asleep." I must have slept without knowing.

"I brought you something," said Monsieur Li, handing me a plastic bag. I unwrapped the aluminum foil inside to find three *fe'i* bananas, cooked in their skin. "Let's go out in the hallway."

I followed Monsieur Li outside the door. "Sit here and eat," he said, pointing to some chairs in the hallway. I peeled one of the bananas and began eating its orange flesh.

"My teacher's nephew arrived," said Monsieur Li.

"He's here?" I asked.

There were rules of negotiation my father had taught me ever since I was very young. Never appear too eager. Never be the first to name a price. Never rush. You waited and you always bargained.

"Did he bring the medicine?" I asked.

You were careful and patient and you always inspected, making sure that the product worked. There were scams and sharks and con artists. Fake merchandise.

"He brought the medicine from China," said Monsieur Li.

The foremost rule was that you never appeared eager.

"The medicine," I said. "Where is it?"

"It's five in the morning," said Monsieur Li.

I didn't care—everything that I had ever learned about bargaining and negotiating and getting the best price, none of it mattered, nothing at all.

"Where is it?" I said. "Where the fuck is it?"

It was six in the morning and Mr. Lu sat with Monsieur Li in the cab of a pickup truck in the hospital parking lot. Mr. Lu was a short man with shaggy grey hair and very white teeth, probably fake. When De Koning and Monsieur Li called him the nephew of Monsieur Li's teacher, I had pictured a young man, but Mr. Lu seemed older than eighty. He shook my hand through the open window.

"You're the cousin." He spoke in the proper but awkward way of someone who usually spoke Mandarin or another dialect, but who had once learned Hakka.

"He's the son of my cousin Cecile's husband," said Monsieur Li.

"But he's the cousin of the girl."

"Marie-Laure Li. Yes, they're cousins. His mother and the mother of Marie-Laure are sisters."

"So you say—the girl's mother is coming to the hospital this morning? Then we can talk. You will leave the hospital and we will talk."

"Do you know the store near Tautira?" Monsieur Li asked me. "Near where the road ends."

"Beyond Taravao?" I said. "I know where it is."

"Meet us there around two," said Monsieur Li.

"You want the medicine?" asked Mr. Lu. "I'll give you a special price."

"Special price?" I asked. "This usually means an expensive price. Something much more than what it's really worth."

"No, no, no." Mr. Lu shook his head. "If I say a special price, I mean a special price. You show me something special—I'll give this medicine to you."

"What do you mean—special?"

"I'll leave it up to you. You decide what you want to show me. This medicine—you've never seen anything like it. You're too young. You've never seen this."

"How do I know it works?"

"I give you my word. I know your cousin is very ill. This medicine will work."

"There are people who sell false medicine," I replied. "They're sharks. They show up when they smell desperation."

"I'm not one of these people," said Mr. Lu. "If you don't like this medicine, I'll give you back everything."

I leaned close to the window. "If this medicine doesn't work," I said, "I'll kill you."

Mr. Lu laughed. "Bring me something special. We'll meet this afternoon."

Chapter 27

There were two Chinese stores near where the road ended in Tautira—and when someone talked about the road, they meant the one that went around the island, ending in Teahupoo to the south and the black sand of Tautira to the north. Monsieur Li was waiting at the Chinese store in Pueu close to Taravao rather than the one further down the road by Tautira. I knew this because Monsieur Li was friends with Jean Foo, the eldest brother of the family who owned the store. When I entered, holding a covered box, Monsieur Li was talking to Jean and another man, the three of them standing by the counter.

The front of the store was a single room, the goods piled on shelves behind the counter, an old-style store where customers asked at the cash register for what they wanted: a jar of coffee, a bag of New Zealand apples, a pack of cigarettes. Jean shook my hand and said that I could put the box in the back room.

"I don't know," Jean said to Monsieur Li. "If they stop and the soldiers go back to France—that's not good for business."

"Chirac should have signed the nuclear ban long ago," said Monsieur Li, but Jean shook his head. My father said that Monsieur Li knew about things that had happened hundreds of years ago, a thousand years past. He knew about books and long, long poems, but you didn't want him running your store. So, of course, Monsieur Li knew about the nuclear ban. He had probably read the whole document several times already, but what did he know about what it really meant, when all the army money spent in the islands went back to France?

"No more jobs in Mururoa," Jean replied. "Not enough jobs here. And all because of crazy people rioting—look what they did, trying to burn down the whole airport. They're crazy, all of them."

"They're not crazy," said Monsieur Li.

"If they have so much time to sit around, shouting and waving signs, why don't you ask them to work for a change? Why don't they do something useful? How about running this store for me?"

"There's a bigger picture than just running a store."

"Just running a store? Is that what you call it? A bigger picture besides just running a store? And while you go looking at this big picture, you can flush business right down the sewer."

"Your store's not going down the sewer," Monsieur Li replied.

I walked into the back storage room and placed the box down on the floor, by the cartons and crates of merchandise. Monsieur Li and Jean walked into the room and then Mr. Lu appeared, from the shed where the roosters were kept behind the store.

"Good roosters," he said.

"You'll give me the medicine for them?" Jean asked.

"Later—we'll try with one first. They're a different breed. Let's see how it works with one. It's not good to rush. A good fighting rooster—you have to be careful. Too much medicine won't work." He shook my hand. "How's your cousin?"

"Still sleeping." When I left, Aunt Georgine and Aunt Genevieve were watching Marie-Laure, the two women sitting with their heads bowed by the side of her bed.

Someone called from the front of the store. *"Allô, allô?"*

"I'm here, I'm here. Just running my store," said Jean, grumbling and walking through the door leading back to the front.

"Okay." Mr. Lu sat down at a wood table next to the garden door and Monsieur Li sat on a chair by the sacks of rice. "Now." Mr. Lu spoke in a loud voice, as if he were announcing the beginning of a show. "Let's see what you have here."

I lifted a cage from inside the box. It was covered with a long towel. I removed the towel, opened the door, and carefully lifted out the python, the cool ripple of her skin moving through my hands.

"A snake," said Mr. Lu.

"A Black-Headed Python." I held the python, letting her head move, undulating in the air.

"We have snakes in China."

"You don't have something like this. A python from Australia. See the head is completely black. You won't find a snake like this in China."

Mr. Lu watched as I held the python, sliding along my arm. "A big snake," he said. "Too big to eat. What am I going to do with such a snake? She'll eat too much. Every day I'll have to feed her."

"She's a very beautiful python." I kept my voice smooth, but not too smooth. A good salesperson had to believe the sales pitch, at least for that moment.

"Beautiful—you can't use that word for a snake. Women are beautiful, not a snake," Mr. Lu replied.

I let the python move back into the cage, allowing her to slither inside and then closing the door.

"Okay," said Mr. Lu. "What else?"

I opened a small box, letting him peer inside. He laughed.

"Some dried leaves."

"The finest."

"I see. *Pakalolo.*" Mr. Lu pronounced each syllable slowly and loudly so that it sounded like a Chinese phrase: Ba ca low low. "Can I keep this?" He picked up the box from my hands.

"It's a gift. If you want something else, I can arrange for it too."

"Something else?"

"You say what you want—I'll bring it here."

"And how do you bring it here?"

"I tell someone and he tells someone, someone with a boat, a fishing boat, a yacht. It depends."

"Small boats," said Mr. Lu. "I see. The ocean is very big—so it's hard to find your small boats." He placed the box next to him on the table and then slapped the table with his fist and laughed. "What else?" he asked. "Show me what you have."

I picked up a larger box, placing it on the table and lifting the cover. Mr. Lu glanced inside.

156

"Okay—now we're getting better." He lifted the revolver in his hand. "You know what this is?" he asked Monsieur Li.

Monsieur Li shook his head.

"You don't know?" Mr. Lu asked. "You haven't seen American action movies? You can make a very big hole in someone with this. Magnum. Smith and Wesson."

"I would be careful with that," Monsieur Li replied.

"Here," said Mr. Lu, handing me the Magnum. "You hold it. Did this arrive on one of your small boats?"

I placed the revolver back inside the box. "My cousin Marie-Laure gave this to me."

"She gave you this?" asked Mr. Lu. "A gift between cousins?" He grew serious, his gaze examining me. "Or something else?"

"It was a gift."

Mr. Lu kept his gaze on me. "You know how to shoot?" he asked.

"I spent two years in the army."

"So show us."

Monsieur Li shook his head. "Guns—they're illegal. If you like, we can go where Marc can show you the Magnum, but we can't shoot it here at the store."

"So it's illegal? Against the law? And his cousin, the girl—she gave it to him as a present? Even though it's against the law?" He leaned forward in his chair. "She gave this to you?"

"Yes."

"Okay," said Mr. Lu, his voice growing quiet. "This gift from your cousin. I think I understand now." He turned to look at Monsieur Li. "I understand much better. Your cousin—you are special to her. Special."

"You may have this," I said. "The Magnum. The *pakalolo*, the python. You can have all of them. But you must show me the medicine."

The smile disappeared from Mr. Lu's face. "I must show you? Must?" he asked. "Do you know what you're asking?"

"You have a medicine that will cure my cousin—yes or no? If not, I'm wasting my time."

"You're asking for a very rare medicine," said Mr. Lu. "Very old. How do you say it—one of a kind. I give this medicine to you, I don't have any left. That's it. No more."

"I'll pay you for it."

"You?" Mr. Lu remained unsmiling and then he burst into sudden laughter. He turned to Monsieur Li. "He says he will pay the price. He will pay the price for his special cousin."

Monsieur Li replied, "You haven't explained the price to him."

"But he says that he will pay it."

"Explain the price," said Monsieur Li.

Mr. Lu laughed again, laughing as if something was very funny. He slapped his hand against his thigh. Monsieur Li waited, not sharing Mr. Lu's laughter. Finally, Mr. Lu stopped and he spoke.

"Special. Yes, yes." He stood up and walked around me in a circle, stopping in front of me. "How old are you?"

"Twenty-six."

He reached out and with sudden swiftness, he snatched a few strands of my hair, holding it between his fingers. "You have long hair." With his free hand, he pulled a small folding pair of scissors from his pocket, unfolding them with another rapid motion. He snipped off the strands of hair and held them up before him, examining the strands.

Monsieur Li was standing, frowning. "You can't cut any more," he said. "You have to explain it to him first."

"Explain what?" I asked.

"The price," Mr. Lu replied. He waved one hand at the boxes on the table. "You see—I'm not really interested in any of this."

"You were going to explain the price to me," I replied. "The price of the medicine."

"The price of the medicine," said Mr. Lu. "It's very simple. You let me cut your hair. All of it. Then I give you the medicine."

"My hair?"

"You give it to me in exchange for the medicine. That is the price."

His words were strange, like I had entered a scene from one of the magic tales that A-tai had told me when I was a boy. I looked out the open door, at the concrete steps leading outside into the sunlight.

"Agreed?" asked Mr. Lu.

"You're not explaining about the consequences of you cutting his hair," said Monsieur Li.

"The consequences." Mr. Lu waved his hand lightly. "They're not so difficult for someone your age."

"There will be consequences if you let him cut your hair," said Monsieur Li.

"You will lose your hair. For a while," said Mr. Lu. "But it will grow back. And I won't cut all of it—just most of it. I'm not a barber, but I will try to make it look not so bad. For someone of your age, it will grow back before you know it. But"—he folded his arms—"there will be a short time before it really begins to grow."

"A few weeks," Monsieur Li said.

"A few weeks," repeated Mr. Lu. "And during that time, you will lose everything. Everything." Mr. Lu shook his head sadly, as if he were already feeling sorry for me. "Except for your cousin. She will get better."

"What is everything?" I asked.

"Your money, your wealth, whatever you have now. All of it."

"I'm going to pay you all of my money?"

"No. I'm not getting any of it. I just get your hair. The money, everything—it's going to go."

"What he's saying," Monsieur Li explained, "is that if you agree to let him cut your hair, then there will be a period of a few weeks afterwards. Two or three weeks—it varies. Nothing longer than a month. But during that period of time, whatever money you have—it will be gone. Perhaps other things as well, but usually it's just all the money."

"Is it dangerous? Will people die?" I asked.

"I'm not that kind of sorcerer." Mr. Lu waved his hands. "But you—when it's all over, you may wish that you were dead. But that will pass. Your hair will grow back. And look at you. Monsieur Li told me about you. I said to him, you have to be careful, you have to find the right man, someone who will do this. And Monsieur Li told me the truth. You're the right man. You'll be able to start over without too much problem. So." He held up the scissors in his hand. "Yes? Agreed?"

"First, you'll give the medicine to Monsieur Li," I said.

"Agreed," Mr. Lu replied.

"Wait."

"Do you want the medicine for your cousin? You will let me cut your hair then."

"And I'll lose everything during a period of a few weeks?"

"All your money. Land. Cash and valuables," Mr. Lu said. "Maybe some other things too."

"Take your time," said Monsieur Li. "You don't have to do this. Think carefully."

"How do I know the medicine will work?" I asked. "Maybe you're just making this up."

"The medicine will work," said Mr. Lu. "Look at me—do you know how old I am? Eighty-two years old. Yes—you don't believe me?" He grinned, showing his teeth. "I look good because I practice breathing exercises every day. Ask Monsieur Li."

I glanced at Monsieur Li, who nodded his head. "He is eighty-two. And he does special breathing, qi-gong, every day. I don't know about looking good, though."

"Bah." Mr. Lu waved his hand at Monsieur Li. "You wait until I cut his hair. Then you'll see the women all over me. Anyway." He turned to me. "You can trust me. I know—you are a good businessman, good at selling things—the way you talk. Your father raised you right. Don't trust anyone in business. You seem polite—but I see you're thinking all the time. Very good. But I tell you now, I am one hundred percent trustworthy. How do you know? Because I am a sorcerer—and I am among people like Monsieur Li here."

"I'm not a sorcerer," said Monsieur Li.

"Okay—you're not a sorcerer. Not a sorcerer, okay, okay. You are—what do they call them now? A shaman, a teacher—you like that better? Anyway, whatever you want to call it, I think you understand," Mr. Lu said. "If I make a mistake, if I cheat them, they will find me. And do you know what they do to sorcerers who cheat them? It's better for you not to think about this. It will give you nightmares. So there. I am eighty-two years old and I am still walking around and I have a good reputation. So you can trust that my medicine will work. So I am going to start cutting your hair now."

"Wait," said Monsieur Li to me. "You can still say no."

I thought of Marie-Laure, the hospital tubes stuck into her veins. "Give the medicine to Monsieur Li," I said. "Then you can cut my hair."

Mr. Lu paused and unbuttoned his shirt pocket. He pulled out a draw-string pouch the color of a rice sack. He handed the pouch to Monsieur Li, who opened it, letting something roll out onto the palm of his hand. He showed me his open palm, a bead resting in the center. The bead looked surprisingly small and plain—I was expecting something more elaborate and impressive.

"Is this the correct medicine?" I asked.

"We'll test it," Monsieur Li replied. "I'll need one of your hairs." He walked to where I stood and Mr. Lu handed him the scissors. "May I?"

Monsieur Li cut one of my hairs and tied it carefully around the bead—it took him three tries, my hair slipping out between his fingers on the first two attempts. He produced a pack of matches from his pocket, struck one and held it to the end of the hair until it caught on fire.

As we watched, the hair burned quickly and crumpled, a tiny lit spark consuming the strand of hair until it reached the bead. The spark went out. Monsieur Li and Mr. Lu continued watching the bead intently. For several moments nothing happened, and then the part of the hair that was touching the bead seemed to straighten, waving delicately like a small worm, and as we watched, the hair grew, renewing itself and lengthening until there was no sign that it had ever been burned at all.

"Ha—there!" Mr. Lu grinned, showing his white teeth.

"All right," said Monsieur Li. He placed the bead back in the pouch and then handed it to me.

"I give this to Marie-Laure?" I asked.

"It dissolves in water. You have to stir it with a spoon and make sure that she drinks it all."

"Good?" said Mr. Lu. "Everything okay? Okay—now I cut." He approached me, the scissors in his hand, and it became clear to me what he was about to do.

I knew then that I had been blind all along. I thought that Monsieur Li had approached me because I had a reputation for selling things that were rare and exotic. Things you couldn't find by walking into a store. But I saw now that it was not that at all, that Mr. Lu was interested in something far different.

There were dark stories that A-tai sometimes told, stories about a black sort of magic. They were usually about someone—an old man, a dying emperor—who wanted a type of life energy, the energy of youth and beauty. The search was always for a young woman or a young man—and if he was a man, he was always handsome and somewhat stupid about his virility. The sorcery was about capturing and distilling this virility down into a liquid, an elixir.

"Don't move now," said Mr. Lu. He took a snip, cutting off a lock of my hair. He nodded at Monsieur Li, who opened a bag and removed a large jar filled with a green-hued liquid. "Bring it here," Mr. Lu said to Monsieur Li, who walked over with the jar. Mr. Lu put the lock of hair into the liquid. I half expected it to hiss, to make a strange magical sound, but there was no noise, no smoke or steam—only Mr. Lu, who held up the jar, examining the liquid with the lock of my hair inside. "Good, good." He dipped his hand in the jar and scooped out some of the contents. I saw that the liquid was a type of green gel, wiggling on top of his fingers. "Don't move," he said again.

"What are you going to do?" I asked.

"Hold still," he said.

"He's going to put it on your hair," said Monsieur Li.

"Why is this going on my hair?"

"It makes it easier to cut," said Mr. Lu.

"No, that can't be the reason." I felt uneasy, a heavy sick feeling growing in my stomach.

"It makes it easier for me to prepare my remedy."

"The medicine for Marie-Laure?"

"No—you already have that. I'm preparing something special for me and the ladies."

The green gel felt cold on my scalp. Mr. Lu was careful, his fingers moving in circles over my hair, pausing to scoop out more liquid and then continuing to cover my head. A tingling spread over the skin of my scalp.

"Good," he said finally. He begun cutting, in small swift snips, stopping only to place the locks of my hair in the jar.

Chapter 28

I washed what was left of my hair in the cement sink behind the store and when I finished, De Koning was standing there, a few steps away, watching me the way you looked at a car wreck piled by the side of the road. The green gel had a strange smell, not strong enough to notice at first, but now that it had soaked through, my hair reeked of it.

"You want a towel?" De Koning asked.

"Do you smell it?" I asked.

De Koning was wearing a tiny backless dress that looked like she had been squeezed inside. "I think Mr. Lu mixed the ointment into regular hair gel."

"Is it out?" I passed my hand over the side of my hair, still sticky in clumps. "Is most of it out?"

De Koning disappeared through the back door into the store, leaving me to wait outside in the heat. A breadfruit tree grew over the rusting skeleton of a car sunk among the vines growing behind the store. Bottles were thrown by the wall and a rooster picked his way among the pile of glass.

"Try this," said De Koning, reappearing with a rag in her hand.

I rubbed the rag over my hair and bent under the sink faucet, letting the cold water run. I turned off the water and straightened, the green leaves of the trees whirling for a moment.

"You look sick," said De Koning.

I felt like I had traveled from a far distance, from someplace strange and unreal. The sunlight poured through the leaves of the breadfruit tree.

"Go sit down," she said.

De Koning went into the store again, bringing out a bottle of mineral water. "I didn't think that you would really do this," she said. "You know, when I talked to you in Madame MuSan's restaurant." She handed me the bottle, watching as I drank.

Mr. Lu and Monsieur Li had followed Jean Foo to the back, the shed where the roosters were kept, so they could talk about the cockfights on Sunday. This kind of talk would take the rest of the afternoon, with Jean tossing different roosters in the air and letting others out of their cages to be examined one by one before he passed his prized fighters into the hands of only those he considered impeccably trustworthy.

"Can I go with you to Papeete?" De Koning asked. "They'll be here for hours, talking about those horrible fights. You can drop me off at my cousin's house—it's not far from the hospital."

"What makes you think that I don't want to stay?" I said, but De Koning was right. I was driving to the hospital, and besides, I had to return the python to Radish.

"Fancy car," De Koning remarked as I stopped at the crossroads at Taravao before turning west towards Papeete.

"It's my father's."

"Odile says that you're his favorite."

"Cecile is his favorite. And she hates me."

"Do you always have this attitude? Odile says that she wouldn't mind working with you."

"They don't need me."

"*They don't need me. I don't need them.* Why don't you relax a little? And you're so secretive. I mean, the Hakka are closemouthed, but you have everyone beat, don't you? Don't tell anyone anything. Is this any way to live?"

At the side of the road stood a table beneath a thatched shelter, jars of dark honey and clusters of *fe'i* bananas for sale. A pair of dogs ambled across the road ahead and I downshifted. My father's car, the Italian import, was amazingly preserved after years in the salty island air that rusted everything—although perhaps I shouldn't have been so amazed since my father kept the car stored in the cool mountain air above Pic Rouge. My father had lent the car to me that morning, handing me the keys while I was leaving the hospital. I was preoccupied, preparing to meet Mr. Lu and

Monsieur Li. I had assumed that he had brought the car down to Papeete for some reason and it was just convenient to lend it to me at that moment—but now, I wondered if my father had not retrieved the car, one of his favorites, as a sort of consolation, the way he once, when I was a boy, bought me a chocolate Eskimo popsicle after a bee-sting swelled one of my eyelids shut. It was out of his usual route to drive from Taravao to the house above Pic Rouge, and he regularly drove more solid, less ostentatious cars. And now that I thought about it, my father had paused in the hospital corridor, reaching into his pocket for the car keys and placing them in my hand, instead of telling me that he had left them somewhere on his desk or tossing the keys to me as he hurried away.

"It doesn't look that bad, your haircut," said De Koning.

"You mean it looks bad, just not that bad. What is Mr. Lu doing with my hair?"

"You don't know?"

"Now you're talking Hakka. *You don't know?* Pure Hakka."

De Koning reached out a finger and touched my hair, carefully, as if it might burn her. "Okay, I was wrong. It looks bad." The car passed a blur of hibiscus hedges and a flamboyant tree with brilliant red flowers blooming over the road. "You don't know? All right, I'll tell you. Mr. Lu is going to make some sort of love potion with your hair. He says it'll make him irresistible to women. That's what Monsieur Li told me."

"You sound skeptical. Don't you believe in this magic?"

"You're the one who sounds skeptical—and you're the one who just signed on the magical line. Your hair for the magic."

It didn't matter what I believed. As long as Marie-Laure awakened. It could be her doctors, it could be Mr. Lu's magic—I didn't care, as long as she opened her eyes. For a moment, I saw the grey-haired men that sold powders and herbs in Chinese pharmacies; it could be in Papeete or Paris—these pharmacies looked the same. There were always the rows of wooden drawers holding mushrooms and odd-shaped fungus and roots that they measured on brass, handheld weights, two saucer-shaped bowls balancing on either side. Even when they were talking, chatting with customers about different maladies and symptoms or whether it was going to rain, there was always a pause, a second of quiet, as they weighed each medicine, placing a piece of metal on one saucer and then watching the two sides bobbing, silence falling for the moment as they held the balance.

Inside my pocket was the pouch with the bead inside.

"Hey, don't drive so fast," said De Koning.

Marie-Laure still slept. Under the hospital lights, she looked drained of life, her face even more bloated.

"Marie-Laure." I spoke into her ear. She continued breathing, without stirring, without any sign that she heard me at all.

Monsieur Li entered the room. "Your father drove me here," he said. "He went to the Chinese store to see if you were still there. Where's De Koning?"

"I drove her to her cousin's house."

Monsieur Li reached over and touched the blanket over Marie-Laure's foot.

"She's been like this all day." Aunt Georgine spoke from where she sat, by Marie-Laure's bed. Another woman sat knitting next to her, her face bent over her needles, the repeated click-click.

"You can't bring that here," spoke a nurse, standing in the doorway.

"All right, I'll let you have half." Cecile appeared, holding a durian fruit in her hand.

The nurse stepped in front of her. "I'm sorry, madame, you must take that outside."

"It's from Papaeri," Cecile replied. "A delicacy. You can't imagine how much I paid for this."

Aunt Georgine stood up and walked quickly to Cecile, kissing her on the cheeks. Cecile handed her the green fruit, its normal fragrance, a pungent rotting odor, drifting through the room.

"No, no, madame. Outside." The nurse took Cecile's arm but Cecile wrested herself free.

"*Mon dieu*," she shouted.

"Outside," the nurse repeated. "It smells."

Cecile put her arm around Aunt Georgine. "We'll eat it in my car. I'll turn on the air conditioning."

Aunt Georgine began to cry. Cecile kissed her gently on the forehead and took her by the arm. She looked around the room and saw me sitting by Marie-Laure. She frowned and pointed to my hair. "What happened to you? You look horrible."

"Please—outside," said the nurse.

Cecile stood for a moment without moving by the door and her gaze fell on Monsieur Li. "Jonathan," she said. "Come and join us."

"Go, enjoy the durian," Monsieur Li replied.

"But I never see you in Tahiti. You're always hiding in the *van-tui,* in Huahine," said Cecile as the women walked out the door.

"You should eat with them," Monsieur Li said.

"I'm fine," I replied.

Marie-Laure remained sleeping, her breathing quiet. The walls of the hospital room were painted a flat, unlovely shade of green. I felt in my pocket and found the pouch with the bead inside. In the quiet of the hospital room, I picked up the bead between my fingers and held it to the light. It was opaque, a yellow-beige color. On one side were two long Chinese characters with lines that hung downwards like arms.

I knew about charms—A-tai had kept jade charms and a long root of ginseng in the shape of a sword. A-tai said that there were charms carved of stones and charms made from bones with ancient characters carved on the surface and that, a long time ago, such bones foretold the future. I didn't like these stories—even when I was a child, listening to the tales of these charms, I felt that there was something malevolent and cruel about them.

"This bead," I said to Monsieur Li. "The characters on the side—what do they say?"

He reached into his shirt pocket and took out a pair of glasses, putting them on to examine the bead. "Mei Zhun. Beautiful Cloud."

"Is this really the only one like this?"

"Mr. Lu exaggerates. I've seen two other beads like this. One in China. One in America. Beautiful Cloud—it's the name of this type of bead."

"How can she drink it?" I asked.

Monsieur Li remained silent, thinking for a moment. He took Marie-Laure's hand and placed it over his own, sliding his hand out and leaving the bead beneath her hand. "It'll dissolve," he said. "Part of it will absorb through her skin."

"I thought you said that she had to swallow the bead. I had to make sure she drank it all."

"But she can't drink now," said Monsieur Li.

I stood and put my hand on Marie-Laure's arm. She slept, drifting in her long, dark slumber.

Chapter 29

Aunt Georgine and Cecile were talking, their voices growing closer as they walked down the hallway to Marie-Laure's room.

"How is she?" asked Aunt Georgine. She had left for such a short time, a half hour at most, but she sat down by the bed and studied Marie-Laure's face for the smallest change.

Cecile entered with Radish's mother, Aunt Annette, a nervous woman with yellowish grey hair, pulled back from her face with two plastic combs. Aunt Annette kissed my cheeks and sat next to Aunt Georgine. "Poor Marie-Laure," she said, her head quivering. "Radish—he told me what happened." She folded her arms in front of her and rocked back and forth as if she were already in mourning.

"She'll never wake up," Aunt Georgine cried.

"She will," said Cecile. "The doctors say this kind of seizure isn't that serious."

"Then why isn't she awake? There's something else—there's something else that's wrong." Aunt Georgine buried her face in Cecile's shoulder and began crying.

Aunt Annette reached over and stroked a stray hair from Marie-Laure's face. "She's looking much better than when we saw her yesterday," said Cecile.

"It's true," said Aunt Annette. "Look here—her cheeks have more color."

Aunt Georgine rested her head against Cecile's shoulder. She grew quiet and the three women sat watching Marie-Laure. Monsieur Li tapped my shoulder and motioned that we should go outside. A group of men passed us in the hallway, one man carrying a guitar. He walked tipped forward with his head bent down, like he was moved along by the thoughts in his head.

Monsieur Li said nothing, walking down the stairway and down another hallway until we reached the entrance doors to the hospital. I opened the door into the hot evening air.

"There's something I have to tell you." Monsieur Li paused as a car passed on the street. "About the bead. Your agreement with Mr. Lu. You can't tell anyone about this. It's how it works."

"I won't say anything." I knew what he meant: the magic worked only if I kept silent—but from what I saw, it was already hopeless. You felt it in the silence as Marie-Laure slept without waking. She was already far away.

"You understand, then," said Monsieur Li. "Go back home and sleep. I'll go see your father."

"I'll stay here," I said, too tired to think.

Cecile was talking on her cell phone outside the hospital entrance. It didn't look like a happy conversation—she was stabbing the air with one finger. I passed by and opened the door.

"Marc," she said, and then she spoke into the phone. "I'll call you back. We'll talk about this later."

I waited outside, letting the door close. The last thing I wanted was to talk to Cecile.

"Marc." She stopped for a moment, before plunging in. "I don't like you. I've never liked you."

I thought that she was going to say something different for a change, but once Cecile started and I knew that it was business as usual, I returned to my normal look around her—looking like I didn't care what she said.

"You know, your father gave you everything," said Cecile. "And what did you do? Throw it away. At the beginning—and this is what I'll never understand about you—when we first started reorganizing the Perles du Paradis, your father really needed you. But you had your own ideas."

"You were the one who reorganized the Perles du Paradis," I said. "You had your own ideas about how to run things and none of these involved me."

"Your father needed you. And you weren't there."

And whose fault was that? I thought, but I didn't see the point of getting into an argument that just ran around and around in circles. A waste of my time.

"Other people have excuses," said Cecile. "But you—I don't understand. You could have done anything, but what did you get into? There's no excuse for it, how you made your money. I don't like you and I never will." She stuck her face closer. "There's something wrong with you. You know, before, in China, there were people like you. You know how they made their money? Opium. They weren't addicts—they let that happen to other people. That's how they made their money. That's what you do. I know your type—you don't do it for pleasure or because you can't help yourself. No, there's something very cold about you. Business, business. In your head, you're just thinking about how much money you can make. You know what? There's no forgiveness for you. None. If it was up to me, I wouldn't let you near Marie-Laure. The most decent thing you can do is to leave her alone. Leave her alone. Leave her in peace." Cecile turned, walked away and entered the hospital.

I stood by the door and stared at the cars parked outside. Two women crossed the street, one woman wearing a green hat woven of leaves, the other carrying a basket. I opened the entrance door and walked inside, along the hallways to Marie-Laure's room.

Someone was crying from somewhere and a nurse was walking, almost running, down the hallway. Cecile, her angry face, kept jabbing my thoughts. Whatever Cecile said, she didn't get it all. What I had done—it was petty, it was nothing. I was a small fish in a deep ocean and there were always much bigger fish. Predators—and they ruled the ocean. And wasn't I making my money now in ways so clean it was boring?

"Marc, *ça va?*" It was Harris, standing in the hallway. He had gained weight and he wore a white shirt and dark trousers, creased and wrinkled after a day's work. "I came straight from the bank. How is she?"

"The same. Still sleeping."

Harris shook his head and walked with me, his hands in his pockets. He was an assistant manager at the bank office across from Madame

MuSan's restaurant. I kept most of my accounts there and we had talked about having lunch, but it was one of those things you talked about and never did. I had heard that Harris had a new girlfriend, one of the Yu sisters—they were pretty, but somewhat lazy.

"You haven't stopped by the office this month," said Harris.

"No, Radish did the deposit." I wasn't in the mood for small talk.

In the hallway outside Marie-Laure's room, a group of doctors had gathered. A jumble of faces—Tahitian, French, Chinese, a few men, a few women. Marie-Laure had been moved so that she was lying on her left side on the bed. Harris made a small sound, of surprise and pity, and sat on one of the chairs by her feet. It seemed that the nurses were no longer limiting the number of visitors—Cecile, Aunt Georgine, Radish's mother Aunt Annette, and my mother were all seated around Marie-Laure's bed. My mother rose to embrace me, saying nothing, her eyes filled with tears.

I bent over Marie-Laure's arm. A black bruise had formed on the back of her hand. Harris looked pale, as if he were feeling ill. The faint smell of death had begun, sweet mixed in with an ammonia-like odor.

Harris stood up suddenly, looking worse, and left the room without speaking. I followed him out and we walked back through the hallways. At the entrance, Harris turned to shake my hand, pausing, trying to say something, but then walked away.

The corridors stretched back inside, the hospital sounds you always heard so that you never really heard them: the crying, the screaming, the silence that descended afterwards. I walked, passing groups of visitors carrying food and a toy—something large and brightly colored. I heard the sound of their flip-flop sandals on the floor as they stopped to look at the numbers on the doors.

I was crying. Really crying. I wiped my nose with the back of my hand. I couldn't stop crying. Some visitors standing around a doorway stared as I passed. I couldn't stop, I couldn't think. I reached Marie-Laure's room and I stood outside.

I heard the silence inside the room—no one was talking—and a feeling of dread tore at me. My aunts and my mother looked up at my sudden entrance. Cecile was holding Marie-Laure's hand. Marie-Laure's eyes were open, staring at nothing, and then she blinked.

Chapter 30

They talked all at once.

"It just happened," said Aunt Annette.

"She's awake."

"Cecile saw her."

"Shhh—you're too loud," said Cecile, still holding Marie-Laure's hand.

Marie-Laure looked without speaking at the faces around her.

"Rest," Cecile said.

Marie-Laure lifted her fingers and Aunt Georgine took her hand and began crying. A doctor entered the room.

"Sleeping Beauty awakens," she said.

A nurse entered and checked Marie-Laure's blood pressure, peeling back the sheet to wrap the cuff around her thigh. "Too many tubes in her arms," said the nurse.

The bedsheet beneath was wrinkled and creased. The Mei Zhun bead was gone, no longer under Marie-Laure's palm. Cecile held one of her hands and Aunt Georgine held the other.

"It's normal," said the nurse, removing the blood pressure cuff and glancing at the doctor, who nodded, picking up Marie-Laure's chart.

Marie-Laure looked up at the doctor and her eyes moved to the side, to where I was standing. "Marc," she said, her voice a whisper.

A machine was ringing in another room and the nurse left.

I drew close to Marie-Laure. The smell of death was still there, a smell that she exhaled together with the scent of something forgotten, arising again and impossibly beautiful. I looked into Marie-Laure's face and I breathed in the smell of death and dreams and life.

"Marie-Laure," I said.

More doctors and nurses appeared, everyone examining Marie-Laure. Her chart, clipped to a metal board at the foot of her bed, was checked and blood was drawn from the tube in her hand.

Cecile assigned different times of the day and night to different family members. "No need for everyone to get sick," she said. "Go home and sleep," she said to Aunt Georgine.

Everyone thought of Aunt Georgine as the youngest—the youngest sister of my mother and the youngest wife of Cecile's father, Ten-kwok. She was lovely, plump and placid, a smooth-faced doll. No one had imagined her as she looked now, grey-faced and red-eyed, her hair unwashed, sitting without moving by Marie-Laure's bed.

Marie-Laure turned to her. "Ma," she whispered. "You look bad."

Aunt Georgine stopped and stuck her tongue out and Marie-Laure smiled back.

"Don't do that," Aunt Annette said.

My mother was talking to Cecile, making a list of who could stay at the hospital. "Odile will be here tomorrow morning," she said.

"Marc should go home," said Cecile. They checked the paper where Cecile was writing, their heads close together.

"What do you want to eat?" Aunt Georgine asked Marie-Laure.

Marie-Laure shook her head, her movements still small.

Monsieur Li and Radish arrived a few minutes later, and while my mother and Cecile were greeting Monsieur Li, I saw Radish studying the two women as they laughed together.

"She's awake," said Aunt Georgine, and Radish went to Marie-Laure, jostling Monsieur Li's arm in his hurry.

Marie-Laure moved her eyes to Radish.

"Hey," he said.

"Hey," Marie-Laure whispered.

Aunt Georgine began crying again.

"Marc?" Marie-Laure asked.

"Over there." Radish pointed to where I stood at the foot of the bed.

Marie-Laure shifted her eyes to me and then she looked back at Radish. "My eyes are funny," she whispered.

"No," said Radish. "It's not your eyes. He's cut his hair."

"Can you see me?" asked Monsieur Li.

Marie-Laure nodded.

"I don't have two heads?"

Marie-Laure shook her head once.

Aunt Georgine blew her nose. "We should ask when she can eat."

"We'll ask one of the doctors," said Aunt Annette.

I bent down by the side of the bed. "Do you want something—some water?" I asked.

Marie-Laure continued looking at me for a long moment. She closed her eyes and moved her head, first slightly to one side and then slightly to the other—no—and she opened her eyes, still looking at me. I sat down on one of the chairs by the side of the bed. She seemed to be weighing something in her mind.

Marie-Laure whispered something, a sound I couldn't understand. I moved closer. Her breathing was steady and quiet and then she shut her eyes and fell asleep.

I wanted to seize her. I wanted to shout *Don't go, don't go.* As if he read my thoughts, Monsieur Li raised one of his hands to stop me. I bowed my head and watched Marie-Laure. She was breathing lightly. She was asleep, only asleep, nothing more.

Aunt Georgine left with Aunt Annette and then Ten-kwok entered the room. Monsieur Li told him that Marie-Laure had awakened. Ten-kwok sat down and watched his daughter sleeping. He sat, gripping the railing along her bed.

Chapter 31

"Did you see your mother and Cecile?" Radish said, his voice low, as we walked through the hallway. "There's talk—they're planning something."

"Who's feeding the python?" I asked.

"Arthur's looking after her. Jacqueline Chow called. She says she has a buyer."

Radish hummed quietly, part of an old tune, "Bora Bora nui." When I was very little, my parents had danced to this song. I remembered them, waltzing at a party, my mother wearing a midnight blue dress, the only time that I remembered them not angry at each other.

"So what about my mother and Cecile?" I asked.

"My father said that Cecile was going to reorganize the Perles du Paradis again," Radish said. "She was investing outside of Tahiti. He said that sooner or later, the economy will collapse once nuclear testing ends."

"We're dogs," I said. "Going around and around, chasing our tails."

I returned to Marie-Laure's hospital room at five in the morning. Marie-Laure was asleep, her face still colorless and swollen, her hands like pale fish. Ten-kwok slept, snoring, in a chair by the bed, his head fallen back and his mouth open.

As I watched Marie-Laure in the silence, a black feeling poured into me, a fear that sucked out the air. Was Marie-Laure really better? Had she awakened only to fall sick again?

Marie-Laure moved her hands and shifted in her sleep. I took one of the chairs along the wall, placed it next to the bed and sat down.

"Everyone's afraid of dying," Marie-Laure had once said. She was standing on the monument, the flat concrete at the bottom of the Chinese cemetery. Ten-kwok and my father were cleaning the family graves up the hillside. I was eleven and it was too hot and I was bored.

"Well, do you think he was afraid?" I asked, pointing to Marie-Laure's feet. No one had really told me where he was buried, the hero of the monument. I had always thought that he was somewhere beneath the concrete, but I wasn't sure if he was buried there at all or if they had buried his head separately, one hole for his body, one hole for his head. I thought of telling Marie-Laure that heads stayed alive after the guillotine chopped them off.

"Of course he was afraid," said Marie-Laure. "If he wasn't, he wouldn't be a hero."

"No, he wasn't afraid," I said. "He wasn't afraid at all."

"Even if he wasn't afraid at the beginning, he was by the time they marched him up to the guillotine," said Marie-Laure. "Everyone gets scared looking at it. That's why they made it—so everyone gets scared."

Years later, Aurore made me take her to the monument, even though I told her that it was easy to find, right at the bottom of the hill where the Chinese cemetery started. I didn't have to show her; she could just drive up and walk around. The monument wasn't anything elaborate.

"Park under the mango trees," I said.

As it was, I drove her at sunset, when I knew no one else was around. She was as bad as Marie-Laure, talking about the historic evidence—as if I hadn't already heard the story a thousand times, from A-tai, from my mother, from my father. Yes—how brave he was, how he had sacrificed himself. I got out of the car and followed Aurore, but when I stood there in the quiet light of sunset, I knew, standing there and looking up at the hillside of tombs, hundreds and hundreds, that he had to have been afraid, terrified, the entire month that it took for the guillotine to arrive from France.

It had happened a long time ago, during the time of the William Stewart plantation at Atimaono when the first Hakka were brought to Tahiti. A Frenchman, a plantation overseer, was killed. The Hakka were told that all would be punished, every last one. Who was guilty? They only had to give him up and everyone else would be spared. A man named Shim Siou Kong came forward and confessed.

"But he was innocent," said my father. "If he hadn't confessed to something he didn't do, none of us would be here."

I told Aurore somewhat sarcastically that you had to give the French credit—they hadn't hanged him right there. The French ordered a guillotine to be brought from France for the formal execution. In those days, it took a month for the guillotine to arrive by boat.

"The French were barbaric," said Aurore.

I always told Aurore that she couldn't hate the French so much. If she did, she would hate herself. I didn't understand it—she was so angry about whatever France had done, saying a hundred times that France had stolen the islands.

"Well, it's true," said Aurore.

"What's the point?" I said. "True or not true, you can't change what happened."

Aurore walked from one end of the monument to the other. She kept her eyes on the ground. A pair of horses grazed among the tall grass that grew among the older tombs, the stones cracked, tumbling back into the earth. Finally, I took her hand—it was growing dark and no one was there so late, out of fear of the ghosts and the spirits, the *tupapa'u,* so I knew that no one would see us.

Marie-Laure coughed and opened her eyes. "What time is it?" she asked. It always seemed to be the same time in the hospital, a time without night, without day.

I stood up from the chair. "It's morning. Almost six."

"Water," she said, her voice cracking.

I poured mineral water from a bottle on the bedstand. She took a sip and laid her head back on the pillow, closing her eyes to rest.

"How long did I sleep?"

"Since last night."

"You went back to your place?"

"I stayed with Radish. He says he'll visit you this morning."

Marie-Laure lifted her hand, moving slowly to scratch her nose, a tangle of tubes following the movement of her hand. "You're going to work?"

"Soon. Not right now. It's early."

Her eyes remained closed.

"I'll be back this evening," I said.

Inside the room, it was still, like the boats that float over the deep sea, the immense quiet beneath the sky. Marie-Laure rested on her back, her hands at her sides. Outside the hospital, it was early, the sun still rising. I sat by her bed and, briefly, I was whole.

PART FOUR

CHESSBOARD

Chapter 32

I was going to lose everything. Mr. Lu had said this. All my money. Cash and valuables. Maybe other things too. The words kept playing in my head, like the words to a song I didn't like but couldn't forget.

Part of me didn't believe in this magic—Marie-Laure was alive, but there were her doctors and their medicine. Who knew what was really healing her? Whatever it was, I had promised to pay a price. I had bought the charm and Mr. Lu was clear that I was going to pay.

I heard enough stories about magic and magicians and their spells to know that you couldn't outsmart the magic. You could be clever, you could think ahead of time, but somehow the magic was going to win out in the end, no matter how hard you tried. The way I was preparing, I was counting on losing my money. What mattered was what happened after that, and all my planning was going into how I was going to get my money back. Hadn't Mr. Lu and Monsieur Li said that the magic's hold on my money was just temporary? My hair would start to grow and then I could start over. They had shaved my hair in the army enough, so that I knew that it took only a few days for a stubble of hair to cover my scalp. I was waiting. Nothing was growing but it was still too soon, only a day after Mr. Lu had chopped it off.

I went to see Harris at the bank. "I'm checking on my credit," I said.

"You don't have to worry," said Harris. "Your credit's fine."

"I'll need a loan."

"I'll get the paperwork going—it's just a formality." Harris turned, his fingers hovering over his phone.

"I don't need the loan now." Without thinking, I touched the side of my head, my fingers smoothing my hair. Like a girl, I thought.

Harris settled back in his office chair, his eyelids like thick half-moons. "You need anything, let me know. You're thinking of expanding, you want a yacht again—I mean, why did you sell the one you had?"

"Too much trouble."

"She was sleek, but the one I'll get you—you'll forget all about the old one." Harris folded his hands, touching the tips of his fingers together as if it required a good deal of thought. "I saw you with Marise De Koning a few days ago."

"She's in Papeete for another week. Because Marie-Laure was so sick, she decided to stay here longer."

"There's something strange about her," said Harris. "You know what I mean—although when I saw the two of you together, she seemed interested enough in you. She's pretty enough, a bit fat." Harris shrugged. "She's too serious for my taste."

"The loan," I said. "I'll fill out the paperwork in a month or so."

"Anytime. Just let me know," said Harris. "You don't even have to come in. Give me a call and I'll bring the papers over."

The air in town was hot and choked with the fumes of cars and trucks and scooters darting like flies through the traffic, splashing up water from the puddles that always smelled of trash. It had rained heavily the night before, but now the sky was empty of clouds.

A car slowed and someone called my name. It was Philippe MuSan, offering a ride.

"I'm walking," I said. "It's not far."

"In this heat? Don't be ridiculous. Besides, there's mosquitoes. You walk around like that, you'll get a fever. There's a bad outbreak going around."

Inside the car, the noise and stench of traffic fell away as MuSan navigated the streets, his hand resting on the steering wheel.

"Corrine found this for me—it's very old. Ancient," said MuSan, showing me the ring on his finger. "You can't find jade like this anymore." The jade was the color of young growth, a brightness you saw in leaves right at the beginning, before time turned things murky and dark. He stopped for two Chinese boys crossing the street, one holding a paint-splattered bucket and the other something long, an extension cord or a rope. They looked no more than fourteen, but with the air of older men going to work.

"My car's parked around this corner," I said. "Just drop me off here."

"Why here? You have a parking spot—and these aren't easy to find this close to the *centre-ville*. Why don't I take you back? That is, if you're going back for lunch," said MuSan driving through the intersection. Uncle Florian and Ten-kwok returned to their houses for a leisurely lunch every day, but I usually ate quickly, a *casse-croûte* from a vendor. "I have some business in Mataiea," said MuSan.

"Why should I go there?" I asked, wondering why MuSan was talking like he knew that I lived with Aurore.

"It's beautiful in Mataiea," said MuSan. "If I lived there, I'd consider myself fortunate. I'd wonder what I had done to earn such good fortune."

"What did you do today?" Marie-Laure asked when I returned in the evening. She seemed sleepy, the slurred drowsiness of medication, her voice thick and hushed.

I ran around all day, doing too many things, doing nothing at all. "I saw Harris at the bank."

"Business."

"Yes."

"You talked about money." She kept her eyes closed, talking in short breaths.

"We talked a bit about a loan. Nothing, really."

Marie-Laure moved her head to the side to look at me. "You must have talked about something. Since you wanted a loan."

"Rest," I said. "It's not important."

"Tell me."

"We really didn't talk about anything. Harris talked about a boat I had—I don't have it anymore."

"Your yacht," said Marie-Laure. "I heard about it. When I was in France."

A machine behind the bed started beeping.

"I'll get the nurse." I rose from the chair.

"Something's always ringing. Tell me about the boat."

"Yes?"

"What happened?"

"I sold it."

"Why did you sell it?" Marie-Laure watched my face.

"Different reasons." I tried to sound vague.

"A beautiful yacht. But you sold it to raise money." Marie-Laure closed her eyes again, thinking several chess moves ahead. "You were buying your place?"

"Yes." If I answered right away, I could slide out like it was nothing, common knowledge.

"The mysterious place where you live."

"Mysterious? What's mysterious about Pic Rouge?"

"No, Marc," she said. "You're not living around Pic Rouge. You're living with someone secret. Since no one talks about it. You bought the land. And maybe you sold the yacht to make the down payment."

"You should rest," I said. I had sold the yacht to make the down payment on the property where Aurore lived, a long stretch of beachfront land. She had been renting all this time—I didn't know until I sat next to Maître Leclerc at one of my father's dinner parties.

"Tell me about the last time. The last time you went sailing."

A nurse walked into the room and turned off the alarm, checking one of the tubes before leaving.

"I heard them talking," said Marie-Laure after the nurse left. "The doctors say I should go to Paris. But the flight's long. They're thinking someplace closer. Auckland, maybe." She sighed. "I hate this. I hate being sick." She lifted her arm, the tubes trailing like tentacles.

"Rest," I said.

"I hate this."

"I'll tell you about the yacht," I said.

There was the sound of something dripping through a tube from one of the machines behind Marie-Laure's bed.

"Okay," she said. "Tell me." Her voice fell to a whisper. "The last time you went sailing."

"We went sailing with Edouard's nephews. We went to Opoa."

"In Raiatea. Did you go to the *marae?*" Another alarm started ringing, quieter than the first. Another nurse entered, checking the machine and pressing buttons before leaving the room. "With Edouard?"

"I went with Edouard and his nephews." Edouard's nephews were around eleven and twelve at the time, chubby boys, unshakably calm and serious. The boys had sat on the bow, guiding Edouard's steering as we slid through the coral blooming all around, the boys shouting directions.

"They've increased the dose," said Marie-Laure. "I can tell. I'm so sleepy." The dripping noise from the machinery stopped and she was already asleep.

Chapter 33

I walked along the black sand, fine as dust. Aurore no longer lived on the stretch of beach near Point Venus, but I found myself driving there, parking under an old acacia tree with a broken trunk, an ugly tree still crowned with a haze of shadowy leaves. A pirogue rested on the beach, brought close to the line of *aito* trees, away from the reach of the water when the tide was high.

Cecile had arrived at the hospital. She had assigned different nights to family members and she made it clear that tonight wasn't my scheduled time. I knew that the only reason Cecile didn't start screaming at me was because Marie-Laure was there, sleeping quietly.

I walked where the line of seafoam glowed against the dark sand, my feet stepping on a stone polished round by the waves. Far away where the lagoon ended, a wall of water, the wave of the deep, crashed against the coral wall of the reef.

Aurore had left several messages on my *vini*. I called back once, to tell her that I was returning soon. She answered with a dozen more messages.

I drove to Mataiea, through the haunted groves of black trees, the kinds of trees that grew only where it was always wet. The door opened and Aurore stepped outside. She was wrapped in a robe and in the night, the robe didn't appear to be any color at all, only a paleness like the stars.

"You're here," she said.

Once I entered, she said, "What happened to your hair?" She made one turn around me and she went to get a pair of scissors. "Sit down," she said and pulled at my shirt. "Off." As she cut, I heard the fabric of her robe rustling as she moved, a fabric that sounded both light and heavy, and I knew this was the way her robe would feel in my hand, light enough to fly away, heavy enough to sink into the places where I wanted her.

Si-ri-so-so—the word for the sound that silk and satin made, a word that was the sound itself. There were many words like this in Hakka. Aurore once said that this type of language tried to make the space between the word and the thing it represented as small as possible.

She clipped thoughtfully, pausing to frown at what was left of my hair before continuing. "There." She straightened, standing before me. "Much better."

When I awoke early the next morning, Aurore was already mad about something. I went to the car and took out a sack of Bora Bora sand.

"What's that?" asked Aurore as I re-entered the house.

"The white sand." As she had asked, as I had promised.

"Don't bring it in here," she said. "It'll drip sand all over the floor. Take it along the veranda to the studio."

I backed out the door, carrying the sack through the garden. Aurore was already waiting inside the studio. "Put it over there." She pointed by the door.

"Have you finished the installation?"

"I don't have time for the installation. I have to finish this painting." The canvas stood covered in the center of the studio, and on the table were paints and cloths smeared with more paint. A purple *pareu* lay draped in a corner. I moved to the table and glanced at her preliminary sketch.

"You can't be serious," I said.

"You can't be serious—what?" Aurore stood by the doorway, her arms folded, her red-nailed fingers holding her elbows. "You're surprised."

"It's your work."

"What do you mean, it's my work?"

"You can paint who you like."

"It's commissioned. It's not a matter of who I like. Why don't you just say it? You're surprised I'm painting Jocelyn Loong."

"You want to paint Jocelyn Loong, go ahead and paint Jocelyn Loong." In the sketches, Jocelyn appeared monstrously beautiful, her skin a bruised purple.

"You don't like her."

Jocelyn was once the fiancée of Harris, but she had dumped him to become the mistress of my father—of course I didn't like her. It was a commissioned painting, but Aurore was selective about the commissions she accepted. She turned down most requests: why had she agreed to this one?

"There's something about her," said Aurore. "She's actually quite fascinating. She isn't a bland smiling doll. There's something deeper about her."

Deeper, I thought—like greed, like a cheap grab at attention.

"She has a certain courage," Aurore continued. "She agreed to the painting. I told her that the painting wasn't going to be flattering, but she still agreed. That's more than most Chinese here would do."

"So you have your painting," I said.

"What do you mean by that?"

"Your Chinese painting. The one you've been bothering me about. Now you have Jocelyn."

"You're being a hypocrite."

"I don't care who you paint."

"You don't care? You're lying. It's written all over your face. You're disgusted that I'm painting Jocelyn."

"You're making something out of nothing. I really don't know her. I saw her a few times at parties when she was going out with my cousin, but that's all. How can I be upset that you're painting her?"

"You're upset that I said something good about Jocelyn, that at least she isn't afraid, that she isn't hiding behind some invisible silence. At least I can paint her. And you're so critical of her. What gives you the right?" Aurore continued, following me through the garden and into the house, her words stabbing the air around me. "Go ahead, walk away. Go ahead. It's easy to be silent. You're just fucking gutless."

"You going to get that?" Radish asked.

"I talked to Jacqueline Chow," I said, letting my *vini* ring. "We're meeting at two."

"You want the python?"

"Let me talk to her first."

"If it doesn't work, Edouard says one of his cousins is interested. He's in Tahaa, so we'd have to take the python there."

We were sitting in the kitchen of Radish's family house, the kettles and bowls iron-black and big enough to feed the fourteen or fifteen people who lived there. A wash basin filled with eggplants sat by the sink. By the walls were two sacks of rice and kegs filled with soy sauce and oil. The smell of cooking oil seemed part of the walls, the pans heated with oil a thousand times a year to cook for so many people.

"Moving the python isn't a good idea," I said. "We'd have to get a boat to bring her to Tahaa."

"I don't like this either," Radish replied. "But you said that we should try to sell her quickly. If you wait, we'll find someone here."

I had a bad feeling, either way.

"Jacqueline said she knew someone."

"Well, let's hope this someone is serious," I said.

Arthur entered with Percival, Radish's youngest brother, lanky, around nineteen and smelling of too much aftershave. My *vini* was ringing again, so I wasn't paying much attention to what Arthur was telling Radish, something about someone coming to talk with him. I was so annoyed, I picked up the *vini*.

"What is it?"

"Marc," said Aurore and, to my surprise, her voice didn't enrage me. All I felt was a rush of tenderness, so unexpected that I knew I had to leave the room, to talk with her. "Marc, I'm so sorry," she was saying. "I'm sorry. Why did I say those horrible things?"

As I left, Monsieur Li passed by, entering the kitchen. He turned to speak to me, but I pointed with my free hand to the *vini* against my ear. Radish shook Monsieur Li's hand as I walked out of the room.

"Can you come here?" said Aurore. "Or I'll come to wherever you are. Just tell me."

"I'll go there," I said.

It was around noon when I arrived back at Mataiea, and the sunlight was sharp, a white glare on the fronds of the coconut palms. The heat was strong and bit like teeth on the skin. Inside the house, it was still shadowy and all the fans turned from the high woven ceiling. Aurore sat just inside the entrance. Her hair was loosened in waves around her face so that her eyes were deeply bright against the dark of her hair.

She began to speak but then broke off and instead took my hands and pressed herself close so that I smelled her skin and the sweat of her sadness. She opened her mouth and I kissed her.

Chapter 34

Radish was now calling me, leaving messages, one after the other: Monsieur Li wanted to see me. Don't forget about my appointment with Jacqueline Chow. Where the fuck was I? On his last message, you could hear the exasperation in his voice.

"Okay, I've talked to Jacqueline and tomorrow's better for her anyway—tomorrow morning, eight o'clock, and don't forget this time."

"He's your wife," said Aurore.

I reached for my clothes, stepping over her books on the floor.

"Next time, tell me when you're at the hospital with your family. I was frantic. I was crazy for two days. I left messages but you never called."

"I called you."

"You called only once. And you left a message and never called back."

"You were the one who told me that Marie-Laure was so ill," I said. "I thought you knew."

"What happened to your hair?" Aurore reached out, running her fingers slowly along the back of my head.

"I felt like doing something different."

"So you went to such a terrible barber? It looks better after I trimmed it, but still. Why did you do it?"

"It's been a while. I'm not that familiar with barbers anymore."

"I don't believe you. Are you leaving?"

"I'll pick up something for dinner on the way back, at Madame Mu-San's. What do you like?"

"You're going to drive all the way to Papeete just to turn around and come back in a few hours? What are you going to do? Talk to your Radish

193

wife about selling something? *'Don't accept anything lower than this price.'* Or collect rent on something else?"

"Don't you have to finish the painting?"

"It'll wait."

"Now you say it can wait—tomorrow you'll be angry at me, saying that I distracted you from finishing your commission on time."

"There's no commission."

I stopped, my shirt in my hand. A motorcycle roared in the distance, along the road to Papeete.

"Yes, you heard correctly," said Aurore.

"What?"

"The commission—there isn't one."

"Who's paying you?"

"Nobody. I made it up."

"What?" I could only repeat myself.

"I was at this reception, a *cocktail*. Your father was there, in fact. Without Cecile. Your father was there with Philippe and we were talking about paintings. Philippe mentioned a commission I had, a few years ago, and for whatever reason, I said that I had accepted a new commission. Maybe it was the champagne, maybe I was bored. Jocelyn was there. She was so obviously your father's latest, even though they weren't standing together. And there was something different about her, different from other Chinese."

"You talk about us like we're cattle—*Oh, there's something different about this one, it's not like the other cattle.*"

Aurore ignored me. "I knew right then that I could get Jocelyn to pose for me. Now you have that disgusted look again."

"How is Jocelyn getting paid? And she's getting paid, I know, or she wouldn't pose for you."

"I've told her she's getting paid out of the deposit I received for the commission."

"But there's no deposit," I said. "Don't tell me you're paying her yourself."

Aurore was examining the tan lines on her arms.

"Why are you doing this?"

194

"You wouldn't understand. You're not listening anyway." Aurore drew her legs in front of her on the bed, resting her chin on her knees like a small child deep in thought. "I really wanted a painting of you, I still do."

Her voice was sorrowful and she was right: I didn't understand. Why did she need a painting when I was there, right in front of her? But she continued gazing past me.

When I awoke, I wasn't sure of the time, and I lay gazing at nothing, at the darkness that swallowed me, until I remembered that it was night and I was alone with Aurore, sleeping on her bed. I always thought that no one knew, that it was our secret, that we had somehow kept ourselves hidden. We were clever, we were discreet. But now I was beginning to wonder if I had been wrong all along.

The island was so small that, sooner or later, people noticed things. They saw your car or they noticed that they didn't see your car. They saw you stopping at the same store for bread, at the Libre Service beyond Atimaono, no longer the plantation where the first Hakka picked cotton a hundred years ago, but the Olivier Bréaud d'Atimaono Golf Course where their descendants bickered and grumbled on the fairway about the latest fluctuations in the black pearl market. After so many years, people knew that I didn't live in town, but no one really bothered to put together all the places where I was regularly seen. And that was it—perhaps Aurore and I were secret because no one really thought about it, no one cared.

"You're not yourself," Aurore said the next morning.

"So you're such an expert on who I am." I drank part of my coffee and threw the rest in the sink.

"Even the way you talk."

"So formal and correct."

"It's still so formal."

"Formal and incorrect."

"You talk, but you never really say anything about yourself."

So what should I say? Should I talk about what I thought about all day, the things that Aurore complained about, saying I spent too much time thinking about work? No, if I started telling Aurore what was really going through my mind, she'd complain even more.

"Marc, listen to me."

Of course I was listening. That's all I seemed to do.

"You never tell me anything." Her voice was very quiet. "Like when you went to see your cousin Marie-Laure. You just have to tell me, you just have to say, 'I have to stay with my family, I have to be at the hospital with my cousin.' Is that so hard to say? Just tell me. Okay, you're nodding, but look at me. Why do we always have to argue about these things when it's really so simple?"

"All right."

"Listen to your voice—you're upset about this." Aurore sighed, resting her forehead on her fingers. "You know, there are men who have this meanness, this cruelty. But you, you're like, you're . . ." She stopped and started over. "When I first arrived here, I couldn't believe the sweetness and kindness. The generosity. And you've been generous. But you don't tell me anything. Even after four years—almost five years—what do I know about you? You keep everything from me. I'm in a well of darkness when it comes to knowing even the smallest thing about you."

I picked up the morning *La Depêche de Tahiti*, scanning the front-page story, a three-car crash in Papeari.

"Aren't you going to say anything?" asked Aurore.

"What do you want me to say?"

"MuSan told me."

"What did MuSan tell you?"

"At least he told me."

"What did he say?" I folded the paper, leaving it on the table. "I saw MuSan yesterday, in the *centre-ville*. He was talking strangely, talking about giving me a ride back to Mataiea. Does he know that I'm living here with you?"

Aurore started to cry. My *vini* began ringing.

"What's wrong?" I said.

After the third ring, Aurore said, "I think you should answer that."

It was my father. "Marc Antoine. Where are you?"

"I can't talk right now," I replied. Aurore was still crying.

"Philippe MuSan," said my father. "Go and see him."

"Why should I see him?"

"You have an appointment with him. At ten-thirty this morning."

"Why do I have an appointment?"

"You don't have time to ask questions. Go to La Présidence. Tell the guard at the entrance gate that you have an appointment with Philippe MuSan and they'll let you enter."

Chapter 35

I followed the guard, entering through the black iron gates of La Présidence. Delusions of grandeur, people said, talking about the new City Hall
with its ornamental balustrades and the private homes of President Gaston Flosse—they all involved bloated construction, overspending, and
overbuilding. You could say the same things about La Présidence, a palace, the offices of the president and his staff, but as I entered beneath its
trees, a dreamlike quiet descended, a detachment from the clatter and the
noise of the everyday. It seemed a long walk, the armed guard accompanying me through the gardens leading to the entrance of La Présidence
and up the curve of the staircase beneath the heavy chandeliers. Why was
I here? It was even more silent inside within the corridors.

"Wait here," said the guard.

There were no sounds, no voices or telephones ringing, none of the
chatter found in ordinary offices. I wasn't sure where to look, everything
around me plush, imposing, and dark. I sat in an alcove set aside from
one of the corridors, and the walls around seemed to press close to where
I sat. The minutes passed and I tried not to think of the solitude, as if
I were forgotten inside the emptiness.

A woman walked out from a hallway door.

"You're waiting for Monsieur MuSan?" The woman wore a long, high-
necked gown in a solemn brown tapa print. She was tall and perfectly
beautiful. "He'll be with you in a moment."

MuSan appeared a few minutes later and shook my hand.

"Marc—let's go through here." He turned a corner and opened a door, revealing an office inside. "Have a seat."

I sat down in front of a long desk carved of black wood. Through the window, sunlight filtered through the trees and there was a flapping sound of something I could not at first identify, something that I had heard every day in the army, the sound of a flag waving in the breeze outside.

MuSan sat across from me and picked up a document from his desk. He read silently and I waited.

I felt a movement and, looking down at my hands, I saw them shaking. I clasped them as casually as possible, keeping them hidden.

"Marc," said MuSan, placing the document down on the desk, "there's a ban against importing snakes. I'm sure you know. The protection of native species. Species without any defenses against imported predators. You understand, of course."

He paused for a moment, glancing back at the document and then at me, before he continued.

"When confiscated, the reptile is euthanized or returned to its native habitat. There's a protocol for such situations." He moved the document to the side, clearing the space in front of him. "Look at the Americans. In Guam, there are hardly any native birds. The reason? Imported snakes. The Americans learned their lesson. In Hawai'i, you bring in a snake, you pay a fine. A heavy fine, and you go to jail. No one wants the islands overrun with snakes. This is why the penalties are severe. In exceptional cases." I felt my heart drumming. An absolute silence surrounded MuSan's voice, relentless and calm. "In your case, there's been a request from the procurators for the maximum penalty. They've raised the point that this is indeed an exception. You see, usually those involved in these cases are ignorant. They're fishermen—they're looking to make some money for their families. People just trying to make a living. You could say they don't know any better. The procurators are raising the argument that this isn't the case with you."

"Who brought these accusations?" I asked, trying to look unconcerned.

"That's confidential."

"With all due respect, I don't know why you're raising this. These accusations are groundless."

"Are they?"

"Has a hearing been set?"

MuSan raised his hand gently. "I'm not sure that you would want a hearing. You have to think about your situation. Everyone knows your father and your mother. You're their son and everyone knows that you profit from two of the most lucrative black pearl empires in Polynesia. People will wonder why you turned to smuggling."

"I don't have anything to hide."

"Let's be frank. You haven't exactly been leading an exemplary life. Drug trafficking. And there's talk of the illegal smuggling of weapons."

"That's ridiculous."

"Look, Marc—I'm on your side. You're here because your father asked me to see you. To intervene on your behalf. The procurators agreed to let me talk to you, to see if something can be arranged to the benefit of all parties."

I glanced around the room, at the ivory-colored walls, the legal books on the shelves. "What's this really about?"

"It's about certain people wanting to make an example of you."

"Who?"

MuSan shook his head. "Why don't you look at yourself? I've known you ever since you were born. You're intelligent, you speak well. You could have finished school. You could have helped your father or your mother in their business. Look at your cousins—they're all working, helping their families."

"What do the procurators want?" I asked.

"They want to put you in Nuutania. They want to show that the rich are not above the law. There's a reason for laws protecting the environment."

"Is this the reason I'm here?"

"Marc," said MuSan, "I'm the only person standing between you and Nuutania. Do you want to go to prison? Take a good look at yourself and how you've been living your life. You see anything there that'll make a judge sympathetic to you at all?"

"This is about Aurore du Chatelet, isn't it? She knew you were bringing me here."

MuSan kept his voice even. "The Marquise du Chatelet."

200

What was this about? *At least he told me,* Aurore had said, and then she was crying. What had MuSan said to her?

"It's time for you to stop blaming other people," said MuSan. "This is about the mess that you've made of your life." He placed another stack of papers in front of me. "Your accounts have been frozen. As well as the accounts of Charlemagne Li."

Radish? "What has he done? He hasn't done anything wrong."

"You'll pay the maximum penalty but you won't go to prison. Consider yourself lucky."

I stared at the pile of legal papers before me. "No," I said. "I want a hearing. The accusations against me—they're lies. If I'm sent to Nuutania for false accusations, then I go to Nuutania. I'm not paying anything for something I haven't done."

"The snakes," said MuSan. "They're already being confiscated. They were confiscated this morning, about an hour ago."

I picked up the papers, tapping them on the table to straighten them. "My lawyers and I will see you at the hearing."

"Your cousin Marie-Laure," said MuSan.

"What about Marie-Laure?"

"For once, think about someone besides yourself. Her health is so fragile. How is she going to react to the news of her cousin being charged and his going to prison? Why do you think she returned to Tahiti? She could have stayed in France—her doctors advised her to stay, to undergo medical treatment there."

"She wanted to come home," I replied. "Her parents are here."

"She came back because of you. Ten-kwok told your father this. And what's going to happen when you stop visiting Marie-Laure because you're sitting in your cell in Nuutania waiting for your hearing date? And it might take months, a year, even longer to wait."

"You're the worst kind of evil," I said.

"I'm not the one bringing charges against you. I'm trying to intervene on your behalf."

"You keep saying this, telling me the same lies."

"All right—I don't have to tell you this. But I will, to show you that I'm not your enemy. Why am I doing this for you? Because you remind me of myself. I know that look on your face. That look that says you don't trust me, that you don't care what I'm trying to tell you. You think that I'm taking advantage of you because you care about Marie-Laure. On the contrary, this is the only thing that'll save you."

"Save me? Save me from what? You're playing games with me."

"I'm telling you the truth. You have to start facing the consequences of your actions."

"Fuck the truth," I said. "What do you know about the truth?"

MuSan sat back without speaking and a complete silence fell over the room. My throat tightened. MuSan was not physically imposing, but in his silence, I felt something shifting within him and I was suddenly, inexplicably afraid. I struggled, keeping my face calm. I had always wondered why MuSan held a continual political appointment at La Présidence— counsel to various ministers, Chief of Staff, the titles varying but his presence never changing. He was my father's friend, intelligent and diplomatic and otherwise seemingly ordinary, but now I knew that his affable appearance was only that: an appearance. It was as if the calm, unimposing ocean had silently gathered itself into a great, dark wave. I knew, too late, that I would soon be swept away.

"All right, Marc. This is the way you want to play it," said MuSan. "I've talked to Marie-Laure's doctors. They say that she seems to be recovering, but they're not sure why. They don't know if it's a real recovery. Her doctors say that they've seen three cases like this—two women who were brought in from the Tuamotus and one boy from Tahaa. They received the best treatment possible. The boy was sent to Paris. The women were sent to New Zealand. None of them survived. In each case, there was a short time when they seemed to get better and everyone got hopeful. The doctors say that Marie-Laure seems to be recovering, but this could be deceptive. It only takes the smallest thing—they're not sure what—and things will change. So go ahead. Gamble with Marie-Laure's health. I'll step aside and the procurators will file their charges against you."

I felt my hands shaking again. I told myself that I was used to people being angry, threatening me, and that this was no different. But I knew the stories—of people waiting imprisoned in Nuutania, waiting for hearings that were months, years into the future. And there was Marie-Laure.

"You'll pay the fine," said MuSan. "You won't go to prison. The other charges on drugs and smuggling—they'll be dropped."

The flapping noise continued outside, the flag waving in the wind. I stared in front of me without seeing.

"You'll sign the papers." MuSan reached over, flipping through the documents. He pulled out a sheet of paper. "Your signature, here. And here."

Chapter 36

So I was free to go. Free to walk, to waste time, to feel the blankness inside my head. I felt like my ears were plugged with water, like when I was a boy walking back from swimming in the sea so that all I heard was the echoing inside my ears. Other kids yelled, people talked at me, their words empty like the inside of a drum.

Radish told me that the snakes were gone, confiscated—the python, every snake we had. "They asked questions," said Radish. "I told them fourteen people lived in this house and everyone stored junk everywhere. They asked me questions about Marc Antoine Chen and I told them that I had about fifty cousins the last time I counted and Marc Antoine was a cousin of a cousin—how was I supposed to keep track of everybody? Then they gave me all this shit about my accounts being frozen. What the hell is that all about? I ask—how is that even legal? Fucking shit. Didn't I tell you that the python was a bad idea?"

Radish sat at his desk in his father's office behind the house. He picked up a pen, tapping it frantically against the desk. "We deposited most of the rents already and we haven't made the monthly payments yet. How are we supposed to make payments if our accounts are frozen?"

"Who told them about the snakes?"

Radish shrugged and glared at the pen, tossing it across the table. "Someone told them—it doesn't matter who. We told too many people. We showed the snakes to so many people. Then we got sloppy about the python, trying to sell it and blabbering about it so that half the island knew. The whole way we went about it was fucking wrong."

I flailed and clutched at things that I couldn't hold, trying to borrow money. I called Harris every hour but no one answered. On the fifth or sixth call, someone picked up the line, saying that Harris was not at the office.

"When do you expect him back?" I asked.

"He's not here," said the voice, turning tense and distant, ending the call with a click.

I visited uncles and cousins and I smiled and shook hands and listened to how it wasn't a good time, the economy was uncertain, nuclear testing was ending and it was bad for business. What if all those soldiers left tomorrow and no one bought things anymore?

"We have to be prudent," said Uncle Alexandre. "It's unwise to over-extend ourselves."

"It's just for a month," I said. "I'll pay you back. I'll pay you interest."

"Why did you take out that last mortgage? What's your rent on those bungalows—and those houses in Paea? You're barely making your payments. Not good, not good. You shouldn't borrow like that. You know your property in Mataiea, the one right on the beach? Yes, it's beautiful. I had to admire you. How old were you then—twenty-four, twenty-five? Why didn't you tell us? Why didn't you ask your father about it? He could have told you. We all knew, but you're too young. It isn't clear."

"What do you mean it isn't clear? I had Maître Leclerc check the title."

"There's been trouble over that title for years. No one's gone to court yet; the family's fighting among themselves. No one knows who really owns that land. Why do you think the Countess, the Marquise or whatever, has been living there all these years? She knows that no one goes there, asking her to pay rent—they're too busy fighting, this brother arguing with that brother. What a mess. There's going to be an investigation into Maître Leclerc. Yes, yes—you aren't the only one. He misled a lot of *popa'a*. You have to be careful who you trust. You act like the *popa'a*—they put too much faith in whatever's written on a piece of paper. Why didn't you ask your father about it? You think you know everything? You're just a kid—no wonder you don't know. It's just a bunch of words. You think it means anything?"

A strange woman broomed the stairs to Aurore's house. It was dusk and the night was falling.

"Please stop," I said, startling her.

"I'm sorry—I'm sorry," the woman replied. She was a *demi* with a ponytail of straight black hair. A-tai always said that sweeping in the evening brought misfortune and bad luck. The woman hurried to put the broom away.

"I didn't know," said the woman, reappearing. "Madame said to be sure that everything was clean. I'm sorry, I didn't know that you . . . I didn't know."

I knew what she meant to say—that she didn't expect the Marquise to be living with a Chinese, someone who regarded night sweeping as a sure magnet for bad luck. She lowered her head and stared at the floor. All around her, the front room was clean and oddly empty of the usual papers that Aurore left scattered around.

The woman began to cry.

"Your father's Chinese?" I asked.

The woman nodded, unable to stop weeping. Her hands shook, hanging at her sides, waiting for her punishment.

"Go," I said, and she fled from the house, swept clean of all good fortune.

A silence seeped across the room. Through the window, the sky was purple, the light vanishing. I walked from room to room, from the front to the kitchen and back to the front again.

In a corner, on a side table, stood a chess set usually half-buried by papers. Aurore had constructed an earlier set out of seeds and flower pods and fanciful pieces of wood. She had invented a new game, telling me her complicated rules and how it was more about strategic cooperation instead of taking this or that piece, but I still thought of the game as chess.

"Don't leave it out," I said, but Aurore had laughed and left it forgotten on the back veranda, left to the mercy of insects who devoured the pieces. After a few weeks, only the rooks were left, a haven for squirming larvae. Aurore then constructed a more durable set, chess pieces of shell and stone, rocks gathered by the sea. This was the set that remained on the side table, a less whimsical collection than the first.

I took the chessboard into the bedroom, placed it on the bed. My thoughts were empty and I moved the pieces without thinking, pebbles for pawns, white bishop, black bishop. Did I love anyone? This isn't what people thought about. This is what mattered: the bad ways that I made my money, how I didn't help my father. How I wasted my good name.

MuSan didn't understand at all. What was it that he said? *You profit from two of the most lucrative black pearl empires.* Lies and lies. Here was the truth: I didn't have any part of the business. My share was just writing on paper that meant absolutely nothing as long as Cecile controlled everything and my mother was busy forgetting about her miserable teenage marriage to my father. They were going to make an example out of me, MuSan said. Sign here on the line so that I could lose all my money. The money that I had earned and borrowed to buy what—more stories and more lies? I threw the chessboard across the room, the rocks and stones hitting the wall, the sound of shells breaking, falling to the floor, books tumbling from the shelves, knocking down more books, crashing down one after another. Something was in my hands and I threw that, followed by the sound of glass shattering. I threw it across the room; there was the sound of more things falling. It fell in my hands and I threw it again and again, one by one, until there was a sort of calmness to the way I was throwing, the sound of falling and breaking and falling again, growing calm and regular until there was nothing left to break.

For a long, confused moment after I awoke, I didn't feel anything. I lay on the sofa in the front room; the pillows were scattered on the floor. It was the end of the night, the hour before dawn, and the roosters cried in the darkness.

In the bedroom, books were everywhere on the floor, some with pages badly folded against the ground, others with pages torn. Glass and things I didn't recognize were scattered across the room, so that I stopped before I entered. There was no sign that Aurore had returned.

I walked through the house, I walked through the garden, to the edge of the property, the sand and the sea. My car was parked by the side of the house. The stars had vanished from the sky.

Chapter 37

I drove in the darkness to Papeete. Radish wasn't answering my calls. He was awake—I knew this. His family awoke before dawn. At this time, the tea was already brewed and Arthur would be training the fighting roosters, releasing them one at a time from the cages, flipping each one over, over and over, watching as they slashed and jabbed. The radio would be on, Uncle Florian listening to the weather report.

I was losing my money—just the way that Mr. Lu had said I would— and my anger spun around like a black, black fire. The way that Mr. Lu talked about it, losing my money was part of the magic, part of the price that I had agreed to pay. It was like placing your money down at a store, but this was different: this was finding out that I had been lied to and finding out that they had thought long and hard about how to cheat me.

But weren't they part of the magic? Weren't they like puppets in a play that I'd agreed to watch?

No—no, this was wrong. This was different. I hated this, I hated losing the snakes and being forced to sign papers and having my accounts frozen. I hated every fucking part of it.

Radish was on his way out, walking to his car when I drove up to his family's house.

"I don't have anything to say," he said.

"What's wrong with you?" I said.

"I'm not talking to you. I warned you—did you listen?"

"We're getting out of this."

"*We?* This is all you." Radish opened the car door, a wave of heat spilling out, even though it was early, the sun just rising. "This mess is you."

"Listen."

"No, you listen to me—I've had enough." Radish slammed the door shut.

I waited and, after a moment, Radish rolled his window down.

"We'll talk," I said. "We'll talk later."

"What's there to talk about?"

"Listen to me," I said, shouting so that Radish jumped a bit, but then he went back to staring out the window, not even looking at me. "Radish," I said, "listen. Listen to me. We'll talk, okay? We'll talk." A rooster crowed from the yard. "I know you're upset. But I'll straighten this out. I'll get a loan. We'll make the payments."

"I saw the papers," said Radish. "They showed them to me. I got to look at the papers with your name on them—and then I got to look at the paper that said that my accounts, every single fucking one, were frozen. They don't have to explain it to me because I know how this works. It's simple: you've pissed off the wrong people. Even though I warned you, you just got yourself deeper and deeper. So tell me. How are you getting a fucking loan? You think a fucking bank is going to risk giving you a fucking loan after all this? What bank is going to be stupid enough to do that? They might as well flush money down a fucking toilet. You think any bank is going to do that? You say you want to talk—about what? What the fuck is there to talk about?" Radish put the car in gear and drove away.

My thoughts slid in every direction, paths that twisted and disappeared, paths that went the same way, repeating over and over, going nowhere. What was this all about? Was this about snakes? Was this about magic? And Marie-Laure was alive—she was alive.

I stood in Marie-Laure's room in my mother's house. The room was cleaned, the mosquito netting tied in a large knot, hanging above her bed. My head felt heavy and there was something else, a clammy chill. I was starting to feel odd, too cold and too hot at the same time. I picked up a notebook lying by Marie-Laure's bed. Spiral-bound, like the notebook she had kept when we were in France.

"Go ahead," she always said. "Open it." In France, her notebook had a pale blue cover, clean and perfect so that it looked as if no one ever touched it. You opened the cover, expecting to see nothing, but instead you saw the beautiful dark lines of her writing inside.

I could look all day at her handwriting. You could tell that the letters flowed out like they were the most natural thing. She didn't have to think about it. Even now, I felt like when I was a kid, holding the pencil too tight until my head hurt.

"It's beautiful, your handwriting," Marie-Laure had once told me. "It really is beautiful—are you even looking at it?"

I didn't have to look; it was my handwriting and I knew what it looked like.

My head felt strange. I held Marie-Laure's notebook, not opening the cover. The heat in the room was choking and I dropped the notebook, back on the nightstand. I was leaving, walking out of the room, but even outside, I couldn't breathe.

The sun, the heat. I walked under the roof. I stumbled and now I knew that I was ill.

I opened the door of the nearest room—a bedroom now empty. I pushed open a window. Dust and spider webs clung to my hand, sticky and dirty. There was a cot with a pile of shavings in the corner, something burrowing in the wood. My head burned. I closed my eyes, but it hurt and there was a terrible sound—what was it? It came from inside my head so that I couldn't make it stop. I lay down and covered my ears. The sound grew fierce. All I could do was wait as it grew, louder and louder, filling my ears.

A voice spoke: "How long has he been here?"

I tried to open my eyes but it seemed that I had forgotten how and I sank, bobbing to the surface for a moment before sliding into darkness.

"How long has he been here?" a voice asked. Darkness swallowed the room except for an orange glow from a lamp by the bed. I opened my mouth, but no words came out.

"Don't speak," said Monsieur Li. "Water?"

I nodded and Monsieur Li raised my head to drink.

"It's night," he said. "You caught a fever." I felt my eyes closing.

I didn't want to sleep. I felt heavy like I had been sleeping for days, and maybe it was days and days.

I was walking someplace—I knew this place but the name escaped me. A city, and it was cold and I was trying to walk faster. I didn't recognize anyone around me. They passed like shadows. I walked faster and then I was running to a corner, frantically looking down the street. A woman was walking away. I had to catch her, but I couldn't remember anything—her name, her face. Who was I looking for? She was disappearing and I wasn't remembering fast enough; my head was too slow. The only thing I did was run faster but it wasn't what I was supposed to do and I was sweating, cold and sweating.

Here, someone said—not who I was looking for, but a voice that I knew. A hand over my forehead and something warm so that I knew that I had been dreaming before, but this was real. It was De Koning.

I opened my eyes and she sat there with a towel on my forehead. I tried to talk, but nothing came out, and my eyes closed again.

De Koning was speaking. I didn't understand her words, but there was something in her voice—fear, the way you'd talk if something was going to burn and you only had a very short time to warn everyone. She was calling "Vaianu, Vaianu." I waited, thinking that someone would do something right away, but nothing happened. No one was listening.

Voices flowed in and out, muffled like I was submerged in water. The room seemed a dark blur. I wondered how long I had been sleeping. I heard De Koning's voice and then an older woman saying, "Turn him this way." I felt hands on my shoulder and the warm odor of tamanu oil.

At first it seemed that I was breathing from somewhere underground, but gradually the voices grew clearer and I could tell that they were speaking quietly—De Koning, Monsieur Li and his aunt Vaianu speaking in Tahitian.

"How did he get this way?" Vaianu asked. "Didn't you tell him this could happen?"

"We said there were risks," Monsieur Li replied.

"*Aita*," she said. "You told him nothing. You sent him out without warning, like sending him to find something in the dark when he knew nothing about the night."

The tamanu oil smelled strong at first, but soon the odor faded. It drifted and I clung to the scent, taking a breath so that it grew stronger again. I could follow this smell and I didn't want to fall back again, into the dark, into dreams that I couldn't remember. I felt my hand resting on the bed and the oil on my skin and something sliding, moving steadily. I lifted my hand and paused; it was moving quietly, one foot after the other, the feet crawling in the same pattern, steadily across my skin, following one another, creeping in the same quiet pattern—I couldn't tell what it was: a type of bug, termites, maybe spiders.

Monsieur Li sat in a chair by the bed. "They're gone," he said.

I couldn't speak. Monsieur Li moved closer.

"The spiders," he said. "You were talking about them, in your dream. Talking about spiders." As I watched, his face turned a deep orange and I wondered if it was from the lamp in the room. His mouth began twitching.

I'm dreaming, I thought. It's all a dream.

Somewhere Aurore was sleeping. In her bedroom, the books lay fallen on the floor. I had to pick them up, to make it right again. How long was it—when did I leave? She didn't know where I was, she didn't know that something had stung me, a mosquito probably, infected with this or that. I felt only the fever, a terrible pain, and maybe I was awake and all I knew was this pain in my head. How the fuck did this all happen? It was there, roaring and tearing and screaming. A howling began in my head, like the winds that sometimes swept through the island, torrents of rain falling until the streets flowed like rivers. My thoughts vanished into the noise and the room lifted and fell.

PART FIVE

HUAHINE

Chapter 38

I sat alone at a table. About ten meters away, a sign by the road pointed to where I sat. *Ici Glace,* said the sign, hand-painted in red. *Ice cream here.* Five empty chairs waited around the table, shaded by a green umbrella. A yellow short-haired dog sniffed in the crabgrass, wild and thick from the road to a *fare* another fifteen meters away. On the other side of the road grew guava bushes and vines and beyond that stretched a seashore of rough sand.

A lone car drove up the road, drawing closer and parking by the sign. The door opened and De Koning stepped out and walked to the table.

I stood, motioning to the circle of chairs, gathered hopefully in the solitude.

"Have a seat." The words drummed inside, heavy and hollow. Ten days since my fever had left and nothing around me felt real.

"*Ici Glace.*" De Koning read the sign. "There's ice cream?"

"There's mango," I said. "Vanilla. Chocolate. *Corossol.*"

De Koning chose a chair in the shadow of the umbrella and we sat down. I whistled between my teeth and the dog lifted its head, looking at me and thumping his tail. "Go," I said. The dog didn't move. "*Allez, allez,*" I said and the dog turned and trotted towards the *fare.*

"How long does it take before someone comes out of there?" De Koning asked.

"It depends. A couple minutes. An hour."

"Your hair's growing," said De Koning.

I watched as the dog poked his head inside the *fare.* De Koning turned, following my gaze. The dog whimpered loudly and sat down, tongue hanging from the side of his mouth.

"I don't think anyone's coming to take our order," she said. "It's Huahine. I don't think anyone's there."

I was in Huahine, not Tahiti, I told myself, but I felt as if I were stuck somewhere else, a shadow world, a nightmare without end. I was nowhere, just going through the motions, trying to act as if everything was still normal.

"Here's someone." De Koning pointed at a woman emerging from the *fare.* The woman walked to us with her head turned sideways, as if De Koning and I were holding something too bright to approach directly. She wore a floral print dress and a pink hibiscus over one ear and she clutched a notebook in her hand. As she grew closer, it became clear that one side of her face was scarred and paralyzed with an eye sealed shut. She turned her head to see with her one remaining eye.

"*Bonjour, monsieur et madame.*" She flipped open a notebook, optimistically thick, anticipating many customers. She turned through the pages until she settled on one. From where I sat, I could see that the pages were all empty. "What may I bring you?" she asked De Koning.

"An ice cream. The *corossol* ice cream."

The woman turned to me. "And you, *monsieur?*"

"The usual."

"Very good. *Café, madame?*"

"Yes," said De Koning. "No sugar."

"Very good."

We watched in silence as the woman walked back to the *fare,* the dog following her and then stopping at the doorstep. A breeze ruffled the grass and two hens pecked at the gravel by the side of the road.

"You come here regularly?" De Koning asked.

"Every day. Three days so far."

The empty road curved to the mountains, the hens disappearing through the grass. I didn't want to see anyone; I didn't care what they said. I had left Tahiti for Huahine a week after my fever ended, enough time to learn that Aurore had left and only envelopes full of legal papers waited in my Boîte Postale mailbox in town. I didn't know where Aurore had gone. She had taken the dog, Georges, and the cat and most of her paintings, including the one of Vetea Tchong.

The woman reappeared, carrying a tray. She placed a glass bowl before De Koning, ice cream decorated with an orchid, purple and white and slightly wilted. She lifted a porcelain cup of coffee from the tray for De Koning and placed a blue cup of espresso before me, then walked away, leaving the dog. I took out a pack of cigarettes from my shirt pocket and shook one out, tapped it twice on the table.

"Since when do you smoke?" asked De Koning.

"You mean tobacco?"

"You didn't smoke in Tahiti."

"I'm here now." *I'm here, right here, with nothing.*

"You've been here only a few days." De Koning reached over, plucking the cigarette from my hand.

"What are you? You're worse than my sister."

"Better than your sister. What's wrong with your parents? They never came to see you when you were sick."

"They didn't know where I was."

De Koning picked up the pack of cigarettes. "You were at your mother's place."

"It's a big place."

"That's not an excuse."

The dog sat by the table. He looked off at the sea, but his ears twitched and moved back and forth, following the sound of our voices. Here I was, I thought. Only one visitor and already we were bickering. A boxy white car approached on the road, tourists probably. In five minutes they would pass again, having reached the end of the road, with no choice but to turn around. A few years ago, Edouard and I had bought property on the island of Huahine, two lots from a cousin of Edouard's leaving for New Zealand. I had bought one lot with a house; most of the plumbing was in bad condition but there was running water and some papaya trees in the back. Wild chickens slept in a mango tree growing near the access road. The sea was a kilometer past the road so there wasn't a view, but the price was cheap.

I picked up my cup and drank.

De Koning fished the orchid from the bowl, holding it uncertainly.

"You should try their chicken with *fafa,*" I said.

De Koning twirled the orchid between her fingers. "You know, I heard a rumor."

"I'm not interested in rumors."

"I'll tell you the truth, then—it's not a rumor. It's something your sister told me. At least she visited you when you were sick."

"My cigarettes." I wasn't interested in small talk anymore.

"Odile said that the Marquise du Chatelet fell in love with you when you were seventeen. You were standing on a street corner and she saw you. Philippe MuSan said that he was there—he was seated in the back of a car with the Marquise."

"Well, I'm twenty-six," I said. "Whatever MuSan said, it was a long time ago, and even then, it was just a story that my sister heard from MuSan who probably told my father, and that's how Odile heard it—you believe what someone told someone who told someone else? What kind of crap is that?"

"MuSan said that the Marquise asked him who you were. He said that Tamerlan Chen—you know, Perles du Paradis—had a brief marriage to a great beauty and that was your mother."

The dog stared at something in the grass. He rose slowly, his body moving but his gaze fixed, hunting something that I couldn't see.

"It's people talking—it doesn't mean anything," I said. "I don't see where you're going with this."

"The Marquise du Chatelet is in New York. She's opening an exhibit this week. 'Ugly Tahiti.' That's the title—can you believe it?"

"I don't care. Why are you telling me this?"

"Your sister said that you'd want to know. She told me that the Marquise left Tahiti while you were ill."

I couldn't look at De Koning. Seven days had passed since I had found that Aurore had left—seven days, a thousand years. I couldn't stay in Tahiti anymore.

De Koning poked at the ice cream with her spoon. "Odile said that it was your big secret. She said that you were the lover of the Marquise for years and years, ever since you were seventeen."

I was twenty-one then, I thought. When I looked over at De Koning, she was sitting with her head bowed, looking like she was praying for something.

"You like being an ass," she said.

"Let's go."

"I'm sorry about the Marquise."

I reached over and picked up the pack of cigarettes. "It's almost sunset."

"Odile said that you gave the Marquise these incredible necklaces. She knew when you paid for them."

"Now you're being ridiculous. Why should I pay? Don't you think I'd get a family discount?" Who was I fooling? Cecile would just as soon slit her own throat as give me a discount on anything.

"Odile said they cost thousands and thousands. She said that the Marquise couldn't hold on to money—it was like some sort of exotic bird you'd always get for her, only it would fly off from her hands, never to be seen again."

When I had first returned to the house at Mataiea, I had looked everywhere for Aurore, and I waited through the day and into the night. In the middle of the night, I opened the closets and every drawer of her armoire, searching through the house. She had left most of her clothes, but the jewelry was all gone. I had once given her a strand of three hundred perfect black pearls, but she said they were too perfect, without the flaws that made beauty possible, so I gave her another strand of five hundred pearls, each with a tiny defect. Five hundred, not four hundred, because I was superstitious, after all, and four was the death number and I didn't want my life with Aurore to die. I was crazy then, but I knew how to hide it—although maybe I was fooling myself and I didn't hide it at all. Did anyone know? Aurore was gone, taking the past with her. Who knew, who didn't know? It didn't matter now. For all I cared, the whole island knew while I thought I was keeping everything secret.

De Koning reached over the table and snatched the pack of cigarettes. "You just started," she said. "So you can stop."

"You don't know anything about me."

"Are you staying in Huahine?"

"For a few weeks," I said, but maybe I was staying forever, going no place at all.

In the night long ago, there were the Walkers, those who guarded memories. They walked through the night and they knew everything that had ever happened. It was how they remembered, by walking from when the sun went down and the moon rose. Memory in those times wasn't little scratches of ink on paper: it was in their footsteps and their legs and their voices, chanting the long histories of the past, and it was in the night and the black ocean and the darkness that always returned.

Chapter 39

The cries shimmered in the night. Ten days had passed since the fever roared through my brain and left, spinning me around like discarded trash. Did I look like I cared when De Koning talked about Aurore? I was alone at night now, and every word tore its bite of flesh out of me. Aurore had left, Aurore was in New York, she had once been obsessed with me, but it was a long time ago, and I wasn't a beautiful seventeen-year-old anymore: I was now part of Ugly Tahiti.

The stale after-fever taste clung to my mouth as I had waited for the flight to Huahine. It was early in the morning, a 5:30 flight. A young woman was flirting with a dark reddish-haired man; she was laughing and leaning into him. A child slept on a seat next to me, a bone-colored scab covering one of his skinny knees. On the other side of the waiting room, a Chinese family overflowed, saying long goodbyes to a young couple encircled with shell leis as uncles and aunts kissed their cheeks. One of the uncles came to shake my hand—I recognized him as a cousin of someone who worked with my father.

"It's my niece," he said. "They got a store in Fare. You going to Fare on business?"

I nodded, saying something vague. The truth was that I couldn't stay at Mataiea anymore; I was crazy with Aurore gone. Monsieur Li had suggested Huahine, saying that I could stay at his house, but I told him that Edouard had a place there. Edouard kept his lot and, a year ago, he bought the one that I had. A rundown ruin of a place—the only reason it wasn't overrun with bugs was the wild chickens who made their own mess, but at least they ate the cockroaches.

221

Huahine

The rats were another matter. I heard them scratching at the roof, fighting over garbage in the yard at night. What did you do about rats? You set traps and cleaned the leaves and branches, sweeping them into a pile and burning the refuse, but I didn't care. I slept during the day and listened to the rats at night.

Marie-Laure had been sleeping the last time I visited her in the hospital. "The doctors say we should take her to Sydney," Ten-kwok said. "She'll be better in Sydney. Her doctors, they've already arranged for her to go."

We sat by Marie-Laure's bed and watched as she slept.

A morning drizzle was falling when I walked out to the tarmac where the plane to Huahine waited, propellers whirring. The Chinese couple climbed the stairs, followed by the redhead and a cluster of boys carrying ice chests. The sky was a blur of rain. The mountains had disappeared.

I didn't return to the *Ici Glace* place the day after I saw De Koning. I didn't do much of anything. I ate out of the cans I bought from the Chinese store. I lined up bottles of beer and drank. Outside, the mangoes rotted on the ground.

Did it matter if I left for Huahine or stayed in Tahiti? Aurore was gone. Marie-Laure was in Australia.

Radish no longer talked to me. He went back to working with his father, not that he had ever left, but now he devoted himself completely to the family business. A good son. And why was I so mad? I wasn't so blind that I couldn't see that Radish could have cut a deal, saving himself. They froze his accounts to make him talk: his money in exchange for more information about me. Radish didn't talk. I knew because he lost so much money. Usually you could work something out. You asked for credit, you promised payment sometime in the future. There was always someone you could talk to, someone who knew someone who knew someone else. But this time, once we missed our monthly payment, every single door slammed shut. That was crazy. It was only one fucking payment, I said, shouting the obvious to anyone who would listen. Then I knew: the same system that always bent this way and that, so that you could always negotiate your way out—this system had clamped suddenly shut. Radish said it: I had angered the wrong people, and they made sure that there was no way out for me but down.

I didn't have to be a genius to guess who was angry at me. Cecile hated me—and hadn't she warned me at the hospital to stay away from Marie-Laure? And there was MuSan, whose motives were perhaps more complicated, something having to do with Aurore—although perhaps it was simple there too: MuSan wanted to show Aurore how quickly my finances could wilt into nothing. Perhaps MuSan had been waiting all this time, ever since the day that Aurore had pointed out a seventeen-year-old as her object of desire. He had the last laugh now that my inexperience showed how financially foolish I was.

"I need a loan," I said to my father. I swallowed my pride, driving to my father's house in Taravao to plead for money as soon as I recovered from the fever.

"You're a free man," said my father. "The way I understand it, you should be in prison in Nuutania."

"I need money to cover my mortgage payments."

"For how long?"

"A month."

My father shook his head and looked off to the side, turning his gaze towards nothing, and then he shrugged. I had never seen my father shrug his shoulders in that way, as if he didn't care, and a strange, cold feeling gripped me.

"I need the money," I said.

My father spoke calmly. "You made a mistake. You imported something illegal."

"So no one has ever imported anything illegal before? What did I do that's so different from what your friends do?"

"You did this now," said my father. "When the economy's so uncertain. Now's not the time to do something foolish."

"I was wrong. I learned my lesson. What do you want me to say? I need a loan. To cover my monthly payments for this month. All the rents were deposited and they froze my accounts so I have nothing. Next month, the rents will come in and I'll make the payments. The banks—I don't understand it—they're playing hardball. They say I'm defaulting on my loans.

Even though I've always met my payments before. It's crazy: what they're doing doesn't make any sense. But to fight it in court—the lawyers need to know that I can pay them. If I don't have the land and my accounts are frozen and I don't have any money . . . Well, how am I going to pay the lawyers to get my land back?"

"I already talked to MuSan and he kept you out of prison."

"Yes. All right." I didn't know what else to say.

"I've already talked to MuSan." My father spoke with sudden force.

I understood then—that my father had made an agreement with MuSan. I didn't know the details, but I could guess the general point: that I wouldn't go to prison, but that after that, my father wouldn't rescue me as I drowned financially.

"I'll work with you," I said.

"Cecile reorganized the business." My father's voice was ordinary, as if he were telling me that he was opening a new store or that he was leaving the next week for the International Pearl Auction. "You'll have to speak with her." He rose from his chair. I watched as he left the room. I sat in silence for a long time before I left.

I awoke and a brown chicken was walking around the front room of Edouard's house, scratching among the papers thrown by the door. I tossed a can at her and she squawked, flapping her wings, but she didn't leave, so I got up to chase her out the door. She pecked outside, cocking her head and watching me for a moment before scratching the dirt again. It was either early in the morning or early in the evening, a half-light among the confusion of branches outside. Bottles lay by the door, the vines tangled with the glass remains.

I walked outside to the pile of bottles. An egg rested by a broken plastic sandal, a dusty blue flip-flop poking out of the ground. I bent down and picked up the egg, still warm. When I was a boy, A-tai sent me to gather eggs and I would crawl through the dusty undergrowth of bushes, thick and tangled with thorns. I hated this—the stupid chickens who hid their eggs, running to the other side of the garden to cluck loudly so that it seemed that they had laid right there, when, in fact, nothing was at their feet but dirt. The chicken was scratching among a tangle of grass, pecking at the ground and searching for bugs.

224

Chapter 40

"Why are you here?" De Koning asked, standing on the doorstep to her *fare*. From the look on her face, she was wary of my unexpected visit.

"I'm not drunk. Do you think I've been drinking?" I waved one of my hands like a magician.

"You have a jar," she said. "Tied with string."

"My great-grandmother used this sort of jar," I said, unwinding the string and letting her look inside.

"An egg," she said.

"It's been simmered in a special sauce."

"You're in your salesman mode."

"I'm not selling anything. I brought this for you—you can have it with bread. Or rice. In fact, I have a pot of rice."

"Whatever you're selling, I'm not interested," De Koning said, stepping back through the door without inviting me in.

I awoke later in the day, a rapping noise echoing in my head. It was hot inside the room, the front room of Edouard's house, and I had fallen asleep on the couch, littered with beer bottles and plastic bags. The rapping noise continued, coming from the doorway.

"*Allô?*" De Koning pulled open the sun-faded *pareu* that covered the top of the entrance. "Oh—I'll be back later," she said when she saw me.

I picked up the bottles with one hand, sweeping a clean space with the other. "You're in time for dinner," I said.

De Koning stood without entering. She was wearing flip-flops that showed the glittery polish on her toenails. She eyed the couch the way you looked at old food, trying to decide if it had already gone bad and should be avoided altogether.

I beckoned towards the kitchen. Through the doorway stood a refrigerator bleeding rust marks. I leaped toward it before De Koning could change her mind. I opened the refrigerator door. "They're in here."

De Koning stepped inside and looked at the glass bowl in my hand. "You made more? Are these Chinese eggs?"

Radish had found the recipe in a cookbook lying around his family's kitchen and he prepared the eggs on occasion, shelling them after simmering in tea and star anise. At the time, I thought that he was being ridiculously meticulous. "You got these from a cookbook—these aren't Hakka," I had said, but Radish replied that they were Chinese and the Hakka were also Chinese, after all.

"They're from an old family recipe," I told De Koning.

She picked up one and held it as if she were examining a jewel for flaws. "They look like they're covered with lace."

"You tap the shell after boiling the egg, then you put it in soy sauce, tea, and some secret ingredients."

"You're so full of shit," said De Koning. "Odile said that you could sell coconuts back to the coconut tree."

"I'm broke." I sliced one of the eggs and a leftover baguette, layering the sliced tea egg on the bread.

De Koning picked up the bread and ate. "What are you going to do— sell these eggs? Why do you bother?"

"Ask the banks in Papeete. I can't get any credit."

"Why won't they give you credit? Don't you have a share in the Perles du Paradis?"

"No, not really."

"I don't believe you. You're your father's only son," De Koning said. "Did you get the eggs from the chickens here? There's enough of them— they make a mess. Doesn't this land belong to you?"

"It belongs to Edouard Ma. He's letting me stay here."

De Koning placed the sandwich down on the table. "So it's true. You've lost everything."

I stood without speaking.

"Monsieur Li told you that you can't talk about it," she said. "But I know about the medicine and Mr. Lu. I was there—remember?"

I picked up the knife and cut what was left of the baguette.

"It's not a bad idea, trading the eggs or selling them."

"Everyone has eggs here," I said, unable to remain in perpetual salesman mode, my voice optimistic and false.

De Koning finished the last bite of the bread and eggs, wiping a crumb from her lip with the side of her thumb.

The next afternoon, De Koning appeared with a melon and a box of mangoes. "*Vī atoni* and *vī carotte*." The tree growing in my yard bore the most common mango, the *vī greffée*, and we grew bored of its spectacular abundance.

"When was the last time you ate a *vī carotte*?" De Koning picked up the vegetable-tasting carrot mango, less fragrant but also less common and so more desirable. She opened the refrigerator and took out a glass jar of the tea-marbled eggs. "These look better than the ones yesterday. They actually look decent."

"Take them," I said.

"What happened to your salesman smile?"

"You said I was full of shit."

"Come on, pretty boy—enough feeling sorry for yourself. Go out there and sell."

It was Sunday, the day of prayer for the faithful, the day of drinking for most everyone else. "You can sell everything on Sunday," Ten-kwok once said. I sliced a platter of the melon that De Koning had left and a platter of the eggs and I stood at the door of the *Ici Glace* place dressed in my Sunday-selling best. I didn't have much choice: I was now completely out of money. The one-eyed woman greeted me and waved me inside where a line of three children were seated at a table set out with breadfruit and canned meat and many types of *poe*. I had arrived in time, she said. She sat me next to the eldest, a girl named Hinerava who was no more than seven years old. Hinerava wore a yellow dress trimmed in white lace and she motioned that it was time to bow my head and pray.

Chapter 41

Abundance grew everywhere on Huahine. Mangoes and bananas, fields of melons—but I couldn't get money out of this type of abundance. People traded a bag of limes, a cluster of bananas, a blue parrotfish for the eggs, but no one wanted to buy with cash. I went to the Chinese store and Vong, the store owner, said, "Aren't you Perles du Paradis?" This is how you talked about other Hakka, by their family business. You called everyone in the family *Aline* or *Bata* or *Ariana*—the name of their family store. "Hey, Perles du Paradis, why you selling eggs?" said Vong.

It irritated me to the point that I snapped back, "That's my father, not me."

Vong said nothing after that, leaving to wait on his customers, and I knew that he was embarrassed for me, that I didn't know any better. You didn't talk about your father that way. You never said that you weren't part of his business. Everyone argued and everyone had their private fights with their father. But if you couldn't be trusted to keep the good name of your father in public, how could you be trusted with anything else?

I didn't exist. That's what had really happened to me. Marc Antoine Chen—he was gone. Something had happened with those legal papers he had signed for Philippe MuSan. It was his accounts being frozen, it was the fever burning up his brain. He had disappeared, vanished into the air, and now I was walking like someone that people saw, but didn't really see. I could talk, make sounds, but it was just noise, something that didn't mean anything.

I cooked the eggs and I wandered around with the jars. Hinerava from the *Ici Glace* place appeared at my door one morning. She wore a white blouse and blue shorts and a book-pack on her way to school. She picked up a jar of eggs and started walking out the door.

"Hey, where're you going with that?" I said. "Not that whole jar. No, no," I started shouting.

"I'm just going down the road," she said.

"No, don't take that," I said, and she walked away.

She returned at sunset and placed the jar, now filled with stewed chicken, on the table. "*Poulet fafa,*" she said.

The next afternoon, she walked up the dirt road with the yellow dog. She swung a sack in one hand. I poked at a pile of leaves with a stick to make sure that it kept burning. Hinerava sat down on the front steps, putting down the sack in her hand.

The dog sat solemnly at the bottom of the steps and watched the smoke rising from the leaves. Some people said the yellow dogs had arrived in the islands with the first canoes. You saw the dogs everywhere, walking by the side of the road.

"Your dog have a name?" I asked.

"Aito," she said.

I dipped the stick in a pail of water. It sizzled, the smoke rising in the golden sunset air.

"The hermit told me about you," said Hinerava.

"The hermit?"

"He said that you were Perles du Paradis, but misfortune had befallen you." Hinerava said this in the singsong voice that school children used to recite dutifully memorized poetry, words that you were supposed to learn even though you didn't really care.

"The hermit said this."

"He lives where the road ends," said Hinerava.

De Koning appeared at my door one day with a package. I looked at the dark, painfully proper writing addressed to Monsieur Marc Antoine Chen and I knew it was from Edouard. We both wrote the same way, like we were still in a classroom following the exact way we were supposed to write our letters because we didn't know any better. I sat down at the kitchen table and unwrapped the brown paper wrapping. It was a box of Yunnan Baiyao, the box containing neatly stacked smaller boxes with the vials of the dark yellow medicinal powder packed inside. Edouard had always carried Yunnan Baiyao when we were in the army. He told me how Chinese soldiers carried this; there was a red pellet you swallowed in case you were badly wounded—it'll save your life, he said—and you used the powder for lesser injuries. Edouard swore by this. He told me that I should carry Yunnan Baiyao at all times: you never knew what might happen.

It seemed like another world, the last time I had gone sailing with Edouard, only a year ago. We had taken his two nephews, eleven and twelve. They were from Raiatea and we sailed to Opoa where the Marae Taputapuatea stood, the yacht gliding through the long passage towards the *marae*. Against the stark blue of the sky, a line of black stones loomed ahead, marking the end of the land.

"What do you want to do?" Edouard asked. A wind blew across the sea, rippling the surface of the water.

"We should go there," said one of the boys. "We can climb on those rocks."

A tree grew from the long rectangle of stones at the center of the *marae*. Even from a distance, I saw its thick roots snaking down.

"No, we're leaving," I decided.

The boys started shouting. "No? Why?"

"Move the boat back," I said to Edouard.

The boys shouted louder.

"We're going back," I said. Once I saw the line of stones, I knew. There were places where you couldn't go.

You called them forbidden. You looked at such a place from a distance and then you left, leaving it alone.

We returned through the passage and dropped anchor, Edouard and I drinking Hinano and the boys swimming in the shallows between the coral. The boys were bitterly angry. They were at the age where they wanted anything bloody.

"Why didn't we go to the *marae*?" one boy said to the other. "They killed people there. Human sacrifice. We can climb on those rocks."

230

Edouard took a bag of plastic bottles and threw a bottle in the sea. The boys gazed indifferently at the green plastic floating on the surface. I took out the Magnum and shot at the bottle and they started screaming and laughing. They sat on the bow, their legs dangling. I handed the Magnum to Edouard, who shot every remaining scrap into nothing.

"It's not a toy," said Edouard.

"Show us," said the older boy. "We don't play with toys."

We went to the deep, dark blue water beyond the reef and Edouard taught them to shoot, aiming at the plastic floating in the waves.

The night sky in Huahine was dazzling. At night, I stumbled outside, wandering even though I saw the road clearly, the sky fiercely brilliant. The CEP had named the nuclear tests after the brightest stars. Aurore always talked about this on the nights when we gazed up at the sky shimmering overhead. At first there was Aldebaran, Betelgeuse, Rigel, Sirius, Altair, Antares, Arcturus. There were so many nuclear tests that they ran out of the names of those stars. They turned next to the names of the constellations and they ran out of those names. They took the names of major figures from mythology and they ran out of those names. Test after test, conducted first aboveground so that the fallout spread on the winds through the air, and then underground, in shafts drilled deep into the atoll of Mururoa. "It was too far away," people argued, or "It was too close," contaminating the fish and the seas. People talked like this, arguing over whether the nuclear testing of the CEP was good or bad. I had no time to pay attention. I was busy, and even if I thought that it was a bad idea, that thought was a pebble thrown into the sea where it sank forgotten beneath everything else I had to think about. But now it seemed that I had nothing left but time to think. I wandered in the night and I had nothing but time.

Chapter 42

I never saw the hermit, although Hinerava told me enough stories about him. He rode a red bicycle and he kept a cat with one green eye and one blue eye. He spoke many languages, or at least he knew words in several languages that he taught to Hinerava so that she could say *kartoffel, tempus fungit,* and *xie xie ni.* I knew enough to tell that there was nothing really special about these words—they were common enough, just in different languages so that I wondered if Hinerava had merely picked them up from random tourists stopping by to order ice cream.

When I was a child, I heard about a hermit called Natura who lived beyond where the road ended in Tahiti. He had been a soldier during one of the world wars—I didn't know whether it was the first or the second—and had retreated into the wilderness beyond Tautira where he lived in solitude for the rest of his life, walking into town sometimes to buy provisions. I wondered when I was a boy how Natura could live in such isolation. A-tai replied that you got used to such things so that, after a while, you didn't think about it anymore.

The chickens ate stale bread and cockroaches and the fallen *vī greffée* mangoes. They were a mix of leghorns and red junglefowl, two white-feathered, one black, and the rest copper and brown. Hinerava said that a *popa'a* couple had brought the leghorns with them when they lived at the house.

"What happened?" I asked and Hinerava shrugged, uninterested in the fate of the *popa'a* couple. I tried a different approach, asking "What did they do?"

"They always painted the house different colors," she said. "The last time, they painted it blue. I don't think they liked this color."

"Why not? They chose this color, didn't they?"

"Because. They spent a long time painting it but then they just left. It wasn't what they wanted."

I came across an occasional pale blue egg, large and oblong. Most of the eggs were white, a contrast from the usual round brown eggs of wild chickens.

"They're still wild," Hinerava said. "You can't put them in a chicken coop. They'll kill each other." At night the chickens slept together in the branches of the mango tree, but by day they scattered, each following its lone wanderings, its solitary trail through the grass that surrounded the house.

"Cecile's in France," said De Koning. She had no news of Aurore, but somehow she knew that Cecile and my mother were traveling to France and then to Antwerp together.

"Marie-Laure is living in Australia," said De Koning. She said that Aunt Georgine was renting an apartment with Marie-Laure, but a few weeks later, De Koning said that Ten-kwok had bought Marie-Laure a house somewhere outside Sydney.

"Are you sure?" I asked. "Ten-kwok isn't Australian. How can he buy land?"

De Koning was vague about the specifics of real estate ownership, saying that she had heard about it from Odile, who knew about these things.

De Koning rode a horse into the yard one morning, a bay with a black mane and a black tail.

"My friend's paying me to exercise her," she said. "She just moved here from Tahiti and she's managing the stables."

"Your friend?"

"Ursula." De Koning turned the horse around in tight circles. She wore sleek pants and long black boots.

"Ursula Chan?" I didn't know her, but Harris had mentioned an Ursula Chan who was buying land in Teahupoo.

"You know how to ride, don't you? Ursula says that she knows your mother and she's really beautiful."

"Are you here to talk about my mother?" They always repeated this story about my mother—how she was seventeen, riding a white horse by the Chinese cemetery, when my father saw her.

"I told Ursula about you. She says that you can help with one of the horses."

De Koning returned a few hours later, riding a black Arabian and leading a saddled chestnut horse by the reins.

"This is Fetia," she said. "He's stubborn. His owner doesn't live here."

I rode Fetia to the sea and it was a battle keeping his head away from the grass along the road. His coat was dull and he was lazy from neglect. The way he ambled, turning his head to snatch at the long grass—he had been left to do what he pleased. Fields of watermelons grew further down from the beach, but Fetia was interested only in returning to the stable. He knew the way back, and he wasn't interested in wasting his energy along the beach.

"Be sure to exercise him," said De Koning, appearing at the house the next day with Fetia. "He's lazy. It's almost summer and he has to be exercised every day. You think you can do that? Ursula says that she's seen your mother riding in Tahiti, in Arue. I lied—I told her that you were really good with horses, just like your mother."

"How much am I getting paid?" All those years, sitting in the back of the dumpling woman's truck to go across town to another tedious lesson near the Hippodrome horse track, the lessons paid for by my mother.

"Ursula wants to see if you can handle him. In case you can't get him to trot, you have to walk him at least an hour and a half."

"He'll be cantering in no time."

"Yeah. Ursula would like to see this. How about along the beach? You can use a stick, but you know how tourists are—they don't want to see someone hitting a horse all the time. So don't hit him, just keep the stick in your hand."

"I don't need a stick," I said.

"I told Ursula that you were really good looking." The way De Koning said this, it was like she was letting me know that she was lying for me again.

There weren't any mirrors in the house—only a pale space above the bathroom sink where it looked like a mirror had once been. After De Koning left, riding the sleek Arabian, I thought of riding Fetia to the Chinese store and buying a mirror. I ran my hand through my hair, and my fingers stuck, snarled in the tangles. I didn't need a mirror to know that De Koning didn't want Ursula to see me, the way that I now looked.

"Carrots and an apple," I told Hinerava that afternoon when she appeared with the usual odd bundle of vegetables—lumpy yams and wilted taro leaves. "Bring me carrots and an apple in the mornings and I'll make you *fong ngung ha* for breakfast. The most incredible *fong ngung ha*. Madame MuSan taught me and she has the best Chinese restaurant in Papeete. Her *fong ngung ha*—so much better than the finest omelette in all of Paris. Light and fluffy with just the right amount of ham . . ."

"Where do I get an apple?" Hinerava asked. "This isn't Papeete."

"All right—carrots, then. The mornings that you bring me carrots, I'll make your special *fong ngung ha*."

"You'll cook me *fong ngung ha* with catsup and mustard."

"I'll make you the best *fong ngung ha*, but where am I going to get catsup and mustard?" I was trading enough eggs to eat regularly, but not enough to get careless.

"At the Chinese store. You're a *tinito*." A Chinese.

"You think that just because I'm a *tinito*, other *tinitos* are going to give me free catsup or free mustard?"

"Catsup. And mustard," said Hinerava.

"Bring me a pair of scissors."

"Why do you need scissors?"

"To trim my hair."

Hinerava rested her elbows on the kitchen table and her chin on her hands, studying my face. She reached into her pocket and pulled out a stretchy circle of pink elastic. "You don't need scissors. I'll bring you hair ties but you have to give me *bon-bon citron*. *Fong ngung ha* and *bon-bon citron*.

"I don't have *bon-bon citron*."

"You need to use shampoo," she said.

"I know how to wash my hair."

"No, you don't."

Why was I explaining this to a seven-year-old?

"Your hair's getting long. You'll get bugs if you don't tie your hair," she said.

The following afternoon, Hinerava brought carrots and I cut them in half, storing them in the refrigerator. The carrots were thick and stumpy, bits of sandy soil clinging to the skin. Fetia eyed each daily offering with his large eyes, my face reflected inside, but his eyes were so completely dark that I saw only the black outline of my chin and the wave of my hair, now tied with Hinerava's pink elastic tie.

"Get me another color," I told her. "Not pink." But she ignored me.

Fetia had a smooth gait and I trotted him up and down the beach. One afternoon, Hinerava walked up the road with a bag of red New Zealand apples. Her uncle was visiting and he had brought Hinerava a bag of apples and a bag of candy.

"You can have the apples," she said to me. "But *fong ngung ha* all week. And *bon-bon citron*."

I rode with Hinerava to the beach. "Why do I have to do this?" she asked.

"You don't have to do anything. You just stand there with the apple."

"He's going to bite me."

"No, he won't."

"He will. Why are you doing this?"

"Because this is the only way he's going to canter and then gallop."

"Your horse isn't going to gallop."

"His name is Fetia." The Star.

"Well, he's no star," Hinerava replied. "That's why they call him Monsieur Fiu at the stables. They didn't tell you that?" *Fiu.* What you said when you were too tired and didn't want to do anything—*fiu*, you said, right before you left. *Fiu*, no more.

"Stay there and don't move. I have to go down to where the beach starts. That will give Fetia room to trot and canter and then he'll gallop. All right?"

"How does he know I have the apple?"

"He knows. He smells it on you."

I turned Fetia and rode away, turning once to see Hinerava standing by the water. I waved but she stared without moving. I trotted Fetia down the length of the beach until Hinerava was a small dot in the distance, but I could tell that she had moved, standing now by the grasses that grew among the drifts of sand.

Fetia began to trot and, to my surprise, he changed to a canter at a very slight movement of my foot, a seamless transition. I heard my mother, talking about balance and not adding weight on the horse, but soon Fetia was flying, the sand turning into a blur beneath us—and where was Hinerava? She had disappeared, frightened perhaps by the speed of the horse, although I intended to slow him down to a walk before I even reached her. The horse sensed my hesitation, his gait slowing, turning less confident. Only the grass and sand beckoned ahead and then there was a man in the distance. As Fetia approached, I saw Hinerava standing near the man. It was Monsieur Li.

Hinerava no longer seemed stiff and afraid, and she smiled as the horse moved closer. The wind blew so that both Monsieur Li and Hinerava squinted against the sun. The way that she stood, plucking at his sleeve—she knew him well, I thought.

"Is this the hermit?" I asked.

"His friend," said Hinerava. "They live where the road ends."

Monsieur Li invited me for dinner at a restaurant in Fare, selecting the one at the end of the main street, the dining room overlooking the water. I tried not to act like I was starving, wolfing down the mahi mahi and fries, but when I finished my plate, Monsieur Li asked if I wanted another.

"I'm fine," I said, but Monsieur Li asked the waitress to bring me the menu again.

He had been in China with my father for the past two months, visiting his friend Jeremy Pelevin, an American lawyer sent to Shenzhen. "We told your father that he should bring you into the business," said Monsieur Li. "How old are you—twenty-six, twenty-seven? Your father's thinking of moving into another line of work, letting Cecile run the Perles du Paradis." Monsieur Li reached for a briefcase leaning against his chair. "He asked me to bring you this." He motioned for the waitress. "Order something else. Do you want dessert? *Gâteau des îles?*"

"I'll have a slice of the *Forêt Noire*."

"*Café*," said Monsieur Li to the waitress. "Make that two. I saw that you've met Madame Poroi's daughter."

"Hinerava? She says you're a friend of this hermit."

"The hermit, yes."

"So he really exists?"

"He does," said Monsieur Li.

"What happened to Hinerava's mother?" I pointed to the side of my face.

"Terrible accident—her hair got caught in an electric generator. She's lucky to be alive."

"Hinerava said her father was in Bora Bora."

"He drives a delivery truck there. He sends money once a month." Monsieur Li pulled out an envelope from the briefcase, placing it on the table between us. "This is for you. From your father."

I opened the envelope and pulled out a milky-white jar. I turned open the lid, revealing two large pearls, perfectly matched in size and color, silver with a slight pink blush. To find two flawless pearls with the identical shade of blushed silver and then to find two of the same exceptional size—you searched through thousands and thousands.

"Your father said that you could sell these if you needed the money. You're very thin, but not quite a skeleton yet." Monsieur Li was joking, I thought at first, making a witty comment, but when I looked at him, I saw that he wasn't smiling. "Have you thought of returning to Papeete?"

"What would I do in Papeete?" At least in Huahine I had the chickens and the horse.

"I saw Mr. Lu. In Hong Kong."

"Does he have a girlfriend yet?" I asked, remembering what De Koning had said, something about a love potion that Mr. Lu was brewing, using my hair.

"The first girlfriend didn't last long, but he has a new one." Monsieur Li felt his shirt pocket, pulling out a billfold. "We'll have dinner again, later this week."

Monsieur Li lived where the road ended, as Hinerava had said. I drove there, the paved road turning into gravel that continued for several meters before disappearing in dirt and brush. "I'll walk," he said. "You can keep my car for a few days."

"You don't need your car?" I asked, but Monsieur Li had already stepped outside. I turned off the engine and followed him.

"It's not far." Monsieur Li stopped by the gravel and pointed into the dark. Insects screeched among the leaves and a quarter moon hovered in the sky.

"Have you seen Marie-Laure?" I asked.

"No, but I spoke to Ten-kwok. He sounded like himself again. You know, shouting into the phone."

I laughed, but even then I felt the darkness, the blind solitude. *How is Marie-Laure?* I wanted to ask, repeating myself. I thought of the nights long ago when Marie-Laure had slept so close to me that I couldn't feel her, like a ring you always wear on your finger so that you forget that it's there at all. Was she better? Was she recovering? I wanted to know this, that there was a good reason for sacrificing all the money I had once had.

"I've heard that she's stable," said Monsieur Li. "She's on medication."

"When she's cured, she won't have to take this medicine anymore."

"It's too early to tell. She isn't improving much. But she isn't getting worse."

"I made an agreement," I said. "With Mr. Lu. I kept my promise. I didn't speak about it. I didn't tell anyone." I was speaking into the night, to Monsieur Li, his face in the shadows.

"Mr. Lu gave you the medicine."

"But how do we know that Marie-Laure took this medicine? She had to drink it all—that's what you said. But she was in a coma and she couldn't drink. We put the bead under her hand."

"And did you see the bead afterwards, when Marie-Laure awoke?"

"No. But I didn't go searching for it." Marie-Laure had awakened, and that's all I thought about, the only thing that mattered.

"But you didn't see the bead," said Monsieur Li.

"Maybe it was still there, rolled someplace else. We just didn't see it."

"Marie-Laure awoke."

"Yes, yes. But how do I know it was because of Mr. Lu's medicine? Maybe she was going to wake up, maybe the doctors were right—she was going to wake up sooner or later. How do I know?"

Monsieur Li didn't answer and the insects continued their screeching.

"I lost my money," I said. "Mr. Lu and you said that this would happen. My accounts were frozen. I lost all my good credit. That part—it went just as predicted. Although maybe, maybe, all that would have happened too, sooner or later. I made some bad deals. I went into too much debt for a piece of land and the title wasn't clear. I wasn't thinking. Maybe I was just being stupid. Maybe there isn't anything magical about any of this. It's just the way it goes."

"Are you returning to Papeete?" Monsieur Li asked.

"No. I already said this. I don't have anything there. I'm stuck here in the *van-tui*." I felt unsteady. I could hear myself shouting.

"It's late," said Monsieur Li.

"You haven't answered my questions."

"It's time to rest."

"I want the answers." I was stuck here and no one really cared. "I want the answers," I said again. Monsieur Li turned away, walking from the road, his footsteps passing close to the insects so that they fell quiet for a while.

I never thought of the *van-tui* as a place to live, the distant lost places where everyone seemed distant and lost to me. I had always lived around Papeete except for a few weeks after leaving the army, when I lived in Paris, a cold, great city, but now I was in a hot, sweltering nothing of a place.

The times when I had sailed through the islands, to the Tuamotus, through the passes into turquoise waters, sleeping in my cabin of teak and mahogany—it was as if those times had never happened. Aurore had talked about the past when there was no electricity and the night was starlight and moonlight, the simple life—pure shit. There was nothing romantic about having nothing, living from day to day, trading eggs for stewed chicken, riding a horse that no one else wanted, burning leaves to keep the rats and cockroaches and centipedes from crawling everywhere. The chickens, the horse—they all smelled. The days were flat, every day the same. I bent over Fetia's hooves, tapping his legs, and he lifted them one by one so that I could clean out the little stones caught around his horseshoes. It was always the same.

De Koning said that I should get a telephone line because they—Odile and Radish—called her asking how I was.

No. I didn't want to talk.

De Koning said that Radish was thinking of buying a boat with Edouard.

"Why don't you call them?"

"Radish always talked about transportation—that's what he called it," I said. "It's his idea."

Others passed occasionally as I rode Fetia along the beach—other riders, locals and tourists walking for one reason or another along the water, too rough for swimming so that people swam on other, more peaceful beaches. People sometimes nodded at me and they watched as I raced Fetia on the sand, but they didn't approach too closely. I knew what they knew—that something had happened to me, that I was once someone, but all that had changed. I was once someone very different from what they saw, but now it was best to keep a certain distance, the way you avoided dogs turned feral, the way you avoided ghosts.

Chapter 43

That night I dreamt of Aurore and when I awoke, the early morning air was grey.

"Go get a woman," said Vong, sitting behind the counter at the Chinese store. He took the tea eggs, the plain boiled eggs and the uncooked eggs and I traded them for rice and catsup for Hinerava's *fong ngung ha*. "It's not good, living by yourself. You'll go crazy. I feel sorry for you—look at you. You look crazy already. This time, I send a girl over. You're too crazy to think right. You thank me later."

"This bottle of catsup—it's no good," I said. "Get me another."

"It's all I have."

"No, you've got that one over there. This one's bad."

"You're dreaming. Going crazy, thinking about this woman," said Vong. "I know, I know, just look at you. There's so many women, but all you think about is this one. You're wrong. You make yourself crazy. Nothing special about this one. She make you cry, she make you crazy. She bring you trouble. You crazy, you crazy already."

All during the past year, Aurore had been angry at the CEP and at Chirac, who had restarted nuclear testing. She was angry at the French and the French military and the Chinese who watched from the sidelines and profited from it all. The last New Year's Eve I spent with Aurore was miserable—there had been a nuclear test two days after Christmas, the fifth after Chirac announced that testing would begin again on Mururoa. Aurore threw out the bottle of champagne that I had brought her, a Dom Perignon.

"There's only five bottles like this in Tahiti," I had said, casually leaving the bottle on the kitchen table. Robert Wan had one, Madame Tonita

Flosse, the First Lady of French Polynesia, had another, and the other two were with the branch of the Sin Tung Hing clan that controlled most of the oil imports into Polynesia.

"Where did you get this?" asked Aurore.

"Sin Tung Hing," I said. My father had been invited to their New Year's Day lunch. One of their cousins had three bottles and I entered long negotiations, promising this and that to obtain one of the bottles from him, all the while thinking about how impressed Aurore would be—although she wouldn't admit it, I knew.

I was wrong: Aurore was furious. "Don't you know there's a boycott of French wines?"

"That's other countries," I said. "It doesn't make sense for the French to boycott their own wines, does it?"

Aurore began screaming, shouting all the things I had heard so many times that I tuned out whatever she was saying: that the radiation would leak sooner or later, that it was already leaking, that this was poisoning the ocean and that was the point of the boycott—an endless black stream of words.

New Year's Eve was grimly sober, and I awoke mid-morning on New Year's Day 1996 to drive to my father's house in Taravao. We were invited to one of the Sin Tung Hing houses on a hillside overlooking the lagoon south of Papeete. Bouquets of peonies decorated every room, the peonies special-ordered via refrigerated airfreight. Peonies were the favorite flower of the family matriarch, and a single lavish red peony in a vase decorated her place at the head of the table. Radish was there, accompanying Uncle Florian who was recovering from an episode of dengue fever. Radish and I were seated on either side of an American lawyer, a distant Sin Tung Hing cousin by marriage. She was around forty and spoke passable Hakka. She drank *verveine* tea, an odd choice for a New Year's lunch—Radish and I each had our glass of imported orange juice mixed with champagne—but she explained that you couldn't find this in California and continued drinking the *verveine*.

When my father and I left, one of the older aunts wrapped three of the peonies in paper for my father to bring home to Cecile, who was celebrating New Year lunch with her mother, Mei. The remaining peonies were distributed to different family members, the aunts each clutching a bloom as they said their goodbyes.

When I returned to Mataiea, Aurore was sketching on the veranda. "How was lunch?" she asked.

"It was all right."

"What did they say?"

"The usual. Nothing, really."

Aurore placed her charcoal pencil down on the table. She rose and walked from the veranda into the kitchen, pausing in front of the refrigerator. I had never seen a nearly empty refrigerator until I began living with Aurore. The refrigerator at Radish's house was perpetually crammed with food on every shelf, with jars of Chinese pickled greens always in danger of spilling every time the door was opened. Aurore's refrigerator was bare and pristine and she was always throwing out the food I put inside, things going bad before we ate anything.

Aurore opened the refrigerator door. She had removed the middle shelf so that a bouquet of a dozen peonies could fit inside. The peonies were white, tied with a dark blue ribbon. The buds were tightly closed, waiting in their refrigerated slumber.

"You ordered this?" I didn't want to tell Aurore what she didn't know—that the Chinese wanted the red peonies and no one would take the white ones, the color of death. She reached inside, taking the bouquet and placing it in my hands. *For Marc Antoine,* read a handwritten slip of cardpaper nestled among the flowers.

"Happy New Year," said Aurore.

When I was fifteen or sixteen, living on the pearl atolls with my father, the silence seemed beautiful. Silence had a color then, the aqua blue of the lagoon, the turquoise of the deeper waters, the color of clouds and all the hopeful dreams I had. I drifted on this silence and it seemed to carry me on a current to places that promised—that promised what? I didn't know, only that there was something that seemed to call to me, something I hoped to find, but in the end, it turned out to be nothing at all.

If silence had a color, it was the color of nothing. I could shout and talk all I wanted, rambling like a madman, but no one was there to hear, so there wasn't any point in saying anything and I might as well fall back into this nothing, into not remembering. That was what I wanted—to forget.

But my dreams weren't empty, and although I forgot them as fast as I could, they reappeared every night. This was my real trouble with Aurore. No matter what she said about how she loved the gentleness of the islands, the generosity and the sweetness, I could feel her in the darkness, in the night, searching for something else. You sleep so well, Aurore said. She said this smoothly, but I felt the resentment, hidden thorns in her voice. You have dreams, she said, and then she wanted to know what they were.

I don't remember, I said. I don't spend time thinking about dreams. She wanted to know more, questioning me, so I said that they were terrible dreams, with monsters and demons.

"You're lying," said Aurore. "You're like a child when you sleep. I'd know if there were any monsters there."

Aurore knew because she had enough monsters of her own, lurking in her dreams. She thrashed around, grinding her teeth as she slept. Her hands tightened into fists, her nails digging into her palms. At first I asked what troubled her so much. Bad things, she said. She didn't want to talk about it.

This is why we were secret. The things that troubled Aurore—they were unrelenting and vigilant and they hunted her in her dreams. I understood then that she had to hide completely. She had to disappear into the dark, without a trace. She had to disappear every night before her dreams began, and afterwards, when the nightmares found her, she had to run and disappear again.

This was all I thought about at night, that Aurore was gone. She wanted this. Make me disappear, she whispered, talking about the secret forest, the girl disappearing into the trees. Make me, make me disappear. A watery sound ran in my ears and I awoke, wondering if it was a sound I heard in my dreams or if it was something outside in the night. Part of the water that ran all through the island, the rivers and the fingers of the sea.

Chapter 44

It rained through the morning, but I drove to the stables with Monsieur Li's car. The rain had stopped by the time I arrived, but the sky remained covered, threatening more rain. I was saddling Fetia when De Koning walked up, accompanied by a woman wearing jeans and a flimsy blouse, held together with the tiniest of ribbons.

"You're riding Fetia?" De Koning asked.

"It's not raining now."

"I'm lunging the horses. My cousin's here to help. Do us a favor and ride Fetia. He's stubborn."

"Stupid and mean," said De Koning's cousin, laughing, and they left to see the other horses.

The dirt had turned muddy and the potholes in the road sloshed with water, reflecting the heavy clouds. I rode Fetia alone by the side of the road. The trees and the vines were vivid green, the leaves drinking the rain. When I returned, De Koning's cousin was sitting in the car, parked by the side of the stables, the windows rolled down. She was listening to the radio.

"Nice ride?" she asked.

I rode Fetia up to the window and he stepped close, flicking his long tail, as if he wanted a better look at the woman who spoke so unfavorably about him. "You're Elodie."

"Yes. I recognized you."

"You live here now?"

"No, I'm visiting. Helping Marise. She's going to Papeete."

"A change of scenery. Something different."

"Your sister asked her to move to Papeete, to live with her," Elodie said, and then she laughed, shaking her head. "You didn't know? You should see the look on your face."

"I'm not into gossip. And you're not telling me anything new."

"Well, it's not gossip. It's fact," she said, her smile easy and smooth.

De Koning knocked at my door later in the afternoon, or rather she knocked at the side of my door, since it was open. There wasn't anything worth stealing inside the house and besides, everyone kept their doors open in Huahine.

"Are you all right?" De Koning asked.

"Is something wrong?"

"I saw you talking to my cousin."

"She said you're moving to Papeete."

"Elodie's crazy. She isn't right in the head."

"Are you moving to Papeete? Because if you are, tell Ursula to assign your horses to me. I could use the extra money."

"What else did Elodie say? What did she tell you?"

"Tell me what?"

De Koning kept looking at me.

"When are you leaving?"

"In a few days."

"You want something to drink?" I asked. We walked into the kitchen and De Koning picked up two glasses from the jumble of odd glasses by the sink.

She sat down at the kitchen table. She sat for a long time before she spoke. "Elodie's unstable and crazy. I wanted to tell you that Odile asked me to move to Papeete."

"Does my father know you'll be living with Odile?"

"What—tell him? Are you serious? He'll never understand. He thinks that I'm just her roommate. You know, your father called Monsieur Li. He wants to talk to you."

De Koning had already told me this, that my father wanted to talk and that I should call him. What was I going to say? *Bonjour,* I'm trading eggs now. *Bonjour,* I get money by riding a horse—and the money I get, I couldn't buy a ticket back to Tahiti even if I saved for months.

"You want a beer?" I said. "You have some choice here: French, Belgian."

"Monsieur Li told me that you were special."

What did Vong the storekeeper say—that no one was special? Or perhaps he was talking about Aurore.

"I've been called a lot of things," I said. "But I've never heard this one before."

"Monsieur Li told me that when you were ten, he went with your father to dig up your grandfather's bones. He explained that this is what the Hakka did in China." When De Koning spoke, it looked like she was speaking to a spot between us on the kitchen table. "They dug up the bones after ten years and put them in jars. Your father decided that this was the right thing to do, even though no one did this anymore. Monsieur Li said that he was telling me something that you weren't supposed to talk about." She paused, looking up at me. "Monsieur Li said that your father decided to take you with them. He told me that in China, people in the village did this all as a group. But here, they were breaking the law, so your father had to do it in secret, at night with only Monsieur Li and you. Monsieur Li wasn't sure that it was such a good idea to bring you along. There were all those stories about spirits of the dead, *tupapa'u.* But it turned out that you weren't scared at all."

"I was with my father and Monsieur Li," I said. "So why should I be afraid? It wasn't like I was there alone."

"Still," said De Koning. "Monsieur Li said that you were only ten. Old enough to hear a lot of ghost stories and not really old enough to know that most of them were just stories. Your father told him that sometimes you slept in this *fare* they built in the garden, by where they put your grandfather's bones. He said that it was strange, your sleeping alone out there."

"They built a pavilion for my grandfather. It was really beautiful. The garden was beautiful too." I began to feel uneasy, that this wasn't something to talk about, and that if you did, you didn't talk about it too long.

"Don't you think that's strange, sleeping there?"

"It was quiet. My father wasn't there in the garden to yell at me all the time. Of course I liked it there." My father was starting out in black pearls then, barely keeping his business from drowning. He was like a rope pulled so tight, it was always in danger of snapping, lashing out at whatever was closest. I learned not to stay too close, retreating to the darkened garden when my father arrived home late after work. It was my father's idea to keep my grandfather's bones there, but he didn't want to be in the garden after dark, and I knew this whenever I entered the bungalow, the *fare* built for a caretaker that my father never hired since he didn't trust anyone outside the family and Monsieur Li to keep a secret.

"Monsieur Li thought it was strange, that you weren't afraid. He told me that there was something about you. He told me this when he sent me from Huahine to Papeete, to see you. He wasn't sure if the medicine would work for Marie-Laure. He told me that he remembers when Marie-Laure was born. He came back from his studies in Paris. Marie-Laure was very small. So small that he could hold her entire head inside his hand. A tiny baby. He told me all this before I left Huahine for Papeete." De Koning tucked a stray strand of hair behind her ear. It had started raining again, the drops falling and rattling on the tin roof. "You know, at the beginning, when I first started learning from Monsieur Li, he wasn't sure if I was right. He said that I was too American and that I grew up in Oregon and I wanted to know about everything. What was up. What was down. But that isn't the way magic works."

I watched her running her finger around the rim of the empty glass. The rain tapped against the window. "Well, tell me," I said. "The way magic works."

"I think it's like love—I know, it sounds stupid, but think about it. You can't ever really know for sure if someone loves you. You feel it, but you can't prove it a hundred percent. I mean, maybe they're just fooling you. Or maybe they want you for other reasons. You never really know, do you?"

You never really know about anything, I thought.

"You can't grab on to anything, even though you want to. It's just love."

"You want a beer?" I asked.

"I'll have the mineral water," she said.

I returned and placed the bottle of water down on the table. We sat listening to the rain pounding on the roof and against the house. The wind toppled something that sounded like a large tin can. I went to the window to find a sheet of metal lying in the yard with leaves and branches torn from the trees. The lights flickered and I fished around the drawers, pulling out two candle stubs in case the lights went out for good. Waiting for the storm to end, De Koning fell asleep on the bed, wrapped in a blue and white *pareu* sent by Hinerava's mother.

Chapter 45

I awoke to complete silence. De Koning stood looking out the windows, by the sofa where I slept. No birds, no roosters crowing. The wild chickens had run under the house when the storm began.

"I should call Elodie," De Koning said. "Storms frighten her."

"Go call her, then."

"I'm waiting. The rain will start again. Can you hear it? It's so quiet. It's spooky."

"Doesn't Elodie have the number of your *vini?* She'll call if something's wrong."

"She's lost."

Elodie seemed fine to me. Armed with enough venom to defend herself just fine.

"She's lost in the woods," said De Koning.

"*La forêt lointaine.* Aurore once told me this story about being lost in the woods."

"The Marquise du Chatelet? Was this about sex?"

I laughed, but De Koning kept staring out the window, her arms folded. "She told you this story only at night. I'm right—you don't even have to tell me."

"What makes you think that she told me this story at night?"

"Because I know. She'd tell you this story and then she'd sleep with you. That's what she did, right? You were her lost-in-the-woods fuck. Nasty and dark."

"Don't talk about Aurore like that."

"Don't talk about Aurore—what, you're upset?"

I got up from the sofa.

"Hey, hey." De Koning followed me into the kitchen. "I'm sorry. Look, I'm sorry."

"You're not sorry," I said.

"I'm sorry if I offended you. I didn't think you'd get so upset all of a sudden."

"What are you talking about? Just go call Elodie."

"Look, look. Why are you so upset? Just think about this for a moment."

"Go," I said.

"Why don't you just tell me this: where is Aurore? Where is she?"

I opened the refrigerator and looked inside.

"Is she here?" said De Koning. "When you were this rich kid, she was all over you. But where is she now?"

"You don't understand."

"No, I do. I was there when you were sick. I was so scared. Even though Monsieur Li was there with Tatie Vaianu. And I know what you're thinking—that Aurore didn't know."

"She didn't know—how could she?"

"Wake up, Marc. She's a goddamn Marquise. If she wanted, she could find out what happened to you. We all knew how sick you were. What about Philippe MuSan? Don't you think she could have asked him? Like she asks him about everything else. He would have told her that you caught a fever, that you were at your mother's house. But she never asked him."

"Don't talk like this."

"You're an ass, but she stayed with you all those years, right until you lost all your money. That's the real reason she's gone."

I flipped on the light switch, the bulb buzzing in the center of the ceiling. A cockroach flew around in a circle.

"I imported these snakes," I said. "I made money from it. I had this python brought in. A beautiful snake, really. You know you can't bring a python into the islands."

De Koning stood in the kitchen doorway and watched the cockroach whirring along the ceiling.

"A python will eat everything," I said. "Eggs. Birds. But I really didn't care. I brought her in from Australia. It was just money to me. That's all

I thought about. That's the reason Aurore left. MuSan probably told her that I was making money from the snakes."

"Don't you think she already knew all the stories about you? How you made your money. I was in Papeete for only one week and I heard enough stories. You know that Aurore heard them too and she still stayed with you, as long as you had money."

"They're just stories," I said. I walked out of the room. I didn't want to listen any more, I didn't want to hear. *She didn't love you, she didn't love you.* If I didn't think, I could keep this voice very quiet, a knife that cut me only slowly.

I drove to the Chinese store to buy a baguette. Leaves and broken branches covered the road and I drove slowly around a fallen tree limb. When I returned, it was raining again. De Koning had boiled water, pouring it into the teapot.

"I talked to Elodie," she said. "She slept at my place during the night."

I took out two jars from the refrigerator. "So you feel better."

"Sort of. Not really." De Koning picked up one of the jars. "Damn. Chestnut puree. You eat like this at breakfast all the time?"

"It's from Vong the storeowner."

"Are we talking the same store? All I find there is overpriced butter and the same three jars of guava jelly he's been trying to sell for years. I know, because one of the jars has this petrified wasp stuck on the bottom."

"I gave him a vial of Yunnan Baiyao."

"What?"

"Edouard Ma, he owns this place. We were in the army together. Edouard always carried this medicinal powder called Yunnan Baiyao when we were in the army. He told me how Chinese soldiers carried this. If you got shot, the powder would slow the bleeding. I gave a vial to Vong."

"Why? Don't tell me he has a gunshot wound."

"No, he has these fighting roosters. I gave him a vial and it saved one of his roosters. I told him I'd give him the medicine, but he'd have to cancel the debt I owed him at the store."

"So now he gives you delicacies like sweetened chestnut puree? No wonder Elodie said we should keep an eye on you." De Koning opened a drawer, pulling out a spoon.

I cut the baguette and handed her a slice.

"I should go home." She talked with her mouth full.

"I wouldn't go out—it's raining again. It'll be pouring soon."

"I'll go to Monsieur Li's place. It's closer."

A rattling hit the roof, the rain turning stronger.

"We have rain in Oregon, you know. It's not just here." De Koning pushed the chair back and walked to the door.

"You have better roads in Oregon."

De Koning stood without moving, like she was pulling a string of thoughts through her mind and didn't know yet which one to follow. The roads were useless in the storm. I could say this a hundred times, but De Koning wouldn't believe me.

"You have a pair of scissors?" said De Koning finally. "I'll trim your hair. Since it looks like no one's driving anywhere."

"Don't you like my hair?"

"It's a rat's nest." De Koning pulled open one drawer and then another. "Here we go." She pulled out a large pair of rusty scissors.

"I've never seen that before."

"What—these?" She snipped at the air, cutting ghostly threads. "They were put here by the couple who lived here before. The woman. I tell you, she was organized enough to put scissors in the drawer. Some oil and they'll be good as new."

The tin roof continued its rattling and the lights flickered, turning bright for a moment before they went dead. The refrigerator stopped its humming, the silence so sudden, it was as if someone had stopped talking in mid-sentence, everyone still listening for the next word. De Koning closed the scissors, laying them down in the palm of her hand.

"How long before the lights come back?" she asked.

"We wait. Could be an hour, could be two days." Could be a week.

A strange howling began outside, the crying of the wind. "I should get a generator." I could talk to Vong, and try to get one on credit.

"I thought you said this place belongs to Edouard Ma."

"He's letting me live here, isn't he?"

If you sat long enough, the dark always turned light. Even though the storm swallowed the sun, it was still day after all. We sat in silence. I thought of candles, but then decided to save them for night, in case the storm lasted that long. You could never tell—the storm could rage and exhaust itself after an hour, and the sun could be shining by late morning, or it could last for days.

"Weren't you and Edouard in the army together?" said De Koning, breaking the quiet between us. "In the Tuamotus?"

"In France."

"Why did you have to go to France? Couldn't your father arrange for you to stay here?"

"And do what? Office work? Didn't Odile tell you about my glorious school days?" If an exam was important, if it really counted, I could never pass it.

"You speak pretty well."

"I've been told that."

"Why do you have so little education?" De Koning was still standing, leaning against the counter near the window, the water streaming down the glass outside. "It's so strange, the Chinese here. I mean, you had a fortune. You made so much money. But sometimes, it's like you're . . . I don't know."

"First Hakka lesson: *van-tui*," I said. "Yes, repeat out loud after me. *Van-tui*. Backcountry. Someone who lives in the *van-tui* is someone who lives far away, out there. Out on some tiny island. Out in the country. Out in the hills. Out far away. It doesn't matter how rich they get, how smart they are about making money—you can tell they come from the *van-tui*. They're not civilized at all. No matter how well they speak."

De Koning stood and opened a drawer and slipped the scissors inside. She was thinking perhaps of how long she would be stuck in the house with me.

"Monsieur Li thinks that you should go into business with your father," she said. "You don't talk much to your father, do you?"

"I'm not a child."

"That's not what I mean. What happened? Is it Cecile? They say you don't get along with her."

255

"Cecile rescued the Perles du Paradis. From the terrible edge of bank-ruptcy. And under the Rule of Cecile, it became an empire, a very successful one."

"So an empire can have only one ruler? Is that it?"

"Pretty much."

"I think you're to blame, too. You act as if everything is black or white—it isn't easy talking to you when you get like that."

"All right. I accept the blame. I am Monsieur Black and White."

"Don't you want to go back to Papeete?"

"And leave this paradise?" I stretched out my arms and the tin roof shook.

"I'm serious."

"Actually, I'm becoming accustomed to the *van-tui.* To the rats and the smell. It's—what do you call it?—spiritual. Yes, spiritual, this kind of solitude."

"You're so full of shit," said De Koning.

"Isn't that why you're here? The sorcerer's apprentice? Now I'm remembering what Mr. Lu said—Monsieur Li isn't a sorcerer. He's a shaman. That makes you the shaman's apprentice. And I'm probably still speaking incorrectly, since you've completed your apprenticeship."

"No—I'm still an apprentice."

"An apprentice, then. I don't know anything about this kind of thing."

"You don't know or you don't want to know?"

"Is there a difference?"

De Koning opened one of the drawers, looked inside, and then closed it. "I have these dreams. You're in them."

"Am I doing anything interesting?" I asked.

"You mean sex, don't you?"

"Okay. What you said."

"Monsieur Li had a teacher. This teacher died when he was studying in Paris, but Monsieur Li saw him, in a dream."

"He's still his teacher, then."

"You could say that. He's his teacher. His guide. That's how Monsieur Li knew that he wasn't an apprentice anymore, when his teacher first appeared to him in the dream. He had finished his apprenticeship. You don't pick your guide. The guide picks you."

"Well, I appear in your dreams. I'm your guide, then?"

"I'm not sure. Maybe."

"What am I doing?" I asked. "In your dreams. Am I eating, walking around?"

"Stuff like that. Nothing too interesting." She talked some more, about how Monsieur Li had waited a long time for his guide and how he gave her papers to read on this subject. "Monsieur Li says the guides are part of this reality, psychoid reality. He showed me a paper, in English because it was presented at this conference in Colorado." She continued talking and soon I wasn't really hearing her words. It was as if she was talking in a classroom, talking about things I didn't understand. What I knew about was loneliness. Being alone and wanting someone who wasn't there. Here she was, on another island far from Odile, and she was right—my father would never understand.

I reached over to some papers lying on the counter.

"What are you doing?" she said.

I found a pencil among the papers and began drawing lines, first a diagonal line from one corner to another, then a second diagonal line crossing from the next corner and then lines dividing the paper into quarters.

"What's this?" De Koning asked, watching as I drew more lines. "Oh— is this Peré Fa'anu'u? I don't really know this game."

"It's played on a board like this. It's drawn on the ground. By the Fautaua River, you can see this scratched near the water."

"It's like a sort of star pattern. How did you learn this?"

"My father taught me. He taught me Peré Fa'anu'u. He taught me Chinese chess and he taught me *jeu d'échecs.*"

"Odile says that Marie-Laure is really good at *jeu d'échecs.* The way Odile talks about it—it's like she's some kind of chess master."

"She's very good."

"Have you played her?"

"Yes. Have I won? About five or six times. She's won a hundred times."

"You know," said De Koning. "Marie-Laure isn't like the rest of your mother's family, and I've seen a lot of them. They're always visiting your mother's house. They're so beautiful. It sort of dazzles you at first, doesn't it? It's like a smooth and shiny world."

"Aren't you going to live in this smooth and shiny world? In Papeete, with Odile?"

"I don't know. It's too easy to slide off that shiny surface. And once you do, everyone just keeps going without you. It's like when you were sick. You slid off the surface. You just disappeared. Even though you were still right there."

"You forgot about gossip. What everyone knows."

"*Radio cocotier*. Yeah, I forgot—everyone turns up there. Sooner or later. It's impossible not to be found, inside the *radio cocotier*." De Koning laughed and then she turned to the window. For a moment, I didn't know why and then I realized it was completely silent. The rain had stopped.

"Do you hear it?" she said. We listened to the stillness. "Do you think the storm is over?" she asked. "Does it change that quickly?"

De Koning stood and opened the front door. A solitary chicken was walking among the wet leaves thrown around the yard. The clouds covered the sky overhead, but they were no longer black with the darkness that silenced birds like it was night. I followed De Koning and we walked outside, among the branches and twigs lying torn on the ground. We walked as if we had just awakened from a long sleep, among the steam rising from the ground in thin white curls.

We stared at nothing, blinking in the light. The way we moved, we went around in circles, in no direction at all.

"We should check the horses," I said.

De Koning bent down and picked up a broken branch. "Look at this. Where did it come from?" She stopped, turning towards the road.

A car came into view. We watched its slow approach. The car stopped by the mango tree and a man stepped out from the driver's side. The passenger door opened and Monsieur Li walked out. De Koning was already halfway across the yard, running towards him.

The driver strode up to me, shaking my hand. "I'm Teva." He was tall, around thirty years old with a black tattoo across his knuckles.

"He's Hinerava's father," said Monsieur Li.

"That was some storm," he said.

"Are you here from Bora Bora?"

"For a few days." He looked back at Monsieur Li and fell silent so quickly, I knew they hadn't driven over just to talk politely.

De Koning was holding Monsieur Li's arm, her face suddenly very pale. "What happened?" I said.

De Koning kept holding on to Monsieur Li.

"There's been an accident," he said. "In Tahiti. The storm passed there first. It's your uncle Florian."

My head spun. "Radish?"

"His brother Arthur. He was driving your uncle Florian early this morning. It was raining, but they went out in the storm. Your uncle had some business; he was meeting someone."

"Uncle Florian and Arthur."

"A car was coming too fast. Arthur must have swerved and lost control." I heard Monsieur Li speaking as if from a faraway place. "The funeral is tomorrow morning," he said. "Your father just called. He's bought you a ticket for the flight to Papeete."

"A ticket." My mind was stunned, stuck in the same place.

"The flight leaves at four this afternoon."

The funeral was tomorrow morning, the burial following immediately. It was always this way: the funeral early in the morning, before the heat of the day arrived and the smell of decay grew overwhelming. They would be there at dawn, all the Li family and all the Chen family.

"You should be there," said Monsieur Li.

PART SIX

NIGHT

Chapter 46

My father was waiting at the airport at Faaa. He and Monsieur Li shook hands and then he turned to me. I put down my suitcase to shake his hand, but my father reached over and embraced me.

Maurice, one of De Koning's cousins, had arrived to drive Monsieur Li and De Koning from the airport to Papeete. I followed my father to his car, a new white sports coupe.

"The flight didn't seem full," my father said.

"It wasn't."

My father and I knew how to talk to each other without really saying anything.

"Jonathan said he was staying here in Tahiti for a week."

"I saw Marise's cousin in Huahine."

"Which one? There's so many De Konings."

"Elodie," I said.

"Is she the crazy one? I thought she was in Raiatea."

"No, she's in Huahine."

My father drove to my mother's house, where Tiurai came to greet me at the door. One of his nephews took my suitcase and Tiurai told him that my clothes should be washed and ironed for the funeral. Tiurai sat with my father at the dining table carved of ironwood.

The sun was setting and I walked to the kitchen, the long table where Marie-Laure once sat while I talked like a fool. Did I think in those days? The same smell was there, the smell of rice and hoisin sauce and the flowers that grew outside the door.

"Marc," said a voice.

It was Radish, dressed in white. He had grown a moustache. He stood without moving by the entrance and I wasn't sure what to do. He sat down at the table and we stared at everything, the walls, the lights.

"I'm sorry," I said. "I'm sorry."

We said nothing, like we were trying to hold our breaths, something that you couldn't do for very long. Radish began to speak and then he cried, like he was gulping air and couldn't breathe.

I drove Radish to his house in the evening. Long sheets of white cloth covered the doorways. The two dark wood coffins of Uncle Florian and Arthur lay side by side in the front room. Mourners had already arrived, laying bouquets around the coffins. Radish moved silently through the room. Aunt Annette sat crying in the kitchen, her hunched form surrounded by a large gathering of women: her daughters Livia and Eleanore, Madame MuSan, Cecile, my mother and Odile, Aunt Suzette, Aunt Melody, her sisters and nieces.

A long stream of visitors arrived until the coffins seemed to float on a sea of flowers. I stood next to Radish as he received the bouquets, the tearful sobs and cries. He was a fine son, the mourners said.

His wife Natasha served endless cups of tea. She had come that afternoon from Raiatea. She had a high, smooth forehead and long fingers like her husband.

Early in the evening, a man appeared holding white roses. "This is Paul," Radish said to me. Paul looked no older than twenty, with sunflecked hair and brown eyes, a golden darkness.

"I'm the pilot," he said.

"The pilot of the boat to Tahaa?" I asked.

"Uturoa to Tahaa."

Another mourner appeared with a bouquet of orchids.

"Thank you," said Radish as she embraced him, kissing his cheek.

"How long are you staying in Papeete?" Paul asked.

"For a week," I replied. "Are you from Uturoa?"

"My mother's family is from Bora Bora. My father's from Milan, from Italy."

264

Radish's youngest brother, Percival, tapped Radish on the shoulder. "Madame Chen has arrived," he said. Radish followed him to the entrance where my grandmother walked slowly, holding my father's arm. My grandmother embraced Radish and wept, the tears streaming down her nose. Radish took her arm and called to Percival to bring a chair for Madame Chen.

My grandmother turned, examining me with her watery red eyes. She placed a hand on my arm. She wore a ring on one of her thick, square fingers, a ring of tiny seed pearls. "Marc Antoine," she said. "When did you arrive?"

"This afternoon," I said.

"Go get her some tea," my father told me.

Natasha stood by the stove in the kitchen, a black kettle on the stovetop. She picked up the kettle, pouring a small amount of hot water into a heavy blue teapot and swirling the water inside before tossing it into the sink and setting the kettle back on the stove. "Radish will take over the business," she said. "They want me to move to Papeete with him."

"Did Radish ask you to move?"

"No. He doesn't want the business here. Have you seen him? He's not really here." The kettle began whistling and she threw a pinch of tea leaves into the teapot before pouring a stream of boiling water. "Why aren't you married?"

"I don't know," I said. "Too busy, perhaps."

"Work, work, and work until it's all over," said Natasha, and she began crying. I took the teapot from her hands. "The guests need tea," she said. "Don't forget. The cups are by the sink."

Madame Chen sat next to my father and I brought them tea in porcelain cups.

"Did you bring tea to your Aunt Annette?" my father asked.

"Radish brought her tea already."

Madame Chen shook her head and cried. "Such a good son."

A group of church singers arrived, wearing white woven hats. They began to sing, slow, beautiful and mournful. Life was heavy with sadness and you didn't have to rush about it. The rooms of Uncle Florian and Aunt Annette's house were crowded with hundreds of guests, family and friends, and all fell silent as the singing began. The coffins rested on the endless flowers, pink, yellow, and purple blossoms and the white of sorrow, the fragrance so thick that the windows were thrown open and the singing drifted out into the night, into the streets where people walked towards the house, their arms filled with flowers.

Chapter 47

Radish and I sat at the kitchen table at his parents' house the following evening. I peeled an orange and Radish ate the slices without talking. He had slept for two hours the night before, sleeping in shifts with Percival so that someone was always awake by the coffins. We rose at dawn for the Mass at St. Thérèse, the funeral followed by a line of cars, pickup trucks with children in white sitting in the back, delivery trucks, and the sleek cars that seemed to come in two colors: white with black windows and black with black windows. All the Hakka community, it seemed, snaking its way up the cemetery hillside to the tomb where Uncle Florian and his son Arthur were buried under a single slab, a temporary covering until the stone of Carrara marble that Radish had ordered would arrive by boat.

Natasha slept in Radish's bed upstairs and Aunt Annette slept next to her daughter Livia since she could not bear to sleep alone. Radish was grey with fatigue.

"Go and sleep," I said to Radish, but we sat silently. I picked up another orange and began peeling it. The house was still, the front room empty. The flowers had all been transported to the cemetery where they covered the tomb. The usual routine of work was suspended and time seemed to float, an uneasy and strange buoyancy.

A door opened and closed. I heard my father's voice speaking to someone. "Ten-kwok?" I asked and then, in answer, Ten-kwok entered carrying a suitcase into the kitchen. Radish stood up and Ten-kwok embraced him fiercely.

"Marie-Laure," I said, turning to the door. Marie-Laure stood in the doorway.

Radish went to her and she took his hands. Marie-Laure had grown very thin and her face had lost its puffiness. She had cut her hair short, above her ears, and she wore a pale grey dress. "You must rest," she said to Radish. "Did he sleep at all?"

"An hour, maybe two," I said.

"So why aren't you asleep?" Marie-Laure took Radish's arm.

"When did you leave Sydney?" he asked.

"As soon as we heard." She waved her hand at Ten-kwok and my father so that they opened the door leading from the kitchen. Radish took a few steps, then he stopped and turned to Marie-Laure as if he had forgotten where to go. "Yes," said Marie-Laure. "You must sleep." Ten-kwok took him by the arm and Radish left, the door closing behind them.

"Where are you staying?" I asked Marie-Laure.

"At your mother's. My father is staying here."

I stood without approaching, as if Marie-Laure would vanish if I stepped too close.

"You can drive me to your mother's house," she said. "Go ask your father for his keys."

It felt unfamiliar, driving my father's car, gliding through the streets. No bending over Fetia's hooves, smelling of dirt and shit, to pry loose the stones stuck around the horseshoes, before easing the bit into his slobbering mouth so I could ride him to the Chinese store.

"I heard that you're living in Huahine now," said Marie-Laure.

"Yes."

"Do you like it there?"

I nodded, not knowing what to say. "Do you want dinner? It's a long flight from Sydney."

"I ate on the plane. Lunch or dinner—I'm not sure what it was."

"How's Aunt Georgine?"

"She decided to stay there. I'm here for only a week."

I stopped at a light and turned to Marie-Laure. She had aged, not so much the age of years but of pain, the sort that seems unending and without time. A pale tautness pulled at her skin and white scars marked the back of her hands, the traces of hospital needles and tubes.

268

"Does it hurt?" It seemed that I was always asking her this question.

"Not now. I'm all right. I'm worried about Radish."

I turned the corner and drove up the street to my mother's house. I parked by the hedge of hibiscus, turning off the engine.

Tiurai stood at the entrance door with Odile, dressed in a sleeveless white shirt and tight white cropped pants.

"Wow—look at you!" said Marie-Laure, and Odile ran to embrace her.

I carried Marie-Laure's suitcase through the main house, to the back and up the stairs to her room under the mango tree.

"They told me you were really sick," said Marie-Laure.

"A fever. Nothing really bad."

"I didn't know."

"You were in the hospital. I wasn't sick for long."

"Odile told me. She said the fever ran for days, over a week. You probably don't want that room again, where you were sick. Why don't you sleep in the main house? Your mother and Odile are there."

"Where do you want your suitcase?" I asked.

"Here, by the door. You look as bad as Radish," said Marie-Laure. "Go to the main house and sleep."

I walked into the hallway and opened the door to the closest room. The room was the same as when I was sick there, a room with dust and ground-up shavings, left by the bugs that ate the wood in the walls. I lay down on the bed and listened to the water flowing through the pipes. It looked like no one had entered the room since I left.

Go to the main house, Marie-Laure had said. The bathrooms there smelled of milk soap and the maids swept all the corners clean early in the morning.

I stared at the paint peeling above on the ceiling. The room smelled dusty, as if no one had ever lived there. I had never seen the hermit in Huahine, the one who lived at the end of the road, but I imagined that his place smelled the same way, the smell of forgetting and being forgotten. I didn't like this, but here I was, in this room again. A brown, soft-bellied spider hung from a corner of the ceiling. A good luck spider, A-tai always said, but I didn't feel particularly lucky. I listened to the water gurgling again in the pipes and I slept.

At dawn, all the roosters crowed over and over. The roosters crowed under the mango tree and the roosters crowed under the skinny seurette trees by the path that led to the sea.

Marie-Laure arose around six, opening the door to her room and walking out on the terrace. I sat by the table under the mango tree.

"How long have you been sitting here?" she asked.

She opened a paper bag on the table. "*Pain coco.* You got this at the store across the Protestant church?" She tapped the coconut bread. I had brought up a thermos of tea, plates, and a knife from the main kitchen. Marie-Laure cut the bread and handed me three slices on a plate.

"I'll go inside," she said after breakfast. The floor in her room had new tiles, a beige pebble pattern. "Neutral tones" was the description I heard from Odile. Marie-Laure lay down on her side; the mosquito netting was knotted above the bed. "Leave it," she said as I loosened the netting.

"Mosquitoes. They come out after the rains. You shouldn't get a fever."

"My father will go to the cemetery this morning," said Marie-Laure, closing her eyes. "He shouldn't go alone." Her voice grew thin and quiet, its early morning brightness falling away. "He was crying, even on the plane. It's hard to lose your brother—it's worse to lose your youngest brother. You should drive him."

I drove Ten-kwok to the graves of Uncle Florian and Arthur. Ten-kwok burst out in lamentation, sobbing when he saw the carpet of flowers, now fading over the tombs. "*Lao-ti, Lao-ti!*" he cried. Younger brother, younger brother.

Monsieur Li appeared, carrying a broom to sweep away the fallen flowers and leaves. He took Ten-kwok by the hand, sitting down on a low cement wall that bordered another tomb. "Why? Why?" Ten-kwok was saying. Three horses walked between the graves, stopping to graze among the grass that sprouted along the tombs. They ambled past, disappearing further down the hill.

Monsieur Li talked about the shipment of marble. Ten-kwok blew his nose as Monsieur Li pointed to a row of tombs beneath the frangipani trees growing at the end of the cemetery.

"Similar to that color," Monsieur Li said. "A translucent white."

"They're shipping this from Italy?" said Ten-kwok.

I walked down the hillside to where A-tai was buried. The urn of sand holding joss sticks had tipped, spilling sand and incense. I picked up the urn, moving it to a corner of the tomb, and I looked around the eaves of a nearby tomb where a broom was usually kept under the roof, but no broom was there. Along the pathways were the infants beneath their tiny tombs and the bouquets of tiny plastic flowers. The first Hakka, those who had arrived at the time of the Atimaono plantation, lay beneath thick layers of grass and stones with the writing worn down by time. From A-tai's grave, I looked at the jumble of rooftops, the graves crowded together. If you didn't know the story of those buried there, maybe this is how the cemetery would appear: a confusion of tombs packed together on the hillside looking over the sea, the wide horizon to the west.

Ten-kwok wanted to buy a newspaper on the way back from the cemetery. "Pull over here," he said. He waved his hand at a corner store owned by a Chinese named Chiang. "Park there." He pointed at a chicken-wire fence next to the store.

I parked the car and opened the door, stepping out.

"Where are you going?"

"To buy you a paper," I said.

Ten-kwok wrinkled his face as if he just ate something too sour. "You don't know which paper I want."

"Tell me, then." On the entire island, there were only three newspapers.

"How do I know what they have here?" He opened the car door.

We walked up the concrete step at the entrance of the store. At the counter sat Chiang, a visor advertising American beer pulled over his head. He nodded, smiling as we entered.

"Chiang! Chiang!" said Ten-kwok, shaking his hand.

"So terrible," he replied, standing up from his seat. "Your brother Florian—such a good man."

"A good man," Ten-kwok agreed.

One of Chiang's brothers emerged from behind the counter. He wore dusty shorts and a toothpick jutted from the side of his mouth. "Ten-kwok," he said.

"Get me a paper. A morning newspaper."

Chiang picked up each of the three morning papers. "Take them."

Ten-kwok reached into his pocket but Chiang walked around the cash register and took his elbow. "No, no. No money."

"You can't give this away," said Ten-kwok.

Chiang put the newspapers in his hand. "No money today. Please."

"It's all bad news anyway," said his brother.

"What do you mean?" Ten-kwok said.

"Business going downhill. Ever since the nuclear ban."

"Terrible, terrible," Chiang agreed.

"That's nonsense," Ten-kwok said. "Nonsense."

"It's bad for business."

"I don't care," Ten-kwok shouted.

The two men looked as if they had swallowed something too quickly.

"The testing. It was all wrong," Ten-kwok shouted, more loudly.

The store fell quiet and even the shelves of boxes and jars seemed to hold completely still.

"I know what you'll say," Ten-kwok said. "You'll say 'How do we know? Maybe it isn't so bad.'" He shook his head and his hands closed into fists. "This is how the worst things start. When you can't point to something, when you can't say 'This is bad.' You can't prove it, but there's something wrong, something terrible. Look at my daughter. Look at my daughter! Marie-Laure." Ten-kwok's voice faltered for a moment. He held out his hands and his arms swept close to the laundry detergent, almost sweeping the boxes from the shelves. "Tell me. Why is she so sick? You tell me! Yes, tell me why. You can't say 'It's this man. Or him—he's the one who did it.' But that doesn't mean that something didn't go wrong. It's wrong! It's wrong! All of it is wrong. It should never happen." He began to cry.

I approached Ten-kwok, taking him by the arm.

"Marie-Laure!" he cried.

"I'll get you some tea," said Chiang.

272

Ten-kwok shook his head. He stopped for a moment at the doorway, as if he were going to say something else, but then shook his head again and left the store.

I drove away, turning the corner where a number of men sat talking and reading the newspaper under a *purau* tree. Ten-kwok sat, looking out the window.

"I know what they're saying," he said. "Back in that store. They're saying 'Ten-kwok is crazy'—that's what they're saying." He made a rumbling noise inside his throat as if he were going to spit. "What do you think they're saying? You tell me."

I didn't have to say anything. I knew Ten-kwok would just keep talking.

"I'll tell you what they're saying about me. They're saying 'Ten-kwok, he was a smart man. Made a lot of money.' Well, they're right about that. A lot of money. You know what they'll say? They'll say 'It's too bad he's so crazy.' And then they'll talk about whether it's better to go to Australia or New Zealand or Canada. They're all talking like this. We're going to leave! No more business here! Every day they say this. Some of them are going to leave. And some of them are going to say this every day until they turn into old men and die right here. You know what? I'm telling you this. Your name—it's out of fashion. Out of fashion! Nobody's going to name their son Marc Antoine or Napoleon—they're all naming them English names. American names. Tahitian names. You're out of fashion. I'd change my name if I were you. You think about it. You heard it from me first."

"So what should I name myself?" I asked.

"I don't know. Anything but the name you have now."

"Another name? Maybe I better stay with Marc Antoine."

"No! It's a bad name."

"Well, that's even better. A bad name."

"Well then," said Ten-kwok, folding his arms and staring ahead. "Don't say I didn't warn you. You keep your name—you're even crazier than I am."

Chapter 48

The household slept in the day, collapsed under the heaviness of sadness and weeping. I walked up the back stairs and opened the door of the room where I had slept. A new *pareu* covered the bed, and then I woke suddenly and it was night. I had fallen asleep on the *pareu* and slept through the afternoon without knowing. I opened the door to find the outside hallway dark. From the main house, there was usually the chatter of people talking or a radio or a television or the sounds of cooking from the kitchen— the sizzle of oil, the stirring of iron pans—but only a thick stillness covered the buildings. By the stairs, cats slept undisturbed, no one passing on the wooden steps. It seemed that everyone slept, the daily schedule erased by grief.

I walked out to the back terrace under the old mango tree where the lights glowed through the narrow windows of Marie-Laure's room. I knocked and Marie-Laure opened the door. She slipped back inside the netting, holding one end open over the bed. "Sit here," she said. I moved uncertainly inside the shelter and Marie-Laure let the netting fall shut over us.

"Did you put the *pareu* in my room?" I asked.

"It's dusty there. At least you can sleep on a clean *pareu*."

I took out the pins that fastened the netting to the wall and moved them higher, forming a larger tent so I could sit more easily inside. The leaves of the mango tree rustled against the windows.

"You're here for a week?" I asked.

"The doctors say that I shouldn't stay away too long. Are you returning to Huahine?"

"Yes. I'm not sure."

"Yes, no—you always talk like this." She reached out her hand, touching the chain around my neck. "Did A-tai give you this?"

"A man living in Papara."

"Was he working in the *mairie?*"

"No, his family farms the land there. Towards the mountains."

"You're working in Huahine?"

"I have some chickens and I'm working for a stable, riding a horse. His owner doesn't live in Huahine."

It sounded terrible, what I did. Why did I tell this to Marie-Laure? I thought it was better not to speak anymore, but Marie-Laure nodded, as if I had just said something interesting.

"What's his name?" she asked. I didn't answer, but she repeated, "What's his name?"

"The owner?"

"No, the horse. What's the horse's name?" she said.

"Fetia."

"The Star."

"It's a common name. He has a star here." I touched the space between my eyebrows and felt the stickiness of my skin. It was evening, the time to shower.

"Where are you going?"

I parted the opening of the mosquito netting and stepped outside. "I'm going to shower."

"Why don't you shower here?" Marie-Laure pointed to the bath next to her room. "I'm not going to look. Okay, if you want, you can use the shower downstairs or in the main house."

I thought of Monsieur Li saying that I looked almost like a skeleton. "I'll shower next door," I said. "I'm not that clean though."

"Oh yeah. Not that clean."

I turned to leave.

"Wait." Marie-Laure stepped out of the bed, lifting a cloth over one of the shelves and handing me a towel.

I walked out on the terrace after the shower, looking at the lights in the main house. More lights glowed from the buildings towards the sea, but the back building where Marie-Laure was staying was dark, except for the light in her room. In the household of my mother and Tiurai, it seemed that everyone had moved to the main house or the buildings closer to the water where a breeze flowed in from the sea. The building under the old mango tree seemed abandoned, a deserted middle ground. The plants growing in the pots along the edge of the terrace had either died or flourished from neglect, some of the pots holding only crumbled sticks and others overflowing with ferns and vines.

Marie-Laure was lying beneath the mosquito netting when I entered her room again. "You shouldn't sleep there, in that other room." She looked through the white filament between us, her hands folded on her stomach.

"Why not?"

We were alone, but she still lowered her voice. "Stay here," she said. "Stay here with me."

Chapter 49

Marie-Laure ate breakfast the next morning in the kitchen by the main house. She chewed on a plain Arnott's cracker and drank tea diluted with hot water. I looked through the plate of star fruit and mangoes in the center of the table.

"*Vī atoni, vī carotte*—do you want this one?"

Marie-Laure placed the half-eaten Arnott's cracker down on her plate. I picked up one of the glasses in the cupboard and poured tea into the glass. I drank, watching Marie-Laure.

"You're not well."

"I'm fine."

"Then tell me why the doctors want you back in Sydney in a week."

"They always run tests."

"So tell me one of these things that they're testing."

"Different things." Marie-Laure leaned over and kissed me quickly on the mouth.

"What are they looking for, with these tests?" I asked.

"They think I may need a transplant."

"What? When?"

"Calm down. This sort of transplant is routine."

"No transplant is routine," I said.

"It's why my mom is staying there," said Marie-Laure, opening the refrigerator and taking out a bottle of mineral water. "She says she'll give me a kidney. I need only one."

"One kidney."

"Can you go to the Vaima for me?"

"The Vaima River?" Why were we talking about the Vaima? "No, I want to talk about this transplant."

Marie-Laure poured the mineral water into a glass. "There's nothing to talk about. Why don't you go to the Vaima and bring me back a bottle of the water? To take back to Sydney." I stood without moving. "A small bottle," she said.

I drove to the Vaima in Mataiea and filled three large bottles with water. It was always wetter in Mataiea than in Papeete. The day was clear, but grey clouds towered over the mountains and the air smelled of rain. There were legends about the water of the Vaima, the water flowing from its springs, a cold clear water. I didn't know these stories well—something about women swimming in the Vaima or maybe it was pregnant women who were supposed to swim there or the other way around, women who wanted to get pregnant. I didn't trust these stories, whatever they said. Marie-Laure was alive but she wasn't well. Maybe I should have bargained with Mr. Lu. I should have been like those lawyers studying a contract, reading every single word over and over before signing. I had forgotten to demand Marie-Laure's complete recovery. I was too young or I didn't have enough experience with magic or maybe I was hoping for something that wasn't possible, no matter what anyone did. They all looked the same to me: Mr. Lu, the doctors in Tahiti, the doctors in Sydney. Marie-Laure was sick with something that wasn't common enough to be predictable and they were all making wild guesses, shooting in the dark.

I drove from the Vaima River, returning to Papeete, passing through Mataiea. I noticed the familiar landmarks: a Chinese store, that *aito* tree by the road, this property with the endless, well-trimmed hedge, the places I had passed every day, driving to and from the land I had thought that I owned when, in legal reality, I hadn't owned it at all—and then I was passing the land itself, my land, the land I never had.

Driving to the Vaima, I was thinking only about filling the bottles with the water for Marie-Laure, but now I found myself slowing, turning my head to look. The gate, the entrance to the property, was just past a row of coconut trees, beautifully aligned. I had always admired this, congratulating myself on being only twenty-five and having such a property.

Nothing had changed. There were the little things—the way the hedge thinned at one spot, a coconut tree leaning slightly more than the others. It was all the same. I caught a glimpse of the house as I passed by the gate and even that was just as I had known it, so much so that I found myself making a U-turn since there was little traffic in the mid-morning. I pulled up to the gate and stopped.

Aurore had never believed in keeping many dogs, even though all our neighbors had several dogs. A property without many watchdogs was a more likely target for theft, but Aurore said that Georges, her one dog, was enough. If they wanted to take her things, that was fine. She said that they could take her books and her paintings but, whether she liked it or not, I kept her jewelry locked and hidden in places that only the two of us knew. I walked up to the gate, expecting to hear the barking of the new owner's dogs, but there was nothing. I opened the gate on impulse and, returning to the car, I drove inside, uncertain of what I should say if anyone appeared—driven only by the desire to see the house again, if only from the outside.

I drove past the coconut trees towards the house. There was the wide veranda and the stairs and I imagined the view from the front room— the garden and the beach just beyond—and then I saw Aurore's car, parked to the side.

I pulled up the car in front of the house and Georges ran out, barking and growling at first, but then whining and wagging her tail. Doves cooed, the repetition of the same call. Why were Aurore's car and dog here? I felt my mind growing cold. I walked up the stairs, Georges racing ahead. I knocked and the door opened.

"Hello, Marc," said Aurore. The dark wave of her hair was swept back and her eyes were intensely green.

I stood in front of the door.

"Why don't you come in?"

I followed Aurore inside to find that the front room was nearly empty. The paintings had been removed from the walls.

"Something to drink?"

"No, thank you," I said, and I heard my voice as if someone else were speaking, a low, angry voice.

"I heard about your uncle and your cousin," said Aurore. "I'm very, very sorry. You must be here for the funeral."

"The funeral was two days ago."

"I'm sorry."

I stepped across the room, glancing at the kitchen through the open door. It too was nearly empty. I wondered if Aurore was moving out or moving in. "Maître Leclerc's trial is in France," I said.

Aurore shook her head. "Marc, what can I say? I'm sorry. I wish you had told me."

"Told you about what?"

"You could have told me about this land."

"And what difference would it have made? You weren't paying any rent before and you weren't paying anything after."

Aurore took a deep breath, holding out her hands slightly as if to stop something from approaching too quickly. I walked around the front room and looked up at the empty walls.

"Did the exhibit go well?" I asked.

She nodded her head. "I sold quite a few paintings. I was surprised."

There was no sign that anyone else was living at the house with Aurore, but I knew that appearances were untrustworthy. "Why should you be surprised?" I said. "You're a wonderful painter."

"How long are you in Tahiti?" she asked.

"I'm not sure yet."

Aurore placed one hand on her head, touching her fingers tentatively to her forehead. "I'm here for only a few months longer. And I was so hoping to see you. I called Philippe when I returned and he told me that you were in Huahine. From what I gathered, things had gone badly for you, although Philippe said that you agreed to a settlement and that you paid a very steep fine." She looked up at me. "Philippe said that you're very good with horses, that you found work at the stables there. You always told me that you hated those riding lessons at the Hippodrome." She took a breath, falling quiet for a moment. "I'm sorry that I left the way I did. I thought it was for the best."

The silence rose, thick and empty, between us.

"Where are you living?" I asked finally.

"I'm staying for a while with a friend in New York. Most of my books are there."

"I damaged some of your books. I meant to come back, to repair them. And your chess set." I had always intended to tell Aurore that I was sorry, to make things right. I had played the words so many times in my mind, but now they slipped away unspoken. "I don't know if Philippe told you I was ill."

Aurore stared at the wall behind me. "No—Philippe didn't tell me." She looked down at her hands.

I took one of the chairs, looking out into the garden. "Why did you leave?"

"I had the exhibit in New York. I told you about it—I did. You don't remember? I had to prepare for the exhibit. As it turned out, it was more successful than I imagined. Many of the paintings sold—can you imagine? Remember the one of Vetea? How I love that painting. The ones of the *moripata*. The *fe'i* series—the entire series." She talked on, about her paintings and how they had sold, so many of her paintings, and then her voice fell suddenly and she stopped speaking.

"Go on," I said.

"You're angry."

"No, on the contrary. I'm happy for you."

She sighed, resting her hand against her forehead. "I dreamed about seeing you again. I waited for this moment."

"Then why didn't you call? I still have the same *vini* number. You seemed to have known that number well enough before."

"It wasn't right."

"Then you didn't want to see me. So don't tell me any more fucking lies."

"I'm not lying."

"Let's start with this land, for one. Didn't I tell you that you didn't have to pay rent anymore? I remember this conversation. It was after dinner and we were here, in this room, pretty much the same way that we are now."

Aurore stood facing the window, her head turned away from me.

"So, at that time, you could have said 'You know, Marc, I've never paid any rent because I'm a *notaire* and I know that the title to this land is such a fucking mess that they've been fighting over it for years. In fact, that's why I'm living here. If anyone bothers to ask for the rent, I just call up any of the many, many people who think they own this and I just watch them fight among themselves. The benefits of my fine legal education.'"

"It wasn't like that," said Aurore. "It wasn't that simple. And I didn't know about you and Maître Leclerc. You didn't tell me that Maître Leclerc was involved. You just said that I didn't have to pay rent anymore—you never told me why. And you never tell me anything. You never explain anything, even if I ask and ask. So by then, I was used to you never explaining anything. So why should I ask you any questions? Did you ever answer anything that I asked?"

"And I suppose that you always told me everything, that the truth always came straight out of your mouth."

"Marc, you brought in a python. You had all these snakes and god knows what else, things I never knew about. I couldn't keep living off the profits of whatever you did."

"Did Philippe tell you?"

"Yes. Yes, he told me. He told me that you were importing—how did he put it?—illegal reptiles. And then you tore apart my room when you returned from your meeting with Philippe. You destroyed my books. I came home that night and saw what you did with my books. You were out of control. I had to leave. What choice did I have?"

I stood up and walked to the kitchen, through the doors to the veranda and the back garden. I heard the door opening and closing behind me.

"Marc," said Aurore.

The waves of the ocean fell in the distance, the familiar sound, the waves rushing along the sand beyond the garden.

"I'm tired," she said. "I don't want to argue anymore. The way things turned out, it's better this way."

"Do you really believe that?"

"You know, Philippe—"

"Fuck him. I don't want to hear about him."

"Listen, listen to me. I'm going to tell you what I should have told you. I should have told you, long ago."

I looked ahead without speaking.

"That first night," said Aurore. "At the party. I met you there on the beach. You know, I saw you before, just for a moment and I couldn't

282

forget you. It wasn't just how you looked. It was strange, it was like I had seen you somewhere, long ago." She stopped for a moment, a dark light in her eyes. "Love at first sight. It wasn't until I met you that I knew what it was. And then you were there. You were walking next to me on the beach. I went crazy inside. I knew that I couldn't ever let you go. You said you'd get me something to drink, champagne. You left the room and I watched you, walking across the garden at night. I couldn't stop watching you. I followed you outside—and there was Philippe. He was waiting for me. Leave him alone, he said.

"I was afraid that you'd return and hear me talking to Philippe so I let him lead me to his car. He drove to the lighthouse at the end of the beach. Philippe talked the whole time, about how he knew your father and how he knew your mother and her cold, cold heart. He told me to leave you alone.

"I told him that I wasn't a child that he could lecture. I told him that I was returning to my party, that I had my guests and I couldn't just leave like that. In the end, Philippe drove me back to the house and that's when I saw you leaving. I couldn't bear it. That's why I asked you to return. I asked you to promise me that you'd return. And you did. You kept your promise. But Philippe was right. I should have let you go. And later, when you came back from the army—I should have left you alone then. But I couldn't. I couldn't.

"I saw you, at that Chinese store near Tautira. You were with your cousin Radish. Poor Radish. You were both so young. People don't understand this. They criticize you for making your fortune from *paka* and then reinvesting it in land. But that was smart of you. They say these things because they're jealous. You were so young and you already had so much money. But they don't see what really went wrong.

"It poisoned you. Our life together. It wasn't real. It was this dream world. Because I couldn't let you go. We were always something hidden. Secret. And that's when it all went wrong. All that secrecy. It twisted you. You asked to go out. You didn't care if we were seen together. But I was afraid. I was so afraid of losing you. Of what people would say—asking why you were with this woman who was older than your own mother. People are cruel. But what I did to you was worse."

"You didn't do anything to me," I said. "I can think for myself. I chose the life I wanted."

"It's what you thought you wanted. Don't you see? You were never treated like—it was always hidden. And if people knew about it, they knew it as something secret. Something no one would talk about." She turned her head, towards the house. "I've returned to get my things. Philippe made the arrangements."

"And how did he manage to arrange for this, with Leclerc on trial in France and the title to this land still in dispute?"

Aurore walked back inside. I stood looking out into the garden for a moment, the neatly trimmed hedges. It would take only a week and the garden would turn wild.

"Who's taking care of this land?" I asked suddenly, following Aurore inside. "I left months ago—but it looks like no one ever left."

"You spoke the truth," she said, turning to me. "When you said that the title was a mess. Fought over for years. The benefits of fine legal machinations. You should stay away."

"Who's been living here?"

"You still have your whole life ahead of you. You said it yourself—all this time, I never called you. And you made your own life without me."

I walked through the house, through the empty front room, and I opened the door to the bedroom. The armoire was still there and the bookshelves. The shelves were full, the books returned and arranged behind glass, just as before. I opened the armoire. It was filled with her clothes.

Aurore stood outside in the hallway. I walked over to her and she took a step back, away from me.

"You're lying," I shouted. "You're not moving out. You're living here just as you did before. Who arranged for this—Philippe MuSan? He's put you here, hasn't he?"

"Why did I return from New York?" she asked. "I could have stayed there. But I didn't. I came back for you. I came back to look for you. I couldn't imagine my life without you. But I didn't know how to look. Who would I ask? I knew that your family would never tell me anything. So polite, but it's a wall. You know this. You know I'm telling you the truth."

My thoughts turned dark. "You're lying. You're fucking lying. Why didn't you call me? And MuSan—he knew where I was. You talk one way and then you talk another. You say that your books are in New York—but they're all here. Like nothing ever happened. You're lying and I don't want to hear any more of your goddamn fucking lies. It's both of you, MuSan and you."

I saw the house so clearly as I walked out through the rooms: the high thatched ceiling, the smooth polished wood. Everything clear, the truth sharp and hard: it was a game. A secret, complicated game. I had thought that I was part of the game, but it turned out that I had never understood anything about how it was really played. I stood for a moment in the doorway. One of Aurore's paintings leaned against the wall, a landscape, a painting of the valley in Papara.

"Do you remember Vetea Tchong?" asked Aurore.

Go to hell, I wanted to say.

"He died," said Aurore. "About a year ago."

"This painting. It isn't what you painted when we visited him."

"This is recent. I painted this when I arrived a few months ago. It's for his family."

"Where is he buried?" I said.

"On his land. His parents are buried there, and one of his daughters."

In the garden outside, the doves fell silent.

"Marc," said Aurore. "Marc, please. Will you sit for me?"

She was crazy—how could she talk like this? "What are you talking about?"

She stood beside me in the doorway, half in shadow. "Please. I know that you don't believe me, but I'm leaving Tahiti. I'm telling you the truth. I'm leaving soon. All right—I'll tell you the truth. I made an arrangement with Philippe MuSan, a temporary one so that I could stay here for a year, but my year is almost over and then I'll be gone. It's the truth. I'm telling you the truth."

I could make a good guess about Aurore's arrangement—that she had made this arrangement with MuSan so that she could stay while the legal proceedings over the land dragged on, far away in France.

"A sketch—it'll take just an hour. Please."

"Why should I sit for you? Give me a reason why I should ever sit for you." I started shouting.

"There's no reason. I'm asking you. Please, Marc. Please. Just one sketch. Just one."

"Why don't you ask MuSan? Ask him."

I drove away without looking back. I opened the gate and turned on to the road without shutting the gate behind me. It was not until I reached the border of Mataiea, entering the district of Papara, that I pulled over, stopping by the side of the road. I slammed my fist again and again on the dashboard.

It disgusted and enraged me. Her words, everything Aurore had told me, lies and lies and the truth tangled together. What was true? It was so twisted, layers and layers of words that might mean this or that or nothing at all, just whatever she needed to say to survive an endless game without any rules.

When I returned, Marie-Laure was resting downstairs in the main house. She lay on the sofa covered with a large green and white *tifaifai*. An anti-mosquito coil burned, the smoke drifting across the sofa.

"I'm not asleep," said Marie-Laure.

I put the bottles of river water down next to the sofa.

Marie-Laure rose, sitting up and picking up a bottle, stopping when she saw my face. "Are you all right? Did something happen?" She placed the bottle back on the floor.

I sat down without speaking.

"What happened?" She reached out and touched my face. "You saw someone."

"It doesn't matter."

"Who did you see?"

I looked around at the empty chairs of the parlor.

Marie-Laure returned to the sofa, lying back down on the *tifaifai*. "Jonathan and Madame MuSan were here. Talking with Radish about how long mourning should last."

"Radish told me he was closing business for a month." The rules were strict and a period of mourning could last for weeks.

"Madame MuSan said it was unrealistic. His father wouldn't have wanted that. She says times are different."

"Everyone says that now. Times are different," I said.

Marie-Laure opened her eyes to glance at me. "They talked about it for a long time. They decided to shut everything for at least a week—that's

286

what Radish wanted. After that, Madame MuSan said he could continue, like talking to his overseas contacts. They talked about it for a while and then Radish got up and left." Marie-Laure looked over at me again. "Are you all right? I'm going out later with Odile and De Koning to pick up some food. Madame MuSan said that it didn't make sense for everyone to stay locked up during mourning."

Modern Mourning, I thought. "Modern rules."

"That's strange—that's what Madame MuSan said. You don't want to go with us? You're going to brood around here?"

The next evening, I was sitting outside on the terrace when Marie-Laure appeared, walking up the stairs.

"What are you looking at?" she said.

"It's a drawing for the tomb. Monsieur Li asked me to look at it."

"Is this a pavilion?" Somewhere on the road in front of the house, some-one was racing an engine. "What a noise," said Marie-Laure, sitting on a plastic chair.

"I have some water here." I pointed to two bottles on the table.

"You went to the store?"

"Odile asked me to go with her."

Marie-Laure reached for one of the bottles. "I was just in the main house, talking to Odile. She didn't tell me."

"Why should she tell you? Going to the store with her big brother? Nothing worth mentioning."

"You're still in that mood."

What mood? I wanted to say.

"Do you have enough light to see here?"

"I'm fine." Here in the dark, yes, I was fine.

"You know," said Marie-Laure, "at first, at the beginning when I got ill, I was really angry."

"You had good reason to be angry."

She opened the bottle. "Some water?"

"It's yours," I said.

"At the beginning—it was the beginning of my being sick, so I still had enough energy. I got really, really mad. Why me? It wasn't fair." She

287

took a drink of water. "But then it started. The pills. The drugs. Pulses, that's what they're called. The medicine goes into the veins, the dose a thousand times higher than any pill. When it goes in, it's like your brain starts melting. You can't think. You start screaming. Not because it hurts, but so that you can hear yourself screaming and you know you're still there."

"You want more water?" I picked up the bottle, not really knowing what to say.

"After a while, you start seeing things differently. Things change. Maybe it's the drugs. They do something to your brain. The things that used to bother you, they don't bother you anymore. So tell me. Because I know that you had to drive past Mataiea to go to the Vaima. People talk." She took another drink of water. "*Radio cocotier.* That's where you lived before, in Mataiea. You saw the Marquise, didn't you?"

"I saw her," I said. "But she doesn't mean anything to me."

Marie-Laure shook her head. "Life passes like a dream. Look at Uncle Florian and Arthur. While they were here, it's like I never really saw them. Then they were gone."

The night had fallen and the sky began filling with stars.

"Love," said Marie-Laure. "The real thing, it's rare."

"It wasn't real, whatever happened with the Marquise."

"I've seen her paintings. In one of the galleries in Papeete. They had an exhibit several years ago. I saw the exhibit twice when I came back for Radish's wedding. I went back, to see those paintings again. The people she drew. And simple things, like mangoes. The things we look at every day, we don't notice them. We say that's real life. But usually it's just a blur. And then you see something like those paintings and when you look at them, it's like stepping into a light and your eyes open and you see. You see and it's real."

Marie-Laure went to bed early, sleeping in her room under the mango tree. I stayed on the terrace. I lit an anti-mosquito coil and watched the night over the mountains above Papeete.

I thought of Vetea Tchong and the land of his family, the rambutan tree that grew there, in the valley of Papara.

Aurore said that a woman had bought his painting, an American woman. The woman had returned for several days during the exhibit to gaze at the painting of Vetea Tchong. I had seen this painting so many times. At different times of the day, at night. It had its own life. There, in the painting, was the land itself. The colors and the light—the shadows so dark that they held a kind of sadness, and the brilliant sky, the deep, deep green, and the colors of the ground, brown and golden and red.

I went to Marie-Laure's room and I lay next to her within the mosquito netting. She breathed slowly and the sound of her breath was one of those things that quieted you, like the sound of a very soft rain. A voice from another house called out, shouting something like a name. A rooster started crowing, startled in its sleep by the noise, and this awoke other roosters so that they crowed in response, even though it was the beginning of the night. I put my hand on Marie-Laure's hair and I breathed in her smell, a mix of sweat and something that was the faint residue of something I couldn't identify, soap or medicine, death and life.

I walked where the sand was wet, along an unfamiliar beach and, for a moment, I knew it was only a dream and that somewhere I slept in reality, but then I saw something in the distance. It waited and I walked. He was real, a horse by the water and sand. *Fetia, the stars,* said Marie-Laure, and I awoke in the night, still hearing her voice in the dream.

Chapter 50

I went to the cemetery the next morning to clean the graves of Uncle Florian and Arthur. A few days after the funeral—not even a week—every flower had wilted in the heat and even the most lavish and expensive bouquets were a mass of crumbled trash. Aunt Annette ran a fever and Radish called a doctor for his mother and stayed at her bedside to assure her that Masses were being said for the souls of Uncle Florian and Arthur, that a novena would start that very day, that the most beautiful marble was on its way from Italy, that all the proper offerings would be made at the temple and that a medium would be called, the very best from Hong Kong.

A temporary wooden structure had been raised over the double tomb, a wooden cross over a rectangular fence marking the boundary of the graves. I arrived with Radish's youngest brother, Percival, and we started hauling away the remains of the hundred bouquets crowded around the graves, throwing the leaves and petals into the garbage pile by the mango trees where the road began. It was early in the morning and the cemetery was quiet, with only the barking of a dog from one of the houses further uphill.

Someone walked up the gravel path from the parking by the mango trees—Philippe MuSan, holding two bouquets of roses. He walked to the head of the graves, placing the bouquets down before the wooden cross.

"You might as well take those flowers with you," I said. "They'll wilt before you walk back to your car. A lavish mess."

"Marc," said MuSan. "I've heard that you're very good at taking care of hens in Huahine."

"Honest work. Something that you're not particularly familiar with."

"I'm not here to argue with you," said MuSan. "I came to pay my respects to Florian and Arthur."

"You weren't at the funeral."

"I was in Paris." MuSan walked around the edge of the wooden structure surrounding the tombs. Percival had finished sweeping and he turned to me, waiting.

"We're finished here," I said.

"A good man, your uncle Florian. A tragedy," said MuSan. "And Arthur. So young." He turned to Percival. "I have something to discuss with Marc."

"I have no business with you," I said.

"Let's not argue. Out of respect for your uncle."

"Wait for me in the car." I handed the keys to Percival and watched him walking down the slope to the car, parked at the edge of the row of tombs.

"I'm not your enemy," said MuSan. "I've told you this before. Things are changing."

People talked about how politics would change now that nuclear testing had ended, and they talked about how politics would remain the same, nothing really changing.

"I've heard good things about you," he said. "My wife is a cousin of Ursula. She says that you're good at handling horses. Fetia—I believe that's what they call him."

"I don't have time to talk," I said. "Maybe another time."

"You're upset about the Marquise du Chatelet."

I looked up at the clouds rolling across the sky, covering the mountains. The wind stirred through the grass among the tombs.

"You don't know everything," he said.

"I've been punished. I accept that. I did something wrong."

"You're angry because you think that you've been punished for the snakes, while others go unpunished for much larger crimes. You're angry because you think you've been treated unfairly."

"Fairness doesn't exist in La Polynésie Française."

"Things would be different in a better world."

"I don't waste my time dreaming about what doesn't exist," I said.

"You know that Aurore hated the CEP. She hated everything it stood for. The defense of France. Nuclear testing. She hated it. You're upset because I arranged for Aurore to stay on the land at Mataiea. It hurts your pride because she stayed there after she returned from New York. Even though you were no longer there. But tell me, where else would she want to live? This is her home. Even though she's agreed to return to France."

"What do you want?" I said.

"I want us not to be enemies. Times are changing. After all, Chirac agreed to the test ban treaty."

"Chirac signed the ban only after hundreds of nuclear tests. That's like saying you won't play with matches after you've burned down a hundred houses."

"Things will change," said MuSan.

"You think that you can wipe the past clean, that you can make the past right just by putting words down on a piece of paper."

"What about the future?"

"What about the truth?"

"I thought you said that you didn't dream about things that don't exist."

"Are you saying that truth doesn't exist?"

"Truth is different for everyone," said MuSan. "Show me a hundred people and I'll show you a hundred different versions of what's true. A hundred different stories."

"What is the story that you told Aurore about me?"

"I told her that you weren't who she thought you were. I told her that you were very smart and clever and that you made money from smuggling. She knew about the *paka*. She didn't know about the snakes. I told her that you were going to inherit more money than most of her aristocratic family would ever see in their lifetimes, so it wasn't as if you needed that money. There was a part of you that chose to go into smuggling. For the thrill perhaps. Or maybe you were bored and didn't have anything else to do."

"I'm not going to inherit anything. Cecile will work her lawyers overtime to make sure that doesn't happen. And you think that we aren't enemies?"

"I think that the likelihood of us not being enemies is small. I am hopeful, though." MuSan extended his hand to me.

"How did you know about Aurore and me?"

"Aurore told me. Long ago. She told me when she first saw you. I told her that you weren't a plaything, an amusement for her."

"For once, you're saying something true. I'm not an amusement."

MuSan said, "Give my condolences to Charlemagne—Radish. And his family. I'll be leaving for Paris again, soon."

"You should talk to Uncle Florian's family yourself. You should visit them to pay your respects."

"You're a smart man, Marc," said MuSan. "Even though you're not as good looking anymore. I'm always hopeful that we'll be friends."

I turned to look at a dog making its way past the tombs, and then I watched the clouds. I knew how to wait, to observe their slow progress across the sky, as if nothing else mattered. I knew how to look calm, the way I had seen Monsieur Li look, sitting next to Ten-kwok so that he would stop crying and blubbering, but I wasn't Monsieur Li. I didn't feel calm inside, I wasn't aloof and tranquil. I was angry and it twisted and stabbed and burned inside my gut. What was the point of it all? As if I really believed there was a point, an explanation, something that you could talk about. And what could you say—that the French army was leaving and everyone was scrambling to save their necks and, while they were doing so, making some money and ingratiating themselves with the new political order? Or was it all some sort of magical illusion, operating under the hidden rules that magicians studied, sorcerers who now called themselves new names? I had thrown away my money and my land for a trinket that would buy time for Marie-Laure—and she was alive, although did I really know for how long? I was beginning to feel that no one really knew anything, and it was just confusion and talk that meant nothing. And I was a fool, really, because no matter how much I knew this, I was always secretly surprised at how pointless it turned out to be, even though I knew how to hide this surprise so that I looked like I never expected anything at all. I kept this sort of look, gazing at nothing until I heard MuSan leaving, walking down the gravel path, starting his car and driving away.

A mist covered the household early the next morning, a fine silvery curtain enveloping the district of Patutoa. The mist surrounded the terrace so that it seemed like its own island, isolated and hidden. Marie-Laure sat at the table beneath the mango branches, a slice of coconut bread untouched on her plate.

"You should see a doctor," I said.

"I'll be back in Sydney in a few days," Marie-Laure replied. "I'm already seeing the doctors there."

"You should see one now."

Marie-Laure pointed to the inner hallway, leading away from the terrace. "When I was little, a cat and her kittens lived there for a while. I used to come here to look for them. Trying to find where they were hiding."

A melancholy weighed on me. "Is it dangerous, your transplant?" I asked.

"There's always the possibility of complications—small, but it's there. It's not very dangerous."

I reached out, tracing my finger along her hair. Marie-Laure smiled, her lips very pale.

"What are you thinking?" she asked.

Already the air was growing brighter and the mist was disappearing, the sun beginning to rise over the eastern mountains. The early morning had seemed so quiet, nothing moving, as if it would always be that way.

"Why don't you go to Australia with me?" said Marie-Laure.

How would I work there? Another country, another language.

"I don't have enough money right now," I said.

Marie-Laure stirred the spoon around her teacup. "I've been offered a lecturer position in Melbourne, beginning next year. After I've recovered from the transplant. The salary isn't bad—there's enough to share." She picked up a book lying on a chair.

I glanced at the English title. "Is this *Fung Liu Meng?*" I asked, speaking in Hakka. *The Dream of the Red Chamber.* De Koning had told me that Odile had bought a five-disc set of a miniseries version on her last trip to Hong Kong for the International Pearl Auction.

"The fourth volume. The English translation."

"People don't think it's weird?" I made vague motions as she stared at me and then I looked away.

"What do you mean? *The Dream of the Red Chamber?*" She thought in silence, looking at her book. "You mean consanguine relationships? Cousins sleeping together?"

"Yes, whatever you call it."

"You're embarrassed," she said, laughing. "I've never seen you embarrassed about anything."

I moved the bread around on my plate. "Well, you didn't go to that party with me."

"What party? Oh. You mean the one when we were sixteen and eighteen—or you were practically eighteen."

"That one."

Marie-Laure closed her book, placing it down on the table. "When I was sixteen, everything embarrassed me. And I knew there would be all those strangers there—staring at me. I got scared at the last minute. I just couldn't go. Listening to people saying 'Look, they're cousins, but that one's so gorgeous and that one's so ugly.'"

"How about 'That one passes examinations like it's a piece of cake and that one can't even get out of grammar school'?"

"I can't speak Hakka the way you do," said Marie-Laure.

"Well, who speaks it now?" I said. "Besides old people." I tapped my fingers against my plate. The air was changing, no longer fresh, the sky turning a hard shade of blue.

"You'll go to Australia?"

I thought of my work in Huahine—I made enough to live, trading this for that. But so little money left to save for an airline ticket.

"You'll think about it?" Her voice grew quiet.

Marie-Laure, don't go, I thought. Don't go where I can't follow. "Don't worry," I said. "Go to Sydney."

The sun had fallen over her face and I could see every eyelash, delicate and separate, and her wide mouth, its definite mark.

"What is it?" said Marie-Laure.

"Would you sit for a sketch?" I asked.

"What do you mean?"

"A drawing. A drawing of you. Before you leave."

She regarded me, weighing her words. "Well," she said. "Why not?"

✣

Marie-Laure decided that she would sit for the drawing at my mother's house and she decided to wear a mourning dress, plain and white. I watched her combing her hair before the mirror in her room. She drew a line of black around her eyes and examined her reflection.

I handed her a jewelry box.

"What is it?" she asked, opening the box and removing the earrings, the pearls, silver with a pink blush. "They're beautiful, this color. Where did they come from?"

"My father sent them to me," I said. "When I was in Huahine."

Aurore waited in the parlor with Madame MuSan, Tiurai Tunui, and my mother. She stood up when Marie-Laure entered and Marie-Laure walked to her, taking Aurore's hands in her own.

Aurore had brought a pair of paintings as a gift for my mother and her husband: two landscapes of Manihi in the Tuamotus where Tiurai was born.

"They're so lovely," said Madame MuSan, and Tiurai drew nearer to look at the paintings more closely.

Aurore and Marie-Laure sat alone together in the parlor for hours, through the afternoon. I drove to Radish's house and Radish sent me to the *centre-ville* to deliver some envelopes, unfinished business left by his father. Aurore's car was still parked in front of my mother's house when I returned. Edouard waited next to a motorcycle parked by the car. Two motorcycles, it turned out, one black and one red. A man who looked around eighteen stood next to the black motorcycle.

"What's this?" I asked. "Shit." Patches of rust ate at the metal and the plastic curled from the seats. You left anything out and no matter how slick and shiny and fast it once was, the heat and salt air turned it to rot.

"Luxury transportation," laughed Edouard.

"Metal crap. Overdue for the junkyard."

"Take the red one," said Edouard. "Hey, Lucien," he shouted at the man who got on the motorcycle behind him. "That's for your uncle Florian and Arthur." He pointed to a carton tied to the back of my motorcycle.

296

We drove to the cemetery and I untied the carton, handing it to Edouard. When we reached the tomb, Edouard made the sign of the cross and Lucien did the same.

"We should pray, shouldn't we?" said Edouard.

I began with the Our Father and Edouard said three Hail Marys very quickly with the words bunched together. He bent down, opening the carton and pulling out two leis of white *tiare,* the fragrance floating over us. Edouard handed the leis to me and I placed them on the cement, a temporary cover waiting for the final slab of marble.

Marie-Laure was waiting in the kitchen when I returned from the cemetery. She drank a bowl of rice porridge sprinkled with dried orange peel. "Aurore left, not long ago," she said.

Marie-Laure had brought the sketches to her room, placing two beside her mirror. One sketch was from the side and the other portrayed her face from the front, its plainness and how her eyes were almost too close together, but the drawing also captured something indefinable that seemed to illuminate her face from within. I stood in front of the sketches, examining the shading and the lines, wondering how it was done, somehow conveying more than the sum of what seemed physically there.

"It's like magic, isn't it?" said Marie-Laure.

I thought that she was going to say something again, but instead she pointed to the desk behind me and I saw more sketches lying there. Black ink on white: Marie-Laure reading, the ordinary way her head bowed over a book; three drawings of Marie-Laure smiling, then starting to laugh, and then really laughing; and last, a drawing of her face turned to the left, gazing just beyond what the viewer could see.

Chapter 51

We sleep and we wake and we sleep again. Some people say that we're usually just sleeping, drifting in things that aren't real at all. We think it's the truth, but really it's just different forms of lies. Or maybe it's all stories that we tell ourselves and some of the stories are told to make you laugh, and others are told just to pass the time. And there are the stories you hear at night, and, on an island, the lights of the towns fade quickly and soon you are far in the mountains or far out at sea with only the ocean of stars overhead and all the stories you heard during the day fall quiet.

Monsieur Li was chopping dried leaves at the kitchen table after the dinner bowls were cleared away. He opened a packet of white paper, revealing something that looked like a pile of seeds inside.

"What's this?" I asked.

"My teacher used to brew this." He divided the seeds, pouring out half into a teapot and rewrapping the paper. He added the leaves to the teapot. "Wait and we'll share this."

"I'll bring this to Marie-Laure," I said, picking up a bowl of soup.

Marie-Laure rested under the mosquito netting. A moth flew beneath the ceiling of her room.

"Your cousin Monsieur Li is brewing some sort of tea," I said. "He says he'll send you a cup."

"It's made from these seeds and a type of leaves—I forgot the name," said Marie-Laure. "He was talking about it earlier."

It probably tasted bitter, like the medicinal tea that A-tai once brewed. You could drink it slow or you could drink it fast, but the taste was still terrible. "I'll bring you the tea."

"You don't sound enthusiastic."

"I saw him preparing this. It looks like mud. You don't have to tell me—I know it tastes bad."

Monsieur Li sat waiting at the kitchen table. Two cups of tea rested on the table. "It's still hot," he said. "We'll wait."

I sat down and stared at the tea. I tapped the side of a cup and little bits like dirt swirled through the liquid. Outside the kitchen, the chickens settled into their cages, ruffling their feathers, and there were the usual sounds: a dog barking somewhere, a car passing on the road.

"Where are you going, once Marie-Laure leaves for Sydney?" asked Monsieur Li.

"I don't know. She asked me to go with her."

"To Australia?"

"What would I do there? I can't speak the language. If I go back to Huahine, I can work. Edouard is thinking of going to Bora Bora. He has a brother there. Radish says he's staying here." I looked into the dark teacup. "Can you read the future?"

"If I could, I'd have won the Lotto already," said Monsieur Li.

We sat without speaking and then I picked up my cup. The taste was bitter. I tried drinking fast, but it seemed that I couldn't swallow quickly enough. Monsieur Li watched from across the table. "We'll meet in Huahine," he said.

Marie-Laure drank her tea under the mosquito netting. She drank it slowly, without stopping. "It's not bad," she said, handing me the cup.

"Is that what she said?" asked Odile, standing by the kitchen table. "Marie-Laure really said, 'It's not bad'?" She had one hand on her hip, the other around her cup. "This stuff tastes horrible. I don't care what Marie-Laure says."

"It's a matter of taste," I said.

"Shit," said Odile. "What happened to you? I used to be able to count on you. Pure cynicism. You were good at that. But now, after all that time you spent in Huahine, hanging out with Monsieur Li. *It's a matter of taste.* Fuck this shit."

"Bring a cup to De Koning."

Odile glared at the cup in her hand.

"You know she'll love this," I said.

"Medicinal tea. The weirder the better," said Odile. "You know she wants to go study again with Monsieur Li. All that shamanic stuff. Getting in touch with the spirit world, she says. Crap. She just likes living out there—why, I don't know."

"I thought she was staying here with you."

Odile looked at me like I had turned into a complete stranger.

"She wants to be with you," I said. "Maybe you can go to Huahine. Don't look at me like that."

"Have you heard yourself talking? What are you doing—giving me romantic advice or something? That's just too weird," said Odile, and she walked away, cradling a cup for De Koning in her hands.

My father and Ten-kwok poured the mud tea into glasses. Ten-kwok held a bottle of bourbon. "This is the way you drink it," he said.

My father poured the tea and bourbon into a third glass and handed it to me. They clinked their glasses together with mine.

"*Manuia, santé,* ching-ching, bottoms up, cheers!" said Ten-kwok, shouting every drinking salutation he knew.

"*Santé,*" said my father. He lifted his glass. "*Manuia.*"

"Is Monsieur Li's tea still there?" Marie-Laure asked.

"It's not like everyone's in a hurry to drink this medicine," I said, touching the white netting surrounding Marie-Laure's bed. Her suitcase lay shut on the floor. "You've packed."

"The flight leaves tomorrow night."

"What's the hurry? That gives you twenty-four hours before you even have to think about packing."

"You probably throw everything into a suitcase right before you have to leave," said Marie-Laure, sitting up. "I was talking to Monsieur Li." She slid out from under the netting and walked to her suitcase, unzipped it open. "I've always thought that we should write down what he knows, but maybe that's not the way it works." She closed her suitcase again. "I know you couldn't tell me about this. They made you promise, didn't they? Whoever sold this to you. You could never tell me."

"Tell you what?"

Marie-Laure entered back inside the curtain of netting and opened her palm. The Mei Zhun bead rested inside. The bead had melted in a lop-sided way, growing smaller than I remembered, and the characters that had once marked its surface had disappeared.

"I've heard enough stories about this sort of thing," she said. "Someone pays a high price in exchange for the magic."

"Where did you get this?" I asked.

"I found it under my hand, in the hospital. When I awoke. Everything was a blur at first and then I felt it, under my fingers."

"You still need the transplant," I said.

"I awoke, didn't I?" she said. "You can't talk about it, can you?" Marie-Laure took my hand, placing the bead in my palm. "I know. This is yours."

I returned the bead to her, folding her fingers around it.

"No. You paid for this."

"Keep it," I said. "This way, I'll see you again."

"In Australia?"

"We'll see each other," I said. Somehow, in a way we couldn't yet imagine. I should know better than to start thinking that it would turn out all right, but here I was, thinking the same thoughts again. And what was I thinking? That it might be different. That you never really knew. Life was unpredictable and sometimes it surprised you with impossible hope.

Marie-Laure left with Ten-kwok on the eight-thirty flight to Sydney. Radish drove them to the airport where family and friends gathered with leis to say good-bye. I placed a lei of tiny shells of many colors around Marie-Laure and she threw her arms around me. Madame MuSan pressed a small box of Chinese medicine into Marie-Laure's palm, in case she didn't feel well on the journey.

"It's so uncertain," Madame MuSan said. Marie-Laure and Odile embraced, and De Koning took a picture of them, then handed me the camera.

"Take a picture of us!" said De Koning.

"Do you have the tickets?" Madame MuSan asked Ten-kwok, who felt around his pockets for a worried moment before producing the tickets from inside a pocket of his slacks. There was another round of hugs and then Marie-Laure and Ten-kwok were gone. I walked out alone to the parking lot.

I heard the voices of my father and Monsieur Li, speaking together as they walked to my father's car. Further away, in the darkness, De Koning was talking and laughing with Odile.

The solitude seemed to crowd against me. Where was I going? I stopped, listening to the voices, and I knew that I didn't know anything, nothing about where I was really going or what waited for me there.

I stared up into the darkness. The stars appeared faintly above, drowned out by the lights of the airport, and then it came to me that I could see them out in the *van-tui,* the remote districts, and the view would be even clearer in the faraway islands. The solitary mountains, the flat slivers of sand, the places you wouldn't find unless you were really lost. It was where the stars shimmered most brightly. They covered the sky, where the night was darkest so that you saw them, up in the void. I took a step and I started walking out through the dark.

GLOSSARY

'aita: (Tahitian) no

bac, or *le bac:* (French) short for *le baccalauréat:* examination required to qualify for university entrance

bricolage: (French) do-it-yourself (e.g., a *bricolage* store)

casse-croûte: (French) snack, sandwich

ça va?: (French) How's it going?; informal greeting

centre-ville: (French) downtown, city center

cocktail: (French/English) cocktail party, a reception

corossol: (French) soursop fruit

demi: (French) someone of two races or ethnicities, e.g., French and Tahitian

expert comptable: (French) the French equivalent of a CPA, a Certified Public Accountant

fafa: (Tahitian) taro leaves. See also *poulet fafa.*

fare: (Tahitian) a bungalow, a small house

fe'i: (Tahitian) a type of banana with orange-yellow flesh, eaten cooked

fong ngung ha: (Hakka) an egg dish, a type of omelet prepared with julienned vegetables. Thinly sliced or julienned meat may be included. Usually accompanied with a savory sauce, mustard or tomato sauce.

Gâteau des îles: (French) a white cake flavored with coconut

Ia orana: (Tahitian) hello

jeu d'échecs: (French) chess, specifically a European version of chess

la belle étoile: (French) literally "the beautiful star," the open air

lang pui shui: (Hakka) cold boiled water; the older generation of Hakka boiled their drinking water and then let it cool to room temperature.

libre service: (French) self-serve; a store where customers can select items themselves. In a store that is not *libre service,* the customer requests items at the counter from a store clerk who then brings the requested items to the counter for the customer.

lycée: (French) high school, secondary school

maʻa Tahiti: (Tahitian) Tahitian food

maʻa Tinito: (Tahitian) Chinese food; more specifically, a dish of pork, beans, and noodles

mairie: (French) city hall

maozhung: (Hakka) useless, a derogatory word for someone considered lazy or worthless

mape: (Tahitian) Tahitian chestnut tree; usually grows to an immense size

marae: (Tahitian) a sacred place

Marae Taputapuatea: (Tahitian) sacred site on the southeastern coast of Raiatea

mautini: (Tahitian) pumpkin

mec: (French) a man, a guy

métropol: (French) a French person from France (to distinguish from a French person born in Polynesia)

moripata: (Tahitian) flashlight

motu: (Tahitian) a small island, an islet

notaire: (French) a type of lawyer

paka or *pakalolo:* (Tahitian) marijuana

pareu: (Tahitian) a cotton fabric, used as clothing or as a household covering or decoration

Peré Faʻanuʻu: (French/Tahitian) a Tahitian game, similar to European checkers

poe: (Tahitian) cooked food prepared from fruit, tubers or vegetables mixed with tapioca starch

popaʻa: (Tahitian) a white person, white people

poulet fafa: (French/Tahitian) chicken cooked with taro leaves

presqu'île: (French) also called Tahiti Iti (Tahitian); Tahiti has the appearance of being two islands joined by an isthmus. The larger "island" is called Tahiti Nui or "Big Tahiti" while the smaller island is called Tahiti Iti or "Small Tahiti." The presqu'île or Tahiti Iti is less populated and retains an aura of being wilder.

purau: (Tahitian) a type of bush or tree

radio cocotier: (French) literally "coconut radio"; gossip

roulotte: (French) outdoor food stand

terrain: (French) a piece of land; property

tiare: (Tahitian) a white fragrant flower, the symbol of Tahiti

tiare lei: necklace made of *tiare* flowers

tifaifai: (Tahitian) quilt

tinito: (Tahitian) a Chinese person

tireur d'élite: (French) a sharpshooter

ti-tis: (slang) breasts, tits

tour de l'île: (French) a drive around the island, literally a "tour of the island"

tupapaʻu: (Tahitian) spirits of the dead, ghosts

van-tui: (Hakka) backcountry, a remote area, distant from towns or cities

verveine: (French) lemon verbena

vī atoni, vī carotte, vī greffée: (Tahitian/French) different varieties of mangoes

vini: (or *vini vini*) (Tahitian) a small bird, similar to a sparrow or a finch; *vini* (slang) a cell phone

Yunnan Baiyao: Chinese medicinal powder

ACKNOWLEDGMENTS

This book has emerged through the support and encouragement of so many. Deep thanks to all of you: Wakako Yamauchi and Joy Yamauchi Matsushita; Laura Pollard Gorjance, who generously provided the space where much of the first draft was written; Paul Spickard for his unwavering, huge support; Rebecca Lawton who read and edited countless drafts; my amazing writing sisters Z Egloff, Lorri Holt, Jill Koenigsdorf, Karen Laws, and Julia Whitty; the wonderful Seventeen Syllables Sabina Chen, Edmond Chow, Jay Dayrit, Brian Komei Dempster, Roy Kamada, Caroline Kim-Brown, Suji Kwock Kim, Grace Loh Prasad, Grace Talusan, and Marianne Villanueva. Special thanks to Garrett Hongo, Mat Johnson, David Mura, and Andrew X. Pham. For their inspiration, friendship, and invaluable support: Rich Aiello, Karen Carissimo, Patricia Damery, Anthony Dragun, Anne Evans, Thomas Farber, Marla Kamiya, Carol McRae, Curt Pham, Noah Sabich, Moya Stone, Susan Wilde, Orit Weksler, Ingrid Wishnoff, Sandra Zane, and the teachers and staff of The Berkeley School, including the Sunflower Thief Mammad Kazerouni, Paula Farmer, Michael Sinclair, Janet Stork, Danette Swann, and Randy Yee. Heartfelt thanks to the generous peoples of the islands who embraced this book during its long journey and many thanks to my editor Masako Ikeda and the University of Hawai'i Press. Finally, thank you to my wonderfully patient family in Tahiti, Hawai'i, and California; to my children, Yune, Vanina, and Tien; and to my husband, Bruno, for making the impossible possible.

About the Author

Lillian Howan is an attorney and writer whose parents immigrated from Tahiti and Raiatea. She spent her early childhood in Tahiti.

She graduated from the University of California–Berkeley, School of Law. Her writings have been published in the *Asian American Literary Review, Café Irreal, Calyx, New England Review,* and the anthology *Under Western Eyes,* edited by Garrett Hongo. She is the editor of Wakako Yamauchi's collection, *Rosebud and Other Stories* (University of Hawai'i Press, 2011).

Tahiti　　法属波利尼西亚第一大岛（澳国中塔
　　　　　　　　　　　　　　　　　　　希提岛及周
　　首府·岛西北 Papeete　　　　　　　边岛组成）

塔希提岛之客家人占大约 5 万　Hakka
　　80% 波利尼西亚籍